Eldritch Sparks

Shadows of Otherside Book 2

Whitney Hill

**BENU
MEDIA**

ELDRITCH SPARKS
Copyright © 2020 by Whitney Hill

Benu Media
6409 Fayetteville Rd
Ste 120 #155
Durham, NC 27713
(984) 244-0250
benumedia.com

To receive special offers, release updates, and bonus content, sign up for our newsletter: go.benumedia.com/newsletter

ISBN (ebook): 978-1-7344227-3-3
ISBN (pbook): 978-1-7344227-4-0

Library of Congress Control Number: 2020913561

Cover Designer: Pintado (99Designs)
Editor: Jeni Chappelle (Jeni Chappelle Editorial)

For everyone who has had to make hard choices about where to give their time, energy, and love...and especially for those who have made harder choices about when or where they can no longer give at all.

Chapter 1

A howl echoed through the trees, and I ran faster, my feet kicking up dust from the moonlit trail, heart pounding, breath heaving. It was only Roman, but that didn't mean I wanted to be caught. My werewolf lover would be in wolfman form; his magic wasn't strong enough to go full wolf, but he'd be deadly all the same. He wouldn't hurt me, of course, but the game was "keep away," and grown Othersiders played a little differently than human children.

We were taking advantage of the full moon and the balmy spring evening. My evolving role in Otherside and my efforts to get the elves, vampires, weres, and djinn to finalize negotiations on our new alliance had me stressed to hell and back. Roman had suggested a run in the forest to get my body moving as much as my mind had been lately.

Eno River State Park was closed, of course. Nobody should have been in the woods after dusk. Budget cuts had trimmed the number of rangers available to keep people out, but even had there been a ranger, Roman and I could have slipped past. As a sylph—an air elemental—I couldn't move as quickly or hear as sharply as Roman, but I could still perform better than a human.

Not that that saved me.

A shift in the wind brought me the faintest whiff of cedar and musk from in front of me. In my rush to stop, I tripped over a raised root and went ass over tits down the path, landing with an undignified thump in front of two huge paws. The backpack I'd been wearing skidded past them. I winced at the bruises I'd have and the thud the pack made as it stopped against a rock then started laughing at my own clumsiness.

"Interesting tactic, babe," Roman said with a toothy smile, the words coming out a little mangled. Wolf snouts weren't meant for human speech, and being stuck halfway through the change didn't exactly help.

Breathless, I tried to scramble back. It wasn't over until he caught me.

With superhuman speed, he bent down, caught my ankle, and pulled. As he leaned over my body in a push-up, he sniffed along my neck and hummed with pleasure. "This has promise."

For all that I, and my body, agreed, I wasn't ready to let him win just yet. He was using his power, so I drew on mine.

"You little—" He yelped as my eyes glowed gold in the dark and a gust of Air pummeled him in the side. Elemental powers and hapkido gave me enough of an edge to hold him off, but he had strength, weight, and reach on his side. Plus, he fought dirty.

"Okay, you win!" I cried, laughing as I tried to fend off tickling hands. He stopped immediately, nuzzling my neck, and I ran my fingers down his back. "If you want to change, we could continue this more comfortably."

Roman's howl of triumph rang through the woods—and was answered. His growl cut straight through to my gut as he looked up and toward the trailhead. "I know that voice."

It had sounded the same as his to me, but maybe that was the telling part. I stood and brushed myself off, tugging a twig free of my tight curls as Roman went behind a tree to shift back to human, still embarrassed by the process and his difficulty. A handicap or a disability, as he saw it, though I didn't.

I had his spare clothes ready when he stepped back out, naked and trying to hide his nerves more than his assets.

"Let's go," he said when he was dressed. We hustled back to the trailhead, the scent of rotted cedar growing and clashing with the piney scent of the night as we got closer to the parking lot and his anxiety climbed.

A single male figure, as dark-haired and light-skinned as Roman, leaned against a big, white SUV in the parking lot.

"Stay behind me," Roman murmured, one arm out to stop me from passing him. Energy crackled and the moon reflected from the stranger's retinas. Definitely an Othersider, likely the answering wolf we'd heard, and from the way Roman stiffened and rumbled deep in his chest, more than dangerous.

"Not afraid of the big bad wolf, are you, brother?" the stranger said.

"Sergei." Roman's response to the mocking tone held taut patience, even as the tension in the lines of his body ratcheted up another notch. "What are you doing here?"

"Nothing permanent. For now." The wolf in CEO's clothing pushed away from the truck with a mesmerizing, purposeful grace. He'd called Roman brother, but that clashed with what little I knew about my lover's family.

The way I'd heard it, the Volkovs had kicked Roman out of pack, clan, and home and expected him to die somewhere between the mountains and here. Magical "runts" like Roman, who couldn't fully shift, weren't very welcome in werewolf society. I shifted my hand toward the backpack I held close in front of me.

"You don't need the gun." Sergei added an inhuman snarl when I hesitated.

I kicked myself. A werewolf could probably smell the oil, especially if he was in touch with his wild side. The full moon made that more than a little likely, and I was three kinds of foolish to forget and risk pushing him into a shift. Roman made a huge wolfman. I did not want to see how big a wolf his brother

3

made. The man was a full six feet tall, taller than even Roman's unusual—for a wereanimal—height, and had to weigh a good buck eighty.

"A weapon, in the hands of something smelling of thunderstorms on a dry summer's day. Not a hint of musk, so not one of the clans. Oh, brother, what trouble are you making for yourself now? You were shifted in the woods, if you can call it that. I can smell it on you."

"She's Otherside," Roman snapped. A bone popped as his hand started rearranging itself. "I haven't broken any of our laws."

"You mean any *more* of them. Bad enough you still live without breaking the Détente and forcing me halfway across the state."

Roman flinched, and a shadow darkened his expression.

I'd had enough of standing at the periphery of whatever long-standing family nastiness was going on here. "If all you're here to do is talk shit, I'm sure Roman and I have better things to do."

"Oh ho, the mystery meat has teeth!" Sergei chuckled, apparently delighted, and extended his hand. "Well then. You have my name. What's yours?"

I didn't need Roman's warning growl not to shake the other man's hand. "Why don't you tell us why you're here?" I said.

"Not very hospitable in this neck of the woods, are we?"

The little witticisms were starting to grate. Between gritted teeth, I said, "Not when out-of-territory wolves turn up unannounced at the full moon, no."

Sergei smirked. "Do you always let your bitches speak for you, Roman? Lupa's teats, I knew you were weak but—"

The *but what* was cut off as Roman lunged, slamming Sergei against the SUV. "Tread lightly, little brother," he warned in a voice almost too low to hear, his Appalachian mountain accent coming through much stronger than I'd ever heard it. "Family bonds only stretch so far. You're in my territory, and I was cast out of the pack. This land is mine, that there female is mine, and you're far from home. If hospitality is in question, I reckon that's your doing. And if you're fixin' for a fight, Lupa forgive me but I'll give you one."

In the moonlight, I could see Sergei's bared teeth as he quivered, fists clenched, with Roman's mouth at his throat. A weak wolf still had teeth, a fact I hadn't forgotten and Sergei had. Roman might have forgotten that fact himself, given how often he deferred to me, but then again, he was usually much more easy-going. He had a temper, sure, but with me it flared and settled without all of...this.

The standoff ended as abruptly as it had started.

"Beg pardon," Sergei said, opening his hands. "Ma said—"

"I know what she'da said. I don't need to be tested, Sergei. Don't try me again." Roman stepped back, not taking his eyes off his brother as the other wolf straightened the sleeves of his suit. The fine dark jacket contrasted sharply with Roman's tatty, oil-stained T-shirt.

"Sure, bro," Sergei said.

"Business?"

"Business."

I blinked, confused by the sudden change in atmosphere as they both turned and ambled toward Roman's trailer, a minute's walk away on End Street. It wasn't friendly, per se, but they weren't ready to fight anymore. "Uh, guys?"

They both turned back and I lifted my hands in the universal gesture of *what the hell*.

Roman extended a hand for me. "Come on, Arie. Sergei won't try anything else tonight."

Somehow, I doubted it. "So, what was all that?"

"Reintroductions."

Sergei snorted and looked at the ground.

When neither of them offered any more explanation, I rolled my eyes. "Whatever."

Sergei's car would be towed if he left it there but frankly, I didn't care. My date night, the first one I'd had in a while thanks to an uptick in my work as a private investigator and my new Otherside responsibilities, had been hijacked by the guy. Unfortunately, my car was parked in front of Roman's trailer, which meant walking back with them regardless.

I angled toward my car when we got there.

"Arden?" Roman asked.

"What?"

"You aren't coming in?"

"I thought you'd want to take care of family business in peace. Seems like it's pretty urgent."

Sergei's sudden focus set me on edge. I didn't like the interest sharpening his tone as he said, "Wait—Arden? Finch?"

I pressed my lips together, unwilling to confirm it, even if he already seemed to have some idea of who I was.

Turning to Roman, Sergei said, "She needs to stay."

I bristled, but Roman just shrugged. "Convince her yourself."

"I thought she was your woman."

"And that works so well for Pops, doesn't it?"

Sergei fidgeted. The porch light revealed the true quality of his clothes—designer, or I wasn't a private investigator—raising a whole lot more questions about how Roman had come to be living in a run-down manufactured home on the other side of the state.

Rubbing the back of his neck, Sergei said, "Ms. Finch—"

"Oh, now it's 'Miz Finch'? I thought it was 'mystery meat'."

The younger Volkov gaped to look more like a fish than a wolf, and Roman was bright red with the effort to keep a straight face.

"I'm a guest," Sergei said at last. "I should be offended that you don't want to stay and welcome me."

"Then you shouldn't have started off being rude. I guess that's good night." My car beeped a welcome as I opened the door and settled into the driver's seat.

Sergei was fast, I'd give him that. Before I could shut the door all the way he'd come around and caught it.

"Please," he said when I lifted my eyebrows at him.

"Now he finds some courtesy," I muttered, glaring as I tapped on the steering wheel.

With a glance at Roman, Sergei knelt, heedless of the dirt and patchy grass that passed for the front lawn. Up close, with the overhead light falling full in his face, he looked a good five years younger than his brother. Leaner in face and form, though still bigger than me, and with hair a shade lighter than Roman's rich brown. They had the same eyes though, a dark grey that flowed from steel to storm with their mood. He looked soft compared to Roman, though.

With what I imagined was supposed to be a charming smile, Sergei said, "My apologies. I came looking for my brother to re-establish ties, at his request. I hadn't reckoned on finding you here."

The mountain accent Roman took on when he was pissed or drunk grew heavier in Sergei's speech.

In a lower voice, he continued. "My family, my pack, sent me to learn whether Roman was telling the truth about a new alliance and the opportunities it might bring. I was told you were crucial to the negotiations, and I would take it as a personal favor if you stayed a little longer."

I sighed and leaned back in my seat, so not in the mood for this. About two months ago, I'd outed myself as an elemental while trying to escape an elven serial killer and stop the conspiracy he led. Long story short, I'd sort of escaped with my life, gotten one of the elven Houses to suspend the bounty on elementals, and managed to free myself from some onerous obligations to the local boss, Callista.

Now I was in the awkward position of being a known neutral party in the Triangle's Otherside community. I'd gone from persona non grata, keeping quiet about my powers and staying hidden, to somehow being the community coordinator. Callista was pissed with me and the fact that everyone in the Triangle—and maybe beyond, now—seemed to want my help with business they should have been able to settle on their own.

A rap on the passenger window made me glare at Sergei to behave as I reached for the window button. Roman leaned in, the car shifting a little with his weight.

"Babe, he's made himself lower than you," he pointed out, looking at Sergei rather than at me.

"Did I miss something?" I glanced over to find Sergei bright red, eyes averted.

"Yeah. You saw what I had to do to get him to submit at the trailhead, and that was just looking aside. He's not as clever as Vikki, but he knows better." Roman frowned. "Speaking of our dear sister, why are you here and not her?"

Sergei pushed up and away, turning slightly so that he could see us but keep his face and chest angled away.

"Ah." The satisfaction in Roman's voice drew my attention back to him. "Beat you to it, hey, little brother?"

My face blanked as the pieces clicked into place. Sergei was supposed to have created a more *physical* tie between me and the wolf pack. I knew Roman hadn't gone to Asheville in person to bring his family the news of the new power balance in the Triangle, so the Volkovs must have had a weak fifteen-year-old in mind. The boy Roman had been, rather than the man they'd forced him to become.

Though I was proud of him for surviving and even thriving on his own, something felt off. Icky. I cared for Roman but didn't like the idea that he had used my influence with the alliance to gain an in with his estranged family without talking to me first. We were supposed to be partners. Why didn't he tell me he'd started negotiations for the alliance? *I've barely gotten my feet under me with the vampires and the elves, and he's rushing?*

With Sergei out of the way, I slammed the door shut and stabbed at the window button. I needed some space to think this through. "I think it's best if I go. I'll call you tomorrow, Roman."

"Do you want everything to go back to the way it was?" Roman said as he jumped away from the rising glass.

That broke through and I clicked the button the other direction to stop it, leaning forward to rest my head on the steering wheel. At the start of the year, I'd been alone. Alone, scared, and increasingly frustrated by the way I was forced to live. Now I was known. I had people. Sort of. But at least I could practice my magic openly and had gotten out from the worst of my obligations to Callista.

I sighed. No, I really didn't want things to go back to the way they'd been—and Roman knew it. Some Othersiders were coming to me for help, but others were after my blood. That was the whole reason I was trying to pull a new alliance together: to be part of something, both to belong and for protection.

"Shit," I muttered, setting aside my feelings. "Fine. But we're going to have a discussion on this, Roman." I gathered up the fancy leather backpack I used as a purse and got out.

He winced and nodded, shoving his hands in his pockets, and strode toward the trailer home.

"After you," Sergei said, watching me intently.

"Oh, no, after you. I insist," I replied between gritted teeth. He puffed himself up as though he was about to protest. I tilted my head and cocked an eyebrow. How badly did he want me to stay?

With a growl I probably wasn't supposed to hear, Sergei followed his brother, tugging roughly at a shirt collar that didn't need straightening, and answered my question. Badly enough that he'd give his back to an unknown Othersider on the full Worm Moon.

.

Chapter 2

Roman knew without asking that I'd want a cup of tea. He was already puttering around in the kitchen, ignoring Sergei's bemused expression. While the water boiled, he reached deep into a cupboard and pulled out a bottle, then grabbed a steak from the fridge. The steak didn't surprise me that much, since he'd already explained that shifting required a lot of protein, but I hadn't seen the bottle before. Roman was a bourbon man.

After pouring a splash of golden liquid into two tumblers and slicing two thin strips from the raw steak, Roman extended one of each to his brother.

"With meat and mead, we greet our guests," he said solemnly.

Sergei glanced at me. I had no idea what was going on but I raised my eyebrows as though I did and he was being rude. Frowning, he accepted and replied, "With meat and mead, we keep the peace."

My stomach did a little flip as they swallowed the meat whole and raw, then threw back their drinks.

"You'll let her see, but not take part?" Outrage tinged Sergei's voice.

I casually reached for the bottle, recognizing the logo on the label from visits to the farmers market. Ginger mead from one of the local meaderies, as potent as wine. I wondered if it would have the same effects that wine would in warding off the power hangovers I got when I called Air, or the same Chaotic effects that made me avoid alcohol in company.

Roman, seeing that I had no interest in getting involved, answered for me. "She doesn't drink."

"Witch?" Sergei eyed me speculatively.

"No," Roman said.

"What then?"

"That's my business," I interjected, relieved that he didn't already know and wanting to keep it that way if I could. I was still having nightmares about being drowned by the elves after being discovered last winter. Still looking over my shoulder for Troy, the prince of House Monteague—and the man who'd done the drowning on the order of an elven terrorist to avoid blowing his deep cover.

I gritted my teeth and gave Sergei a level look. If Roman hadn't told his family about that when he'd contacted them, I wasn't keen for the rumors of my nature to spread west. Bad enough that half the Triangle seemed to be talking about elementals. Val, my dea friend and the only other elemental I knew, wasn't super pleased with having to take extra precautions against discovery. The other local elementals avoided me entirely, thanks to my connections to both Callista and the elves.

"Your business?" Sergei said, low and slow, after waiting for me to add more. When I accepted the cup of tea from Roman rather than elaborating, he scowled.

"Speaking of business, what brings you here in person?" Roman said into the awkward silence as he leaned against the small dining table. The folding leaf clattered. "I thought I was dead to y'all."

"Technically, you still are."

I grinned. "Oooh, a super secret mission."

"Yes, actually," Sergei said. Now that he knew neither Roman nor I would be bullied or seduced, he dropped both threat and charm, settling into an anxious uncertainty. Werewolves aged slowly, but something about Sergei was starting to make me think he was as young as he looked. "The clan doesn't know I'm here. Pops wanted it kept quiet to avoid setting a bad precedent."

The slackening of his posture and energy brought my shoulders down a bit. I still didn't trust him, nor did I like how he'd just turned up, but I'd listen to him if he wasn't trying to throw his weight around. Having Callista and two-thirds of elfdom against me was enough to worry about without adding the most powerful wereclan in three states.

Roman went to pour another drink, topping up Sergei's glass when he nodded. "I'm not in the mood to sniff down trails," Roman said. "What does he want?"

"What he always wants. More." Sergei studied me again but continued speaking to his brother. "Pops is pissed that you had the balls to reach out but more that you held back what she is and made yourself the key to the deal. Power shifts are bad enough without unknown players."

"And he's always the wary one, I know."

"So. All you said was that you, Torsten's coterie, the Monteagues, and a handful of djinn had come to an agreement facilitated not by Callista but by one Arden Finch."

If I hadn't had years of practice not reacting to outrageous statements, I might have turned to glare at Roman. He'd told them about my involvement but didn't say anything to me? Bitterness stung through me. He knew how much trouble I'd had juggling the vamps and the elves.

Unfortunately, the control I maintained over my reactions apparently didn't extend to my scent because Sergei sniffed and frowned at me. "Something in there is not quite right."

"Close enough," I said, playing along until I could discuss it with Roman in private.

Sergei grunted. "I see. What do the Volkovs need to do to join?"

The shift of Roman's eyes to wolf silver undermined his bland tones as he named the price. "Be ready to stand with the rest of us when we're revealed to the humans."

Goosebumps raced down my arms, despite my having had a little over two months to get used to the idea.

Our guest went ghost pale, his eyes shifting and a ripple shuddering over him, the way Roman reacted when he was fighting the change. "When—what?"

"There's a start-up in RTP. Healthtech," I drawled, as though I was completely accustomed to everything happening here. They would both be able to hear my heart racing, but in Otherside—and especially with wereanimals—attitude counted. "They're on the verge of developing a test that will out us. Callista wants to get in front of it."

"You know this how?"

"I'm a private investigator."

A sneer twisted Sergei's lip. "You're a snitch."

I couldn't help laughing. "Nah. I solve problems for humans. Pure serendipity that I was hired for that job." Tilting my head, I gave him my best dead-eyed stare. "The snitching comes in when I act as a Watcher."

His eyes widened, and he took a step back before he could catch himself. Face flushing and fists clenching, he looked at his brother and snapped, "Is this a joke or a trap?"

"Neither," Roman said as he eased between me and Sergei, protective as ever. "Arden has a knack for dropping into the middle of things."

Sergei gritted his teeth. "And this Reveal? Why weren't we consulted?"

I took a step to the side, wanting Sergei to see I could stand on my own two feet. He needed to keep wondering what kind of Othersider I was to be tapped as a Watcher, privy to Callista's plans, and powerful enough to get the master of Raleigh and an elven House to play nice with the wereclans after thirty years of restrained tension. "Callista has her reasons."

"Meaning you don't know."

"Meaning since when have any of us had a say?" Roman pointed out. "Isn't it time we changed that?"

"Be careful, brother. That's dangerous talk from a cur with no pack."

"This cur managed to survive fifteen years alone and win friends of influence. Be careful yourself."

They stared at each other, a dominance battle I was already bored of. Finishing my tea, I gave them both my back as I went to drop the tea bag in the trash and rinse the cup.

"Arden!" Roman shouted, but the deep-chest growl from behind had warned me. My hearing wasn't werewolf-good, but it wasn't human, either.

I hauled open the fridge door just in time for Sergei to crash into it. He bounced off with a yelp and tripped. I pounced, riding him down with a throat jab pulled short enough not to crush his windpipe but not short enough to avoid hurting him.

"Don't try me," I warned over his bark of pain and surprise.

"Bad move, Sergei," Roman said in a bass growl. "You've broken peace."

"She—never drank," the wolf cringing beneath me rasped.

I needed to establish my own dominance, or I'd be looking over my shoulder for this one as well as Troy. "We won't have any more problems, will we, Sergei? Or I'll show you what I learned on my last visit to the Crossroads."

Neither of them knew the only thing I'd learned in the Crossroads was that I'd drawn the attention of the old gods somehow and didn't want to go back. It wasn't something I talked about. But rumors of the Crossroads were dark enough to make Sergei nod enthusiastically, or try to, with his bruised throat. I waited until he went still and bared it to me entirely, having learned from tickling wars with Roman to look for the gesture.

"Good boy," I mocked when he offered it, waiting another second to make my point before rising and going to lean against the counter.

He bared his teeth as he rose, and for a moment I thought I might have pushed him too far. Then he shook himself and backed down again.

"You staying in town?" Roman asked in a deceptively calm drawl, pulling his brother's attention away from me.

"Yes, though I was hoping for some fast food."

Roman shook his head, the drawl firming. "No."

"No?"

"You're not hunting in my woods. Not when setting me up for an out-of-season kill can score you political points back home. If I find out you did anything other than buy mundane food from a real restaurant or store, you'll regret it." He stared his brother down. "And I will find out."

Sergei's smile had an edge to it, and I didn't know if it was because he'd been caught plotting or simply that he was pissed at having to obey an exile. "Perhaps you could spare a steak then. It is the full moon, after all."

"It's time to go, Sergei," Roman said, glowering.

"He's not shy about asking for things, is he?" I grumbled.

Roman shrugged. "You don't ask, you don't get. Or you have to steal it. 'Scuse me." He leaned to kiss my temple. "I'll just walk him to his vehicle."

With Roman escorting Sergei out, I had a minute to myself. Did I want to be angry about this? *Yeah...I think I do.*

Roman had no control over Sergei turning up unannounced, but he hadn't mentioned anything about having spoken to his pack, let alone dropping my name into it. My understanding had been that he was waiting to see what Torsten would come back with before taking the massive step of reaching out to his family. Now it looked like he'd gotten ahead of himself and dragged me in behind him.

Footsteps crunching up the gravel path gave me a last few seconds to prepare for the coming fight—ahem, *discussion*—with Roman. They did nothing to prepare me for the psychic wail that ripped through my consciousness.

Every muscle in my body spasmed at once. A scream tore free, dragging all the air from my chest until my insides crumpled like an empty chip bag. When there was nothing left, I toppled.

The world went black then flashed to white. I writhed, face down in fine-grained nothingness, pins and needles pricking every one of my nerves.

The Crossroads.

None of my limbs worked. Moving hurt. So did not moving. I opted for the former, pushing through immateriality until I found my feet. The Crossroads was not a place I wanted to be and not a place I should be able to reach on my own. The djinn could reach it. So could Callista.

And so could the old gods.

"She felt it. How curious."

I whirled, time passing like molasses even though I faced the other direction in half the blink of an eye. A dark-skinned woman leaned on a *was* staff and twirled an ankh round her finger. Arrow shafts poked out of a quiver at her hip, and a bow rode on her back. A strip of red cloth held long locs away from her face, and her red kilt fluttered in an unfelt wind under strip-leather armor.

"Curious? More disturbing," her black-masked companion said. He was striped in red and white paint, with deer hoof spools dangling from his ears, and the Milky Way glimmered where his eyes should be. The last time I'd been here, he'd shot me with an arrow that had crackled with lightning when I pulled it out. I still had it, buried deep in my closet, and I never wanted to touch it again.

Fear gripped me by the throat. That arrow had fucking hurt, and none of the gods had been on my side. On the contrary; they'd been willing to let me be a sacrifice of blood and bone because I couldn't summon enough Air to suit them after having been metaphysically beaten within an inch of my life and fighting back to kill a terrorist.

"Nothing to say?" The goddess circled me, still whirling her ankh.

The god smiled, raising a hand to bounce a ball of flame from fingertip to fingertip. "Perhaps she is to be a sacrifice after all."

"Fuck that," I gasped, taking a step backward in a jerky, fast-slow way. I didn't remember that from the last time I'd been here, but last time, a djinni had framed the Crossroads for me.

"Some spirit! Excellent." The ball of flame bounced faster.

"What do you want?" My voice was unsteady, but I think they liked it. Fear was as good as adoration to them, I guess.

"Only to examine you for a moment. You're still weak but growing stronger, and the time is coming," the goddess said. Neith, I thought, recalling the research I had done after the first time I woke from a nightmare of my last visit here, and the god was Mixcoatl.

18

I couldn't keep an eye on her and Mixcoatl at the same time. They could move here. I couldn't, and I was going to dislocate a knee trying to turn quickly enough to keep them both in sight. "What time?"

"She did not feel that a moon ago," Mixcoatl said, ignoring me and clenching his fist to extinguish the flame.

Neith's gaze seemed to weigh me. "No, I think not."

"Feel what?" I asked, unable to help the natural curiosity that came with being a private investigator, even though my heart thudded.

They grinned like cats, already fading.

"The magician," Neith said.

Then they were gone, and with a jolt, so was the Crossroads.

Chapter 3

Four silver eyes stared down at me when I found reality again, and two disastrous things happened. First, as soon as I found breath, I reflexively pulled on Air and forced it outward, blowing the predator eyes away in a gust of wind as I pushed myself backward and out of reach.

Second, Sergei lost control, went full wolf faster than I would have thought possible, and launched himself at me.

Snarling and snapping erupted as Roman met him, changing even as they collided. The wall of the trailer bowed as they crashed into it. The coat stand overturned with a clatter when they rolled into that next. Someone was going to think there was a dogfight going on and come to investigate or call the cops. If that happened, we were in breach of the Détente and fucked six ways from Sunday.

"Enough!" I forced a wedge of Air between the two and ripped them apart. Roman had the sense to stay where he was thrown. Sergei gathered himself for a leap.

I'd been right. He made a massive wolf with intimidating teeth and claws that gouged the already scuffed linoleum floor. That only mattered if he could reach me though.

"Stay," I snapped, making a grabbing motion with my right hand. I didn't need gestures to do my magic, but I'd found they focused my intent more.

Sergei halted, wrapped in loops of solidified Air, not tight enough to hurt but enough to keep him where he was.

"Arden," Roman murmured.

I turned, and he winced at whatever was in my face—or maybe it was the glowing gold of my eyes, giving me away as an elemental as much as the wind had.

"Your hand, babe." He quivered, trying to force a reversal of his shift when there was too much fear and adrenaline in the air.

My right hand, directing my magic, was fine. My left dripped blood where I'd dug my nails into my own palm. I opened my fist and stared at it, unable to look away from the swelling beads dancing as my hand shook.

A vicious growl drew my attention back to Sergei. With a thought, I muzzled him, looping a breeze around his snout and stiffening the air molecules.

"You need to learn manners," I said, "Before someone has to teach them to you, or worse, calls the fucking police."

The wolf stilled and whined.

"Do. Not. Fuck. With. Me." I punctuated each word with a pointed jab of Air in his ribs to make my point. "If I can survive the elves and kill a fucking elven prince, I can bury you without breaking a sweat." That was only partially true, but hey, I was still here and Leith Sequoyah was dead at my hand.

Sergei whined again, and I let go of Air. He clattered to the floor, landing in an ungraceful heap of long limbs and grey fur before slinking behind the couch. I shuddered at the sound of bones rearranging in both him and Roman, who managed to convince his body to shift back as soon as his opponent was out of sight.

"Bleeding mother of the twins," Sergei said in a growl from behind the sofa. The sound of the shift continued. "She's an elemental. I thought they were myths or that the elves had killed them off. Roman, how the hell did you get mixed up with one of those?"

"I'm right here," I snapped. "Don't you talk about me like I'm not, and don't make me remind you about manners."

"Yes, ma'am. Sorry." He popped up just as his eyes returned to a solid grey that could pass for human. He flushed, making him look even younger. "It's just—I mean—"

Roman cleared his throat.

Sergei glanced at him, then at my raised eyebrows.

"I'll get you some pants," Roman grumbled as Sergei rolled his eyes and grabbed the car magazine on the side table, holding it in front of himself.

Sergei and I waited. He glanced around the trailer while I looked anywhere but at him. I don't think either of us had a problem with his nakedness in principle, but it was weird seeing my boyfriend's little brother in the nude on our first meeting.

"This was not how I planned on this meeting going," he said as the silence grew heavy.

I glanced at him, smirked at the frustration in his expression, and started picking blood out from under the nails of my left hand. "That's too bad."

"It's not normal. Roman, I mean."

"Seems pretty normal to me." When he didn't answer I looked up again, long enough to catch him scowling. Whatever he might have said next was lost when Roman reappeared.

He hurled a pair of sweatpants at his brother. "Don't come back here, Sergei," he said. "I may be packless, but at least I still remember courtesy."

Sergei blanched as he caught the mess of grey cotton and avoided both our eyes as he dressed. When he was clothed, he said, "We're not finished."

"We are for tonight." Roman rubbed his temples. "Get out. I'll call you in the morning."

After a last sullen look, Sergei found his wallet and phone amidst a heap of silk then left. The scraps of his designer suit littered the floor where he'd shifted in them, the tattered fabric making a hell of a statement about the evening, and it wasn't even over yet.

As Sergei's footsteps faded from our hearing, I squared up to Roman.

"Before we have that discussion, you wanna tell me why he came back inside?" That wasn't what I was really mad about, but it meant I'd shown what I was before I was ready. Again.

"Shit. I can't, Arie, not tonight. Can we not do this now? That hand needs tending." He reached for it, and I jerked away. It'd heal fast enough on its own; it was a few nail marks, not a knife wound. My healing abilities had ramped up as I used my powers more, and I was not in the mood to be distracted.

"Seriously?" I'd just started getting comfortable with the idea of being in a real relationship. To me, that meant talking to each other, which was why I'd avoided a relationship in the first place—because I hadn't been out to him as an elemental when we'd started sleeping together and it hadn't seemed right to call myself his girlfriend when I'd been hiding my true nature.

He hadn't said a word to me about contacting his family about an alliance I was supposed to be facilitating. Not only did it hurt, it potentially put me in a bad position with Torsten and House Monteague.

My temper flickered when he didn't answer. "That's awfully convenient after I stayed to help you deal with whatever the hell *that* was."

"Come on, babe. You, of all people, know how much it would mean to me. Reuniting with my folks. Having a pack and a clan again. You *know*."

I closed my eyes and clenched my jaw to stop myself from saying something I wouldn't be able to take back. Roman's presence drew closer, and I stepped away.

"Arie…"

I resisted the desire to wrap my arms around him. "No. You don't want to have a conversation now, and I definitely don't feel like falling into bed anymore, not after that."

We stared at each other, each with our own painful past. When he didn't look away, I crossed my arms and lifted my chin. I might have fallen in love with him, but that didn't mean I'd be a doormat.

"When did things get so complicated?" he asked.

"When we agreed to start telling each other the truth." I gathered my backpack and stalked out, letting the door slam behind me. A neighbor protested, hollering a threat out the window of the trailer across the way. I ignored it, focusing on the woods. Sergei might have gone back to his car, but he might be waiting in the dark. Even if he wasn't, lots of things went bump in the night, and too many of them were aware of me these days.

Nothing came at me. I made the drive home in record time, fueled by outrage and aided by a dearth of cops. Tires kicked up gravel as I pulled into my driveway a little too fast. The stones crunched under my feet as I got out and slammed the car door behind me.

"Arden!"

I jumped and lashed out with Air, having been too wrapped up in my thoughts to have noticed Zanna. The strike passed straight over her head.

The kobold had moved into the crawlspace under my house while I'd been working on the Sequoyah case and declared herself my landlord when I returned. I paid her with a weekly six-pack of beer, preferring that expense to offending one of the sprites. Besides, she was better than a guard dog. Just as wary and able to tell me what she'd seen while I was out instead of just barking.

"Hey, Zanna. Sorry. Long night."

"Wolf problems?" Her curls sprang out in all directions, her bearing giving them the impression of a mane rather than untidiness, and her smile was sly.

"Yes," I said, still annoyed. "How's things?"

"You had a visitor."

"A visitor?" The list of people who knew where to find me and would bother—or dare—to stop by was short, especially of late.

A deep, rich voice called, "Hello, Arden."

I whirled.

Zanna snarled and said, "That one. That one was here! Came on *my land*. Didn't ask permission. Didn't offer tribute. Disappeared!"

Nebuchadnezzar stood behind us, his long wool coat hanging straight down even in the light breeze. He wore his favorite form, that of a tall, thin, young, Black man with even features and laughing eyes the color of dravite.

"Duke," I said, trying to keep my breathing even. I hadn't seen any of my childhood guardians since my first visit to the Crossroads in late January. Callista and Grimm, a djinni who I'd learned was my cousin, had taken exception to my budding alliance. I'd assumed that Duke, another cousin, had been punished for getting involved on my side, but I hadn't seen him in so long that I'd started to think he might have decided to side against me. "What are you doing here?"

He grinned, teeth white in the dark. "You know me. Can I come in?"

I exchanged a glance with Zanna. I wasn't sure if we were friends, but she was definitely more than just a random kobold squatting under my floor. Not only that, but I'd need her goodwill if I didn't want to be cursed out of my own home. "Zanna, would you like to come in for a drink?"

The kobold pulled herself up to her full two-and-a-half feet of height. "So kind. Yes. Thanks."

My pointed stare made Duke sigh.

He turned to my housemate, aware of the courtesies even if it annoyed him to follow them. "Zanna, may I join you?"

I hadn't thought it possible for her pride to grow, but it did. Her chest puffed out as she said, "Maybe. If you learn guest courtesy."

Duke blinked. The djinni was thousands of years old and had lost the knack of humility. At last he managed, "Thank you."

Shaking my head, I climbed the stairs of the front porch and stepped over the block of Air I left in front of my door. As it was elemental magic, I was the only one who could see it. Zanna followed my step with exaggerated care, and Duke went misty to walk through it. They'd both learned the hard way that I liked a warning before someone knocked on my door. I ignored Zanna's mutters that I'd moved it again and waved them inside.

"So. You're here," I said once I'd poured everyone a glass of Malbec and gotten them seated at my dining table. I usually avoided boozing in company, but Duke knew all of what I was and Zanna wouldn't care as long as I paid the rent.

"I'm here."

"Not in the mood for riddles tonight, Duke," I said. "What do you want?"

Zanna looked between us, catching the tension and wise enough to keep silent and observe.

Duke sipped from his glass and hummed in pleasure before fixing me with an intense look. "Have you ever been bottled?"

I frowned. "You know the answer to that."

"Then you have no idea what an outrage it is."

"No, I suppose I don't."

His gaze flicked from dravite to their natural carnelian as rage simmered behind his eyes. "Lucky half-breed."

I stiffened. "Half-breed" was an ugly term regardless of the context, but the fact that my father had been an elf was new knowledge I was still coming to terms with. My hand rose to clutch the onyx-and-gold pendant I wore—my father's pendant, the only thing I had left of him—without my conscious thought. I don't know why the djinn had let me keep it if they hated my tie to the elves so much. "Do you have a point?"

Duke gathered himself with a deep inhale, settling back in his chair. His eyes darkened back to gold-shot black, and I relaxed. Djinn in their true forms had eyes in the shades of red gemstones: carnelian, ruby, garnet, coral, jasper. They couldn't affect others with Aether, as elves could, but they were supernaturally strong and could make a hell of a mess with shapeshifting and teleportation. "My point is, I'd like to take a moment and enjoy this wine before we get down to business."

First Sergei and Roman, now Duke. Apparently this was my night to deal with family squabbles, and I wasn't in the mood. "Some people need to work for a living, Duke. I've got a case starting in the morning, so how about we get on with it."

"One might think you weren't happy to see me."

"One might be unclear as to where you stand these days." I held his glare. "Bottled or not, you hid shit from me. Big shit.

27

For almost twenty-six years." I tugged my pendant to make the point.

"And?"

"And I'm not cool with it. So you need to tell me what you're doing, showing up twice in the same day." I glanced at Zanna, who nodded in confirmation. "Or you need to go do whatever unbound djinn do these days." Okay, so the half-breed comment stung worse than I'd thought. Why was I on hot coals with everyone I called a friend?

Oh. Because they'd used or lied to me, or gone behind my back, when I was trying to build something for everyone. That's why.

"How was the Crossroads?" Duke asked in too light a tone.

I went rigid, flashing back to the endless white, to Neith and Mixcoatl playing cats' games in the eternal nowhere.

"I thought so. You sensed the sorcerer."

"What if I did?" Denial is the mother of easy sleep, but I had to figure out what was going on.

Duke *tsk*ed. "Be careful, Arden. I don't know what happened tonight, but the edge of fate has sharpened."

"The last time you turned up in my driveway talking like that, I was drowned."

"Yet here you are."

"What can I help you with, Duke?" I asked through gritted teeth.

"The Djinn Council has agreed to negotiate with your alliance. *If* you guarantee that you will fight for our interests as vigorously as you have fought for those of the elves."

I pushed away my wine, propped my elbows on the table, and buried my face in my hands. Of course it came down to the djinn versus the elves. That was why I'd spent the first part of my life hiding what I was. The elven Houses had imposed a death sentence on elementals, thinking us too powerful and still blaming us for the elven deaths at Atlantis—the whole plot having been driven by the djinn for reasons only they remembered.

We laid low now, which was easier for weaker elementals like my friend Val. First-generation, trueborn elementals like me, the forbidden offspring of a djinni and an elf, were not so lucky—if you can call that lucky. We were much rarer but far stronger, our magic undiluted by generational distance and prone to strange permutations. Our greater ability to manipulate the elements made us wild-cards too dangerous to be left alive, according to the elves.

Unless you strike a deal with an elven Darkwatch agent-slash-prince and get a stay of execution from one of the high-blood Houses, at the cost of your life.

Yeah. This past winter had been all shits and giggles. I'd even missed my birthday in all the excitement, though Roman had made it up to me later.

When I looked up again, Duke was gone. He'd taken his glass and the rest of the bottle with him.

"Your friends. Rude," Zanna said.

"I know, right?" Rude didn't even begin to cover it. Prophetic, disturbing, and self-interested was a start. For the good ones.

"The Big Reveal. Updates?"

I winced. My personal responsibilities had eclipsed events in Otherside in the last couple of weeks, but that wouldn't slow the pace of Callista's plan to bring us—or some of us, at least—out into the open. "I haven't heard anything, Zanna. Sorry. But I think you'd be safe. You don't eat people."

Her grin showed sharper teeth than I remembered her having and I lifted my eyebrows as she said, "You think."

"Remind me not to piss you off," I muttered, finishing my glass. She stared at me, unblinking, as I rinsed it out and headed for my room. "Night, Zanna."

"Good night, tenant."

"Ah yeah. Rent is by the door. New brewery in town, let me know if it's any good." I hated beer, but the kobold preferred it. Her scampering footsteps and the slam of the front door, followed by a growled curse and the clatter of bottles as she tripped over the block of Air for what had to be the twentieth time, brought my shoulders down. Shit was weird here, but at least nobody was trying to kill me.

For now, anyway. Between the Crossroads and Duke, I had a sinking feeling that was about to change, real fast.

Chapter 4

This month's case was disappearing bodies. The human cops didn't know that I was an Othersider, and my work as a private investigator had always focused on mundane—human—cases: tracking down skips, following cheating spouses, the occasional corporate espionage job. Now I was being brought in to bolster manpower and help clear backlogs for Raleigh's mundane police department.

A few cemeteries had been hit. This morning, I'd been woken bright and early with a call about the morgue. The police were keeping it out of the news, spinning some tale about the medical examiner's office being closed due to a public health concern. I guess you could call it that. I called it acting.

As in, act like I wasn't completely creeped out by the magical residue at the morgue and do my job.

Dried, dead bushes and flowers ringed the building. March had been rainy so that was weird, as was the pattern. Something had carved a path to the door, yellowing the pine needles on one side of a tree, turning half a bayberry to brittle twigs and leaving morning glory blooms to droop on the vine. I shifted the backpack on my shoulder. *What could have caused that?*

The same sense of dread that had accompanied last night's psychic scream oozed from the morgue and extended out to the parking lot. The pleasant spring weather made a jarring counterpoint to the lingering horror, making each step slow as molasses. I wondered if humans could feel it or only Othersiders. Would a sensitive like Doc Mike be affected?

I was about to find out. With a deep breath, I pushed the door open and stepped inside. The sensation was worse in here, concentrated somehow and not just a miasma of fear. Streaks of evil shot through it in a path from the door to the back room.

Doc Mike was standing at the beginning of the hallway that led around to the staff lockers, peering at something out of my line of sight.

"Hey, Doc," I said.

Doctor Michael Miller, suave silver fox, unflappable medical examiner, and the closest thing I had to a friend among the humans, jumped about ten feet in the air. He glanced at me, then back at whatever he'd been looking at around the corner, face pale. "Arden! Did you see that?"

Nothing mundane would have spooked him that badly. He had a steady personality and too much experience with weird deaths, some of which I'd consulted on in my capacity as a private investigator and, secretly, as a Watcher. Part of the job was making sure humans didn't find out about Otherside, and when Othersiders got sloppy, I had to help misdirect the mundanes.

I reached for the Ruger in my inner pants holster, and he stared at it with wide eyes when I pulled it out. Shaking my head to say, "Not now," I eased around the corner and down the hall.

A flicker of shadow caught my eye. Had I been alone, I might have walled it in with Air. With Doc Mike in the next room, I had to keep myself in check.

"Get out of here, if you don't want to see the other side," I said, hoping the wordplay would make my point before a bullet had to. I hadn't carried a gun before this past January and I was reluctant to shoot it outside the range. Not that it would do much if it was the wrong kind of Othersider. Lead bullets would be fine if it was an elf. Anything else would need silver, bronze, or meteoric iron.

A man-sized shadow moved, catching my eye. I recognized that particular brand of magic, as much by the look of it as by the scent of meringue lurking under the stench of antiseptic and dead human flesh. An elf—and if they could command shadows, one of the Darkwatch.

Shit. Something was definitely kicking off again. The Darkwatch only got involved in the juicy stuff.

The burnt marshmallow smell grew as the intruder drew on more Aether. Most Othersiders wouldn't be able to sense the rising power, but being half elven had to have some kind of benefit.

"Don't. I'm a Watcher," I said under my breath, choking down a spark of fear as a flashback of the confrontation with Leith Sequoyah hit me with the smell. It was half a truth but better than the alternative. The elf would be able to hear me. Doc Mike wouldn't. "Whatever is going on here, I'll handle it. The doctor is under my protection."

Such as it was, but Doc Mike was good people and there weren't many of those in my life. I had to try, even if it would probably get me in trouble.

The growing magical pressure hesitated as the shadow edged in the direction of the back door. I tracked it, my gun following its path but pointed toward the floor. We did this dance to the exit. When the door creaked open and shut behind it, I slumped against the wall. That could have been death for more reasons than one.

"What. The devil. Was that."

I jumped. Doc Mike stood at the end of the hall, eyes wide and jaw slack.

33

"Uh…what was what?" *Shit.* The medical examiner was the perfect Southern gentleman, soft-spoken and polite. He never swore or even hinted at a swear. That he had now meant he'd seen too much.

"Don't, Arden, please. It's bad enough that my own office is giving me the willies without having missing bodies and—and *that.* That *shadow.*"

I holstered my gun and scrubbed my hands over my face. "Doc, I really wish you'd stayed in the front."

"You know. You know what it is." He stared at me, gears of thought turning visibly. "You knew about the bodies back in January as well, didn't you? They weren't copperhead bites, and you knew it. Were they even drugs?"

"Doc…"

"What are you covering up? Who do you work for?"

"Come on, Doc. This is not—"

"FBI? NSA? Who? Are you even a PI?"

"Yes!" That question, I could answer safely. "Yes, I'm a private investigator. The license is real."

"Then what is all this?" He rubbed his arms, and I knew it wasn't from the cold but from the lingering evil that he shouldn't be able to sense. Would that give me enough of a loophole that I could explain all of this enough for him to keep trusting me, without betraying Otherside?

With my arms spread and my hands open, I slowly approached Doc Mike. He steeled himself, muscles tensing as he resisted the urge to take a step back. He was lucky I wasn't one of the Othersiders who ate people; his fear was palpable.

"Look, Doc. There are—there's more to life than what you know, okay?"

"Life. Like biological life, not philosophical."

"Yeah."

"So what was that?"

"That was something you shouldn't have seen and isn't my place to tell you about. Something you cannot talk about. Ever. Trust me, you don't want to cross them."

"Why do you know about them?" His reserve was unraveling by the second, his eyes darting as he sought the source of the psychic threat his sixth sense told him was there.

"Can you lock up and get a coffee with me? I can tell you why you've got the creeps right now."

He stared at me, fear warring with a painful desire to know in his brown eyes.

"I shouldn't. But it's not like it's been business as usual today. Okay."

Doc Mike sat silent as we drove over to the café on the other side of Wade Avenue. I was too busy composing what to say to break it. We got our beverages—black coffee for him, chai for me—and found a table against one of the windows, away from the morning bustle at the counter.

"Right," I said when we couldn't put it off any longer. "Where to start…"

"Let's start with you."

I winced at the snap in his tone. Doc Mike had helped me out with a case more than once. He probably felt betrayed. I'd had enough experience with that in the last few months that all I could do was sigh tiredly. "Me. That's complicated."

"Why?"

"Because even among the others I'm a special case."

"The others. Arden, why invite me for a conversation if you're going to beat around the bush?"

He was right. I slouched in my chair, really not wanting to do this. "Fine. There's a parallel society that most humans know nothing about and are fortunate enough never to learn of."

Doc Mike took a long sip of coffee, his hand shaking as he heard the implications. "And if they do learn of it?"

"They are killed," I said bluntly. He needed to understand the gravity of the situation. "Or made to forget or brought over. Depends who of us the mundane—the human—stumbles across."

"Is that a threat?" he said with a snarl. Defiance flared and his face flushed.

I rubbed my temple, the lingering warmth from my mug offsetting the chill of the overdone air conditioning and helping to soothe my growing headache. It was too early in the morning even without dealing with this. "No. It's not. Like I said, I'm a special case, and I have no interest in killing anyone."

"Then what happens to me? What did I see?"

"What happens is this. We talk. You shouldn't be able to sense the evil in your office. The fact that you can confirms something I've suspected for a while, that you're some kind of sensitive, and that gives me—gives us—options."

"Sensitive? Wait—have you been watching me?"

"Too many questions at once, Doc. Bear with me." I blew on my chai and took a sip. "Yes, I've been watching. It's part of my job. Some of the community get sloppy or bold, like this winter. We can't have the wrong kind of news getting out."

"Did you bury my report? About the bites?"

"No. I made the case that you should be left alone. Somebody else took it upon themselves to bury it. It was that, or you would have had an accident." When he didn't ask more questions, I continued. "You're a sensitive. I don't know what type. Could be run-of-the-mill psychic, could be something more interesting like a latent necromancer, given your choice of occupation."

Doc Mike scoffed and set his coffee down. "Psychics. Necromancers? Give me a break."

"After what you saw this morning, that's the incredible part?"
He opened his mouth. Shut it. Frowned.

I took advantage of the lack of reply to get some more chai into me before it went cold, then fiddled with my pendant. "This isn't the first time you've had a funny feeling, is it? Maybe you felt a nudge to look again when you were ready to wrap up an autopsy. A cause of death jumped out at you that everyone else missed. Or maybe it was a family member who gave you a bad vibe despite how broken up they seemed at the death."

He paled. Nodded.

"You had a funny feeling about me at first, as well. You got used to it, but something about me probably sets you on edge when you stop to think about it."

With an uncomfortable glance away, he said, "I, uh…I was afraid it was, you know…racist or something."

I laughed. I'd experienced racism from humans more than once. I presented as Black or mixed race, with a warm sepia skin tone, dark eyes, and tight, espresso-colored curls. But I'd never gotten the sense that he was like that. It explained why he'd fallen over himself to be helpful in the early days of our acquaintance though. "No. You sensed that I'm Other. Truly other, not the lines humans create between themselves."

"Well, that's a relief." He slumped, blowing his cheeks out. Then the bit about him being psychic, or me not being human, hit him and he sat up ramrod straight. "Let's say I buy all this. What—" He swallowed.

"What was in your office? Not the shadow, but the feeling?"

"Yes."

"Something corrupted. That's why it feels evil. Given what I—what *we* sensed, I'm willing to bet that it's related to your missing bodies."

"Evil wants dead bodies?"

I shrugged. "This evil does." A smile cracked my face before I could stop it. "Gotta admit, Doc, you being kind of in the know is going to make investigations a hell of a lot easier. I was pissing myself over those bodies in January."

His gaze grew avid as he leaned forward. We both carried out investigations in our own ways, and he had the same natural curiosity I did. "Come on, Arden. What were they? The puncture wounds. They were bites, right?"

I weighed the pros and cons of telling him. He hadn't run screaming this morning and had taken in everything I'd just told him with only a case of the shakes. Later might be another story though, once he'd had a chance to sit down and pour a drink. "Given what I've told you, I think you can guess. But it's not something we're going to talk about today. Let's get back before you're missed."

The medical examiner was pensive on the return trip, almost subdued. He shivered as we re-entered the morgue, almost a flinch, before squaring his shoulders and leading me to his office.

"What are we dealing with?" he asked when he was settled behind his desk.

"I don't know yet. I'll still need to investigate, like with any other case. I just don't have to misdirect you at the same time." I smiled weakly, hoping he'd see the apology in it.

He frowned. "Hmm. Well. I guess I should start with the first time the security systems were tripped."

I pulled out my voice recorder, notebook, and pen, clicking the recorder on before asking, "This was a few days ago?"

"Yes. Sunday. The security cameras only showed a figure in a hoodie. Short, slim. Probably white and male. Walked around the building and scrawled something in the dirt, then left."

"Did you get a picture?"

"No, the lawn service cleared it away. They get here first thing. Didn't recall anything when Raleigh PD checked on it."

So far, that matched what the file I'd been provided said. I switched off the recorder to test our new understanding. "What's your gut say?"

Doc Mike looked away and shifted in his seat. "It felt like today but...less."

"Interesting." If last night's scream was the becoming, the scratching in the dirt could have been the prep. That had me worried. Wayward witches tended to raid graveyards for parts, not whole bodies, and not a whole morgue's worth. This was something else. Something far worse. "What did the cameras catch last night?"

"Nothing but static."

"Damn." I chewed the end of my pen, considering the options. The Darkwatch had the tech to scramble video. A few witch spells could disrupt magnetic or electronic fields. The djinn's magic could only affect themselves, although helping another group wasn't outside their sphere of mischief. They could have teleported into the morgue's security suite and disabled something. I didn't know enough about the range of vampiric powers, but they and the fae relied heavily on glamour and illusion, respectively, and wouldn't have the magical chops to manage this. I mentally reviewed the witch covens in the area, trying and failing to recall if they'd had any members lose the Way recently.

"Does that help?" he asked.

"Maybe. Honestly, Doc, I don't like the possibilities. Is there anything else?"

He fidgeted. "How long until it feels...normal?"

I winced as I packed up my notes and recorder. "Hard to say. I've never encountered anything like this before. Might be able to find someone to cleanse it for you though." It would mean going to Callista if I couldn't find a witch to help, but I couldn't stay away forever. Our new understanding—that I'd continue to Watch for her but on my own terms and with payment—was still tenuous.

"Okay then. I guess I just need to figure out what to tell the families of the missing."

On second thought, I'd rather see Callista than deal with that job. In the meantime, I had a whole lot of research to do—and if whatever had caused the corruption at the morgue didn't give a shit about the Détente, I didn't have a lot of time to find answers. This was not what I needed with a new werewolf in town and an alliance to build, not when I was already feeling the pressure to build a power base that could rival Callista's.

Chapter 5

I had no idea where to start with this case. Usually, the mundane cases were just that—mundane. My work as a Watcher had been focused on preventing threats to Otherside, not investigating our own. Now that I was out in the community, I didn't have an excuse to pass on this one. My reluctance to go to Callista with it meant I could either make more work for myself or beg a favor.

I was not in the mood to beg favors.

Frustration with my inability to find a lead on body theft in Otherside lore soon had me changing tacks. I scrolled through local news sites, looking for something—anything—else that could point to what this was. All I found was a surprising uptick in arson and car crashes over the last few days. The weird thing was that it was all concentrated around west Raleigh...starting near the morgue, the night before the bodies had gone missing. I scribbled a few notes and then slouched in my chair, tapping my pen against my lips.

"Why so glum, sugarplum?"

I jumped at the amused voice. Maria stood in the doorway, wearing a broad sunhat and shades, linen trousers, and a lightweight, long-sleeved top. I hadn't heard her footsteps or the door opening.

"Um…" I glanced outside, where the sun still held sway, its beams adding a diffused warmth through the privacy frosting on my windows.

The number-three vampire in the Triangle laughed as she came all the way in and closed the door behind her, her berry-bright lips an odd complement to her emerald green hair. "Oh, darling. Don't tell me nobody told you."

"Not trying to be rude, Maria, but…" I gestured at the sunny window.

She edged around the glow of sunlight and into the darkest corner before taking off her sunglasses and nibbling on one of the arms. A sharp canine flashed. "They really did keep you ignorant, didn't they? Oh, dear. Now I've gone and put your back up."

I glared at her, wondering what the hell Grimm, Duke, and Callista had neglected to educate me in now. I hated being afraid, but being ignorant surpassed even that on the list of things that put me in a shitty mood. My job—both my jobs—were literally defined by me knowing or finding things out. I *hated* when it didn't happen on my own terms.

Maria grinned, enjoying seeing me off-balance.

I warmed as my temper heated. "Were you going to tell me what was worth the drive up from Raleigh in the daylight, or did you just want to look at me?"

"My dear, I always want to look at you." She grinned even wider and gained a dimple in her left cheek. "I'd rather taste you, but I'll take what I can get. Unless I can tempt you away from your wolfman?"

My unfinished conversation with Roman flashed through my head. I kept my face straight, but like Sergei, she could read more than visual cues. Unlike Sergei, she had the grace and tact not to comment. Her coffee-brown eyes flashed in amusement, but that was all.

"You're avoiding getting to the point," I said, wrenching my mind back to thinking and not reacting. She'd swanned into this same office a few months ago and pressed her teeth to my neck to get my attention. "You're not here for Torsten, are you?"

She grinned. "Perceptive."

"Kind of my job."

"So it is. And speaking of, I have a job for you."

"I don't take jobs in Otherside."

"You took one for that serial-killer elf."

I rubbed my temples, trying to fend off the unfurling headache. "Sequoyah thought he'd compelled me with Aether. If I didn't play along, he'd have discovered me even earlier than he did."

"You took one for Torsten."

"You had your fangs at my throat."

"I also had twenty thousand in cash. And, oh! Look at this. I have more." She tilted her purse toward me to show neat stacks crammed in tight.

Frustrated, I stalked around my desk and threw myself into my chair. The police departments were slow to pay, and cash in hand was always welcome. Plus, Maria threw me off my game. She always did. Seduction and flirtation flipped to bullying and browbeating as soon as the first method proved unsuccessful, then back again. None of it was personal, but all of it pushed my buttons. On top of that, I needed to keep my reactions balanced or risk tripping her instincts. Her glamour wasn't quite enough to snare me, but her natural allure compensated for it, not to mention her persistence.

As though being an especially charismatic vampire wasn't enough of a weapon, she was also something of a warrior. I didn't see her twin blades now, but that purse could easily hold a gun in the side pocket. Tiny as she was, she was not a being to trifle with.

"I knew this was going to happen," I grumbled. "Fine. I will *listen*, and that's all I'm promising. Just like I would for a mundane client. But you should know I'm on a case already and that one has priority."

Maria smiled and pulled herself up, cat-like in her satisfaction. "All I'm asking is a fair hearing."

"Fine. Shoot."

"It's actually two jobs."

"Maria…"

"I need information about someone. Another vampire. Or several of them."

I frowned but decided to go with it. I'd promised a fair hearing. "You can't get this information yourself?"

She shrugged. "Two heads are better than one." When I just stared at her, she huffed and tossed her head. "Fine. They're exceedingly secretive. They've established a secondary nest somewhere and likely secondary funding. They'll see me coming."

"Maria, please don't tell me you're dragging me into vampire politics. I got dragged into elven politics and practically died."

She grinned wide enough to show fang. "Don't worry, I'd bring you back."

I shook my head, exasperated. "I don't even know if—You know what? Not important. Why the hell should I take the job?"

"Because if you don't, there's going to be a power struggle in Raleigh right when you need me to argue the case for an alliance with the elves and the weres. Oh, and get Torsten to sign on with that little Reveal."

"Shit." I tilted my head back to rest it against the chair, risking taking my eyes off of her to give myself space to think. "Coup?"

"Near enough. You know I'm now the number two *moroi*?"

"*Moroi*? And no."

She flapped a hand, waving it off even as the skin around her eyes tightened. "Vampire. Don't tell them I told you. Anyway. Aron was our number two. You remember him, no?"

I nodded, wincing, and rubbed my throat. Aron had gone mad and become a rakshasa. He'd escaped whatever minders they'd put on him and nicked the skin of my neck, which meant Torsten owed me a favor. As far as I knew, the only way to move up in the vampire hierarchy was for the one above you to die or to change coteries.

"Aron grew unmanageable. We had to put him down." She said it with less emotion than most people used for their dogs. "I moved up. Not everyone is happy about that."

"Why?"

"New blood." Her lip twisted. "With new ideas. They don't just agree with Callista's plan—they want to take it further. And that's just one point of their damned manifesto."

She slumped, all artifice falling from her. "I'm *tired*, Arden. I need *help*. Do you realize what that means, for me to ask? It's what earned me my first death to begin with."

I wanted, more than anything, to probe for details, but her past wasn't my business. "So, Aron's gone. You moved up. But some in the coterie don't want to play by the rules, and you're running out of both time and options."

"More than that. I've fought off four contenders for my rank in the last week, all of them younger than fifty years in death. They know they can't win, but there are enough of them that they're taking me in turns. Wearing me down. Someone is coordinating a plot and using some of the weaker ones as cannon fodder."

"Clearing other elders from the board with expendable youths before toppling you and pushing this manifesto?"

"Precisely. Goddess save me, somebody finally gets it. Torsten says I'm being paranoid."

"I hate to ask, but are you?"

She scowled and drew breath to reply, then gathered herself and sat back. "No, I don't think so," she said after a minute, still frowning but calm in her distance as she stared across the room. "I wish I was. This change will be challenging. Announcing to the humans that we're real? I wish I could say that I'm just afraid of being hunted again. But these…these *children*, are acting like we should be rock stars. They'll be our end, not our salvation."

"Speaking as one who's still got a death warrant open with two elven houses, I feel you."

Her gaze came down, and she smiled wryly, the first one I'd seen without artifice or flirtation or threat. "Yes, I suppose you do. Does that mean you'll help?"

Turning to my monitor, I jiggled the mouse to wake up the computer and pulled up my case notes. "I meant it when I said I'm already on another case."

"It wouldn't happen to be about the missing bodies at the Raleigh morgue?"

I blinked a little too rapidly as I looked up at her.

"Is that a yes? Because that would be *so* convenient for the second job."

"I'm not supposed to talk about other cases with uninvolved clients." Not that that would stop me from all but admitting it if it would get me the break I needed to move the case along.

"You're not supposed to…but you have no idea what would make every body in a morgue walk out or why it feels like the filthiest sort of evil." Her soft tones and sharp expression contrasted with her earlier playfulness.

Chills raced over me as I strove to be casual in my lean backward. "*Walk* out? Is there something I should know?"

"There's something I could tell you, if you agreed to help me with both cases."

She had me, not that I'd admit it. Of course, my scent, pulse, and a dozen other involuntary bodily tells probably did that for me. "My ongoing case takes priority."

"Certainly. But it will go so much faster this way."

"Fine. I will look into your *moroi* conspiracy."

She flinched as I said the super secret word for "vampire" but rose, sticking out her hand. "Then we have a deal."

I slipped my hand into hers, unable to help a short gasp at its warmth, and made the mistake of looking into her eyes.

She nearly rolled me.

Jerking free, I stood and got the chair between us, trembling with my hands on its back.

"Almost," she mused, pupils dilated. "I'm growing stronger again. That's good to know."

"Fuck that. If we're working together, Maria? No. Games."

"You might enjoy them."

"Don't give a shit. That's not my job. My job is—"

"The morgue. And now me." Maria's delight tried my patience, but I needed to figure out what the hell had happened at the morgue. It wasn't just the police department now. Doc Mike was counting on me to find a way to cleanse the place.

"And now you," I said, sighing as I sought the silver lining. Getting paid twice for the same work wouldn't hurt, especially when the vampires would pay a hell of a lot more than Raleigh PD.

"Excellent!" With a clap, she resettled herself in her chair. "You're dealing with a sorcerer. More specifically, a lich."

"A lich."

All good humor, she tilted her head as though I was being especially dense. "Mmhm."

After counting to five, I said, "I was given to understand that I was looking for a magician."

"Magician? How elementary. Who—oh. You went *there* again? Yech."

I glanced away, unwilling to discuss my recent trip to the Crossroads even as I made a mental note that 'magician' was not in common use anymore. Duke had said something about a sorcerer as well, although he'd neglected to say anything about a lich. Did that mean something?

"You must be desperate," Maria said. "Didn't you come back with an arrow in your shoulder last time?"

"You know I did." The shoulder in question ached with the memory and I resisted the urge to roll it.

"But I suppose it's been a few hundred years since a lich was last seen."

My head spun with the jumps in her statements, even for someone used to dealing with the excuses of deadbeat parents and cheating spouses. "Are you going to get to the point?"

She slouched and looked at me from under the brim of her hat, somehow managing to look composed even with the sloppy posture. "The djinn are involved."

I stared. Assuming she was telling the truth, I'd just seen Duke. He'd only given the barest hint of a sorcerer. He knew I was pissed about them hiding things, and he hid something else?

Dropping my head to my hands, I said, "Treat me like I'm only a few decades old and not however many centuries. What do the djinn have to do with a lich, the missing bodies, and the evil at the morgue?"

"The djinn are the only ones who know the making and unmaking of a lich. All I know is that it involves a sorcerer.

Liches call the dead to them. The unnatural act leaves a taint that other evil can ride across planes."

I leaned forward onto the desk, my stomach clenching at the idea of what might cross the planes on the amount of evil that had tainted the morgue. The thought that followed brought my head up. "Why aren't you more concerned about an Othersider that can control the dead?"

Maria tilted her head coquettishly. "Because I'm already *un*dead, silly goose. If the lich turns out to be a lich *lord* then I'll be worried. That's why I want you to start looking into it now." The charm oozed from her expression as she considered that, and she was back to looking tired. "Whatever it is, I can't let the coterie fall to pieces right as the humans are about to learn fairy tales and legends are real. That means figuring out who's funding and leading these little pissants. If you're already looking into the morgue, then we divide and conquer."

"What if I find the lich? How do we get rid of it?"

Maria shrugged and rose. "Find the djinni who made the spell."

"That's it?"

She scoffed, smoothing her linen trousers. "'That's it.' No, silly. That's just step one, and you're going to have to do the rest."

That figured. I crossed my arms and looked at my desk. It felt like I was being used again. Maria wasn't Leith, but I was being pulled into something I wasn't sure I wanted to be involved in.

Too late. I'd gotten involved when I took Doc Mike for coffee.

My eyes fell on my notes. "Could a lich cause a spike in violence?"

"With as much evil as would trail in its wake? Entirely possible. Now. Is my down payment paid?"

"Add a grand for up-front expenses, and your retainer is." I might not be excited about the vampire politics side of things, but with the elf at the morgue I would have spent at least a few days barking up the wrong, deadly tree. "I'll invoice you at my standard rate. *After* I give my other case enough to work with."

"I accept," the vampire said, for once keeping an appropriate distance between us as she dropped a single stack of bills and a neatly folded sheet of notepad paper on my desk. "Start with those names." She turned to go.

"Enjoy the weather." I was irked and knew I shouldn't be. I wanted a group of my own—not just a power base, but friends. I'd be naive if I thought I could build anything without putting in some work. That didn't stop me feeling salty at the idea that I was just being used again. I didn't know where Maria and I stood. Maybe I'd hoped that I was something other than hired help.

"It's not deadly, the sun," she said over her shoulder. "It gets more dangerous as we grow older and more sensitive to ultraviolet light damage, but even Torsten wouldn't burst into flames walking down the street. He might wish he had though, with the sunburn he'd have."

She pulled the door open and strode out, her long, emerald locks bouncing behind her.

Chapter 6

As frustrating as Maria's visit was, at least I had a lead. If a sorcerer was involved, I needed to arrange a meeting with the local coven. But first, tea. Fortunately, the coworking space in which I rented my office had a well-equipped little kitchen area.

While I waited for the kettle to boil, I smiled blandly at the humans also making use of the space. They smiled back with no idea that I wasn't one of them, equally non-committal in their nonverbal office etiquette. We'd all seen each other around and exchanged a few words, maybe had a vague idea of what the others did, but I avoided the mixers and didn't know everyone in the space as well as I might have. Sometimes I debated the wisdom of that choice, but I was used to keeping a low profile.

With a cup of oolong in hand, I headed back to my office and scrolled through my phone, trying to figure out who would be best to contact. The witches tended to keep to themselves, following the Way in peace and not bothering anyone. I hadn't had to deal with any of them in over a year.

Janae, I decided. She ran an online magic shop catering to humans, the kind that sold crystals, hoodoo herbal preparations, tarot cards, and books on esoteric and spiritual topics. For those in the know—mainly Othersiders but also the occasional enlightened or sensitive human—she also dealt in real magic. Janae wasn't magically powerful enough to be a coven leader, but she was well-respected in both the Otherside and human communities and strong enough in her sense of self that she could probably manage the morgue cleansing.

When it came to evil like that, self-belief would outweigh power nine times out of ten. Besides, Janae's family had been in Durham since before the Civil War. Her blood tie to the land would make up that last tenth. If I could get Janae on board, I could avoid asking Callista for a name. I still needed to see her, but coming as a supplicant would weaken my already precarious position.

I shut my office door and leaned against it while I dialed.

Janae picked up before the first tone had completed. "Miss Arden, to what do I owe the pleasure?"

"Blessings of the Goddess to you," I said politely. The older woman was even more of a stickler for respect than most of Otherside. "Why do I get the feeling you knew I'd be calling?"

"Call it witch's intuition."

"Right. Is this a good time to ask a few questions?"

"About the evil in Raleigh, Callista's plan, or your new alliance?" Her tone had gone from warm to sharp, a grandmother welcoming you in before calling you to task.

I winced and rubbed my forehead. Too much was getting out too fast. "Door number one."

"Mmm. And if the cost of door number one was to open the other two?"

"Then I'd ask to throw in a personal favor as well. For balance and all."

Janae hummed again, a considering tone. "For balance, then, I will accept, but I don't commit to your favor until I hear what it is. Ask."

"I'm told it was a lich. What—"

Her hiss of outrage cut me off. "It can't be."

"I understand it can't be the best news," I said, treading lightly. "But I have no reason to think my source lied." When she didn't answer, I added, "Ms. Janae, I'm sorry, but I don't know what else would scratch a hex in the dirt, make off with all the bodies in the morgue, and leave a taint that evil. And the scream alone—"

"You sensed it?"

Her sharp interruption put me on edge, and I kicked myself. Like almost everyone else, the witches didn't know what I was, other than that I was an Othersider. I'd just admitted I had a connection to nature magic. Mine was elemental, where hers was tied to life forces, but none of the Aether-users would have sensed it.

"I did," I admitted between stiff lips.

"We have more to discuss than I thought."

"Be that as it may, ma'am, are there any witches who may have lost the Way? Anyone from out of town?"

"Come to see me tomorrow, and we'll discuss it."

Which likely meant that she had to run it by the local coven leaders before sharing it with outsiders, but I'd take it. Striding to my desk, I checked my calendar and said, "Sure. How's...two?"

"I will see you tomorrow afternoon at two. And Miss Arden, I do hope we won't be playing any games."

The line clicked off, and I buried my face in my palms, hoping that I wasn't about to complicate the alliance or the Reveal further. *It'll be fine. You're doing fine.* I closed my eyes and focused on my breath, then on all the little eddies of air stirred by the air conditioning.

I checked in with the Raleigh Police Department, letting them know that I had a possible lead to follow up tomorrow, then finished my tea and headed out. I couldn't keep avoiding

Callista and call myself a bad bitch. Our estrangement after the events of the winter was a constant weight on my back, a knot in my belly, and a burn in the crevices of my mind.

Odds were good that she already knew about my mini alliance. Acting like it was meant to be more than me looking for shelter would be like showing weakness to a hungry bear. I'd told the Monteagues, Maria, Roman, and Duke that I could handle Callista. If I wanted to be a force in Otherside, and if I wanted to keep my word, I needed to face her.

* * *

The late afternoon pressed down with unusual warmth for the season. It was just humid enough that my sweat refused to evaporate completely, making my jeans cling to my legs and my black tank top stick to the damp line down my spine. I regretted walking over by the time I arrived at Callista's bar. Making matters worse, heavy metal was the music choice of the day. I hated the stuff. It messed up the airwaves and always threw me off.

Callista looked up from where she was chatting with a customer, leaning against the bar on one elbow. The pleasant look dropped from her spring-green eyes as the wood-framed glass door shut solidly behind me, trapping me in an over-loud hell. She turned back to her customer and made a last comment, patting his hand before making her way over to the end of the bar with a smooth grace.

"I wondered how long it would take you to find your courage." The bite in her words belied her broad smile.

Swallowing my immediate reply, I took a seat on the closest stool. She plunked a highball onto the counter, pretended to splash rum in it, then filled it with cola before dropping a lime in and sliding it over. Our usual ruse, me pretending to drink in public, her indulging me.

"I'm here now," I said after taking a sip. The soft drink was too cold on top of the change in temperature from outside, triggering a brain freeze.

"I see that."

Her attitude pissed me off. She'd admitted to using me and shaping me into what she needed. Had celebrated my flexing my power with Air and making myself a more useful tool. Now she was mad that I wasn't doing her bidding anymore?

Of course she was. That's what people like her did.

Leaning forward and keeping my voice low, I said, "Look, Callista. There might be a lich in the Triangle. I'm sure we can find common ground on *not* wanting that?"

"A lich," she said tonelessly. She sat perfectly still in her chair, a snake trying to determine whether the rustle in the grass was prey or a threat. "Where did you hear that?"

"Source on a case."

"Tell me."

"No. It's a case. I'm not working it for you. I'm here as a Watcher, but that's no longer boundless. As we agreed."

"Stubborn." She scowled before forcing her narrow face into a more pleasant look. "Well, I suppose it's to be expected. You've come into your power. Now you seek to exercise it. Just don't push me too far, child."

We stared at each other, each getting a sense for the new balance of our relationship.

"I will help with the lich, if that's even what it is," I offered, not wanting to be too far on her bad side. The alliance wasn't finalized yet, which meant I was still on my own.

"Very well. What else?"

I blinked, not sure how she'd guessed that I wanted something else. "The Reveal." I sipped my drink as a cover for my pause. "I've got more of the community asking about it."

"Serves you right."

"I might need to trade information to find out about the lich. Information I'd bring back here."

Callista considered that, grabbing a rag to wipe up the ring of condensation left by a patron leaving a space farther down the bar before coming back to me. "It will be the elves first," she said, lips tight, as though that would stop the words from coming out. "I have an agreement with House Sequoyah. Compensation for Leith's misstep."

Misstep. That was a hell of an understatement, but all I said was, "And healing runs stronger in that house than the rest."

Her narrowed eyes told me I wasn't supposed to have seen that, but she didn't say anything about it. It made sense, though. House Sequoyah ran closer to the human imagination of what elves looked like—tall and blond, with light eyes—than the other Houses in the Triangle, and their affinity for healing could be spun as a benefit to humanity, a reason not to hunt the rest of us down or press too hard for answers, lest the gift be withheld.

"Can I get you anything else?" she asked in a louder tone, playing the bartender again while giving me a pointed hint to get out. She'd spent too long with me, but she lingered over each patron at some point or other. It wouldn't look that weird.

I pulled out my wallet and dug out a few dollars. "That's all for today. Thank you."

Callista swiped the bills and stalked away without a backward glance, leaving me even more unsettled than I'd been when I came in.

I thought about the discussion on my walk back to my office. She hadn't been surprised to hear about the lich, which could have been because she had other Watchers. What bothered me was how quickly she'd let it go. My stomach cramped, and I shivered as I realized she was plotting something that touched on the lich. Shit. Did it have anything to do with Duke having been bottled? Or the old gods in the Crossroads?

Too many unknowns. I scowled as a blast of cold air hit me on re-entering the coworking space. Sylphs may be cold tolerant, but it didn't mean I enjoyed the human tendency to waste energy completely overcompensating for the season. It was only late March. There was no call for that much air conditioning, even with the early warmth and humidity.

I spent the rest of the afternoon trying to piece together where the lich, if that's what this was, might have gone. A morgue full of bodies doesn't just disappear, even when magic is involved, and even when they might have walked themselves out. Raleigh PD had provided a USB drive with plenty of security and traffic cam footage to sift through. Having hit a dead end on lore and news articles for the time being, it was good old-fashioned detective work I fell back on.

The morgue cameras had been blown, so that blocked the easiest checks. Fortunately, there were a lot of state government buildings around the medical examiner's office, all of which had recorded video of a large, white van traveling toward and away from the area at around the time the cameras glitched out. Unfortunately, the police had already determined that the license plate was a fake.

As evening shifted the shadows in my office and painted it orange, a knock pulled me out of another grainy image.

"Come in!" I hollered, scrubbing my face to find a professional, friendly expression as I rose.

I'm not sure who I was expecting. Certainly not Roman and definitely not Roman with a small ZZ plant balanced on the palm of one big hand. He'd never come to my office before.

"Hey," he said, taking in the space. The baby blue T-shirt he wore was clean for once, as were the tan cargo shorts and grey sneakers. His dark hair was freshly cut, and he almost looked dressed up.

Crossing my arms, I leaned against the side of the desk and tried not to let the sudden sourness in my stomach show on my face. I wasn't sure whether my indigestion was because I was still mad or because I didn't want to be despite feeling like I'd had a right to know he was going to name drop me the Volkovs. "Hey, yourself. What are you doing here?"

"I'm sorry about last night, babe." When his gaze finally landed on me, it flicked away before settling on my face.

"You're sorry." It was a start, but fuck it, I guess I was still mad. We were supposed to be *partners*. It was hard not to feel like he'd turned around and used what I'd been through on the Sequoyah case to get himself an in with his toxic family. I got it, but that didn't stop the hurt squeezing my heart.

"Yeah."

"What are you sorry about?"

"Can we maybe not do the investigation part? I brought you this." He hefted the plant, eyes and mouth tight.

"It's nice," I allowed, appreciating the effort. "But if we're going to be a thing, we're doing the investigation part."

Sighing, he took another step in and shut the door behind him before finding a home for the plant in the same corner I would have put it.

"I'm sorry I took advantage of the elf shit to reconnect with my pack," he said, tone sullen and eyes flashing silver as he rested unusually elongated hands on his hips.

58

I fought to keep my face blank. Roman's control was usually excellent. Then it clicked. It was only the day after the full moon with his little brother in town, and I was pushing buttons. They needed pushing but maybe not when we were both feeling justified and pissed off. I needed to step back. Lose this battle and take it from a different angle later.

Taking a deep breath, I forced myself to drop my arms and take a less hostile stance. "Look, Roman. I get that this was important to you. I'm just frustrated and upset that you didn't talk to me first. I'm still learning who I can trust with what I am. And I thought we were partners in this—that you would, I dunno, *talk* to me first. It sucked to meet your brother like that."

His eyes settled into a less stormy grey and his shoulders came down a notch. "Yeah. I see that now." His hands popped as they returned to normal, and he stepped closer to rub them along my arms. "I *am* sorry, Arie. You know I'd never mean to do something to upset you or that put you in danger."

That he was sorry for upsetting me, I believed. That he was apologizing when he didn't think he'd really done anything wrong still bothered me. We'd come back to this, just not tonight.

"Okay," I said, giving in to the delicious werewolf scent of cedar and musk and leaning in to rest my head on his chest. "Thanks for the plant."

"And maybe dinner?"

I leaned back. "Dinner too?"

"I haven't taken you out in a while. Look, the shirt's even clean."

"I noticed," I murmured. I'd also noticed how well it fit him, showing off the smooth muscle of his arms and the breadth of his shoulders. Yummy. My stomach predictably took that opportunity to rumble. "Dinner sounds good."

Roman's arms tightened before he let me go and took my hand, kissing the top of it. I leaned over the desk to grab my purse out of the drawer and locked up on our way out, hoping dinner would be enough to smooth things over for a little while.

Chapter 7

We made it through the meal without incident. Sergei was still in town, so Roman was on edge, checking the door every time it opened and keeping an eye on the windows. That he'd taken me out and tried to make things right when he was so obviously disturbed by the presence of his brother softened my attitude, and I agreed to follow him home.

"I'm glad you're here," he said when we were inside his old trailer. He peered down at me, something haunted yet hopeful behind his eyes. Tree frogs peeped in the soft rain outside, and Roman grabbed the sweatshirt hanging from the coat stand to dry my hair. His gentle tugs at the ends of my curls tilted my head back, and his lips hovered over mine.

I closed the small distance between us, meeting the offered kiss. His musky cedar scent intensified as he dropped the sweatshirt and wrapped his arms around me, encouraged by my acceptance. Our tongues danced, and our bodies pressed together, awakening in me the passion that had fled last night.

"Roman," I gasped, clutching the waistband of his jeans and fumbling at the button. He dipped to grasp me under my thighs, lift, and pin me against the door with a solid thud. A pleased growl rumbled in his throat as he dipped his head to kiss my neck. Giving up on the jeans, I tugged his shirt up and skimmed my hands along his flanks before dragging my nails back down.

That earned me a nip to my shoulder and another trail of kisses back up to my mouth. The next time we came up for air, he said, "Bed?"

With a smile, I nodded and kissed him again, challenging him to find his way in the dark with his arms full of me. I was the one distracted, though, and a small yelp of surprise escaped when he dropped me onto the mattress and followed me down. We tore off clothing without a care. Something ripped and was thrown to the side.

He freed my breasts and nuzzled them before taking a nipple into his mouth to make me arch back. This is what we'd had before everything got complicated by a relationship, this easy, fiery lust and pleasure in each other's bodies.

"I'm glad I'm here too," I admitted.

Roman claimed my mouth again, more forcefully than before, as he slipped a hand between us to test my readiness.

I did the same, pumping my hand along his length and enjoying how it made his breathing ragged.

He jerked the nightstand open and reached inside. Condoms snaked out when he withdrew his hand, still connected to each other as he grabbed one, and I laughed. "Optimistic much?"

"With you? Always." The sound of tearing plastic accompanied the scent of lubricated latex as he ripped one off the string and tore the packet open. "I could never get enough of you."

The sentiment stole whatever little quip I might have made as he rolled the condom on. Then he was kissing me again, his body barely held above mine as he pushed in.

We both groaned. He gave me a minute to get used to him again, resting his forehead against mine, until I rocked my hips. Then he moved, slower than we had when it was just a thing on the side, but more intense.

Ecstasy grew. Our movements quickened.

"Let go, babe," he murmured. "All the way."

I didn't know what he was talking about until he blew a stream of air from my chest up to my jaw. Distracted as I was, it called my power forth. I stiffened, breaking our rhythm as I scrambled to maintain my shields.

"Hey. Relax. Just be," Roman said, pausing and pushing up so the only place we were touching was where we were joined.

I panted, caught between passion and panic. *How the hell did I manage this before?*

"Arie. Just. Be." A strategic movement of his hips combined with a caress of my breast to bring everything tumbling down. Something toppled from the nightstand as Air burst from me in a gust and I flushed, glad that he couldn't see my embarrassment in the dark room.

"It doesn't matter. Listen to me. Just be. You and me," Roman prompted. He moved again, slowly, carefully, invitingly.

For once, I let go, crying out as I relinquished the part of my brain that always had to be in control and paid more attention to our bodies.

He growled and picked up the pace. "There you go. Just like that."

I reached up and tangled my fingers in his hair, pulling him down to me in a deep kiss as we connected on a whole new level.

Another slip of Air escaped as we climaxed, my eyes glowing gold, his shifting to a luminous silver. He shivered as it tickled the sweat clinging to him in the now-stuffy room but stayed where he was, showering me with kisses.

"There's my girl," he murmured as he withdrew and tugged off the condom, dropped it over the side of the bed, and pulled me to him, back to front. "That was okay, right?"

"I wish you would have warned me," I grumbled half-heartedly.

"If I had, you'da overthought it."

My temper flared, and I tensed, ready to fight him on it. Then I thought about it, remembering the times I'd lost an orgasm because I'd been wound tight and afraid of losing the rest of me. "You're right," I acceded, relaxing into his embrace. "You still should have asked, but you're right."

Roman huffed a sigh, tension leaving him when I didn't pick a fight. "You were always so scared before. I could smell it on you, but I didn't know why. A bad ex? A subconscious warning about me being a wolf? I never knew. Then I started to wonder if it was…"

"Having to hide what I am?" I could hear the bitterness in my own voice, both for having to hide it and for the rift it had caused between us.

"Don't worry about it, babe."

For the first time in a long time, I didn't. The cracked window let in cool night air scented by rain and grass, damp woods and the distant, water-filled quarry. It blended with the smells of us, salt sweat and static and musk.

He pulled me closer, enveloping me.

"No matter what happens with Sergei or the others, I'll protect you. Believe it, babe." His words slurred with sleep, but I could tell he meant them. His arms tightened once more before they slowly went slack.

I lay completely exposed in the arms of a sleeping werewolf and, for the first time in my life, felt safe.

"He's getting stronger," a disembodied voice said.

My eyes snapped open, and I found myself not in Roman's bed, but in the endless white of the Crossroads. Neith leaned over me, scowling. I jerked backward, managing only to half-bury myself in the nothing-sand that formed the basis of this place between the planes.

Before I could ask what she meant, another psychic scream tore through my mind. I flinched and slapped my hands to my ears, too slow and yet too fast, the broken movement making me box my own ears so that my head rang as much from the blow as the scream. I didn't know what the goddess wanted, I didn't know where the scream was coming from, and I'd be fucked if I laid here and took it.

Air fought me when I reached for it, but I was a trueborn sylph. Even the suggestion of the element was enough for me. I dragged it to my grasp and forced it into an explosion of outward force.

Neith staggered backward. Instead of being angry, her eyes lit with interest.

"Well done!" She whirled her *was* scepter in a complex loop and jabbed it at me.

Snarling, I swept it aside with another burst of Air.

"Very well done!" The goddess grounded her staff and leaned against it. "Much better than your first visit. I am pleased. Go. Hunt this magician. See that he does not steal that which belongs to us." She pushed her hand forward, as though she was doing a palm strike.

I choked as the ethereal sand buried me then snapped awake with a gasp and sat up, blood surging as I reached for Air again.

Roman gaped, hands up where they'd sprung away from me at my sudden movement. The morning sun tried to make its way through the blinds, striping his face as he blinked at me. "Sorry, babe. I was just—you've never stayed the night before."

Sighing, I flopped back onto the pillows then rolled to kiss him, hoping to take the hurt out of his eyes. "It's not you, Roman. Or us. It was the Crossroads." I hadn't mentioned the lich to him yet. With Sergei in town and the moon full, I wasn't sure it was the best idea. My heart thudded.

"Shit." Roman didn't push. He never had. Gratitude filled me as he simply gathered me closer and let me use his familiar scent to calm my racing heart. "I hate that this is happening to you."

"Has your life been any less messed up?" I asked, my lips moving against his pulse.

He slid a hand up to my hair and plucked at a curl. "Maybe a little. With Sergei here…"

I waited for him to finish, but he didn't. We laid there as the morning sunlight grew stronger, taking solace in the present.

His stomach rumbled, pulling us from our thoughts.

"Breakfast?" Roman offered.

"Tempting."

"But?"

I wrinkled my nose. "I don't usually eat breakfast. Too much in the belly makes it hard to think."

"*Nothing* in the belly makes it hard to think. Although there's another distraction this morning." He skimmed a hand up my side, hinting.

I leaned into him and stole a quick kiss before easing out of bed. "Also tempting, but I picked up a second case yesterday and got a tip on the first one. There's things to do today." *Like research liches.* I had to get home.

With a scoff, Roman said, "You work too hard, Arie."

"Hey, someone's gotta get the job done." When I'd finished dressing in the jeans and black top I'd worn yesterday, I bent to give him another quick kiss. His arms snaked around me to make it a longer one.

I wrinkled my nose at him when he freed me. "Jerk. I'll see you later."

"You love it."

I stuck my tongue out at him because he was right. After hiding for so long, being desired as my whole self made butterflies flutter in my belly. I'd never been that kind of woman, or girl, for that matter. Everything was changing so fast, but maybe that just meant I was finally finding the belonging I'd always ached for.

I let myself out. Gravel sprayed as I gunned the engine, anxious to get home and dig into whatever the hell was going on with the lich and the gods. A white Range Rover barreled around the corner onto Howe Street as I reached the end of the road. While the Triangle had its fair share of the flashy SUVs, I'd only ever seen one at the Cabe Lands trailhead.

"Fuck off, Sergei," I muttered as he braked and blew the horn at me, waving out the window for me to stop. When I turned onto Sparger without acknowledging him, he kept on toward Roman's.

Whatever that was about, I was glad to have missed it. The suspicious side of me wondered if that was the reason for Roman to offer breakfast and sex, the thought immediately chased away by guilt. He meant well. Right?

My first stop was home to shower and change into a fresh pair of denim shorts and a close-fitting teal tee. I tucked my pendant into the scooped neck of the top. Ever since Leith Sequoyah had shown enough interest in it to tear it from my neck, I was wary of letting it show. Especially after discovering a similar one around his neck before I killed him. Not that I would take mine off, but we all have our failings. Holding on to a necklace I should probably hide in the bottom of a drawer was one of mine.

Zanna was out doing whatever it was kobolds did on spring mornings, so the house was blessedly quiet and completely mine. I made a cup of tea and plotted out my day, scrawling circles on one of the notepads I kept scattered around the house.

I didn't need to meet Janae until this afternoon and I had no intention of jumping back into a Volkov family squabble, leaving the morning free to do more research on liches. Maria's first case would have to wait. I'd already told her I had other priorities, and digging into the lich would help the second case.

My phone buzzed with a notification: drinks with Val this evening. I got the feeling she'd been assigned to keep tabs on me by the rest of the local elementals—who I had yet to meet— but I didn't mind. As a dea, Val's affinity for Fire blended easily with mine for Air, and she'd become the closest thing I had to a friend with the djinn gone.

The djinn. What is Duke hiding? Determined to find out, I snagged my laptop and my mug and headed out to the deck to do some research.

My deck was small but cozy, stained a golden mahogany that almost matched my skin tone. A small table with blue-and-white mosaic patterns sat between two cast-aluminum chairs with an open X back. I snagged one of the cheerful, palm leaf-patterned seat cushions on my way out, dropping it onto the chair with the best view of the yard before taking a seat. I loved my deck, with its tinkling windchimes and squirrel-resistant bird feeders swinging over the railings. As was the case with most of my furnishings, nothing matched other than having a reasonably similar pattern and being mostly in blues or greens.

The table sported a thick layer of the pollen that got everywhere starting in mid-March. I couldn't be bothered with wiping it off, so I propped my bare feet up on the table and settled the laptop on my legs. A chickadee scolded me from the gutter overhead, and a titmouse whistled hauntingly, its flock joining in from the surrounding trees. An early hummingbird buzzed at the nectar feeder, guarding the food from her fellows in between sips.

I had work to do, but this was the closest thing I'd had to a break in weeks. I tilted my head back and closed my eyes, enjoying the dapple of late morning sun on my cheeks and the kiss of the light breeze cutting through the humidity.

The tickle of a sugar ant scaling my foot brought me back. I brushed it off then flipped open the laptop and got to work. I'd have to speak to one of the djinn eventually, but I wanted to have a starting point for my questions. It would cost me too much in favors or information otherwise.

While the internet was generally long on bullshit and short on facts—especially about Otherside—the key to any investigation was finding the linking threads, the details common to every story. With liches, everything from mythology to roleplaying game guides agreed that they were powerful sorcerers, linked to the dead, and as intelligent as they were before becoming a lich. They evaded their own deaths, either by being undead themselves or through some magical means. Even if I took everything I read with a giant heap of salt, there was too much lore connecting them to sorcery and the dead—just as Maria had said.

I didn't write any of this down. Rule number one of Otherside: leave nothing behind that could hint that it even exists.

"What does it want with the bodies at the morgue?" I muttered aloud, stringing my pendant back and forth along its chain. A few of the roleplaying games had "army of the dead" as a power. That seemed wildly implausible...but then again, so had an elven conspiracy to take down the queens and end the matriarchy.

A stone settled in my gut at the idea of an army of zombies in the Triangle. If the gods were hassling me over it, maybe the idea wasn't that farfetched.

Chapter 8

Imagining the worst-case lich scenario had me on edge as I arrived at the west Durham house where Janae lived and ran her business. Taking a deep breath, I got out of the car and tried to shift my mind away from the vision of a swarm of zombies making their way down I-40.

"Let it go, Arden," I grumbled to myself as I approached the door and knocked. The white trim was spotless despite the pollen, and not a single cobweb haunted the corners. My porch was coated in even more yellow than my deck table, and spiders seemed to be running a bed and breakfast out of every crack in my house. "That has to be magic."

"It is," Janae said as she opened the door. "A gentle suggestion, nothing dramatic or harmful."

I blushed at her knowing smile, not having intended to be heard.

"You best find another place for that negative energy before you bring it in here," she said, the smile morphing into a frown as she took my measure.

"Blessings of the Goddess on you and yours." I meant it, and let the intent behind it chase away the last of my dark thoughts. For now.

"Better." Janae stepped aside to let me in. I shivered despite the lack of air conditioning as something, not elemental magic, not Aether, but *something*, prickled over my skin as I passed the threshold. She narrowed her eyes. "Hmm. You've grown far more interesting than the last time I saw you, child, if being here gives you chill bumps."

"So I've been told." Thinking of the old gods made me wonder if she might be able to help me there as well, but I needed to tackle one problem at a time and wasn't keen on letting more people know about my visits to the Crossroads.

When I didn't elaborate, Janae waved for me to follow her into her parlor. Two old-fashioned wingback chairs in a deep purple sat opposite a long sofa of the same color, and a matching chaise longue sat in a beam of sunlight against the far wall. The cream-and-gold, damask-patterned wallpaper added to the stately elegance of the room. A simple pot of tea on the coffee table scented the room with mint.

"Please sit down," she said.

I slid to the end of the sofa with murmured thanks, waiting to say more until she'd settled into an armchair, then poured and served the tea. "You said that the cost of telling me about what happened in Raleigh would be information about Callista's plan to reveal us and...my...new alliance."

"Oh, good. A Watcher who abides by her word. I am so pleased that we won't have to play silly games."

I frowned. Torsten had said something about Watchers showing disrespect when I'd visited him this past winter, and I wondered what Callista's other agents had been tasked with to irritate so many of the Triangle's key Othersiders.

"Why waste time?" I said with a shrug as I filed that away for later. "I'm sure we both have better things to do."

"We certainly do." The sharpness of her gaze made me wonder if she was talking about more than I thought, but all she said was, "Tell me what you can about this grand Reveal and the status of your alliance, and I will share what I may about your lich concern." Her mouth twisted on the last two words, disgust tightening her features, but she didn't deny it again.

"You sent someone to look into it," I guessed.

"After you, child."

"The elves go first."

"What House?"

"Sequoyah. They owe a debt, and healing magic is easy to spin, as long as it doesn't get out what else they can do with it." My voice cracked, and I involuntarily clenched my fists, remembering how Leith Sequoyah had warped his magic.

She narrowed her eyes at me. "Sounds like somebody found that out the hard way. Hoo, boy, that would be a heck of a lesson."

"Yes, ma'am, it was." No use dissembling with a witch I hoped to exchange information with. I swallowed, setting my cup of tea down to hide the tremble in my hand at the memory of Leith ordering his opponents' bodies to shut down and die, and the heat of his blood washing over my hands.

"What brought all this about?"

"I was tasked with bugging a healthtech start-up. They've developed some new technology, something that Callista thinks could finally out us. An elf sent in as a test last month was flagged as a genetic anomaly, so I think she's right. It's measuring something the other tests haven't managed to catch yet. They don't know what it is now, but they will sooner or later."

"Well then. Makes me wish I still smoked." She patted one of the hip pockets on her floral-patterned dress, where I assumed she'd once kept cigarettes. "One way or another, the end times are coming."

I tensed. That was almost what Neith had said in the Crossroads. "What does that mean?"

"Child, you've gone pale. What have you seen?"

"What—" I stopped. Gathered myself and let the breeze from the ceiling fans calm me. "Ms. Janae, what do you mean the end times are coming?"

"A change is coming, my dear. A big one. My cards warn me about it every time I cast for answers. Could be this Reveal is it. Could be it's just the start. Goddess, do I wish I had a cigarette." She sipped her tea instead, leading me to suspect menthols had been her favorite. "Now. What have you seen?"

"The Crossroads." The words tumbled out before I could stop them, and I flinched when she set the cup down with a gentle but firm clack on the table.

"And who did you see there?" Each word was spoken quietly and with care, not doubting for a second that I'd been there despite her not knowing what I was or how I'd found it.

"Them." I glanced at her and away, wishing the prickle of magic would stop, wishing I could keep my big mouth shut and stop giving away my secrets.

Janae leaned back into her chair. "Be easy, child. Be easy. I keep to the Way, and no harm will come to you here."

"I'm sorry. I know the energy isn't good, but—"

"I understand. May I take your hands?"

"What are you going to do?"

"A reading of your aura. Nothing invasive or painful."

I studied her seamed brown face, lighter than mine and framed with stray curls of white hair. She looked like someone's grandmother. It didn't fool me—many Othersiders looked far more harmless than they were—but I didn't sense in her the evil I'd felt at the morgue. Still...

"Sorry, I'd rather not."

She frowned. "Very well. Tell me about your alliance then."

That I could do. I outlined the agreement Maria, Troy, Roman, and Duke had taken back to their respective peoples, leaving out the fact that Sergei was in town. Whatever was going on with the Volkov family wasn't her business. I didn't even want it to be my business.

"You didn't think to ask the covens if we would join?"

"None of this was my idea to start," I said bluntly. "So no, I didn't think to ask y'all. But it seems everyone is looking to me to get this done, and if it means safety and allies?" I shrugged. "Does the coven want in?"

"They may. Would we be welcome?"

"The more the merrier, as far as I'm concerned. The others will want assurances that you'll be there to help if and when needed."

"We will not do violence. But we could serve in other ways. Healing, refuge, succor, divination, for a few examples."

"I can take it to the rest."

"Do. And I will bring this before the assembled covens."

Fair enough. That put them at the same level of commitment as the elves and the vamps, so I nodded.

We both took advantage of the natural break in conversation to drink some tea and refill our cups before she said, "I will consider your side of the bargain fulfilled. Ask your questions."

"Thank you, ma'am. I guess to start, you seemed offended that I'd call you about a lich. Why?"

"It is a disgusting heresy, a sin against the Way and a corruption of all we believe. To become a lich requires a witch to become a sorcerer first. Do you understand?"

I shook my head no.

"To use death magic. To kill, to end life, and steal the soul of a being rather than borrow energy. It is…" She shook her head and closed her eyes. When she opened them again, the kindly grandmother was gone, making me glad that I hadn't given her my hands. "It. Is. *Evil*. And that is what you sensed at the morgue. The twisting of our gift to its worst application."

With a deep breath, Janae closed her eyes again, regaining her composure. "It has been a long time since one of us has lost the Way so badly."

"I'm sorry." After waiting a respectful moment, I said, "How does a sorcerer become a lich?"

"In a ceremony that twists our traditions. I understand it involves the djinn, somehow."

That matched what Maria had said, and I nodded. "I hope I haven't caused offense. I just hadn't even known they existed before now. The humans think someone broke into the morgue and stole a bunch of bodies. A source hinted they may have walked out, and the last thing I need with the Reveal coming is zombie rumors. If I don't know the truth, I can't give the mundanes a believable fiction."

"No. No, I suppose you cannot. And we must preserve their fictions, at least for a little while longer." Janae sucked on her teeth. "Hard times coming."

I pondered my next question carefully before asking, hoping that it wouldn't cause more offense. "So it sounds like a sorcerer could be somehow more powerful than a witch?"

Janae rocked in her chair as her face tightened. "The range of our magic is limited by the life energy it can pull on. Greater spells need more life, or even death. It's part of why we seek balance and harmony. If there is no more life, there is no more magic, at least for those who follow the Way. Even that does its part for balance. But you're correct. Limiting our impact limits our power. And we accept that. Most of us, anyway." She waited until I nodded my understanding to ask, "Did you notice anything dead? Other than the humans."

"Every plant in a path from the door and a good way around the building."

"No animals?"

"A ground crew had been in earlier that morning. I could check with them."

"Do. If the deaths weren't there, they were somewhere else. I'm not sure what is worse in all of this."

"What do you mean?"

"Is it worse that this lich killed to empower his evil? Or that the innocent dead were pulled from the Goddess's sleep?"

Personally, I thought the worst thing was that there was a super-powerful, super-evil corrupted witch running around with a bunch of dead humans in the back of a truck somewhere, getting ready to do Goddess knew what, but there was no need to piss on her beliefs. I shrugged, then frowned as something occurred to me. "Ms. Janae, if witches don't do violence, how do you deal with a sorcerer?"

"Those who lose the Way are Severed. I will say nothing more."

"I…see. Thank you." Now I knew more about the mechanics of being a lich, but I still didn't know how a witch—or a sorcerer, rather—became one other than that the djinn were involved. "Is there anything else you can tell me?"

"Not that I can think of, no. I did share your question with the coven. We will be watchful and stand ready to give aid."

The witches self-policed then, as did everyone else in Otherside. I suppose I shouldn't have been surprised, but they'd always struck me as such pacifists. My mistake to assume that meant sitting around and letting others solve their problems.

But speaking of giving aid…

"Would you be willing to send someone to cleanse the morgue?" At her suspicious look, I added, "The medical examiner is a sensitive."

"And a friend of yours?"

"Yes," I admitted reluctantly. "He's new to all of this. So, someone subtle?"

"I'll go myself, if he's so important to you. A secret shared is a secret kept, a trust not to be broken."

Relief made me slouch against the sofa, though only for a moment under Janae's sharp eye. "Thank you, and for the tea. Consider us even—the cleansing for the information. I'm sorry about all the negative energy I brought. Or caused."

Janae waved it away. "I can cleanse my home as easily as the morgue. You've brought much to think about, child."

"Thank you, and blessings."

"Blessings on you."

With that, I speed-walked to my car, glad to finally be leaving the hungry prickles of life magic behind. My gut soured as I realized I'd have to call Duke and trick or trade for information he almost certainly wouldn't want to give.

Chapter 9

With my callstone shattered in a fit of anger, I'd have to summon Duke in a more roundabout way. Fortunately not the one that required blood, given that I already had a talisman, but I'd be breaking a promise not to do this to him. Broken promises could have serious consequences with a djinni.

I sighed. Nothing I could do about that except pay the price. I had to find this lich.

A small box carved from black walnut sat pushed to the back of one of my bookshelves. I'd only used it once, during practice, the time Duke and Grimm had decided I should understand this particular aspect of my heritage. I figured they were more interested in seeing if I was djinni enough to be summoned.

Spoiler alert, I wasn't.

Grimm never gave out her true name, so Duke was the one I'd summoned. Neither of us had enjoyed it, given that a summoning was tied to obligations and banishment. A summoned djinni couldn't just pop out mid-conversation, as they were both prone to doing with me. Needing answers wouldn't cover my ass, especially with Duke mentioning he'd been bottled. A summoning on the heels of that punishment would have him feeling his heritage a little too strongly for either of us to be comfortable.

Nothing for it. I need answers, yesterday.

Tucking the hand-sized box under my arm, I grabbed a bottle of wine, two heavy glasses, and the iron fire poker before heading outside. The sun was just setting, casting golden rays over the parts of my backyard it could reach through the surrounding trees. Lightning bugs flickered from the elderberry bushes lining the deck, unbothered by my presence or my mood as they signaled for mates.

After setting the box, glasses, and wine on my mosaic table, I stepped down to the yard. Keeping a lush carpet of grass alive under so much tree cover was both impossible and a little more bougie than I was comfortable with, so I couldn't call the sparse, weedy patches a lawn. That had never bothered me though. It felt more natural this way. It also made it easier to scratch the eight-pointed star of the Goddess in the dirt with the poker.

That done, I rested the poker against the deck and fetched the box, opening it to withdraw a cuneiform-etched bone. There were some crystals as well, for other purposes, but I stayed away from divination and any magic that wasn't strictly Air. The two halves of Aether were blended in me thanks to my parents, and the resulting Chaos was, well, chaotic. Djinn could tell the future and see visions. Despite having the crystals that should allow me to pierce the veil I left it to them. The way I saw it, not being summonable meant attempting other pure-djinn tricks was futile at best and dangerous at worst.

I placed the bone in the middle of the star, careful not to scuff any of my careful lines, and stepped back out.

"Nebuchadnezzar, come to me," I said. The simple request relied on what I now knew was a family tie. As my cousin, Duke—and Grimm, for that matter—would always hear me as long as I observed the forms with the star, the bone, and a true name. I didn't need blood or spells or any of the other nonsense a human would need.

The sun was nearly below the horizon when Duke materialized. I had sat down to wait, knowing that without a callstone he'd have no idea why I wanted to talk to him and would put it off if he could out of djinn contrariness.

His face was hard and cold. "Arden."

I winced at the clipped pronunciation of my name. "Sorry. I know we agreed not to do it this way. But—"

"You broke your callstone losing your temper like a child and you need to know about sorcerers."

"Yeah." I hated when he finished my sentences, doubly so when he did so in the least flattering way possible. "Be free in this place," I said formally. The conventions still applied, but at least he wouldn't be trapped like a captive while we talked.

He shivered as the joined power of the star-trapped bone released, stepping around the talisman with a sneer.

I rose and led the way up the stairs to my deck table and poured for two before taking a seat. "Don't take the bottle this time, okay?"

"Is that a command?"

"Come on, Duke. I already apologized. And you came to me first. Was I supposed to do nothing?"

He sat down and sipped, staring at me without answering. For once, the laughter always lighting his expression was extinguished.

Fine. I refused to cater to whatever mood he was in, which meant getting down to business. "I know about the lich."

"I thought you might. Fate's edge grows ever sharper."

Goosebumps raced down my arms, despite the muggy warmth of the evening. "I hate when you do that."

"I know." A spark of amusement finally lit in his dravite eyes. He'd forgive me if he could scare me or tweak my pride.

"I also know creating a lich requires a djinn. Why didn't you mention that on your last visit?"

Duke leaned back in his chair and sipped. "Your bitterness is almost as rich as this wine. Better vintage than your usual, little one. Work's going well then?"

"Don't call me that." I took a breath as subtly as I could, grounding myself in my element. "Talk to me about making a lich."

"But you *are* little. So very young. So very unaware of what you're bumbling into with your investigations."

I sipped from my glass to buy a minute, not liking the darkness in Duke's tone or his implications. "You didn't come here to talk to me about sorcerers, even though you knew that's what I'd be asking."

"Oh, I did. But not only." A smile flickered. He was pleased that I'd seen through him. He'd always appreciated cleverness.

"What?"

"Ask me."

I leaned back, scrubbing a hand over my face. Duke didn't mean about the sorcerer. I'd already asked about that. He wasn't ready to answer yet. I could compel him, but it would add to the strain summoning him had already put on our relationship—whatever it was, these days. *What the hell—oh.*

"Why were you bottled?"

Duke toasted me with his glass and sipped again. "For knowledge."

Twenty questions. Again. Another geas? A curse like that would keep him from answering me on pain of death, but sometimes they could be gotten around with clever phrasing. I glanced at the carved-bone talisman still laying in my yard. I could compel him, but I really didn't want to know what would happen if that compulsion smacked up against a geas. Duke hadn't always been a kind guardian, or a gentle one, but I didn't wish him harm, despite discovering that he'd helped hide the truth of my past from me. It would have to be twenty questions.

"What is the topic of your knowledge?"

"You."

"Me. And?"

"Your heritage."

I pressed my lips together and squeezed my pendant. "Tell me."

"I cannot. But it pained me to see you feeling so betrayed."

Reading between the lines, I thought he might mean it had hurt plans of his. He'd never indicated regret or remorse before, not even when he'd beaten the living daylights out of me for drawing on Air in my sleep. Djinn were, above all else, practical. Regret wasn't practical, so most had no use for it.

I cast my mind back over the last few months, considering what I'd learned from Val and in the course of the Sequoyah investigation. "My heritage. My father? The Chaos magic? The Crossroads?"

The flash of Duke's eyebrows told me what it was.

"The Crossroads. And bumbling. And my heritage." Grimm had said that having an elven father was why I couldn't reach the Crossroads on my own. It wasn't a talent the elves had. I still seemed to find myself there often enough.

I slouched, rolling the round pendant between my fingers. "You know something about all of it. But you're prevented from telling me?"

"You always were cleverer than Callista gave you credit for."

That stung, even though it shouldn't have. "You can't tell me because…"

"Reasons."

"But you want me to be aware."

"I want you to remember this conversation when fate's edge is a blade in your hand and the time comes to pick a side."

"A blade? Wait, whoa, pick a side? Duke—"

"Liches are created when a sorcerer makes a deal with a djinni."

"Oh, come on!"

Duke's eyes flashed carnelian, their natural color, and stayed that way. He didn't like this, but I wasn't going to get any more than he'd already given me.

"What kind of deal?" I asked flatly, signaling my acceptance that this was how it had to be. Maybe I should have fought harder or tried to compel him, but Duke had been the closest thing I'd ever had to a brother, even before I knew we were kin. *What side do I pick when everyone has an agenda that involves either using me or lying to me?*

The djinni sipped his wine, savoring it before answering. "Heartsblood and soul's breath."

"That sounds fucked up."

His answering shrug suggested that I was alone in that opinion. "Maybe I would think so, too, had I only a quarter century. Now?" Duke finished his wine and topped up his glass. "Now it might seem a good trade, were I in the market for such things these days. Even given the consequences."

"What consequences?" Goosebumps prickled when he didn't answer, defying the warmth of the summer evening. "What consequences, Duke?"

"The hastening of world's end." He winced at the soft-spoken words, as though that was more than he should have said, and my stomach plummeted. Glaring as though it was my fault, he said, "You did *not* hear that from me."

I stopped myself from saying that Janae had made a similar comment as my mouth dried. "What else do I need to know about liches?"

"It takes a long time to corrupt a witch so thoroughly. Longer than a natural lifespan. Hints and doubts whispered over decades or more. Temptation delivered drop by drop, building in a soul like a stalagmite built by dripping water in a cave."

"You've done it," I said, feeling green around the gills.

Duke toasted me again and drank some more. "Usermaatre-Meryamun would have done anything to end the Sea People. Tiye and Pentawer putting an end to him saved me a great deal of trouble. Ishtar blessed me with a profit on that deal."

That was just gross. My skin crawled at the realization that what I knew of my guardians was only as deep as the topmost grain of sand on a beach. Duke watched, impassively drinking his wine, as I gathered myself. "What else? Other than slow and steady corruption."

He held up his fist, pinkie raised. "First, necromancy, to defeat death." The ring finger joined it, followed by the middle finger. "Second, soul magic, to pierce the ethereal planes. Last of all, an amulet, severing soul from body and mind, a repository for life eternal—and of course, collection."

I grimaced. "Collection?"

"Do you have any idea what a soul goes for on the *sūqu*?"

I shook my head, disgusted by the idea of trading souls on the djinn version of the black market. I didn't have loads of scruples beyond consent and individual sovereignty, but a body's soul was their own.

"More than you can dream of, little one. Especially since soul magic—death magic, really—was outlawed by the Détente."

That caught my attention, and I jerked upright in my chair. "Hang on. Are you saying we have a rogue djinni to deal with, in addition to a soulless sorcerer?"

"That, plus whatever zombies the lich will have created."

"Zombies." My heart plummeted as pieces came together. Blood drained from my face so quickly I swayed. "Doc Mike. The morgue."

"Already? Well then." Duke almost looked merry as he finished his glass of wine and refilled once more. Djinn delighted in chaos. It birthed opportunity. "The sands of time flow ever faster."

Hopefully he'd take that information as payment. "How do I stop a lich?"

"The amulet, of course."

I had no idea how soul magic worked, not even having known it was a thing until five minutes ago. "What about it? Destroy it?"

"Mhmm. This wine is spectacular, Arden dear."

"Don't you change the subject on me. How do I destroy it?"

He started to reply, then flinched as though slapped. Wine sloshed and spilled plum-red droplets to stain my deck. "That touches on matters I cannot talk about."

"Go, Nebuchadnezzar." I couldn't look at him anymore, or the frustration burning in my gut would give me an ulcer. "Your obligation is fulfilled. You are needed no more this night. Go wherever you call home." I should have been more specific, but strain still tugged the energy flowing between us. Ordering him somewhere would have worsened it.

Duke finished his wine, downing it faster than I would have. "I'll let you know when I need a favor in trade, little one," he said as he dematerialized. His carnelian eyes and wide grin were the last things to go, like the Cheshire Cat.

Sighing heavily, I couldn't help but feel like Alice tumbling down the rabbit hole. I'd come a long way since breaking free of the box Callista, Duke, and Grimm had raised me in, but there was still too much I didn't know. I kicked myself all over again when I realized that I hadn't asked him about his progress with the Djinn Council on the new alliance in the Triangle.

"Shit." I slumped and took a swallow of wine almost as large as Duke's last had been. I was supposed to be coordinating this whole mess, providing a neutral third party in the face of all the confusion and distrust associated with bringing the major local players in Otherside together, and I dropped the ball every damn time. I had no idea what Duke and the djinn or House Monteague were doing. I'd forgotten to reach out to the witches. Roman was using me as a negotiating point without speaking to me first. Maria was the only one involving me with shit, but she was also deep in the shit from the sound of things.

I needed to get on top of this. Fast. It wasn't just about wanting a group of my own to belong to anymore. The vampires, the witches, and now Duke had all confirmed that something evil had come to the Triangle. I hadn't really wanted to be in charge of this alliance back in January, but it was my best shot at having somewhere to belong and gathering enough power to stand alone, independent of Callista. I'd be damned if I let that pass me by—or let my home be destroyed.

Chapter 10

I had time to kill before I was due to meet Val. The white van speeding away from the morgue had been a dead-end, and my conversations with Janae and Duke hadn't really told me all that much. That meant turning back to the vampire angle.

Body-stealing liches aside, there was still the sheet of paper Maria had left on my desk. A list of names in a vampire coup waiting to happen. Whether it was a coincidence or a symptom of the issue with the lich, I didn't know, but maybe changing gears would get my brain thinking in new patterns.

As I pulled into the parking garage and tapped my monthly pass, I asked myself how much I really wanted to be involved in vampire politics. "Not at all" was the answer, and yet, that was the price of having allies.

Then there was Maria herself.

I shook off the memory of her hand in mine, irritated by the allure of vampire glamour as I strode into the coworking space. I regretted leaving my zip-up hoodie in the car as soon as I was through the doors. My personal office would be warmer, but the rest of the building seemed determined to re-enact the Ice Age.

Maria's list still waited in my locked desk drawer, folded into quarters. I tugged it out and woke my computer to start researching the first name on the list. We Othersiders might hide our true natures from humans, but that didn't mean all of us hid completely. Open source intelligence gathering was an important step to any investigation, and these new vampires might as well have been human for all they attempted to hide themselves—which was to say, they made no effort at all.

I found social media profiles for the first three names on the list in less than ten minutes. Those three were all connected to some degree to the rest of Maria's list, enabling me to sketch out a web of relationships, interests, and recently visited locations. Connecting those dots led me to a few more individuals I suspected were either vampires or blood junkies.

The more I found, the more concerned I grew. If any one of these fools was outed as a vampire, the whole coterie might fall. They needed to watch themselves.

I compiled my findings into a tidy Google Sheet and shared it with Maria so she'd see I was taking her seriously. That her master, Torsten, seemed inclined not to believe her bugged me for a reason I couldn't put a finger on. Sexism, maybe. I didn't want vampire politics to be my problem, but I had to stop thinking like that if I was going to pull off this grand new alliance. I'd do my part. I'd been a Watcher too long to be able to let this nonsense pass, and if these young vampires screwed the Reveal, Torsten's coterie wouldn't be in a position to help anyone. Especially not me.

With the initial round of work for Maria done, I called Doc Mike.

"Arden?"

"Hey Doc. Good time?"

"Sure, one moment, please." Quick footsteps, the thud of his heavy office door closing. "Is this about…you know. What we discussed?"

"Yeah. I found someone to come by and cleanse the space. She's powerful, but you don't need to be afraid of her, okay?"

Silence. I imagined he was rubbing his temple the way he did when he was thinking hard. "Okay. What should I look for?"

"Little old Black lady, slightly overweight, smoker's lines. Probably dressed in purple. She might *feel* the way I do but a little different."

"Is there…I don't know, some kind of password or something?"

I grinned and started a quip, then bit my tongue. His tone suggested he wasn't best pleased with me, and I didn't want to rile him. "Actually, it can't hurt if you just wish her blessings. Her beliefs are different than yours, but it's the intent that counts."

"I see. Well. Thank you, Arden," he said grudgingly.

"No worries. And Doc? I had to tell her about you. The sensitive thing, you know?"

"Oh."

I winced, feeling as though I'd broken his trust again somehow. "Sorry. But trust me, it's better than both of you meeting blind. Welcome to Otherside."

"I see. Well. Thank you for the warning."

"Sure thing, Doc. Still working on finding that van, but we'll get there. Take care."

"And you. God bless."

It had been years since Doc Mike had invoked religion with me. He must have been more shaken than I'd thought, and I debated whether I should drive Janae down myself. Would my presence make things better or worse? Worse, I decided. He was obviously still sore about my lying to him about Otherside things. It stung, but I understood.

Nothing for it. That energy couldn't hang around the morgue, not if Maria was right about evil crossing the planes in its wake. The last thing we needed, on the verge of the Reveal, was Goddess-knew-what coming over from the ethereal plane and sending humanity into a panic. Here in the South, that could turn to Bible-thumping and Rapturing real fast in some parts—and they already had passages about not suffering a witch to live. What the more conservative and religious elements of society would think about the rest of us was anyone's guess, but it was safe to say it probably wouldn't be good.

That didn't even consider the rest of the country, or the world, for that matter. Cell phones and the internet meant the Triangle's Reveal would be global in minutes, a reality that made me sweat when I stopped to think about it. Did Callista have counterparts in other cities? Others like her? I refused to believe she was a goddess. She didn't have the vicious detachment exhibited by the gods in the Crossroads. Vicious, yes, but not detached. Everything she did was somehow personal. *Maybe a demi-god? Are those a thing?* Maybe I had more to ask Duke than just how a lich was made. The price for that information would probably be more than I was willing to pay though.

Sighing, I slumped back and chewed on a fingernail, wondering when things had gotten so complicated in so many parts of my life.

When an elven prince walked into your office and hired you, I decided. It was all Leith Sequoyah's fault, the bastard. He was the first and only person I'd ever killed, and I didn't lose a wink of sleep over it. Troy had drowned me, but it had been Leith behind it all. Did I think Troy should have stood up to him? Hell yes. At the same time, Troy had been in deep cover and surrounded by Leith's cronies.

I wasn't quite over what had happened and I didn't like Troy, but I'd gotten my revenge in the end. Sequoyah's prince was dead, and the House was in shambles after Callista used the information I traded for my independence.

Footsteps approaching in the hallway and an itch at the back of my skull pulled me out of my musings. My office was the only one occupied in this section since the tiny house start-up had moved out and the software developers had relocated to a larger space in the building. If it had been the sales manager with a prospective tenant, I'd have heard his overly upbeat chatter all the way down. With the frosted glass of my office door closed, I could neither see who was coming nor read the air patterns.

Most people knocked before coming in. Apparently, knocking was not a thing elves did.

A whiff of burnt marshmallow reached me as the door swung open. The scent triggered a slew of visceral memories, all bad, and I was out of my chair with the Ruger aimed before I could think.

Troy Monteague fixed me with cool eyes the color of moss on sandstone, his gaze flicking over me and pausing on the gun as he slipped into the room and shut the door behind him. I could have been holding a bouquet for all the concern he showed.

Of all the assholes I could have had to deal with today, this was the one who walked into my office.

Glaring at Troy, I lowered the gun but didn't holster it.

"What?" he said as he kept coming, glaring right back, as secure as ever in his elven sense of superiority.

"You, walking in as if you have every right to be here. You don't."

"I'm Darkwatch."

"And this is *my office*. You think you can just turn up?" I said. Maria did, but Maria hadn't pulled the same level of bullshit Troy had.

His expression said "so what?" more eloquently than words could have, and I pulled on Air. He stopped, then backed up at the glow of my eyes, putting space between us and a hand over his shoulder. Probably to the hilt of a blade riding along his spine, hidden by the popped collar of his polo shirt and the shadows that never quite seemed to leave him.

I got ready to thin the air in the room. "Monteague, you need to tell me what you want or get the fuck out."

"You're not in control here."

"Are you serious?" I hissed. "My name is on the door. All I have to do is scream and give them your description. You really want to have to pull Darkwatch tricks to get in here every time you want to talk to me instead of just walking in like a preppy-ass mundane?"

For a few heartbeats, I thought I'd have to follow through on my threat. I drew breath, and he threw up a hand.

"Fine," he said. "What in the name of the Goddess were you doing at the morgue?"

Shock hit me like a slap in the face. "You have got to be shitting me. That was you?"

His scowl said that yes, he had been the elf I'd chased off the morning after the first psychic scream. I almost cursed my luck. Then I decided it would have been worse if it had been an elf who didn't already know that I was an elemental.

"I'm on a case." Adrenaline spiked as I considered my options. Fighting him wasn't one, and Troy was the stubborn sort of ass who put his mission first, the law second, and every other consideration far behind. I'd have to talk my way out.

"A case," he said.

"Yeah. I take a lot of those, you know, being a PI and all. Sometimes they involve dead people."

"Why did you take the medical examiner to coffee?"

"What—Did you follow us? You, what, sat in your car spying on us or something?"

He only stared at me, and I kicked myself. He'd marked me with some kind of magical tag back in January to make it easier to keep track of me. I'd been so focused on keeping Doc Mike in order that I hadn't been paying attention to my surroundings. Between his magic and my scattered focus, following me would have been easy, even if he hadn't come all the way into the café. Amateur mistake. Shit.

"He was shook by the sight of a walking shadow," I snapped. Doc Mike being a sensitive was none of the elves' business. If I told Troy, he'd tell the rest of them. And besides, I just didn't like him enough to share info like that, alliance or not.

Troy narrowed his eyes. "Is that all?"

"Yes."

"Are you lying?"

"What were *you* doing at the morgue?" Maybe flipping the question around would get me some answers.

"I told you once before, Finch, I won't be questioned by you."

"Then go fuck yourself, but get out of my office first."

This time, he did, glancing once more at my gun. As he eased out, he said, "See you around."

I didn't doubt it. The idea made me sick all over again. I slumped into a heavy lean against my desk, releasing Air and letting the gun clatter to the surface, my arms trembling as fear caught up and adrenaline crashed. Despite the nightmares, I'd thought I wasn't afraid of him anymore, not after our parking lot meeting shortly after the Sequoyah case wrapped up, but I'd been wrong.

This was the first time I'd seen him in the flesh since then. I hadn't heard any updates regarding the new alliance and assumed he'd been working on the terms within House Monteague all through the rest of winter and early spring, plus whatever the Darkwatch had him doing.

I'd suspected sometimes that he kept an eye on me, but whenever I turned around, there was no one. Not a surprise. I'd only heard his footsteps in the hallway because he wanted me to. His version of a statement of peaceful intent, I guess, given that he could move soundlessly.

I need to get out of here. A glance at the wall clock next to the door told me I had half an hour before I needed to walk over to the bar where I was meeting Val, but fuck it. I could do some more OSINT work for Maria's case on my tablet.

Chapter 11

The bar at Mangum and Main was only a minute or two away, walking. I shook off the lingering funk from Troy's visit, looking forward to the meeting. Val was my guide to everything I'd been cut off from, in addition to being one of my few friends. We tried a new bar every other week, and she taught me more about what it meant to be an elemental.

This was one of the fancier spots. An entire wall was lined to the ceiling with bottles, locally sourced entrees like confit duck and hanger steak graced the menu, and the cocktails were craft. Nineteenth-century posters in fancy frames lined the brick walls, hanging over plush leather benches.

As good as the cocktails looked, I went with my usual virgin Cuba Libre—Coke with a wedge of lime. Val had been the first person to understand why, without me saying. She'd even given me a name for it.

"The curse?" she'd asked on the first of our get-togethers.

I'd stared blankly, embarrassed without knowing why.

"Too much drink moves you to dance. But sometimes when you dance, Chaos rises. Maybe awkward things happen with people you mighta thought about or who mighta been thinking about you. Ya know...romantically?"

"How did you—"

She'd winced. "You're a maenad. Shit, Arden. Been ages since we've had one on our hands. But it's been ages since there was a trueborn elemental, so…yeah."

I'd blushed even more deeply, more uncomfortable than ever, even as I was relieved to have an explanation. I wasn't a bad drunk or bad with magic. It was a *thing*, and apparently there was nothing for it other than what I was already doing: being careful about how much I drank in the company of others.

Pulling myself out of the memory, I found a corner table where I could see the door and got to work on my social research. I was still working on it forty-five minutes later when the door opened and I looked up to see yet another someone who wasn't Val.

"Where the hell is she?" I muttered. WRAL had plenty of news about vandalism, assaults, and thefts but nothing about a fire, so she probably wasn't on duty at the fire station. It was supposed to be her day off, anyway. When I tried her cell, it went straight to voicemail.

"Hey Val, it's—me." Paranoia stopped me from giving my name. She'd know my voice. "I'll wait for another fifteen minutes and then head out. Hope you're okay. Call me when you can."

Twenty minutes later, Val still hadn't appeared, but a nest of snakes had settled into my belly, writhing with the weight of dread that settled over me as I left.

My phone didn't ring in the twenty minutes it took me to get home. I told myself to calm down, that Val might have had a personal or family emergency and was probably fine. But I couldn't shake the feeling that something was wrong.

"Trouble?" Zanna asked, rising from her seat on the porch as I stomped up the stairs.

"Val didn't show for drinks." I unraveled the block of Air and moved it as I passed, not thinking of the kobold following close on my heels.

Zanna grunted as she tripped over it, glared at me, and for once, withheld comment.

"I'm worried," I said with a wince of apology. "Monteague showed up at my office, and with a lich in town—Hey, do you know anything about them?"

The little kobold shrugged, a sudden seriousness making her look old. "Stay away."

I sighed, tugging my hair out of its tidy bun and fluffing it. "I can't. Everyone except Roman has—Shit, Roman." I pulled out my phone. I should have called him earlier to find out why Sergei had been barreling down Howe Street, but I'd been distracted by Neith's demand then too focused on my caseload.

As I thumbed through the call menu on my phone, it lit up. I considered not answering the incoming call, but I'd already taken Maria's money. There wasn't really "after hours" on a vampire case.

"Hawkeye Investigations, Arden speaking." I used formality to build a wall against whatever had passed between us when she'd left my office yesterday.

"Good, you're in work mode. Get down here." The brusque flatness of her demand clashed with her usual honey and spice.

"Excuse me?"

"We've had an incident at the bar. The kind that needs investigating. Now."

"Accepting your case does not put me at your personal beck and—"

A stream of invective in another language—Spanish, maybe, but not modern—cut me off. "Honestly, Arden, do you think I would have you come all the way to Raleigh just for my hunt?"

"I didn't—"

"There's blood on the floor, and if you want this alliance to stand, I need you here, *now.*"

In the next five seconds, I asked myself if the alliance was worth the pain in the ass of driving forty minutes to become more enmeshed in vampire politics when I would rather have checked in with my boyfriend. Maybe I could kill two birds with one stone?

"I'll be there. But I'm bringing backup."

"Fine."

The call ended, and I immediately swiped over to Roman's number. "Hey, you free?"

"Hey, babe, whatcha got in mind?"

"Not what you're hoping for, from that sexy little growl." I smiled, despite the way my night was going. He'd never been shy about wanting me. "You up for a drive?"

"Sure." His long drawl told me he heard some of what I hadn't said. "Your place?"

"Yeah. I'll drive us from here."

"What're we hunting?"

I hesitated, not quite sure of that myself. "Load for vamp."

"See you in ten."

That right there was what made it so hard to stay mad at Roman and made me feel so guilty for being mad in the first place. He might have gone behind my back dragging me into his family business, but when I called after dark and asked him to come packing, he didn't fuss. He just turned up.

By the time we arrived at Claret, Roman had wound up into a bundle of bristly werewolf. He kept his shift in check, but the air around him prickled like static and his eyes shone wolf silver. My driving was enough to put anyone on edge, especially with all the night construction going on down I-40. Then I'd told him about Monteague's visit to my office, Val's missed drink, Duke's words, and the fact that we were heading for a vampire bar that had had "an incident."

"I don't like any of this, Arie," he said as I snagged a parking spot on the street a couple of blocks down from Claret. "Val's a big girl, she probably got caught up in business with the collective again. But that Goddess-damned elf turning up at your office?" He growled low in his throat.

And yet you didn't think that someone from your family would turn up looking for me when you dropped my name to them. I gritted my teeth to keep myself from saying it aloud. We were still close to the full moon, and I needed backup, not another distraction. I filed it in the back of my mind to use as an example later, whenever we got around to discussing our relationship like the grown-ups we were supposed to be.

Whatever had happened at Claret, it was impossible to tell by the upstairs, which still throbbed with sultry jazz, heat, and heartbeats, most of them human from the smell. A subtle metaphysical pressure told me Torsten, Maria's master, was in residence. I wondered what his role was in the night's events.

"I know Sergei came to see you," I said as we eased through the crowd to the curtained hallway leading to a door that went down to the club's basement. "If you want to talk about it when we get home, you could, you know...stay."

Roman snapped around to look at me and some of the edgy prickle eased, which had been my intention. "I've never slept at your place."

"I know."

"Well then. Okay." Satisfaction rolled off of him, which was a much better emotion for a vampire bar than tension. Maybe we could even have that talk in the morning, when we were both cooler-headed.

I squeezed his hand before nodding at the skinny guy standing next to the heavy velvet curtain. A sign over his shoulder read, "Staff Only." Up close, the metallic scent of vampire was there, but faint enough that I wondered if he'd fed recently.

"Hey, hi, Maria sent for me?" I held up my PI license, shielding the motion with my body to keep it discreet.

Bouncer vamp didn't even look at it before tossing his head for us to pass. Odd, considering there weren't usually guards on this passageway, but Maria must have told them to expect us.

Roman rested a hand on the small of my back and guided us through. As the curtains drooped closed, he glanced behind us then reached for the gun tucked behind his waistband—not to draw it but for reassurance. "I smell blood," he muttered. "Lots of it. And something worse. Way worse."

"Great. Fantastic." I knocked on the door at the end of the hall. Both of us had our hands visible and empty when it swung open. Another unknown vamp, this one a similarly thin woman with straggly blond hair, completely strung out with black eyes and fangs dripping saliva, scowled as she waved us through and down the metal spiral stair.

Without the door to block it, the scent of blood hit me. Blood, and something darker and deader, accompanied by a wave of the evil I'd sensed at the morgue. The door must have been spelled for me not to sense it earlier. Roman jerked like he'd been slapped but said nothing.

"Well, shit," I muttered as we reached the bottom.

"Shit is one word for it." Maria stood with her hands on her hips amidst carnage, a nightmare of dismembered bodies and broken chairs lit by a single overhead lamp. Chunks of something spattered her white sundress, stained dark with blood, and the hilts of her twin katanas jutted from over her shoulders. Fury radiated from her and snapped in her tone. "What took you so long?"

I didn't answer, too busy trying to figure out what the hell had happened and why there was a weird little tug on my awareness all while being completely overwhelmed by sights and smells my brain didn't want to process. Roman shouldered past me, sniffing cautiously and ignoring Maria's glare.

"Of course, you brought your puppy," she sneered. "I hope he's housetrained."

"Back off." I swallowed my gorge and stepped around a severed head. That, my brain made sense of, and I kind of wished it hadn't. I'd seen violence in my time as a private investigator but not anything like this. I'd been too far removed from the rest of Otherside to see any of the excess we could be capable of when it was fresh, and it was nothing like the cold, sanitized view I got at the morgue, after the corpses had Doc Mike's attention.

The smell alone threatened to overwhelm me and I had no idea what use I could be here. "Goddess, Maria, when you said incident, I was imagining something less...Biblical?"

"If you think this is bad, you should have seen the auto-de-fés back in the bad old days."

I shuddered. "No, thanks."

My brain would not make sense of what I was seeing, and I moved away from the staircase, trying to find a clearer area. Roman, looking grim, waved me to a corner the blood hadn't reached yet. I picked my way over, glad I'd had the sense to wear an old pair of sneakers.

"Talk," I said to Maria, unable to keep from hugging myself.

She smirked, dark humor flashing over her as she took creepy-slow, delicate steps through the mess that had been someone. Several someones. "Your first bloodbath?"

"You wanted me here. Talk." When I spoke, the stench coated my tongue. I gagged a little.

"How boring," she said as she reached our corner. Shadow hid her eyes, but the tightness of her features warned me that she was walking a fine line. "Fine. The lich case has escalated." She reached out toward a stray curl that had sprung loose from my bun.

Fine line or not, I slapped Maria's hand away as Roman growled and edged closer to me. Her simper had a twist to it as she blew him a kiss before refocusing on me. The fine line might be more like a knife's edge, but nobody touched my damn hair.

I frowned at her in warning. "Escalated how? It feels like the morgue." I rubbed my fingers together, trying to get a sense of the skin-crawling evil. "But maybe less, somehow."

That weird pull on the back of my mind was still there as well, turning me into a bundle of upset. "Can we talk somewhere else, or do I need to be looking at all this for our conversation?"

"I suppose you've seen enough." With faster clockwork-jerky steps, Maria led us to a plain door I hadn't noticed on my last visit to Claret. She entered the digits into the numeric keypad securing it with a vampiric speed that prevented my making a note of the code. She lifted an eyebrow when she caught me looking, but waved us through ahead of her.

The hallway was lost in darkness a few paces in, and I hesitated, wondering how safe our alliance made Roman and me.

"After you," Roman said gruffly, his eyes shining silver as he stared at the vampire.

I half-turned to tell him it was fine and bit my tongue. Whether it was the state of the room, Maria's off-kilter mood, or her reach for me, he was in full-blown protective alpha mode, born to it even if he'd been robbed of the position and exiled because of his stunted magics. Turning back to Maria, I tilted my head and lifted my brows.

"So bold," she hissed, the anger returning. "Giving me directions in my own nest. You're growing up, baby doll."

"Imagine that," I said, not so bold as to object to the little nicknames and pick more of a fight with a predator running hot and hungry.

With a toss of crimson-sticky emerald locks, she stalked forward.

Roman pushed me ahead of him again, growling when the door swung shut behind us. "Don't like this, babe."

"Neither do I. Thanks for being here though."

"Wouldn't miss it."

Maria's scoff, too close in front of me, made me stop short. "You two are sickeningly sweet."

The click of a switch preceded the sudden flooding of the room with light.

If it had been intended to throw me off-guard, it failed. I might not be djinni enough to be summoned, but enough of my mother lived in me to let me adjust to changes in light far faster than the night-bound werewolf and vampire. Maria moved, familiar with the room, and so did I, having recovered from light-blindness quickly enough to dance around a massive couch upholstered in red silk jacquard. The thick shag rug it rested on muffled my steps.

I couldn't help my shit-eating grin when she looked to where Roman still stood, scowling as he blinked with gun in hand, then did a double-take when I wasn't still standing next to him.

"How intriguing," she said as her eyes traveled over me. "What other little tricks do you have, elemental?"

Chapter 12

I flinched at her interest, glancing around the room to make sure we were alone. "Enough games, Maria. It's late for us day-living folks, and I want my bed."

"Then be seated, both of you." She made the invitation sound like an indulgence, waving a hand at the rich couches while she threw herself into an oversized armchair of the same material, careless of the blood and bits still clinging to her clothes and hair.

I came around the couch and sat more carefully. Roman perched on the edge of the couch, between me and Maria. Since she didn't start speaking right away, I glanced around. The rest of the room was a cozier version of Torsten's throne room across the hall. This was a more intimate space, even as the crystal chandelier overhead and the tapestries on the walls made it feel richer than Torsten's gloomier, more austere chambers.

She was smiling at me when I pulled my attention back to her. "Always investigating. Tell me, poppet, what do you see?"

"A transition." I pointed to a piece of blue painter's tape just above the baseboards, the exposed wiring of the chandelier where it hadn't been completely installed, and rubbed the sofa, which still smelled new. "Your new digs? Part of your promotion?"

"Yes. As are tonight's problems."

"How so?"

Maria's annoyed glance at Roman told me she wasn't happy about him being present, but neither of us moved. With a huff, she said, "If he stays, this becomes alliance business. I'll expect to call on the wolves. Especially given that hunky morsel in town. A brother?"

"Stay away from Sergei," Roman growled, as protective of his asshole brother as he was of me.

"Pity. He looks like he'd go down a treat. I will have your cooperation, if not your pack's. Understood?"

Roman shifted in his seat and looked at me. "Only for as long as Arden's case runs."

I shifted and reached for his arm. "Roman—"

He swatted my hand away much as I had Maria's. "This was the agreement, Arie. Those things outside were dead before they got here, which means this is bigger than Torsten's coterie. You know why I need this."

"Yeah." I sighed, sick at heart but unable to do much about it. I'd asked him to come along, but I didn't get to choose the capacity in which he participated. "Fine. Good enough for you, Maria?"

The vampire inclined her head, looking like a queen despite her dishevelment. "Your pup is correct. Our invaders were dead on arrival."

"Zombies," I said. "Which means the lich."

"Very good."

"And it was an inside job."

"Even better."

"Come on, Maria, that's a deduction a child could make."

"But not an effort a child could pull off. And yet, one did."

I lifted my eyebrows, assuming that what Maria considered a child might well be older than my quarter century.

She flipped a hand. "Fine, a matter of perception. But a newly risen fledgling was at the head of the attack, unheeding of any of his master's calls."

"Who let them in?"

"Someone smart enough not to wait for the battle's conclusion." Maria seemed to notice the gore caking her for the first time and picked off a few of the larger chunks, dropping them to the rich rug. "Too many of the Modernists, as they call themselves, live away from the nest. It will take me the rest of the night to account for them. I didn't even recognize the one leading the zombies. Maybe Torsten will finally listen."

The last statement was delivered sadly and under her breath, as though she'd forgotten Roman and I were there. He and I exchanged a glance, his face tight and his lips pressed into a thin line. Torsten's coterie was falling apart, and he seemed oblivious. Not that either of us would voice the thought aloud with the master of the city across the hall.

"Maria, why did you call me here?"

"Because if I'm right and that fledgling was being controlled by someone other than his master, we're dealing with a lich lord, not just a lich." The corner of her lip curled into a snarl.

"You're scared," I said.

She fixed me with a stare that I didn't dare meet. "Yes. We're not exactly corpses. We still have our higher mental faculties. It takes far greater magic to corrupt an active vampire than it does a rotting, inanimate carcass."

I swallowed past the bad feeling in my gut rising into my throat, trying to think fast. A piece fell into place. "So you, what? Kickstart things with the alliance by having me appear in a crisis? Knowing I'd bring Roman."

She flashed dark eyebrows, a salute.

Annoyance flared at her playing me. I tamped it down. It was a good play, even if I'd been used. Again. "And dangle a motivator for me. Clues for my case."

"I want to be the middle ground, Arden. It's not truly in me to give, but the *moroi* can do more than just take. The old ways are dying, but the Modernists want something too radical for us to survive. Not and keep our culture intact. Our laws."

"Which presumably keep humans safe. And Otherside concealed," I said.

Maria nodded. "You will leave here with any and all artifacts and photographs collected by my people."

"Do you trust them?"

"Only those who live by my blood are present. I scattered the rest."

I had no idea what "live by my blood" meant, but assumed it was pretty solid if she already knew they were betrayed. "And in return?"

"You get this alliance going before I lose my head. Because Arden, poppet? You're entertaining as all hell, but I'll take *your* head and deliver it to whomever offers the best price if it saves my skin. I've survived too much to fall now."

Roman growled. She ignored it and rose, the movement abrupt now that she wasn't trying to seduce or reassure and was simply acting according to her nature. Roman and I stood more slowly, taking the cue that the private audience was over.

Maria's chosen were waiting outside the door. Plastic zippy bags of varying sizes, filled with whatever small trinkets the walking dead had had on them, waited on a table. I didn't know what the hell I was going to do with this shit—which was technically evidence in a corpse-robbing case, something I should turn over to the police yet couldn't without explaining its provenance—but I collected it without debate. Maria had exposed herself in that audience and I had a feeling that throwing it in her face, with gore and despair and paranoia coating the room, would get my throat torn out. Roman's too.

* * *

Back at home, out on the deck with sweating glasses of sweet tea, Roman said, "You should be more careful with Maria, babe."

"I am, but what makes you say that?"

"You were showing off when we got there. Sassing her, showing what you can do when you're not hiding that you're an elemental. Everything that would push a vamp's buttons. You may not be able to smell her desire, but I can. You're her next hunt."

"I know," I said softly, afraid of what that could mean for Roman and me, for the alliance, for the balance of power in the Triangle and Callista's jealous guardianship of it.

After a few minutes of silence, he said, "You can look them in the eyes, can't you?"

It wasn't really a question, and I winced. "Sort of? If they're lower in the pecking order."

"Is that an elemental thing or a you thing?"

I shrugged. It might be a djinn thing, but I didn't know for sure. We hadn't ever discussed my mixed parentage, and given how much he seemed willing to do to get a ticket back to his family lately, it wasn't a topic I was keen to explore with him. "Can't everybody, if the vamp is weak enough?" I mumbled.

"No. Not weres, witches, or elves. Not sure about the fae or the djinn." Roman drew me closer and kissed the top of my head. "You are somethin' special though."

"I just want to be *me*. I got along perfectly well when nobody noticed I was special. Being special has had me in hiding nearly all my life. I mean, shit, it got me drowned." I wrapped my arms around myself, the remembered bite of freezing lake water chilling me in the late spring night. "Special is not a good thing."

We sat in silence, listening to night sounds, hands linked. I tilted my head to rest on his shoulder, then sat back up with a start when I realized that I'd never pinpointed the source of that weird tug on my mind at Claret. That hadn't just been paranoia. It had felt like magic.

"What is it, babe?" His hand tightened around mine and he inhaled, scenting the air for what had startled me.

I squeezed back. "Just thinking." I couldn't frame my thoughts into the right words, so I didn't want to voice them yet. "Case stuff. Hey, what happened with Sergei this morning?"

His sideways glance and quirked eyebrow told me he didn't quite believe me, but he usually acted like I was the alpha in this relationship. He let it slide. "He has a proposition."

"A proposition that you don't sound convinced by."

"I reckon what I've accomplished here is worth more, yes," he said, almost defensively.

I ground my teeth to stop from asking what exactly he'd accomplished, given that I was the one who'd been the go-between for all the other parties. It stung that he seemed to be claiming credit for what I'd bought in blood and tears, but maybe I wasn't understanding him. "What'd he offer?"

"For me to be an official representative of Blood Moon in the Triangle, howling with their voice and running at their direction."

"Representative of the clan? But not welcomed back home by your family?"

"Exactly." Roman squeezed my hand again, a bitter smile thinning his lips. "It sounds good on the surface, but it's a cur's offer. My father's offer, I suspect. My mother or sister would know better."

"And you were born to lead," I murmured. Roman would have been next in line to be the alpha of both the Volkov pack and the Blood Moon clan if it wasn't for the—in my not at all humble opinion—backwards inconvenience that he was considered a magical runt by his people. His wolfman form was a partial shift which, I'd learned, meant he was considered incomplete, less than whole, unable to commune fully with the spirit of Lupa.

"I was. Plus the fact that I'm still here despite…despite everything they did." He sighed, still unwilling to share the cruelties he'd been subjected to as a teen. "I've earned this, Arie. This and then some."

This being his birthright. Leadership. A ticket home, purchased with his ties to me. Given that all I wanted was to belong somewhere, it felt petty and low to begrudge him wanting the same thing. I just wished that he didn't have to use me to get there. Or that I didn't feel like it somehow cheapened our relationship that he did.

Let it go. I couldn't keep working myself into fits over this and be with him. If I was going to be with him, I had to choose to accept this or let him go. Since I wasn't ready to do the latter, I had to embrace the former. "So, what happens next?"

"We negotiate again. This time, I play hardball. I didn't use you this last time." He glanced at me, acknowledging my unspoken but obvious feelings. "If this fails, I go wide. The leopards and the jaguars are allies, making them the largest single were force in the Triangle. Terrence and Ximena will want concessions though, so they're a hail Mary play."

"This party just keeps getting bigger." I filled him in on Janae's questions about whether the witches would be welcome. "Roman, I don't know how much longer Callista will let this go or why she's ignored it up to now. I'm shitting myself over this by itself, but then I try to focus on work and it's not any better. It's a cluster all around."

He grunted and tugged me closer. I leaned into him, reminding both of us that our blood was still hot and in our veins, not spilt across a concrete floor in some basement or in the mouths of our enemies.

"Tell me what you need, and it's yours." Roman's lips moved against mine. I smiled against his.

"Comfort." I rose, tugging him after me back into the house. He wrapped his arms around my waist as we went, making our steps awkward as he pressed up behind me and nibbled on my neck.

"I'll do my damnedest," he said between nips.

Chapter 13

I pulled free and spun to face him, drawing him backward toward my bedroom. Nobody had ever been there other than me. It was my most private, most sacred space, and I hadn't been able to trust anyone enough to welcome them there.

Roman must have read that in my eyes, because he used his grip to pull us to a halt as we reached the threshold. "Arie, you sure you want me here?"

My heart fluttered, and my stomach clenched. Did I want this, when I hadn't ever offered it to anyone else? I searched his storm-grey eyes, reached up to run my fingers through his hair, now clipped short at the back and sides. He gazed back, neutral, undemanding, calm.

"Yes." I kissed him, full and deep, trying to tell him with my actions what I couldn't with words. That I loved him, despite the mess we faced with his family. That I trusted his good intentions even if we were still working on their execution.

He pulled back and cupped my face in his hands, searching my face as I'd searched his, eyes narrowed. "Definitely?"

"Yeah."

Roman flowed back into me with a strength that told me he took this as seriously as I did, that he recognized what I was offering and wanted it all for himself. The force of his passion pushed us over the threshold, and I guided him to the bed, glad I'd tidied up a little the night before.

My legs hit the mattress, and I tugged his shirt over his head. Our mouths met with enough force that one of us split our lips. At the scent of blood, the night's horrors flashed through my mind. I froze. He paused.

"I would never let anything happen to you, babe. Come hell or high water." He eased off, planting gentle kisses along my jaw. "You're safe."

Reassurance returned. With a tug at his jeans, I leaned back and pulled him down on top of me. Roman stuck with his gentle foreplay, stripping my clothing off like he thought I might bolt. Normally, I preferred a faster pace. Tonight, after seeing a severed human head staring up at me from the floor, I'd take it slow and remind myself that we were both still alive.

An hour later, when he'd teased and loved me to within a slow, careful, inch of my life, I curled up against him, my face buried in his chest. The room smelled of our satisfaction, crisp cedar and the faintest hints of a thunderstorm. I thought about switching on the bedside lamp to ask him about Sergei but decided against it. I could ask my questions, and he could see the room, in the morning, when the sun illuminated all. Sleep stole over me as Roman's arms wrapped me in safety.

"You're getting closer," Neith said.

I jerked, eyes flying open, to find myself in the empty, white expanse of the Crossroads again. This time I was paralyzed. I couldn't move anything other than my eyes. Couldn't breathe. The usual sensation of fine sand under my fingers was gone.

"I'm dreaming," I said aloud without moving my lips.

"So you are," the goddess agreed. "Sometimes dreams are more powerful. Have you ever hunted in a dream? Killed in one?"

Fear closed my throat. I couldn't answer.

The quorking of ravens drew my attention. The two child-sized creatures I'd seen on my first visit soared overhead, more like vultures than corvids.

"Pay them no mind. Odin is nosy as ever." The goddess glared up at the birds, whose calls sounded eerily like laughter this time, and whirled the odd staff she always carried. Turning back to me, she said, "Have you discovered the magician?"

"No." I forced the word out in a croak.

"His creations?"

"Yes."

"And?"

My heart thundered. I suspected, "And what?" would not be a suitable answer. I said nothing.

Neith bent and slapped me. I gasped, nearly managing to throw myself out of the dream but failing as she gripped my throat. "We won't be denied our hunt. Not by a magician. Not by anyone. If you *are* to be our huntress on the earthly plane, you'll need to do better than this. Look. Deeper."

She slapped me again, harder. The ankh looped around her wrist on a leather thong swung against her palm and cut into my cheek.

I sat up in my bed with a gasp that tore my lungs to shreds. A warm trickle coursed down my face. I swiped at it, wincing when my fingers touched broken flesh. Magic scented the air with a hint of lotus and tingled in the cut on my cheek.

"Arden!" Scent of rotted cedar and spoiled musk. Eyes glowing silver in the dark. No ravens. No goddess. Only Roman, on his knees beside me, hands hovering as he held himself back from touching me. "Holy—breathe, babe. You're okay. You're safe. I'm here."

I took another shuddering breath, looking at my fingers in the moonlight. A liquid sheen tipped them.

"What happened?" he asked.

"What did you see?"

"You stopped breathing. Then your head snapped and your cheek split, and you woke up."

"I was here the whole time?"

"Yes. What. Happened?"

"The old gods," I said, still staring at my fingers. "The Crossroads. I wasn't all the way there this time, not that it seems to matter." My cheek throbbed, and I rolled, reaching under the bed to grab my discarded tank top and press it to my face.

Silver eyes reflecting moonbeams flicked from my face to my fingers and back. A surge of metaphysical hunger beat at me before it recoiled, drawn back toward Roman. I caught my breath then switched the hand holding the shirt against my face and held my bloody hand out to him.

He caught my wrist. "Don't offer me this if you don't mean it." His mangled voice cut to my core. He was fighting a shift.

"What does it mean?" I asked.

"It's a promise."

"Of what?"

"If you were pack, fidelity and faith. It's a binding. A commitment. It wouldn't even be valid back home, since you're not pack. But Arden, the power in your blood…they might make an exception, especially with the alliance in the balance. Lupa's breath, I don't know how I missed it before. No wonder Maria wants you."

I wavered. We cared for each other, I knew that, but what he was saying sounded akin to a marriage and a fetish wrapped up in one. We couldn't even have a discussion, which meant I couldn't make that offer.

With gentle fingers, Roman curled my fingers into my palm, hiding the blood. "It's not time yet."

I nodded, and shivers raced over me at what I'd almost done.

"You gonna be okay? Need anything?" he asked.

"I'll be fine." I probed my cheek gently, finding that it had already stopped bleeding. "Was just a scratch."

With a gentle kiss on my clean knuckles, he eased from the bed and headed for the bathroom, shutting the door behind him. The shower hissed on as I fell back against the pillow, weirdly guilty that I wasn't there yet but relieved not to have had to make the choice.

I slipped out from under the sheets and went to the kitchen for some ice. The frozen bite against my cheekbone matched that in my stomach as it occurred to me that this binding might have been what Sergei had had in mind when he arrived. Nothing I'd seen said he had the self-control to do what Roman had done, and I shivered from more than cold. For the second time in less than a year, my ignorance of the rest of Otherside was dragging me in over my head, and none of my other so-called allies had a fraction of Roman's restraint.

And none of that even came close to the danger of a disappointed goddess who wanted me to hunt down a lich for reasons of her own.

***

Roman wasn't shy about making himself at home in my kitchen the next morning. The presumption irked me for reasons I couldn't put my finger on. Maybe it was just too much new—the first time someone spent the night, now the first time someone else cooked at my stove. I sat at my table and nursed the cup of white tea he set in front of me while he scrambled eggs and buttered toast, muttering about the lack of coffee or breakfast meats.

"Barbaric," he muttered.

"I could always kick you out next time. Then you wouldn't have to worry about it."

Glancing over his shoulder, Roman grinned and shoveled the sloppy, undercooked mess of far too many eggs for one person onto a plate, dropping the toast on top before settling across from me.

"You're healing fast." He gestured to my cheek with his fork before scooping a jiggling yellow heap atop a corner of toast.

I gingerly dabbed at the scab on my left cheek. "Yeah. I'm not vamp or were fast, but faster than human."

"Good. Shit's gonna get worse before it gets better, babe."

"You mean Sergei?"

"Him and likely everyone else, especially with the Reveal coming. Power is shifting. Nobody—"

The "Bad Boys" ringtone on my phone interrupted him and I said, "I need to take this. Cops."

Roman nodded and shoved another bite of toast and eggs into his mouth as I tapped the answer button. "Hawkeye Investigations, Finch speaking."

"Arden, it's Tom Chan. Raleigh PD says you're working the zombie case?"

Roman froze and I nearly choked before reminding myself that Detective Chan wouldn't have been referring to the zombies we'd seen last night but rather making a morbid cop joke about the disappearing morgue bodies.

I shook my head at Roman and made a soothing gesture. "Hey Tom, yeah. Whatcha got?"

"White van abandoned at the edge of Mason Farm Biological Reserve. That's under my jurisdiction, but a toe tag from the Raleigh morgue was found not far from the dump site so they're calling it linked. That place is accessible by permit only with all the research going on and the scientists want it sorted yesterday. Problem is, the K-9s won't go near it."

"Anything strange about the scene?"

"I wouldn't think so, but one of the geeks was having a hissy about some dead plants."

Oh shit. Dead plants plus skittish dogs? A sinking feeling told me this was my guy. "I'll be there in thirty, forty tops."

"Thanks, Arden. Doctor Mitchell says you're good on the weird ones."

I laughed weakly, hoping that was all Doc Mike had said. "Sure thing. And hey, Tom? Friend of mine missed drinks and hasn't answered calls or texts. I don't have any reason to think she's avoiding me, so I'm worried. She's a firefighter in Durham. Off for the next two days, so it'd be a while before she was missed. Could you keep your eyes peeled for news?" It was too early to report Val missing, but first responders looked out for each other.

"Sure thing," Tom said, his echo of my words grim. "Text me when you get to the reserve. Stay safe, Arden."

The call ended. I rubbed my temples and pushed my tea away. I should have mentioned all the evidence Maria had given me, now sitting in my freezer alongside a ready-made beef pot pie for lack of a better place to put it, but that was one problem too many just now.

"I need to get to work," I said to Roman.

"Need company?"

The offer tempted me. Roman's nose and ears were better than mine. He might pick up something I'd miss. But he was also an unlicensed civilian, and I was just growing my name—and reliability—with the larger police departments rather than the handful of individual relationships I'd cultivated. At least, that's what I told myself. Mostly I just wanted a little space. "Wish I could say yes. See you later?"

"Meeting Sergei later, but you're welcome to join. Might be helpful, actually."

His way of asking while trying to respect the fact that he knew I really didn't want to see Sergei again. I sighed as subtly as I could. Our relationship couldn't be just about what I wanted or needed. Plus, I had Maria breathing down my neck over this alliance and Janae and the witches curious about it. Something needed to move. Time to put on my big girl boots and get to moving it myself. "Text me when and where."

"Thanks, babe. Go on, get dressed. I'll tidy up." Roman's smile and lifted posture made the future dealings with his brother worth the inevitable trouble.

I kissed his forehead before heading to the bathroom to wash up in the sink and then change into a clean T-shirt and jeans. It was going to be too warm for denim, but better to be a hot, sweaty mess than a tick magnet. The biological reserve was mature woods and fields, probably full of Lyme disease-carrying vermin. I pulled my curls back off my face, wrangled them into a poofy ponytail, and tucked my pendant back behind my shirt.

Roman was waiting by the front door with my hiking boots when I stepped out, having washed the dishes by hand and set them to dry on the rack. After a last goodbye kiss, he left, stumbling over the block of Air I always left tied off with a muffled curse before thumping down the stairs. I smirked as I tugged on and tied my boots, then sobered as I wondered what fresh hell I was about to step into.

Chapter 14

I'd thought the auratic residue at the morgue and Claret was bad, but it had nothing on the evil oozing from the van abandoned at the biological reserve.

Every nerve, sinew, and hair in or on my body tried to rip itself free and crawl away when I arrived at the main parking area. After texting Tom to confirm my arrival, I stood at the back of my Honda Civic hatchback for a full five minutes pretending to get my gear in order before I could find enough spit to swallow the fear and speak to the officers on scene.

"Arden Finch with Hawkeye Investigations," I said as I approached, my private investigator's license held up in one hand and the backpack with my gear extended in the other. They looked twitchy. Not surprising. With the amount of bad juju in the air, even a magical null would feel something off.

One of the officers took my license, and the other took my bag and rifled through it with a tense expression.

"Detective Chan said to expect you," the heavyset Black officer with my license said as he slapped the card against his hand. "Said you're good with the weird ones."

"That's what they tell me," I agreed.

"Better be," said his equally heavy white partner, whose name plate read "Johnson." "The dogs won't even touch this one, after all the trouble we went through for them to be allowed in."

"Any idea why?" I asked.

The two exchanged glances and shrugged, their motions seeming choreographed. They handed back my stuff, and I tucked my license away before slinging the pack over my shoulder. The one who'd checked my license said, "Parton says—"

"Oh, don't start, Davis."

"*K-9 Officer Parton says* that the scene gives her the creepy-crawlies."

I focused on Officer Davis. "And the dogs wouldn't track?"

"No, ma'am. Not hide nor hair. Hers was extra jumpy, too. Jinx is usually a steadier dog than that. It's weird." He gave Officer Johnson a pointed look.

K-9 Officer Parton sounded like another latent sensitive, one with an affinity for animals. She and her dog probably had a minor feedback loop that made them especially effective on any cases that didn't involve Otherside, and fifty-fifty on those that did.

I gave my best not-bad-Obama face for Johnson's benefit, committing to neither belief nor disbelief. "Could I see the vehicle?"

"After you." Officer Johnson gestured toward where the taint of evil was strongest. The van itself was nowhere to be seen, hidden down a dirt track that ended in a mixed stand of beech and sweetgum. I could have found it on my own if I wasn't playing human, following the stench of death and evil. Officer Davis settled back into an antsy parade rest, watching the dirt track leading up from the creek ford to the parking lot.

Plants had died in the vicinity of the van, leaving an uneven ring of yellowed, brittle growth and a thinner trail leading deeper into the woods. The pattern matched the one I'd seen at the morgue, with a sharp delineation between the dead plants and the living, sometimes cutting halfway through the same tree or flower. The lich had either done some magic here or was somehow storing up the stolen life for later—assuming this wasn't just a sign that he was getting stronger.

The taint of evil worsened the closer I got to the van, wave on wave of nauseating, mind-numbing horror emanating from the vehicle. Nobody had mentioned that the van had blown a tire and crashed into a tree, answering why it had been abandoned. The evil had everyone off their game.

The weird little knot of whatever had bothered me last night pulsed in the back of my mind. I latched onto it, scrabbling for something to focus on besides the intense desire to start vomiting and never stop. I had a job to do. Hurling was not part of it. Nor was fear.

"Why here?" I wondered aloud, fumbling with my backpack with numb fingers in an effort to do something to take my mind off the psychic sensations.

"Who knows. Crazy son of a bitch."

I glanced at Johnson then got out my DSLR, slung the neck strap over my head, and adjusted the settings for the low light making it through the overcast sky and thick tree cover. "Seriously, though. There are woodlands all over the Triangle with acres more space than this. Areas that are a lot less of a pain in the ass to get into than a permit-only biological reserve. I mean, we had to cut through a golf course and ford a creek just to get up here. So why this place?"

"Look, lady. That's why you're the PI. You figure it out."

Typical. Though frustrated, I tried to give them some grace— if this whole thing was weirding me out, they'd be well out of their depths. I started taking pictures of the scene, narrating to my voice recorder about each shot and what about it had drawn my attention. My voice shook, and my mouth was dry on the first attempt. I dug in my bag for my steel water bottle and took a swallow, a splash falling ungracefully over my chin. Officer Johnson didn't notice, too busy leaning over to inspect a young pine tree that was half-dead in a clean line down the middle.

I tucked the bottle away and snapped pictures of a large, shallow boot print, suggestive of a tall but thin man, given the depth and size. Next was the gore in the back of the van, dried to a blacker sheen than blood usually did, with only my better-than-human nose telling me that it was blood—the same type as the zombies in the coterie's nest.

A scrap of torn paper lay in the passenger seat, with two letters on it—SV—and the numbers 828 trailing off into ragged edges. I frowned as an ugly suspicion wormed through me, temporarily cutting through the fear. *It can't be.*

Service on my phone was down to one bar, but that was enough to do a Google search. *Shit.* One of the area codes around Asheville was 828. And there was someone in town who just happened to be from there, with those initials.

Sergei.

I pocketed it after checking that the cop still wasn't looking at me, afraid all over again of what it might mean. I'd gotten lucky. The police had either missed it, or their crime scene tech had been too sensitive to be able to focus long enough to see it. How the hell could Sergei be involved in this case?

Maybe I was just looking for a connection because I disliked the man. With the unsettling new clue in mind, I forced myself to go over every inch of the scene then down the trail, looking for something else to corroborate or disprove it.

Another concentration of dead plants outlined an area of disturbed ground, a deep hole about the width of a dinner plate dug into it.

"Weird," I muttered, snapping photos before kneeling to peer into the reddish dirt. It had started filling in with groundwater, making it impossible to tell what might have been dug out. After steeling my courage, I took a deep breath and reached in, patting through the mud at the bottom and finding nothing. I wasn't sure if that was a relief or a disappointment. I wiped my hand clean on my jeans.

"What were you looking for?" I mused aloud.

The earth and trees gave no answer, so I made my way back to the parking lot, collecting Officer Johnson along the way. A wiry, white-haired woman in what looked like the outdoors store's summer catalogue was waiting with Officer Davis when we arrived. "This here's one of the biologists," Davis explained, edging away from the irate-looking woman. "Thought you might wanna talk to her."

"Thanks, Officer," I said.

I took Dr. Mary Manning's statement by voice recorder, not clear on why or whether the lich might be interested in rare native plant species or university experiments but trying to be thorough.

I broke in when she started repeating her outrage for the disturbed experiments. "Dr. Manning, is there any other reason, outside the experiments or rare plants, that someone would come here and dig a hole in the ground?"

"Well, I suppose it could be the reserve's history. Most of the area hasn't been disturbed since the 1730s, and we occasionally turn up old relics in the midst of restoration work."

"Old relics?" That sounded promising.

"Things from the original farm, or Indigenous artifacts. Mostly arrowheads."

"I see. Anything else?"

She frowned, considering. "It's not likely, but I suppose enslaved Africans might have passed through on their way to the Underground Railroad in Greensboro. They wouldn't have had much, but these woods still have secrets."

"Thank you, Dr. Manning. I appreciate your time and will be doing my best to track down whoever disturbed the reserve."

Her sharp nod was as much acceptance as dismissal. I spun slowly in place, trying to see if I'd missed anything as a thunderstorm blew in, stopping only when a threatening rumble suggested a lightning strike would be more trouble than missing a piece of evidence. My power pulsed under my skin as it tried to rise up to meet the gusting winds, and I gritted my teeth as I kept it close.

As I splashed back across the ford, I turned over everything I'd seen. *Janae might know more.* I dialed her number.

"I was just thinking of you, child. Blessings of the Goddess be on you."

"Blessings, Ms. Janae. Are you free this afternoon? I'm just leaving another scene where the sorcerer's been, and it's worse than before."

"I have clients this evening but could spare an hour if you can make it here in the next thirty minutes."

"Yes, ma'am, I can. I'll see you soon." I stepped on the gas, hoping to outrun the storm. Aside from the deadline, Chapel Hill tended to flood.

I made it in record time. Janae was waiting for me, rocking in the swing on her front porch and watching the first raindrops fall. She shuddered as I approached the porch and held up a hand for me to stop, ducking inside the house when I did. I waited, eyeing the new bottle trees decorating her lawn, until she reappeared with a lit bundle of juniper.

"Ah. Right. Sorry," I said, bowing my head and trying to find inner peace as she circled me, apparently unbothered by the worsening rain.

"That's better," she muttered after circling three times and invoking the Goddess. "Hoo, boy, that's a nasty one."

"It really was." I tried not to think about it, not wanting to bring the negativity with me into her home.

The prickles started up again as soon as I crossed the threshold behind her. We sat in the cream-and-gold wallpapered parlor again, although the tea was hawthorn this time. I sipped as I filled her in on the zombie attack in Raleigh last night and today's encounter at the reserve. "It feels like he's getting stronger."

"He? You're sure it's a man?"

I shrugged. "That's the police department's best guess based on what little they got from video surveillance at the morgue."

Janae leaned back in her chair, sucking her teeth. "He's definitely getting stronger. An attack on the vampires? Bold. Worryingly bold. That or Torsten has weaknesses."

Keeping my face straight was not easy under her piercing gaze, but I managed. "My question is, what was at the reserve? And how'd he leave if he abandoned the van?"

"You're assuming he's working alone, child."

My jaw dropped at my own stupidity. "Are you saying there are two sorcerers?"

"He might have an accomplice. One of our young people stopped attending coven meetings three months ago. My cards are pointing at him."

"Can I have his name?"

"No."

"Ms. Janae—"

"I said no. We'll handle this young'un our way."

The look on her face told me there was no use arguing. I bit my tongue on a saucy reply, instead saying, "Any ideas what he might have been after?"

"That's what troubles me." Wrinkles in her forehead slid together, furrowing deeply. "The Masons were members of our coven. We haven't been able to recover all of their ritual items."

"Sh—sugar," I said, backing away from the swear when she raised her eyebrows. "You're telling me there are magical objects lost on the grounds of the reserve?"

"There could be, lost or buried as part of a spell, or returned to the earth at the conclusion of one. If the lich recovered one, it could be the reason for the increase in evil taint you sensed. The Masons were powerful, more than any of us living now."

I scrambled to think through the implications. "Raleigh was a test. Maria won without losing a single vamp. The lich needs more power."

"I see no flaw in that logic."

Heaving a sigh, I finished my tea and replaced the cup before slumping back and scrubbing my hands over my face, trying desperately to find a silver lining. There was none. "Is there anything else you can tell me?"

"Not about your case, but I have spoken to the coven leaders about your alliance."

I popped back up, guilt that I'd invited myself over and focused on my problem making me wince. "And?"

"We would like to speak with the rest of the ringleaders."

"I see." Imagining Janae, Troy, Maria, Roman, and Duke in a room together made my head spin. Too many power players with too many diverging interests. But this had to happen. The lich situation was only getting worse. If Sergei and a rogue witch were both involved, I had to get it moving immediately. "I'll let everyone know and get back to you by the end of the week with an update."

She nodded, stately as a queen in her purple wingback chair. "There's one other thing, child. Your aura."

"What about it?"

"When I cleansed you, not everything left." Concern pinched her brow. "There's something anchored to you. Not necessarily malevolent, but definitely there."

"I think I know." There was only one thing it could be: the Aether tag Troy had put on me last winter.

"Do you need assistance with it? It feels different than the last time you were here, as though it's evolving. I can't tell for sure without touching you."

I frowned and tried to read her, but she was an inscrutable old woman with a face that stayed placid unless you disrespected her or her home. "Only the…the anchor. Nothing else," I said, holding out my hand.

"Of course." She took it and inhaled deeply, then exhaled, closing her eyes. "There." Opening her eyes, she studied the area around my head. "Aether, with the taste of herbs and roasted marshmallows. Elvish magic? You do live dangerously."

"Yeah." I squirmed as the goosebumps the house's magic gave me intensified.

"Whatever he put on you, it's sympathetic magic. And it's evolving. I can't say how." She released my hand.

"Sympathetic magic?"

"It acts on you both."

My stomach fell. "I was under the impression that it was only supposed to act on me."

"Maybe at first. But whatever you are, girl, your magic is changing it."

"That's not at all comforting." Bad enough that I had elven tracking magic lodged in my aura somehow without it evolving all on its own.

"At least you know now. I suggest you act on it."

"I plan to." And I would, as soon as I figured out what was going wrong.

Chapter 15

I had too much to worry about with Val still missing, elven magical bullshit, the alliance, the fallout with Callista and the djinn, and now a strengthening lich with a possible accomplice. I hadn't heard from Doc Mike since I'd called to let him know about Janae and was starting to worry. But I'd promised Roman I'd join him to talk with Sergei, and it was time that I gave a little more, so that had to trump a bubble bath with a glass of wine this evening.

Roman's text came in while I was walking through the door to my office. They'd be meeting for a late dinner at the Argentinian steakhouse on Ninth, a fancier place than Roman's usual selection. Sergei had probably chosen it. The nine o'clock reservation gave me plenty of time to get some administrative work done and file some selective updates with Raleigh PD.

Calling around got me in touch with the groundskeepers who'd cleaned up the hex at the morgue. They didn't remember anything except that they'd had the heebie-jeebies that day. Dead end. I was reviewing my notes on the disappearing bodies for anything I'd missed when my phone rang with the ringtone I used for the business's Google Voice account.

"Hawkeye Investigations, Finch speaking." *Who overlaps on both cases other than Sergei?*

"How much does your puppy dog mean to you?" The voice was low and aggressive, with a Midwest accent, probably male, though it was hard to tell. It sounded muffled, like he'd put a cloth or a hand over his mouth.

"Excuse me? I don't have a—" *Roman.* That's what Maria had called him, my puppy. My chest tightened. Someone was threatening Roman. Probably a vampire. My pulse leapt. "Who is this?"

"Would be a shame for him to be put down."

I put the phone on the desk and switched it to speaker with a trembling finger before switching my voice recorder on. "I said, who is this? Why are you calling me?"

"Bring your dog with you again, and you'll be burying him. You can't stop us. Not when we've got wolfdogs of our own."

And there it was—the piece of evidence tying Sergei to the splintered vampires, the rogue witch, or both. My stomach plummeted as I sat in shock.

With a click, the call ended.

"No!" I slammed my palms on the desk then pushed out of my chair to pace the room, too upset to sit still. "Get it together, Arden. You're supposed to be a bad bitch. Investigate."

Taking up the recorder, I stopped and saved the snippet before playing it back again. Almost definitely male. Again, listening for background noise this time. Nothing distinctive came through. "Fuck." All I had was a vague threat and the shortlist I'd created for Maria's case. It could be any of those people or any of their associates. I even tried calling back, only to get an automated voice telling me the number had been disconnected. A burner account, probably Google Voice or one of the many apps anyone could use for that purpose.

I called Roman, still pacing, my skin crawling. "Pick up, pick up…"

"Hey, babe. What's up?" His deep, easy tones settled me somewhat, but not enough.

"Roman!" I answered him too fast, my words tripping over each other. "Are you okay? Are you safe?"

"Of course. Why?"

"I got a call just now, saying that if I bring my 'puppy dog' with me again, they'll kill you. I think something is gonna go down with the vampires." The line was quiet for a few moments. "Roman?"

"I'm here, Arie. It's just been a long time since I mattered enough to be worth threatening. I might be flattered."

"Yeah, well, that's not all of it." I paced, wondering if he'd believe me about Sergei. "Whoever the fuck this was implied they had a wolf of their own."

"Did they, now?" He sounded like he didn't quite believe me.

"You need to watch your back. How far do you trust Sergei?"

"He's my brother, Arden. Watch it."

I winced at the hardening of his tone and the use of my full name. "I get that. But he also tried to pull some shit when he arrived—"

"He wouldn't pull this. That was *show*. Posturing. Two alphas establishing pecking order."

"Roman—"

"He *wouldn't*. Don't push this."

I frowned at the belligerent certainty in his tone. Usually I was the bossy one. "Okay," I said reluctantly, reminding myself that I needed to give a little more with him than I had been. "But this is Otherside shit. I can't take it to the police. So I need you to be careful while I dig into this."

"I can defend myself."

"I know you can." I sighed and slumped against my desk, trying not to sound clingy as I said, "I'm sorry, I just—Look, I'm not used to caring, this much, okay?"

Roman made a low whuff of amusement. "That might be the sweetest thing you've ever said to me."

"Yeah, well, don't get used to it." I squirmed in my chair.

"I'd like to." His voice had softened away from gruff irritation and into something warmer, more hopeful.

"I know. I'm working on it," I said softly. "I'll see you tonight."

"All right, babe. Later."

The threat on Roman's life lit a new fire under my ass as I tackled Maria's conspiracy list with a new angle: someone on the list, or close to them, might have been at Claret for the zombie attack if they were calling Roman my puppy. If the zombie attack and the rogue witch were linked—and I was almost certain they were—that someone had probably been there to watch and report back on whatever the lich had been testing. That didn't tell me how Sergei was involved, but it was a start. I called Maria for the duty roster for that night, fending off her usual flirtations with the news of the threat and my assumptions.

"I'll email it over. I need a resolution soon, Arden. I'm running out of time," was all she said before hanging up.

"You and me, both," I muttered to absolutely no one.

I got so lost in cross-referencing vampiric relationships and work schedules that I almost forgot to clean up in the coworking space's small shower facility and change into the emergency little black dress I kept in the tall cabinet in my office.

Roman and Sergei were both seated with wine by the time I arrived. My heart thudded, and adrenaline surged as I avoided looking at Sergei.

"Sorry," I said with a wince as I slid into the seat next to Roman, smiling as I took in the shirt and slacks he'd put on for the evening. "Work. You look nice."

"No worries, babe." Roman looped an arm behind my chair, resting a hand on the back of my neck and squeezing in what could have been a massage but felt more possessive than relaxing. I allowed it, not trusting Sergei's intentions enough to shrug it off or frown. We needed to present a unified front.

"We were just talking about concessions," Sergei added.

Definitely needed to show unity.

"Concessions?" I tried to keep my voice steady as Roman kissed my temple and reached for the bottle of wine. I held up a hand to stop him. "Just water, thanks."

The Malbec smelled perfect, but I needed a cool head and no Chaos. Roman reached for the carafe of water instead as I allowed myself to study his brother. The younger Volkov wore another designer shirt and had slicked his hair back. Was this what Roman would have been, had he grown up at home?

Sergei was studying me in turn. "Pops has agreed to let Roman return to pack and clan, if we can secure certain adjustments to the current balance of power."

The waiter appearing saved me from having to answer. I bit my tongue and tried not to look as though I'd been punched in the gut, burying my nose in my menu and deciding quickly as the men ordered. It was futile to try pretending—even with all the scents in the restaurant, Sergei's smug little smile told me he knew what a blow he'd just dealt at the suggestion that Roman might go home. I needed one goddamn minute to process the nuances of what he'd said on the heels of the earlier revelation.

Roman squeezed the back of my neck again, lighter this time, and I dug my nails into his thigh in warning before ordering the filet mignon au poivre with a side of sautéed broccolini. "Thanks for getting dinner, by the way," I said to Sergei with my best fake smile. "What adjustments did y'all have in mind?"

Sergei's momentary scowl at my pre-emptively handing him the check smoothed. "It's my pleasure. You're looking lovely this evening, honey." He let his gaze travel from my lips to my breasts, the pervy smile curling his lips leaving no question that the offense was intentional.

"Excuse me?" I snapped as Roman stiffened.

"I said—"

"Oh, I heard what you said. It's not gonna fly."

"It will if you want the Volkovs to sell this deal to the rest of the clans."

Roman trembled at my side, and his hand slipped from my neck to fist on the table. "That was not part of our discussion."

"Call it an agent's fee then."

Outrage stole my words.

The waiter came back, opened his mouth, then winced and slipped away on feet so silent he might have passed as an Othersider.

"Let me get this straight," I finally choked out. "You're hitting on me."

"Bright one, eh, bro?" Sergei turned mocking eyes on Roman and sipped his wine, looking every inch the entitled brat of a wealthy, powerful family. "Think she'll give it up as quickly as Ana did after you got run off?"

I grabbed Roman's bicep as he moved to stand, the interplay telling me more than I wanted to know about the Volkov family history.

"I don't know who Ana is, and I don't know who the fuck you think you are." I kept my voice low to avoid making a scene. Othersiders fighting in public would accelerate Callista's Reveal in a way that would have all three of us executed by the more bloodthirsty of my colleagues among the Watchers. I hadn't reported Sergei's presence, but I had no doubt that Callista knew he was here and was having all of us Watched.

"She was his betrothed," Sergei said with a nasty smirk.

Roman's muscles went rigid under my hand. "Don't."

"Oh! You didn't tell your new bitch? Well, then." Sergei's grin widened, and he swirled his wine. "Ana was given to the Volkovs to ally the two biggest packs on the East Coast. She should have been Roman's, but when he showed himself to be less than an alpha male should be..." He hitched up and slouched in his seat, flashing his eyebrows as he sipped from his glass.

"I'll kill you," Roman snarled, pulling his arm free of my grip.

"Roman. Roman!" I glanced around, anxiety flooding me as I saw that some of the other diners had noticed our spat. "You need to either cool it or go for a walk, before we get the wrong kind of attention."

He didn't answer. If looks could kill, Sergei would be on the floor with his throat torn out.

I leaned in to speak into his ear. "I'm serious. We're probably being Watched. If you go for him now, if one of you shifts, that's all three of us dead."

"Listen to your bitch, big brother," Sergei said.

"Excuse me." Roman stood so quickly I had to catch his chair and stormed out.

The restaurant quietened. I waited, face flushed with both embarrassment and indignation. Fury crested in me, and my blood pounded in my veins. My faint smile said I was ready to partake in some vigilante justice. It warred with the darkly satisfied smirk on his. The front door opened and shut. Conversation slowly picked back up and the waiter made his way back.

"He and I are gonna need ours to go." I indicated Roman's empty place. "Leave the check with our friend here, please."

"Of course, ma'am."

When he was out of earshot, I said, "You're a real fucking piece of work."

"I'd love to work you over."

I shook my head and scoffed as the whole fucked up situation became ridiculous. Sergei wasn't some master planner. He was a kid in over his head. I could trap him and get the confirmation I needed right from his own mouth.

"You don't get it, do you?" I said.

"I get that I was sent here to bring my lost big brother in line. I'd say I've done that. I'd also say it's none of your fucking business."

"If you're really here to negotiate for the alliance it is my business, but go off, I guess." I watched him process that, watched the frown pull his brows down as he started looking beyond getting his brother out of play in the negotiations. "See, I didn't like you to begin with, but I figured dealing with *my boyfriend's* bratty little brother was part of the price of being in a relationship. Then there's the fact that I'm trying to get literally everyone in the Triangle to play nicely when they all have their own agenda. Do you know what you just did, Sergei?"

"Go off," he said, throwing my phrase back in my face.

"You pissed me off and made it personal, which means I'm finna get this done in spite of you and everyone else." He rolled his eyes and I added, "And all this confidence? Pissing on your brother's turf? You just made yourself my number one suspect for the furbaby collaborating with the drinkers making trouble."

My shot landed. Sergei sat up straight, and sweat broke out on his upper lip, the body language proclaiming his guilt as much as his strangled, "I have no idea what you're talking about. What would make you think one of us—"

"Everything about the last fifteen seconds. Then there's the paper I found with your phone number on it and the call I got about Roman just before coming here. What the hell are you playing at?"

Sweat had broken out on Sergei's brow. "Did you really think you could just set up your own hustle without consequence? Without anyone *important* taking notice and doing something about it?"

My heart raced, and my mouth dried. *Callista knows. This is her doing.* "She had you fund the group in Raleigh."

Blood drained from Sergei's face before he flushed. We stared at each other for long heartbeats before he settled back, smugness washing over him. "You can't prove that, and Roman will never listen to you without proof."

"In exchange for what, though? And who else are you working with?"

His lips firmed into a thin line. "Looks like you're not *that* clever, bitch."

Two boxes appeared at my elbow, and I gave the waiter a genuine smile as I reached for my purse and pulled out a twenty. I wouldn't put it past Sergei to stiff the guy on tip, and I'd have paid more in time or bribes to get the information about who was helping the vampires. "Thank you so much for making it fast."

"My pleasure, ma'am." He glanced at Sergei as he pocketed the twenty, swallowed, then left a leather folder at his elbow.

I gathered the boxes. "Some free advice: don't come to my town and think you own the place just because you reckon your dick is big out west. I've been pushed around by much bigger bitches than you, and I'm done with it."

As I turned to go, one of the women at the next table said, "Well, bless his heart. You go, girl."

Those in hearing distance laughed, hiding behind their hands or turning away from where Sergei sat alone and red-faced. I smiled, feeling like I'd won the exchange despite the icky clench of my heart and the knowledge that my boyfriend's brother was working with Maria's enemies.

Did that definitely mean he was helping the lich too? Could I get Roman to see it?

I found Roman halfway down the block, scowling at traffic with his hands in his pockets. "Here." I extended his box of food. "I figured we'd both had enough of him for one evening."

"Thanks, babe." He took it, then squeezed my free hand. "I'm sorry about that. I should have stayed."

"And done what? Gotten us all killed?"

"I dunno. Kept my temper." He rubbed his thumb over my knuckles and avoided looking at me. "Defended you."

"Don't worry about it. Everybody's itchy these days. Must be something in the air. Besides, I can defend myself." I went on tiptoe to kiss his cheek. "And sometimes you too."

He stiffened, drawing away. "It's not—"

His withdrawal stung. I tamped down on my hurt. "It's done, Roman."

I thought about telling him my revelation about Sergei's relationship with the Modernist vampires, but decided against it. He'd made it crystal clear that he wasn't willing to entertain the idea, and I wasn't sure if Sergei's ham-fisted attempt to steal me had changed anything. Now wasn't the time.

"Okay. If you say so." He avoided looking at me as his expression darkened. "About Ana—"

"I really don't need to know about your exes." Hurt made my words come out sharper than I'd intended.

"She's—you know what, fine." He dropped my hand, and we stood there, looking at each other. Tension hummed between us, worse than it had in the restaurant, tightening the lines of his face and body. He wasn't happy, but neither was I.

I rocked on my heels, too full of nervous energy to stand still and wanting to be anywhere else. "I got a lead this evening. I'm gonna head back to the office. That threat against you worries me."

"Sure, babe." He walked off without so much as a goodbye kiss, and I stared after him, feeling like something was broken and not liking that he was acting like it was my fault.

Chapter 16

Everything about the evening was still bugging me when I swung by my office and shoved my untouched dinner in the mini-fridge. I tried to find connections between Sergei and my narrowed list of vampires, but if they were there, they weren't jumping out. Neither was a text or call from Val. And still nothing from Doc Mike other than a text saying that he was fine but still processing. Reasonable or not, that hurt. I knew firsthand the pain of having people you trusted hide things from you, but I'd hoped he would understand, that we could talk about it.

I sat down to work then stood right back up again. Compartmentalization only went so far when one friend might be missing, another wasn't talking to me after a bad scare, and my boyfriend's family business was becoming way too personal.

"I need a night off. I've *earned* a night off," I told the plant Roman had bought for me, mad all over again at the fact that he seemed to be mad at me. Rational? No. But I'd used up all my rational talking Roman out of bringing Callista and the other Watchers down on all our heads by breaking the Détente.

Shit. I hadn't said anything to Callista about the zombies. Or the trip out to Mason Farm. Or Sergei, or anything. But if she'd made Sergei an offer to destabilize Torsten's coterie, she definitely knew. If she didn't want it to happen, that meant she saw it as a threat.

My skin prickled. She saw *me* as a threat. One strong enough that she didn't risk coming after me without picking away at my allies first.

Understanding whirled through me like a spring storm, staggering me. Tapping Sergei to do her bidding accomplished three things. It made the Volkovs feel important and trusted, tying them to her. It destabilized Torsten, weakening my ally. And it drove a wedge between me and Roman, right when I needed his support.

As evil plans went, it was beautiful. It also meant a timer had started ticking on my life again. If I wanted to survive this one, I had to outmaneuver her. That started with playing ignorant.

Fear choked me, taking me back to the days I'd lived hidden and alone, isolated by powers I couldn't use for fear of elven hunters. I shoved it aside as I locked up and started walking toward Callista's bar a few blocks north of downtown. My stomach clenched, and that weird feeling at the back of my mind was back. Paranoia at its finest.

I hadn't come up with anything clever by the time I reached Callista's. A rush of frigid air slapped my bare arms as I entered, but it had nothing on Callista's glare. Momentum kept me moving forward, and habit had me sit at the bar. "The usual, please," I said, pushing past a sudden hoarseness.

Callista radiated disapproval and didn't pour me a drink. "Back room. Now."

When I hesitated, her raised eyebrow reminded me of my few, short, futile childhood rebellions with her as my guardian. We might have made a new arrangement, but I was the one who'd brought the information about the lich. It was on me to follow through, and I hadn't, too caught up with the alliance I'd thought beneath her notice. I rose and made my way back, heart hammering as I punched in the numbers on the door's keypad and sank into the familiar, creased leather chair. I should have just stayed away. Why was I even here?

Anger at that last thought began to mix in with anxiety and apprehension. I'd never asked to become a Watcher. The obligation had been bestowed on me when I'd turned eighteen. "It's time to repay what you owe," Callista had said. I'd had nothing and no one else. Now I'd committed the crime of wanting out and had painted a target on myself and everyone who'd pinned their hopes of a new arrangement on me.

I jumped when the door shut with a firm thud and interrupted my thoughts. Callista settled into the roller chair behind the desk, a green-eyed snake coiling as she considered a strike. Her aged desktop with its huge monitor flashed to life, ignored as she stared at me. I clenched my jaw to stem a tumble of babbling words that might not even be related to what she was mad about, a habit I'd learned early on in her guardianship.

"Are you sure you're still a Watcher, Arden?" Callista asked in the softly ugly tone that said she meant business.

No, my mind urged. The compromise we'd settled on still gave her too much power, but the idea had been to ease my way out. "Yes." I summoned some courage and tried to be smart. "For now."

"How interesting. Is that why I've had to expend resources on you lately, rather than my interests in the rest of the territory?"

I didn't know how to answer that, but I'm sure the blood draining from my face did it for me.

"My patience is wearing dangerously thin, girl. I agreed to no more orders, freebies, or threats, as you put it. But *you* agreed that you would still contribute. Consider this your more-than-fair warning that my patience has reached its limits. Do I make myself clear?"

"Yes, Callista." Something inside me curled up and died, while another part exploded in rage. I wasn't a child. I was powerful in my own right. Just not powerful enough to stand alone yet. I didn't know if I could best a being that Duke had implied was something akin to a goddess.

"Report."

Straightening, I cleared my throat. "I have suspicions that the lich is allied with the vampires."

Her eyelid flickered. She hadn't known that, which meant the vampires were playing her as much as she was using Sergei to play them. What a shitshow.

Reassured, I pressed on, throwing her something real in the hopes that she didn't want a lich to succeed in overthrowing her. "There was a zombie attack at Claret last night. I think the lich is testing his power."

Callista leaned back in her chair, face blank, hands folded. "What else?"

"Roman's brother is in town. Sergei."

"Oh, that, I know. A Watcher with more dedication than you already informed me."

I couldn't help wincing.

She stared at me, waiting for me to add something else, and I stared back. The angry part of me was starting to assert itself, and I didn't owe her everything. Not after nearly dying to get intel last winter, and not after we'd struck a new understanding.

"What else?" she demanded.

"That's all I have for you." True, in its way.

She stared at me for even longer moments. My stomach roiled, but I refused to answer further or look away.

"Fine. I want this lich situation resolved before we move forward with the Reveal." With a fake smile, she said, "Report again in no more than a week. With progress, Arden. I'll transfer your finder's fee tomorrow."

I had no idea what the implied threat entailed, but I wasn't feeling brave enough to challenge it, even if the order went against our agreement. At least I wasn't working for free anymore, and had learned something about the game she was playing.

My feet carried me out of the bar before I realized I'd stood. Spring sunshine enveloped me in its embrace, clinging to my skin as I made my way back downtown. The cheerful decorations of the Tiki bar on East Chapel Hill Street pulled my feet toward it, drawing me with a promise of distraction.

I'd flubbed Doc Mike's intro to Otherside. The nagging feeling that Val was in trouble kept growing. Roman was inexplicably angry with me, his brother was an asshole of epic proportions, and I could not catch a break on Maria's case or the lich. Every time I checked the news, violent incidents had increased again. Oh, and I was on Callista's shitlist.

None of my efforts in the last few days had paid off. Maybe it was time to stop making them and have a damn coconut pineapple shrub with a cute umbrella before going home and dodging my self-appointed kobold landlord to feel shitty about everything in peace.

A couple was leaving the bar as I walked in, and I snagged one of their seats. As I took a quick glance at the food menu in the hopes of making up for my missed supper, a whiff of herby meringue made me sit bolt upright.

Troy slipped onto the stool beside me.

"No. No, I do *not* need to deal with you today," I hissed as he settled in.

"Cute bar." He flicked his eyes dismissively over the beachy decorations before looking back at me. "Not where I thought you'd go after whatever happened at Callista's though."

I glared at the casual reminder that the Aether tag meant he could find me whenever he wanted. "What do you want, Monteague?"

He flicked a finger to signal for a drink.

"Monteague."

The bartender floated over, all smiles and good hospitality propped up by an ornate moustache. Troy ordered a glass of the bar's homemade cola and, with a glance at me, added, "And whatever she's drinking."

"Sparkling water," I snapped. No way was I drinking anything more revealing around House Monteague's prince and a top Darkwatch agent.

We sat in silence while the bartender poured and served. Muscles flexed under taut, tawny-brown skin as Troy reached for the glass the bartender set down and handed over a credit card to pay for both drinks. I looked away, studying the bubbles in my water and reminding myself that he wasn't here to hurt me. Probably.

"A bit boring for a PI, isn't it?" He sneered at my water.

"None of your beeswax, Monteague. What. Do. You. Want?"

"My grandmother wishes to see you."

"No."

House Monteague's queen frightened the ever-loving bejeezus out of me. The last time I'd been in her presence, she'd ordered a teenage elf in her care killed as retribution for a slight against her house. Troy had wielded the blade, piercing the heart of his little sister's crush without a question. Then Keithia had tried trapping me in a mindmaze to cover up the exposed corruption—a maze I'd broken out of later, unbeknownst to them. I still had nightmares.

"You can come, or I can take you." He sipped his cola and smiled cheekily, looking every inch the convivial hipster trying to convince a chance-met woman to go home with him.

I looked him over, trying to figure out where he was hiding all of his knives. My lead-bladed elf-killer was in the bottom of my backpack, too far for me to reach even if I could use it in the bar. I went with bravado instead. "You can try."

"Don't tempt me, Finch," he murmured.

I scoffed and sipped my water.

He leaned closer to my ear, and I shivered as he said, "I gave Leith the clue to taking you down before. Our agreement protects you from death, not anything else, and I carry bronze now."

Outraged, I turned so that we were nose to nose and said the only thing I could think of to get him to back off. "If you get any closer, I might kiss you, Monteague."

He recoiled, eyes darting to the distant bartender. "You'd regret that."

"And then who would meet with Keithia?" I simpered, drinking more of my water and taking my attention off him to scan the rest of the bar. Callista had to have a Watcher here, and I did not want to know what she'd make of an elven prince chatting me up at a Tiki bar.

Troy huffed a sigh. "You're a pain in my ass, Finch."

"Your royal ass? Or have they finally disowned you?"

His glass clinked as he set it back on the counter harder than was strictly necessary. "You'll come with me, or the alliance is over before it's started."

That took me back a pace. Angry as I was with Roman, and him with me, he needed the alliance. It wasn't in me to be so petty as to throw it away just to needle Troy. And hell, I needed it for myself now, to get all the way clear of Callista and the threat she represented. Still, I hated to give in that easily. I spun my glass on the bar, hesitating.

"Good to know it matters to you," he said.

"Fuck off, Monteague."

"There's no shame in choosing to serve something greater than yourself."

"I wouldn't know. I was never allowed the option before."

The weighing look he gave me made me hyper-aware of all the air currents in the room, currents I could pull on to smother Troy, or at least knock him on his stupid smug ass if he tried something. Not pulling on Air took all my control. This was a human bar. I was in no position to risk exposure.

"Are you done?" Troy asked, eyeing me before taking another long sip and shifting to face me full-on.

"What does Keithia want?"

"She has concerns about the recent troubles."

"It's not like I caused them."

"All the same. Your presence is required."

Sighing, I propped my forehead on my palm. Troy hadn't tried Aether on me, hadn't even reached for it as far as I could tell, despite the fact that we both knew he could sting past my shields and force the issue if he wanted. Shieldbreaking was a talent of his house in general and him in particular. I wouldn't even feel it, though I'd know he was preparing if I smelled the heavy, burnt-marshmallow scent of a powerful elf drawing on Aether—which I didn't. This conversation was a courtesy, not a request, and we both knew it.

"Fine," I finally said. "When?"

"Now."

"Are you kidding me? I have shit to do tonight."

"No, you don't. Not unless your boyfriend has changed his mind after whatever happened earlier."

It was my turn to draw back. "How long have you been following me?"

He shrugged. "I do my duty."

I leaned close. "Fuck your duty, and fuck you too."

Troy made no response as he finished his cola, stood, and gestured toward the door, smiling lopsidedly with another glance at the bartender. I understood the ruse, and I didn't like it, though I'd have to play along if I didn't want our interaction commented on. Forcing my face smooth, I finished my water and slid off my stool.

"Don't touch me," I muttered as I squeezed past him and the new couple angling for our seats.

"Don't flatter yourself," he snarled back. I guess his bared teeth could be taken as a smile in the neon lights over the bar, but the two of us knew the truth.

"I'll follow you there," I said when we reached the street, turning to where I'd parked in the garage next to my office.

"You'll ride with me."

"Like hell."

We stared at each other, close enough that most people would be fighting or kissing.

"I'm not getting in a car with you," I said in a low voice when he wouldn't back down. "You want me there, we go on my terms." I smiled, going for flirty since that was his ruse in the bar. "Or you can see if you can get bronze on me before I scream bloody murder and have all the mundanes thinking you're trying to force me. Think a Good Samaritan would jump in?"

"If you get *lost* along the way, I'll call it a breach of our agreement and have you hunted down."

Tears sprang into my eyes, and I jostled him with a shoulder as I shoved past before he could see them. I hadn't needed more entries on the ledger of personal shittiness today, but count on Troy Monteague to hand me a big one.

Chapter 17

I'd pulled myself together by the time we arrived at the Chapel Hill mansion that served as the local seat of House Monteague and its queen. Keithia scared the living hell outta me, but after meeting with an angry Callista and reminding myself that the elves tended toward the lawful end of the alignment spectrum, I found enough resilience to face her with dry eyes and a lifted chin.

It was a façade, of course. The last time I'd been here, I'd killed Leith Sequoyah just before, ending his dreams of forcing the elves to a patriarchy and war. I was blamed for the subsequent loss of his corpse in the Crossroads, where Callista and Grimm had dragged me after discovering us. One of the old gods—Mixcoatl—had sent me back the hard way, with an arrow of lightning lodged in my shoulder and no corpse for the Monteagues.

That shoulder ached now, and I rubbed the scar as I followed the butler through the long hallway with its ugly, old-fashioned paintings and overdone lily arrangements. Troy's little sister, Evangeline, didn't come running this time, for which I was grateful. Leith's missing body meant her crush, Keithia's ward, was killed to settle the blood debt owed to House Luna. She'd seemed like a nice girl, for an elf. I couldn't remember her boy's name now, and I couldn't decide if that bothered me.

The butler gestured Troy and me in. Troy crowded me when I hesitated. "Now, Finch."

With a queen ahead and a prince behind, I didn't have a choice, no matter how much my heart thundered.

The rug Evangeline's crush had died on had been replaced with one in an ugly yellow. Or gold, I guess, since it was fancy, but I'd sooner burn it than have it in my house. I kept my attention away from it, since I wasn't supposed to remember the entirety of my last visit here.

Keithia waited for us in her same chair as before, a graceful diadem resting amidst piled curls of silver-threaded black hair. It should have looked silly, like a *Toddlers in Tiaras* mom playing dress-up, but her bearing made it impossible to laugh. Her four bodyguards and their guns made it pretty difficult too.

My pulse quickened in dread. "Evening, boys and girls." I stayed as close to the door as Troy would let me. The room reeked of Aether, making my skin crawl.

"The elemental, as requested, my queen." Troy shot a glare at me as he bowed.

The snap in Keithia's purple-green eyes betrayed her fury at my refusal to kneel. I sidled away from Troy's attempt to bring me down alongside him, reminding myself that we had an agreement. They couldn't just kill me. Janae, I greeted with respect because I respected her. Keithia...she could die angry. Especially after sending Troy to track me down.

Yeah, it stung that Troy of all people had seen the weird moment with Roman, and I was just tired enough of Otherside not to care if refusing to bow to an elf queen might be problematic.

"You rang?" I cocked a hip and crossed my arms.

"Finch," Troy said in a tone heavy with warning.

Keithia glared at us. "It certainly has grown bold these last months, grandson."

"I'm sorry, my queen. She—"

"*She*," I said, "would like to know why she's been summoned. I have two cases, and you're not paying me to investigate either of them. I'm here as a courtesy, seeing as there's no alliance yet."

Troy made a grab for me, which I dodged, dancing away from him and then from the bodyguard I nearly crashed into.

"Enough," Keithia snapped. "It will have to be bold to fulfill our charge."

I blinked. "Your—Excuse me?" The bitch had a fistful of nerve. "I'm not anything to you to be given a charge. Use your grandson. He's the Darkwatch agent."

"It will hunt down the lich that is causing all the violence in the Triangle," Keithia said, as though I hadn't spoken. "The creature is causing imbalance. I will not have it."

I stared, shocked into speechlessness, then spluttered, "I am already—"

"It's not working hard enough."

The queen had addressed all of her comments to Troy. My temper snapped. "If you're going to try demanding I do whatever shit the Darkwatch can't handle, the least you can do is look me in the face when you do it."

Every elf in the room went still as Keithia stared thunderously at Troy and spoke in a dangerously soft voice. "Take it in hand. Or we will take it for you."

Troy flushed. "The Darkwatch can handle this," he said. "We don't need her."

"Then why is it not handled? The Conclave gave its orders. Now, I give you another." She leaned forward and pointed imperiously at me. "Get this filthy creature to hunt, or you'll share its fate. It would be much more agreeable to negotiate this new alliance without it, and if you can't be effective, perhaps your sister can be."

"Hey!" Outrage clenched my fists and made me take a step forward. "We had a deal! You can't just kill me like I'm—"

"An elemental, living at my sufferance, in breach of elven law?" Keithia finally looked at me, and my guts froze at the hate in her eyes. "Otherside is poised for the greatest shift in generations. Neither my grandson, nor Callista, nor anyone else will stop me if my price for cooperating is one. Elemental's. Head." She paused to let that sink in. "It pleased me to indulge my grandson's giving his word, but now you both vex me. Pray vexation does not become ire."

I opened my mouth. Closed it and swallowed as wisdom finally caught up with me along with the rising scent of burnt marshmallow. I'd kept my head down for twenty-five years before being discovered. I could find the knack of it for five more minutes if it kept me alive. But as I ground my teeth and glared at the fugly rug under my feet, I discovered what I wanted from the new direction my life was taking: enough power to force even elven queens to respect me. Not power derived from an alliance but from within myself.

"Good. It finds humility at last," Keithia said in biting tones meant to wound. "Now get out. You have until the new moon to end the lich and its zombies, or we kill the elemental and go to war."

Troy grabbed my arm and propelled me out. I let him, a dizzy, sick feeling washing over me as I counted. I had ten days before my hard-won deal was reneged and I either had to get out of town or fight elves from three high Houses and who knew how many lesser ones. The old, bone-deep fear I used to live with every day settled itself deeper in my chest, squeezing as we left the house.

"Are you suicidal or just stupid?" Troy snapped in a low voice as we exited the house.

I stopped on the porch and stared at him.

"All you had to do was kneel and keep your mouth shut."

Translation: all I had to do was keep being less than everyone else. My skin prickled, and something hollow grew within me.

"Fuck that sideways with a broomstick," I said, filling the hollow with a quiet rage and scrabbling for dignity.

His brows lifted, and I deflated at the reminder that we were still on his family's doorstep.

Numb, I turned away and headed for my car before he could say anything else. I needed to go home and find refuge in a drink and my cozy armchair.

Someone was leaning against my car when I got back to it, slim and a little taller than me. They'd chosen a spot shadowed by the redbud tree alongside the road, and a cap hid their face. I stopped, mentally cursing the fact that my Ruger LCP was secured in the glove box for this visit. I didn't dare draw on Air in front of the Monteague family mansion, which left scraping up enough charm to talk my way out.

"Can I help you?" I called, stopping a few paces away and trying to catch a whiff of scent. The wind blew from behind me though, and I got nothing.

The figure uncrossed their arms and tugged the cap off, allowing the nearby streetlamp to reveal Troy's face done in feminine lines. Her lilac eyes seemed to pull in what little light there was and glow faintly with it.

I frowned. "Evangeline?"

She snarled, and a second row of teeth slid down from her gums, viciously pointed. "If I ever hear my name in your mouth again, I'll kill you."

I stared in shock, not having known that elves had secondary teeth, and fucking sharp ones at that, before shaking it off and easing into a hapkido ready stance. "I'm not looking for trouble. If you step away from my vehicle, I'll just get myself on home."

"He's dead because of you," she snarled in a thick voice. "Why should you get to go home in one piece when Clay is dead?"

"Why don't you talk to your brother about that?" I let all the nastiness spoiling in my heart out on her.

"You fucking—"

"Enough, Evangeline!" Troy's shout made me jump, and cut short his sister's lunge for me.

She whirled on him instead, drawing back for a strike. "Bastard!"

He let the slap fall, steadying his stance and loosening his neck and shoulders instead of blocking it. Even let his head turn when it landed.

I hope that hurt as much as it looked.

"You were raised better than to brawl in the street," Troy said, softly but sternly. "I won't apologize for doing my duty."

"Then do it, and kill that!" Evangeline hissed. Her hand trembled as she pointed at me.

"Shut. Up. And get inside." He stepped closer and lowered his voice further. "Put your teeth away. You're too old to make a slip like that. If the police are called, they'll be on her side. And you've just given anyone watching a juicy story to share if she does turn up dead. You're smarter than this, Evie."

Evangeline glanced at me, petulance blending with hatred and predator's teeth to make her the most dangerous-looking teenager I'd ever seen. I needed to find a library with books about elves. Old books. Nothing I'd ever read or heard whispered suggested anything like this.

She flexed her jaw, and the teeth retracted. "I hate you both. I'll see that one dead, even if it breaks your oath. *Especially* if it does." Her long, black braid whipped behind her as she spun and stalked back to the house.

Troy waited until the door slammed behind Evangeline to turn back to me. We stared at each other.

"Y'all must love Shark Week," I said to break the silence.

"If I hear whispers about this, I'll know who they started with, and then our deal is off. *Nobody* can know."

Morbid curiosity made me ask, "You have them, too?"

He stared at me, stone-faced, and I took that as a yes.

"Ishtar save me. Y'all let everyone think you had pointy *ears* so you could misdirect from the fucking *teeth*?"

"Go home, Finch. Now."

"Is she going to tell? I'm not going to let you kill me because your sister hates me and cut off her nose to spite her face. Or bit it off, whatever y'all are into."

"The trouble she'd be in if anyone else found out wouldn't be worth it. Now leave."

"Fine. We're not done with whatever the fuck *that* was." I waved in the general direction of the house. "But I have had a hell of a day and I don't need any more of you in it."

Troy watched me get in the car and drive away, looking as close to worried as I'd ever seen him.

Chapter 18

It was the middle of the week, but I gave myself the next morning off. I'd been running from one disaster to the next so fast my head was spinning. A morning on my deck with a cup of iced Tulsi and rose tea was the least I'd earned. I half expected Troy to be waiting around when I woke up, given the order to work with me on the lich, but I was pleasantly surprised to find the driveway empty. The morning's disappointment was no overnight text from Roman, and still nothing from Val or Doc Mike, although Janae had sent a text confirming that she'd cleansed the morgue. That was a relief, but it was too small to settle me.

I tried calling Val one more time. No answer. It wasn't like her to not call back. Something was wrong.

Val was a private person with good and reasonable concerns about my connections to Callista, the djinn, and the elves. That she'd broken from the other elementals and agreed to keep meeting up with me made me feel like I owed her, beyond what I'd feel for another friend. I wrestled with invading her privacy before going back in for my laptop, notebook, and pen and setting up on the small patio table on my deck.

I didn't know anything about her family, only that she had a sister named Sofia. I'd never wanted to pry before, but I'd also never had reason to. I'd start with family and go from there.

Google told me Sofia Pérez was two years younger than Val, a PhD candidate in UNC Chapel Hill's Environment, Ecology, and Energy Program with an MS in ecology and a specialization in urban ecology. Given her areas of study, if she was an elemental like her sister, my guess was that Sofia was an undine or an oread—Water or Earth—rather than Fire like Val.

I called the university. Invoking the Raleigh Police Department got me transferred to the university department head, who told me Sofia hadn't checked in with her advisor two days prior and had missed a lab.

"I'm sorry to hear that. I'm a private investigator working on a case that I'm afraid might be related." Small fudge, but with the weird uptick in violence in the last week, who was to say it wasn't? "Is there any way you could help me with another number to try next?"

"I really shouldn't give out personal information."

I jumped on the anxious tone in the other woman's voice. "I know, and I'm so sorry to ask. We're just hitting dead ends, and with folks acting so strange lately, I'd hate to find out later that something happened." *You're a naughty PI, Arden Finch.*

"How about this? Sofia's girlfriend stopped in yesterday and left her number. She asked us to call her if we heard anything. I'm sure this qualifies?"

"That'll work. Thank you so much." I scribbled down the number, one with an out-of-state area code as so many of them were in this part of North Carolina.

I called the girlfriend, almost surprised when she picked up after I'd left so many voicemails for Val. "Hi, this is Arden Finch with Hawkeye Investigations. Am I speaking to Nazneen?"

"Oh my gosh. Have you found Sofia? Is something wrong? Is she okay?"

I'll take that as a yes. "Nazneen, I'm trying to find Sofia's sister, Val. It sounds like nobody has seen either of the Pérezes in at least a couple of days though. Is there anything you can tell me?"

"She never came home on Tuesday night. I thought she was just mad and went to stay with Val."

"Did you fight?"

"Yes, but it shouldn't have been a big deal," Nazneen said, guilt tinging her words. "She was just stressed about something with her family, and then this dissertation. She's just...well, she didn't mean it, and neither did I."

"What happened after you fought?"

"She stormed out. She does that sometimes when she's stressed. Goes to find—" Nazneen stopped talking.

"Find what?"

"Um. We call it—we call it the other side."

Otherside. Is Nazneen one of us or only Sofia? "I think I understand. I spend a lot of time on the other side as well."

"You know," Nazneen whispered in a blend of relief and fear that gave me goosebumps. "Are you...like her?"

"Some questions are dangerous to ask and more dangerous to answer," I said gently, getting a strong feeling that Nazneen was mundane and Sofia was breaking the Détente in telling her partner. "But she must care for you very much if she shared something with you." The old guilt at my not having told Roman until forced to tried to claw its way up, and I shoved it aside.

"She does, she really does, and that's why I'm so worried. Something happened with her sister the day before she went missing. Sofia started acting scared and then snappish."

"Where does she usually go to find the other side?"

"We live together off MLK, across from Carolina North Forest. She usually goes on one of the hiking trails there or sits by the creek. It's walking distance, so I already went to check if I could, you know, find anything."

"Did you?"

"No. I just felt really, really creeped out as soon as I crossed the road. Like icky. Worse than when some perv is watching you at the bar, hoping the lesbians will kiss."

"Shit."

"What? What does that mean?"

Nazneen had just told me that the cases were indeed connected. She went missing the day of or after Val, was upset and scared about something to do with her sister, and there was a creepy feeling at a place where she could easily have been snatched.

"It means you've just given me a clue, one I can use to help find her. Last question—do you know how I can reach either of their parents?"

"Their parents are dead. It happened a little over a year ago now. Sofi doesn't talk about it, but I think it's part of why she was so upset about her sister."

Val had never told me about that. A pang struck me as I realized my obligations to Callista meant she'd probably been keeping things even closer than I'd thought. Like the other local elementals, Val didn't like or trust the Triangle's de facto leader, and I now wondered if it might have something to do with her parents. Or with me.

Pushing that guilt aside, I said, "If you don't hear from her by tomorrow, file a missing person's report. I'll do the same for Val and work with the police to try and find them, okay?"

"Thank you." Nazneen sounded a little steadier. "Good luck."

I put the phone down and scrubbed my face. The morning had already warmed up to the point where my satin robe clung uncomfortably, and I shrugged out of it as I scribbled some notes.

Val, a confirmed dea, was missing. Her sister, likely an oread or an undine, was also missing, both of them within days of an unknown artifact being dug up in the woods at Mason Farm and a dozen bodies going missing from the morgue. Some of those bodies had been used to attack Claret, where someone had seen Roman with me and felt threatened enough to menace us both.

"But what's the connection between the lich and the vampires? And what does this fucker want?" A shift in the air currents pulled my head up. Zanna was approaching.

She hopped up on the other chair, crossing her legs as she cracked open a beer. It should have been weird to see the child-sized sprite drinking a cold one at ten in the morning, but Zanna was probably ending her day. I didn't really know. I owned the deed to the house, but she claimed it as her own, protected it, and made her own rules that I didn't dare cross. Nobody wanted to be cursed out of their house by a slighted kobold.

"Wanna know what people want? Ask," she said.

I winced. "Can't this time. I think it's the lich."

"Oh. Then no need."

"What do you mean?"

She shrugged, looking both wise and weary as she sipped her locally brewed IPA. "It wants control. Over living. Over dead. Over all. Bad times. Might need to go."

The slight warmth of the morning chilled. "What do you mean, go? Why?"

Zanna cocked her head at me, her expression suggesting I wasn't thinking straight. "This's his town now. He takes bodies. Takes…something else? Some*one* else?"

"Yeah. Something was dug up on the biological reserve, and two people have gone missing. Two people like me." We'd never spoken directly about what I was, but she knew. The blocks of

Air were a dead giveaway, and I was pretty sure she'd overheard enough conversations with Roman to put the facts together.

She hissed. "Bad. Very bad. You find him soon, kill him, or we all go. Or die."

With that ominous comment, she slid down from the chair and headed for the hidey-hole she'd made for herself in the crawlspace, taking the can with her.

"Wait. Zanna?"

She paused and looked at me over her shoulder, her mane of curly hair hiding her face.

"How do you know all this?"

"I'm old. And heard things from older. But don't know more."

As she hopped down from the deck, I decided it was time to drive down to Raleigh. Zanna wasn't the only old Othersider in the Triangle, and while I didn't know if Torsten was older, he was rumored to have a library whose books might be. Torsten owed me a favor. Maybe I could trade it for a look at the library?

My phone rang, interrupting my thoughts. The call was coming to my personal line from an unknown number, which was strange because the only people who had my unlisted personal number were my friends—all people whose numbers would have appeared on my caller ID.

With a sinking stomach, I grabbed my voice recorder, set it to record, and answered, setting the phone to speaker mode.

"Hello, Ms. Finch."

The voice gave me the creeps. It was creaky and slow, like the loose porch step at an abandoned house. It took me a second to find my voice. "Who is this?"

"I think you know."

With that voice, it could only really be one or two people. I just didn't want it to be. "The lich."

"Indeed."

"What do you want?"

"Rude. But that seems to be the way of this time. Very well, I will be direct. I wish for you to join me."

My whole body went cold. "You what now?"

"Join me."

"Why the devil would I do that?"

"Because the devil has nothing on the hell I could rain on Earth, starting with your precious Durham."

My thoughts raced as I sought a way through this. I tried bluffing. "Half the Triangle wants me dead. What makes you think I care?"

"My associate has a theory about your keeper of the dead. He is…special, is he not? I am told there is a tingle of necromancy around the morgue. So much potential, locked away so deeply in a cage of Christian denial that he isn't even aware of it."

Keeper of the dead. Shit. "You stay the fuck away from Doc Mike."

"Your Doc Mike will soon be mine. I also have three more of your kind."

For a moment I couldn't answer, an invisible fist closing around my throat at the confirmation that Val and Sofia had been kidnapped. It had to be them—and someone else. Now Doc Mike was next. I should have found him a guard, insisted that he check in with me.

My heart stuttered, though I kept my voice firm. "What the fuck do you think you know about my kind?"

"Language, nasty girl. Language. My goodness, this time is so uncivilized." When I held my tongue, he said, "The undine broke. She told me what her sister had told her, that you're a sylph of unrivalled power in this age. Join us, and your power will grow with ours."

"No." *Oh Goddess, he tortured them.* My breath came short, and eddies of disturbed air swirled around me, rustling the elderflower bushes.

"Surely you have a use for it."

I didn't answer, heartsick and confused.

"You have no enemies to overcome? No one you wish to outmatch? To vanquish? I was told you had enemies. You said yourself that half the locality wants you dead."

The breath I took to answer caught in my throat as Keithia and the Monteagues, Sergei and the Volkovs, the Modernist vampires, and Callista swirled through my head. The damn lich himself. House Luna and House Sequoyah, who had to know who and what I was even if they hadn't moved against me yet.

"No," I whispered, sick at the thought of what Sofia and Val must have gone through for the lich to learn all that.

"I can taste the lie, girl, even over this electronic device. Come to me. Meet with me. Talk to me. Know me. You're a private investigator, no? Reasonable. Logical. Someone who puts together the pieces before making her own decision. A discoverer of truth."

"I...That doesn't mean—"

"It means everything." His voice lowered and became even more beguiling, took on a pull I fought to resist even as I wanted to succumb. "Come now. I offer you partnership, if you come of your own will. Freedom from all of the petty demands and concerns of those who would kill you if you weren't so useful."

I wavered on the edge of a precipice as every word struck the knot of fear and resentment living in my core. "You're wrong. There's nothing you could offer me to make me join you."

I had to grit my teeth to stop from asking where my friends were. I'd already given away that I cared when I'd demanded he stay away from Doc Mike, a rookie mistake I wouldn't have made if I'd been focused on the case and not on personal issues.

"I am right, and you know it. How many times will you be used before you find yourself drained, cut to the bone, heartless enough to pursue your own wants, your own needs? How many times will you find yourself broken before you pursue your own power, embrace it, push it to its limits as you were born to do?"

Tears stung, and goosebumps raced over me. Had he plucked all that straight from my heart? The admonishment to be careful what you wished for struck me like a lash. "Never. Not like that. Not for you." I forced the words out between lips stiff with falsehood.

"Now I know you're lying. Come. Talk to me."

I didn't answer.

"Very well. If you haven't contacted me on this device in two days, I will call on you again for your answer. You'll come, or your friends will suffer as much as I can make them without killing them. And my dear, I have had such a very long lifetime in which to practice."

The call ended, and I switched off the voice recorder, gasping with the sob I'd been holding back. The lich had called me by what I truly was—sylph—and having the recording was a breach of the Détente. But I needed *something* to go on. Something I could take to Roman…if he would help. The werewolves would be split between Roman and Sergei, and I didn't know if I had enough combined support with the rest of the weres to count on them. Probably not, given that I hadn't even really spoken to any of the other wereclans.

Of course Roman will help you. He might be mad about something, but he's still your boyfriend. He still cares about you. If nothing else, he needs you for his own shit. I held onto that thought, centered myself around it. If he wouldn't help, I wasn't sure I had anyone else.

The djinn wouldn't get involved. The Monteagues would take the excuse to break our agreement and kill me if I didn't finish this job. Torsten would find a way to twist his repayment of a debt into my owing him if I didn't use the knowledge gleaned from his library to bring down the lich.

I was on my own, again, and both allies and enemies were forcing me down paths I didn't want to explore.

Again.

I pulled up Roman's number and wavered, my thumb over the call button. I'd called him after the last creepy phone call I'd gotten, the one threatening his life, and shit had gone sideways for reasons I still didn't get. I mean, yeah, his brother was a douchecanoe, but why had he gotten mad when I'd insisted I could take care of myself? Or was this about my not letting him explain Ana? I really didn't want to hear about his ex-whatever—it being both none of my business and, in my opinion, unnecessary drama—but we needed to talk about it.

I still didn't want to.

I'd done enough, deflecting Sergei, keeping us all from being executed by a fellow Watcher if Roman pushed the issue, as had seemed likely, and trying to figure out who was threatening his life when he refused to see that his brother was involved. Resentment burned through me. I'd call him, but not to try playing kiss-and-make-up. It was time to get the alliance to the table.

I had two days before the lich came for me and nine before the new moon brought Keithia's deadline. I'd dragged my feet on leading this alliance long enough. It was time to take charge.

But first, I had to warn Doc Mike.

Chapter 19

I debated calling ahead for all of the forty-five-minute drive and didn't. I'd just stop in to see if Doc was okay, tell him to watch himself, then leave him to continue his processing. He'd need protection as well, but getting him to see it would mean getting him to speak to me.

The plants were still dead in their unusual pattern when I arrived, but the place no longer felt like evil had gone and taken a shit on the lawn. Janae's cleansing had probably given Doc Mike a whole new level of supernatural to deal with. Maybe that was why he'd been avoiding me.

"Hello?" The crash of furniture breaking interrupted my greeting.

I drew my gun and held it pointed at the floor as I jogged for the back, trying to sense in the air flow what might be happening. Dread curdled in my guts as I skidded around the corner and found the doctor's office.

"Stop!" I shouted at the hoodie-clad figure menacing Doc Mike, pinning him in the corner. "Get away from him!"

The figure turned, and dread hit me full-on when angry blue eyes met mine, like I'd felt on my first visit to the morgue but less.

Blood rimmed his mouth. "Fuck off, lady. You don't want to be involved in this."

"You don't want to hurt my friends." In my peripheral vision, Doc Mike slid down the wall, hand pressed to his throat. *A vampire? They* are *working with the lich!*

The man lunged. His wordless roar showed fangs. I got a shot off before he crashed into me, but it went wide and splintered the already suffering desk. Another went into him point-blank as we hit the floor hard enough to knock the wind out of me. As I gasped and tried to roll over, he ran past me, clutching his gut, and out the door.

I slammed my hand to the floor in frustration and pushed myself up, checking up and down the hall and listening for more trouble before going back to Doc Mike.

"Where are you hurt?" I said.

White-faced, he lifted his hand long enough to show me two neat punctures. "That your copperhead?" he asked, referencing my weak excuse when he'd examined vampire bites last winter.

I flushed with embarrassment. "Yeah. Shit, Doc, it shouldn't be bleeding like this."

He grew even paler. "Am I going to—"

"I don't know. But I can call someone." I squeezed his arm and stood, peering out the door again before dialing Maria's number. "Shouldn't someone else be here with you? It's the middle of the afternoon."

"My assistant was in a car accident last night, and we're still hiring for the other position."

"Got it." The phone clicked over. "Hey, Maria. We've got an incident at the Raleigh medical examiner's office."

"Hello, sugarplum. What's wrong with your pet doctor?"

"He's vamp bit, Maria."

"How problematic. Did you see who?"

"Medium height, medium build. Tanned, but it's fading, so he's gotta be a baby. Blue eyes. He's got a gunshot wound to the gut. We're gonna need your cleanup crew. You owe the doctor a desk."

"Be there soon. Text me a picture of what we need to replace. Don't go anywhere."

I hung up and did as she'd asked, then grabbed some tissue for Doc Mike. "Do you have a first aid kit in here?"

He tucked the wad under his hand, then pointed to the shattered remnants of his drawer. I broke it some more to pull out the small kit, opening it to find alcohol wipes and gauze. The way he tensed when I reached to clean the bite told me he didn't really want me to touch him, and I ground my teeth in annoyance.

"Who was that?" he asked.

"Someone who's going to help clean all this up."

"I got that," he snapped. "God bless it, Arden, that couldn't have been a…"

When he didn't spit the word out, I murmured, "Vampire?"

"It's daylight!"

"Yeah. That was a surprise to me, too." *Who else is going to wear a hoodie and jeans in eighty-degree heat?*

The bleeding had slowed but not stopped, and I handed him the gauze. "This is unusual. They've got a coagulant in their saliva that should kick in within seconds of the attack stopping."

"We need to call the police." With his free hand, Doc Mike started patting his pocket for his phone.

I snatched it as he pulled it out. "Nope. No way."

"Beg pardon?"

"This is Otherside, Doc." I tried my best sympathetic look as my heart hammered. We could *not* involve mundanes in this clusterfuck. "My contact will arrive with a team to clean everything up. It will look like nothing happened, and you can't tell anyone else. Ever."

"Or what?"

I'd never seen this belligerent side to him and paused, not sure how to deal with it or what response would make him least likely to fly off the handle and do or say something that would get him killed and me punished. "Or someone will pay you a visit. Someone less friendly than that guy. They'll pay me a visit too. I discovered you, so I'm responsible for you." I stood and walked over to put his phone on his desk to give him some breathing room without looking like I was running away. "Speaking of, why won't you talk to me? I was worried."

He glared, and something in my heart broke to see the expression on the closest person I had to a friend among—well, he wasn't wholly human, in the end. But I'd thought we were on friendly terms before.

"You lied to me, Arden."

I winced. "Goes with the job, I'm afraid."

"Private investigation?" he said, sharply ironic in his bitterness.

"Being a Watcher for Otherside." I shrugged and looked away. Normally, lying to humans didn't bother me. Lying to friends did though. "There are *rules*, Doc. Rules enforced by people I don't dare cross more than I already have to keep you safe."

He gave me a look like I was fooling myself. "Are you trying to say you were protecting me?"

"Yeah. I am. I'm sorry that meant lying, and I'm sorry you don't like how I did it. But Doc, I do what I have to do." I fixed him with a steady stare, refusing to give in to my guilt and his anger. "Always."

After that, we sat in uncomfortable silence until a shift in the air currents from the front told me someone was here. I stuck my head out of the office, gun ready. It was Maria, followed by a man.

"Arden, Noah. Noah, Arden," Maria said briskly as they approached. She wore a long-sleeved maxi dress made of thin, white linen, the floppy sunhat she'd had at my office, and big round sunglasses. From the smell, she was slathered in sunscreen. The dress had pockets, and she wore ankle boots that seemed better suited for autumn than early summer.

Noah shucked his hood and ballcap to nod politely. "Ma'am."

He was attractive, looking like he'd been born Black or biracial, with rich brown eyes, tight curls cut short, and a golden skin tone faded from avoiding the sun but retaining the kiss of melanin.

"Hi. Thanks for coming," I said. "Although I hadn't expected you to come in person."

Maria scowled. "This might have to do with the Modernists. You've got a bite victim?"

I winced and backed out of the doorway to let them join Doc Mike and me in the office. "Yeah."

She studied him, nostrils flaring at the scent of his fear. "Turn or kill?"

At her question, Doc Mike pulled his attention from Noah. When both vampires grinned wide enough to show fang, Doc paled.

"Neither," I said with a sigh. "He's Otherside. A sensitive."

"Sensitive?"

"A psychic of some kind, I haven't narrowed it down yet. We only found out earlier this week."

"Shame," her companion said, toning down his grin to something smaller and more intimate. "I like him. He's got...presence."

"Thank you. I think." Doc Mike frowned as he pushed to his feet. From the way his eyes flicked between the two, he was sorting out how he felt about discovering vampires were real.

"Well. If we can't eat him, he can help clean up," Maria said briskly. "Noah, get the details on whatever all this used to be and get to work."

Noah approached slowly. I watched long enough to be sure neither he nor Doc Mike was going to do something stupid before turning to Maria.

"Noah is my best. Don't worry," she said.

"You really would have turned him?"

She shrugged and smiled up at me, flirty and coy. "Noah would have, but yes. A gift for my favorite el—"

"He doesn't know what I am, and I want to keep it that way," I interrupted in an undertone, turning her so that our backs were to the two men. Doc Mike seemed fascinated enough with Noah that I doubted he would have heard anything Maria or I said, but it wouldn't hurt to be careful. "Is there anything you can tell me about the vamp who attacked him?"

Maria's mien grew hard and furious. "Noah will confirm, but if the bite didn't close, your pet's attacker must be witch-born. It is *forbidden* to turn witches, and for very good reason. Several, in fact. It must have been one of my opponents among the Modernists who did it, because nobody past their fiftieth deathday would be so foolish."

Looked like I'd found Janae's wayward witch and possibly the connection between the vampires and the lich. "Doc isn't my pet. Why forbidden?"

"The *moroi* virus doesn't work with magic-users. Only those who can't manipulate Aether or draw on life will turn properly. A were will die outright." She frowned and pursed her lips. "I suppose elementals would be excluded from a proper turn as well. But you understand what I mean about drawing on life?"

"Yes, Janae explained the basics. Will Doc Mike experience any side effects?"

"He might carry the virus. He might not. I'm curious about why this *moroi*-witch was here and why he'd bite the good doctor."

I wrestled with telling her more. Val and Sofia being in danger loosened my tongue but not enough that I'd blab about the doc's being a necromancer. "If I told you that I suspect the lich kidnapped a few people—live ones—would that shed light on anything?"

Maria tapped her lips. "Mmm. It might. I could check Torsten's library."

"I need to join you. Please." Averting the attack on Doc Mike had me anxious to find my friends and prevent another attempt on him.

Her slow smile made me shiver. "And owe me two favors? Darling, you move so fast."

"One favor, Maria. Pick which of these cancels out Aron's biting me."

"*And* you let me choose? You are a tease, Arden." She studied me. "The library cancels your existing favor. Access to Torsten's library to pay for his rakshasa." Waving a hand at the room, she added, "This, we will do because it was one of ours who attacked him. I won't have it said that we're stingy."

I let out the breath I'd been holding and touched her arm briefly, relieved enough to let my guard down. "Thanks, Maria. I need to find the connections to close this case."

"Oh. Well. You're welcome." She glanced at my hand, blinking as though flustered, before turning back to Noah and Doc Mike. "Noah dear, are you ready?"

"Yes, ma'am. Samuel is on the way with a new desk and laptop, and I'm headed out now to fetch the rest of the boys."

I raised my eyebrows at Maria, surprised by her discretion, and she smirked. "Doctor, would you be so kind as to disable the cameras and wipe the footage of our arrival?"

Doc Mike blinked. "I don't know how."

"I'll do it," I said. Everyone stared at me. "What? I know some things."

"So you do. Clever girl," Maria said. "Go, Noah."

I followed him to the front and unlocked the computer with the password I'd watched Doc Mike type in with his hunt-and-peck style for years. As I disabled the cameras, a sour sense that times were changing curled through me. We'd gotten lucky with the morgue being short-staffed today, but it was getting harder to be lucky and keep Otherside hidden. With the lich and the Modernists flouting every law and agreement, we might not make it to Callista's carefully planned Reveal—and the way things were going, it'd be me who broke the Détente.

"What is it, doll?"

I managed not to jump at Maria's question, too close as she approached on silent feet amidst my worried thoughts. "We're running out of time."

"Don't worry. The boys will be in and out soon. See?"

Noah led the way back in with a boxed laptop, followed by two more vampires in hoodies, hefting a desk identical to the shattered one between them.

I shook my head. "No. I mean, for the Reveal. The lich is moving too fast. The fucking elves threatened me over it last night, you're running out of time with the Modernists, someone in your coterie has dragged the wolves into the wrong side of it, people are missing, and everyone's looking at me to fix it. Again. I mean, even the gods are after me."

"You have a knack for finding this kind of trouble," she said. When I didn't look at her, she lifted my head with two gentle fingers. "Arden, think. All of the players and all of the pieces are coming together. Solve one problem, solve them all. No?"

I peered into the depths of her dark brown gaze and let her slip past my natural resistance to glamour and lull me. "Yes."

"All set," Noah said. "Oh! Sorry. I didn't…"

"You're fine, Noah. Go on. I'll be out in a minute."

When she looked away, I shook myself and broke the glamour, feeling like I was coming out from under water.

"That was nice." Maria sounded completely sincere. "You should let me do it again sometime."

"Don't count on it." I understood better now why someone might get addicted to the peace in a vampire's gaze, but I couldn't afford it. And something about it seemed intimate enough that I felt a little like I'd cheated on Roman somehow. "I'll be by Claret in a bit. I want to make sure Doc Mike is okay and not going to talk."

She grinned. "See you later, alligator." Her dress swirled, and with faster-than-human steps, she was gone.

Chapter 20

I reactivated the building security, logged out, and went back to Doc Mike's office. It looked like it always did, and so did Doc Mike. I squinted at where the bite had been. Gone.

He flushed, as though I'd caught him at something intimate. "They...uh...well. I couldn't—"

"I get it. No bite, no questions." I wondered if it had been pretty Noah who'd healed Doc Mike's neck. It seemed rude to ask, and I wasn't all that comfortable with my own vampire moment just now. I could ignore his. "Are we good, Doc?"

He crossed his arms and pressed his lips together, giving it a good think. "I guess we're going to have to be, aren't we?"

"I know things can't just go back to how they were. But, Doc, please believe when I say I have your best interests at heart." I crossed my own arms and looked at the carpet. "After all, you're one of the only friends I've got."

"Now that *is* tragic."

When I looked up, he was giving me his old silver fox smile. Not one that was meant to seduce—Noah was much more his type—just a friendly, teasing smile from an older gentleman.

"I know this is a lot," I said. My shoulders eased as some of the tension flowed away. "But I'm here for you. As much as I can be, without giving away secrets that aren't mine to tell."

"After what just happened…hell. I guess I just don't have much of a choice in getting used to this new world, like it or not."

"Trust, Doc, everyone is gonna have to get used to it soon. Otherside can't stay hidden much longer."

He frowned. "What are you talking about? My report?"

"That's one example. Technology is advancing too fast for us to hide like we have been. If it's not something like this happening when we can't cover it up, it'll be a healthtech start-up with a new genetic marker." I thought of Verve Health Solutions, the place I'd bugged in January, wondering if they'd figured out what their test was telling them yet. "Or it'll be someone with a video made on a cell phone that we can't hack from YouTube in time. We've kept up for the most part, but we're at the tipping point. Plus, humans reproduce faster."

"When the time comes, I'll help."

"Thanks, Doc, but—"

"No. That's my price for staying quiet. I want to help. I can pass for normal—"

"Mundane." Normal was a point of view.

"Mundane. Maybe I can…I don't know. Be a voice." His eyes gazed into the past. "I know what it is to be the other."

I couldn't help myself. I crossed the room and hugged him, maybe for the first time in our acquaintance. He hugged me back, and I choked back tears.

Finally, something was getting better.

Leaning back, I said, "You're a good guy, Doc. Just be careful it doesn't get you killed. And make sure you're not alone here anymore, okay? I'm gonna go try to find out who attacked you and why, but you're still in serious danger. I think I know what took the bodies, and it might be back. For you." I didn't have it in me to tell him that he might be a latent necromancer just then, not when he was still reeling from a vampire attack and not when I'd have to explain where I'd gotten the information. "Take time off and get outta town, if you can."

He waved me off. "I'll be more careful. Be safe and God bless."

I let him go and forced a smile before leaving, my heart a little lighter even if I hadn't told him that the bodies he'd tended so thoughtfully on their arrival here had been violated with evil spells and made to attack a vampire bar before being hacked to pieces. Or that the evil that had done it wanted him next.

***

Torsten's library must have taken up a full city block under downtown Raleigh, and had two levels—a feat I'd thought impossible given the Triangle's heavy clay soil, the depth of the frost line, and the tendency of the area to flood anytime the suggestion of a hurricane passed through. It should have been damp and dank, the walls leaking or beaded with condensation, but it was surprisingly pleasant. Tightly fitted stone lined the walls, and the whirr of a dehumidifier protected shelves upon shelves of books, scrolls, stacks of paper, and even a few tablets in stone or clay.

I spun, taking it all in. "Maria..."

"Impressive, isn't it?" She took my hand and tugged long enough to encourage me to follow her deeper but didn't test me by keeping it. "Torsten isn't the oldest *moroi* in the country, or even on the East Coast, but he's powerful in glamour and knowledge. This is part of the reason why Giuliano or Luz would kill to take over this coterie."

"They'd inherit the library."

"And me. Mustn't forget me."

"You?"

She twirled, grinning from ear to ear as the dress flared around her ankles. "I told you, my powers are growing again for the first time in, oh…three hundred and fifty years? It's rare, Arden." The look she threw at me then had more than a little heat in it. "And with more powerful blood, who knows what else I could unlock?"

"As long as you mind your place, fledgling."

Maria and I both jumped out of our skins at the deep, masculine voice that was our only warning before Torsten appeared. Air molecules seemed to hit me in a mini-shockwave at the suddenness of his movement.

The short, spare man had a hard, wiry strength about him, with long brown hair pulled back into a braid and the golden torc from my last meeting with him around his neck. His appearance and accent made me think he was a Viking, which would put him at close to a millennium in age. I averted my gaze from his sparkling green one. Maria, I might take risks with, but Torsten had almost captured me once. Something told me he wouldn't have Maria's surprisingly modern notions of consent if he did.

Maria knelt. "Master. As we discussed—"

"The elemental is here to view my library." Torsten looked at me, smirking when I couldn't stop the wince that he knew what I was. Maria would have told him, of course; I'd expected it. That didn't mean I was used to what seemed like the whole world suddenly knowing. "Given that it means I have another opportunity to engage with her, it seems a fair trade."

"Thank you, Master," Maria whispered.

Torsten dismissed her with a nod then drew himself up, looking like a warrior king addressing his council. "My fledgling and second thinks there are plots against us. What think you?"

I darted a glance at Maria.

"Don't look to her. I want *your* opinion. Part of the price of all this." He swept his arms wide and turned, claiming what was obviously the pride of his life here in Raleigh.

"I agree with her."

Maria glanced up long enough to show me wide eyes before looking back at Torsten's brown leather boots again.

"Oh?"

"Yes…sir." I was *not* going to call him Master, but I didn't want Maria to be punished for my disrespect.

"Explain." He started circling me, and I clenched my fists, fighting the urge to keep him in sight. We were playing vampire games, and turning around would only amuse him. At this proximity, I don't think any of my powers with Air would stop him before he had my throat out.

"I—I doubted Maria as well, at first. Or at least questioned the likelihood of what she said. But there have been too many coincidences and overlaps between my lich case and Maria's request. Then, last night, I received an anonymous call threatening my boyfriend."

"Your *werewolf* boyfriend," Torsten said, as though that was somehow significant. Maria flinched.

"Yes. The caller said something I've only heard Maria say and referenced the, um, the event here."

"The filthy death-spawn of the draugr that invaded my nest. My *home*."

I jumped again at the snap of rage in his voice. "Yes."

"Rise, child," Torsten said to Maria. "It pleases me that you've found a worthy hunt. You have my permission to pursue the sylph."

"Thank you, Master." Maria rose, darting an uncertain glance at me before looking at the floor again.

The master of the city turned to me again. "As for you, I charge you with seeking this draugr and killing it. I won't have this in my city. Call it the first test of your new alliance."

I gaped like a fish, too furious to answer, before shaking it off. There was only one answer I could give when I was underground in a vampire's lair at his second's invitation—if I still wanted a look at the library. "Of course. It's already on my to-do list."

His nostrils flared and his smile was mocking as he said, "I am pleased. Enjoy the library."

He left in a blur of movement as fast as that he'd arrived in.

I glared at the door when it had shut behind him. "Fuck's sake, between him and that bitch Keithia…"

"You spoke to Keithia?" Maria asked lightly, looking at me sideways.

I grimaced. She hadn't needed to know that. "You have his permission to hunt me?" I said, indulging both my anger and my fear. "What the hell does that mean?"

"Oh, come, sugarplum. You already knew—"

"Don't. Just don't. It's not going to happen. Point me to the lich section so I can get the hell outta here."

Hurt flickered across her face and was gone so quickly I might have imagined it. She spread the folds of her maxi dress in a curtsy that belonged to medieval Europe. "Of course. If it pleases milady to follow me."

And now I alienate one of the few people who might have been on my side in the alliance. Goddess damn…everything. I started to apologize, then held my tongue. I was the one with the least amount of political power in every relationship I was in. Pissing off allies wasn't clever, but just then, I wanted to indulge in being pissed off. The alliance wasn't even formed yet, and I had the werewolves, the elves, and the vampires making demands I wasn't sure I could deliver on. Three months ago, nobody had known I existed. Now they wanted me to fix everything. The pressure weighed heavier with each request. They might as well get used to being disappointed early on.

Maria pointed at a shelf and left me to figure out which of the dozens of books on it were related to liches. I might have deserved it, but all it did was add to my general irritation with Otherside.

Most of the books were old, some old enough to be bound in crumbling leather, and none gave an indication of the contents on the spine. I probably should have worn those white cotton archivist gloves to handle everything in the room, but none had been left and I'd be damned if I wasted time going to look for some.

After an hour and a half of careful page-turning and line-skimming, I had a stack of ten books and a scroll that had been left resting atop one of them. Figuring that was enough to start with, I carried them to a small, two-seater table set against the wall with an antique Tiffany reading lamp that would offset the otherwise dim lighting in the room.

Poring through the books got me two pages of notes in my little notebook. As Maria had said, a djinni was needed to create a lich. I confirmed that liches could call the dead to them, leaving a stain on creation that other evil could follow across the planes—demons, malevolent ghosts, anything not at peace and with a bone to pick or a homicidal level of boredom. My blood froze almost as cold as it had in the lake last winter at the idea that a demon might cross over.

Djinn were ambiguous—some good, some bad, nearly all stubbornly independent and self-interested but not outright evil. More like mundane humans than they'd care to admit but with an infinite lifespan and the ability to manipulate Aether. Demons though? Demons just wanted pain, and fear, and death. We'd call it evil because everything they did revolved around hurting others for nothing more than personal pleasure, though that was a moral yardstick they didn't follow.

Shaking off the thought of demons, I turned back to my notes. As Duke had said, liches were created when a sorcerer made a deal with a djinni, selling heartsblood and soul's breath. The process required a thorough corruption of the being, the learning of necromancy to defeat death, and soul magic to defeat the ethereal planes, plus an amulet to store the sorcerer's soul, severed from body and mind.

Their affinity for the dead meant liches preferred to be in places where bodies were concentrated, the older the better. The morgue would have been too new, though it was a great source of practice corpses. It seemed newer corpses took less power to resurrect, though they also offered less as soldiers. Older corpses would take a hell of a lot more power but be nearly unstoppable. Dismemberment wouldn't work with an older zombie as it had for Maria during the attack on Claret. Something old and powerful would have to die by fire, acid, or another necromancer. That had to be why the lich was so interested in acquiring Doc Mike.

The second to last book in my pile confirmed my suspicion that the amulet had to be destroyed. "Two things only may destroy the power in the gem: the undoing of the magic by the djinni who made the amulet, or the primordial forces of creation," I read aloud, frowning. *Primordial forces? Like lava?*

The book was written as though the reader already knew what that meant. I sure as hell didn't, so I'd have to find whichever djinni it was who created the damn lich in the first place.

There was no way that djinni would do me the favor of destroying the soul-amulet, even if I could track them down by my new moon deadline. Not without my trading something of equal value, which could only be my own soul or that of someone I knew intimately enough to provide the key to their heart's true desire. Probably both, given the djinn would want to make up for the lost time invested in the first deal. As Duke had said, the damned things were worth three life fortunes on the *sūqu*, the djinn black market.

I pushed aside the book and took up the scroll, frowning when I realized it wasn't about liches. It was about the old gods and the Wild Hunt. I thought back to my dream the other night, the one where Neith had said, "We won't be denied our hunt. Not by a magician. Not by anyone. If you *are* to be our huntress on Earth, you'll need to do better than this. Look. Deeper."

The scroll didn't explain much of anything that I could decipher. If my Latin was right, it said that the gods of the hunt would return and the world would be destroyed and made anew. A hunter would ride with them, reshaping the world.

My breath caught. That sounded too close to the descriptions I'd read of Atlantis's destruction and the flood myth that popped up in ancient mythologies around the world.

That sounded like elementals.

Chapter 21

Exhausted by reading crabbed writing in old books, stifled by the iron-and-ash scent of vampires and the mind-numbing whirr of the dehumidifier, and generally feeling disheartened, I slumped down to the table and rested my head on my arms. The weird paranoid feeling niggled at the back of my skull again, fainter than it usually was lately but still infuriating.

"Ishtar, can I please, *please* catch a break?" I whispered to the table. I rarely gave a name to the Goddess because she had as many faces and names as she had aspects. I just hoped that invoking the face most frequently worshipped by the djinn might turn that facet my way and grant me the stroke of luck I needed.

"Interesting choice. It's not often that you pray to Her in particular."

I barely caught my chair from going over backward with me in it as I whipped my head up. "Fucking—Grimm!"

"Hello, honeysweet."

I gaped at her. It had been months since I'd seen her, and the last time had been when she'd forced me into the Crossroads for the first time, then held me down by the shoulders while Mixcoatl lined up a shot with an arrow made of obsidian and lightning. My hand crept to the scar it had left under my right collarbone, the arrow placed to hurt, not to kill. "What are you doing here?"

"Oh, trust me," she said smugly. "I'm as surprised as you that it was so easy to get in. Torsten has this place warded against casual entry but not against blood ties. I'd never have found it without you."

I hadn't even known it was possible—or necessary—to ward against blood ties. I also didn't know how close a cousin Grimm was, or Duke, but they *were* cousins. They'd always been able to drop in on me, though with the exception of Duke appearing at my house the other day, it hadn't happened since winter.

"I told you we shouldn't abandon her," Duke said, popping in alongside Grimm. "Especially given she was asking about liches." He leaned forward to peer at the messy piles of open books on my table and flick the scroll. "It looks like you've found something."

"Are you kidding me?" I hissed. "Get out of here!" Ignoring their apparent interest in my research, I dashed to the end of the row of books to peer at the door. No vampires were pouring into the room so it appeared no alarms had been triggered, but I was on shaky ground with Torsten and had slighted Maria. I didn't need them discovering that I was apparently an interplanar channel into Torsten's precious library.

"No." Grimm's smile mocked me and, accompanied by her refusal to shift her ruby eyes to something more mundane, was completely unsettling. I'd thought her my closest friend once. Sometime long before the arrow to the chest.

"Arden, cousin, we're worried about you." Duke turned to peruse the nearest shelf, not looking very worried at all.

"Really." I couldn't keep the sarcasm out of my voice as I moved back to the table and tried to block Grimm's view of my notes, though they'd had enough time to read everything.

"Really. Asking about liches is serious business." He fingered the rotting leather spine of a book and pursed his lips.

"Even when there's one somewhere in a fifty-mile radius?" I said.

"*Especially* when." Turning to face me, he arched an eyebrow. "And given your meeting with House Monteague—"

Grimm whirled on Duke, eyes flashing as she snarled to show pointed teeth. "She *what?*"

"How did—" I stopped myself too late.

Grimm's outraged look turned from Duke to me as my aborted sentence told her it was true.

"Explain, *cousin.*" The fire in her eyes had me half expecting the library to ignite.

I opened my mouth, then shut it and crossed my arms while leaning against the table. "You know what? No. You held me down while one of the fucking Old Ones shot me with a lightning arrow. *Lightning,* Grimm. Do you know how much that hurt to pull out?" I tugged my T-shirt aside so they could both get a good look at the scar it had left, knotty in the center and with spiderwebbing Lichtenberg figures sprawling in a hands-width radius around it. "*You* did this as much as Mixcoatl."

"Don't blame me for your poor decisions, honeysweet. I told you not to pursue that case."

"And you knew I would anyway."

"Ladies—"

"Silence, Nebuchadnezzar," Grimm snapped. "You did well to tell me about our cousin's pursuit of this lich, but I'm still vexed with you."

Duke subsided, and I glared at both of them, still not sure what the fuck was going on but certain I wouldn't like it. "Fine," I said. "You know I'm looking for the lich, which means you must also know that I need to find the djinni responsible for it."

Grimm paged through one of the books, wrapping a blood-red curl around her finger. "Have fun."

"Do you want a lich loose in the Triangle? Violence has spiked almost two hundred percent and it's getting worse. People are losing their damn minds!"

"Not my problem," Grimm said, still studying the book.

"Not your—are you serious right now? What's Callista going to say when he lets the zombies go after a more public target and screws her Big Reveal?"

"Also not my problem."

Narrowing my eyes at her, I slapped her hand away from the book to get her full attention. "And if I tell you the gods want it gone as well?"

She sneered. "I'm not responsible for what the gods want. They didn't ask *me* to get rid of it. Sounds like that just makes it even more *your* problem."

I looked at Duke, baffled, and he shrugged, rolling his eyes. A few months ago, Grimm had appeared to be Callista's right-hand djinni, and she'd been willing enough to do the gods' bidding before. Looked like something had changed, which was as confusing as it was concerning. For me, at least. Duke seemed willing to chalk it up to self-interest.

"Why are you here then?" I asked.

"The library, course. You just happened to be my way in. But since we're both here…" Her hand moved too fast for me to react, and I rocked back from her slap landing on the same cheek Neith had struck. It flamed into pain. "How *dare* you work with the elves."

"Who are you to stop me?" I held a hand to my cheek as much to keep tears in as to soothe the sting. Childhood games and laughter with Grimm flashed through my mind, making my face burn even hotter. I'd been so naive, and that made me angry. "You know what? Forget you. I'm doing my best, and literally every power player in the Triangle either wants to use me or kill me. *Again*. If you don't want to help, then get the fuck out."

"Make me," she sing-songed childishly.

Without knowing her truename, I had one option, and it wasn't good. I took it anyway. "Maria!"

"Bitch." She tried to reach around me for the scroll, but I was watching for her move this time and snatched it first. Fixing me with a baleful glare, Grimm said, "You've chosen your side then."

Before I could point out that she'd chosen first, and it wasn't mine, she vanished.

Duke rubbed a hand over his head, his dravite-colored eyes without a hint of laughter. "The knife edge of fate grows keener. This won't end well."

As the door slammed open and running footsteps approached, he pressed something hard and round into my hand and dematerialized.

"What? What's wrong?" Maria skidded around the last shelf. She held a bared katana at the ready, eyes darting.

"You need to tell Torsten to beef up his wards."

"What's wrong with them? Are you hurt?" She sniffed the air and frowned.

Only my heart. And my pride. I held up the callstone Duke had given me, an enchanted hematite ball polished till it gleamed and strung on a leather thong. "Djinn were here."

"Impossible. This place is warded."

"They used me as an anchor to pull themselves through the wards. They wanted this." I held up the scroll I'd kept away from Grimm. "I'm sorry. If I'd have known, I wouldn't have risked coming in here."

Maria studied me, a hint of anger pinching her brows. "Fine." She lowered the katana. "What is that?"

"It was shelved with the lich books, but it mentions the old gods and the Wild Hunt. Grimm's playing a bigger game, Maria. We need to be careful."

"We can start with you leaving."

"But I'm not—"

"Now. I'll finish reviewing the books and send over anything that seems useful."

This is why I should have found more tact. I slumped, disappointed but not really in a place to argue. "Okay. Thanks for the help."

I gathered my things, trying to figure out how I could clean up the messes I'd made of all my closest relationships.

The drive home passed in a blur. As soon as I got there, I made a mug of chamomile tea and curled up in my armchair, feet perched on the edge of the mismatched ottoman, and sipped the herbal warmth.

I didn't feel good, at all, about the way things were going right now. In trying to do and be more, I kept pissing people off. Was I trying too hard, or not hard enough? I didn't know, and I needed to escape for an hour or two. The big, comfy chair was my refuge. I'd spilled tea on one of the arms, staining the blue fabric. It only sort of matched the green and amber furnishings in the rest of the room, but it was my favorite thing in the house.

With the hand not holding my tea, I skimmed Google for old graveyards, wondering if any were old enough to be attractive to a lich.

I could just pretend to join him. That would mean going in alone though, which hadn't worked out so well when I went after Leith. If this thing was powerful enough to set off the mundanes and control weaker vampires, I needed to go in with allies. Which meant having something to bring to the alliance, and getting everyone together in the first place. No amount of practice with Air would have me ready to confront a lich lord, his accomplice, a demon, and whatever undead army they'd assembled before the new moon.

One thing at a time. I sighed and sent a frustrated swirl of Air through the room, then went back to searching. Given that the disappearance of bodies from the morgue and the biggest spike in crime were both west of downtown Raleigh, with the incident at the biological reserve marking the northwest-most point of activity, I narrowed my search to a band between the two.

Obvious options like the Oakwood Cemetery or the City Cemetery of Raleigh, I ruled out. Though they were among the oldest recognized burial grounds in the area, they were too public. Both were within blocks of the State Capitol building, and while my opinions of mundane elected officials were generally low, they hadn't yet stooped to fistfights in the Governor's offices as I suspected they might if a lich's influence was that close.

A little digging turned up the North Carolina Office of State Archaeology, which had a cemetery protection program. Not only did it encourage citizens to report damage to the local sheriff's office, it also took a survey of suspected lost or abandoned cemeteries across the state. All of the records of the North Carolina Cemetery Survey were publicly available in the Search Room of the North Carolina State Archives, which itself had a page where I could request research to be conducted for me and provided via email for a small fee if I had a specific record. If not, I could go in and look for myself.

"Bingo," I whispered, taking a celebratory sip of tea.

The threads of an idea started weaving themselves into a plan. Get a list of reported abandoned cemeteries from the archives. Sort by age. Call the sheriff's departments about the oldest and most rural ones to see if any had had damage in the last few weeks and strike them from the list. The concentrated presence of evil and fear leaching from a lich would deter most humans and many Othersiders from approaching, keeping it safe from damage but likely giving enough people "funny feelings" on driving past that someone would have heard something. The magical effect was too broad, rippling out for tens of miles from wherever the lich had been recently. I tried not to think about what that meant in terms of his growing power. Then there was the fact that I still needed a djinni to break that damn amulet.

"Shit," I muttered, feeling like I was back at square one for all the planning I'd just done.

Would Duke help me? He'd given me the new callstone. I dug it out of my pocket and considered it. Djinn never did something for anyone's best interest but their own. His giving me the stone could simply be because it was more convenient than being summoned and my having done it once had him planning on me doing it again.

My cheeks flamed as I remembered that the damn things also made it easier for a djinni to listen in on you. There were wards of protection that I could set, but I didn't have the control of Aether that a full-blooded djinni had in order to set wards around myself. I'd need an elf or a witch to do it for me.

Annoyed, I rose and put it in the black walnut box with the rest of my occult items. I wouldn't be foolish enough to break it, as I had the last one, but I also wouldn't be naive enough to keep it on me. The box only had a light warding, but it was better than nothing.

I paced the room, too full of crackly, nervous energy to sit back down again. The air plants swayed in their glass bulbs overhead as I released my tight control over Air and let myself play with the currents in the room again. If I couldn't count on the djinn to help me break the amulet, I'd need another way of making the lich vulnerable.

Maybe getting the amulet away from the creature would be enough. How much distance did you have to put between a soul and its body before you could burn the body to ash and have it stay dead?

I'd find out later. For now, I had to get my alliance together and try to fix things. If I couldn't find a way to break the amulet, it would take all of us to stop the lich.

Chapter 22

If someone had told me that I'd be sitting at a picnic table in the woods at Raven Rock State Park with a vampire, two werewolves, two elves, a witch, and a djinn, I'd have asked if they'd recently experienced a head injury.

But there I was, squeezed in between Roman and Maria, with Janae, Troy, and Evangeline opposite. Sergei leaned against another picnic table, looking foolish and out of place in preppy, branded camping clothes while the rest of us wore our everyday exercise or street clothes. Duke leaned against a tree, with us and yet apart, his dark skin cast in golden-red hues with the light of sunset and his black eyes sparking with gold.

I hoped the setting sun wasn't an omen, but twilight started at about seven-thirty and the park closed at nine, leaving us a nice set amount of time where Maria would be comfortable enough not to be cranky and we could wrap up our business before the park rangers kicked us out.

We'd had to drive an hour outside the Triangle to find ground neutral enough that everyone would come, private enough that humans weren't likely to overhear, and open enough for everyone to scatter if we were attacked—or started attacking each other, as had nearly happened when Janae had set a spell to deter casual approaches and encourage hikers to keep moving. No magic had been one of the agreements, but she'd refused to be cowed and I hadn't stepped in except to tell the elves to back off. This was for our own good, and I didn't see the harm in it.

"Everyone cool now?" I asked, meeting each person's eye in turn. Everyone except Evangeline, anyway. She hadn't looked at me since arriving with Troy and yanking her arm away from the hand he'd extended to steer her to her seat. I had no idea what was going on there and was dying to know. A schism between the prince and princess of the unofficial leading elven house could only be to my benefit.

"I'm fine," Janae said, somehow looking both polite and unshakably powerful at the same time. When everyone else nodded or mumbled an agreement, she said, "Why have you called us together?"

I shrugged and tried to keep my voice light. "Because I'm tired of playing messenger girl and running between all y'all trying to meet this one's demands and that one's favors when we're all trying to get the same thing. I will facilitate, but I want something too."

"You want something for refusing to do anything?" Sergei said with a mocking smile. "I told you my price."

Roman growled, and Evangeline shook herself out of her funk to look between the brothers with narrowed eyes.

I frowned at him, annoyed and wondering why he was so cocky when I'd figured out his game. What had Callista offered the Volkovs? What did she know? "I want something in exchange for my part in redistributing the power balance in the Triangle and setting all of you on equal standing with Callista." Maybe that would be a juicy enough offer to set him back.

"A dangerous game," Duke murmured. I glanced at him, but all I got was what passed for his neutral face—laughing eyes and a small grin just shy of cheeky.

"Nobody said anything about Callista," Maria said. "My master's concerns are elsewhere right now."

I flicked a glance at her, trying to decide if she was still mad at me. Roman was; he'd driven separately and hadn't greeted me with the usual kiss. I had the feeling he was only sitting next to me to keep Sergei from doing so.

When nobody added anything, I said, "But it's what y'all wanted when this collaboration was proposed, or certain of you wouldn't have dragged me into being your arbiter. The witches could have been your neutral party." I nodded at Janae. She inclined her head in return, eyes sharp as she waited for me to make my point. "Or Callista herself. If you didn't want to go to her, why choose me?"

"Convenience," Maria said.

"Upset the balance of power and risk breaking the Détente on a whim of convenience? Nah. I call bullshit." Again, I looked at everyone in turn, trying to read them and the bitterness of all the long decades of bad blood, broken deals, and interspecies war that had been set aside to hunt Leith but had seeped back in since January. This was my fault for putting it off, and now I had to fix it if I wanted to get my friends back. Taking a deep breath, I tried to find calm and inspiration. "We could be more than this. All of us."

Roman, Maria, and Troy exchanged mistrustful glances. All of the camaraderie that had pulled them together earlier this year had evaporated. Duke just kept smirking, watching to see where this went.

"I'll bite, bitch, if only to get to what *I* want for helping." Sergei looked not at me but at Roman. "How?"

"We do what Callista can't. Or won't. We take out the lich. Together."

That cracked the masks on every one of their faces.

"What?" I said. "Half the people here have been involved in a demand that I do it. The other half have provided advice or information."

"And you dug your heels in," Troy said. "Which, I assume, brings us to what *you* want."

I glared, wishing he hadn't pointed that out, but I guess you had to be sharp to be both prince and Darkwatch agent. "He called me."

"Who called you?" Roman leaned forward to catch my eye. "The lich? What did he want?"

I crossed my arms and shivered at the memory of the conversation. "Yes. The lich. He made an offer, couched in threats if I don't give him the answer he wants in two days."

Tension ratcheted up, and the clearing seemed to spark with it. Both elves drew on Aether so hard my teeth hurt, and the cloying scent of burnt marshmallow chased away the smell of pine needles and dusty sand. Duke flickered between his human shape and his djinni true-form, smoke and fog with carnelian eyes, before settling on the form of a lean Black man with eyes like lava. The saplings at the edge of the clearing grew half a foot as Janae's aura flared, and both wolves' eyes silvered. Only Maria didn't visibly react, though the tang of iron and ash grew stronger. I winced, hoping any passing humans wouldn't notice.

"What answer is that?" the witch asked.

I looked at her and willed her to see the pain I'd been trying to wall away.

"Oh, child. Oh, no. You can't."

"What?" Sergei snapped, coming out of his lean.

"He wants her." Evangeline rose and leaned on the table, her loose black curls falling over her shoulders. "Doesn't he, bitch?"

Troy laid a warning hand on her arm. "Evangeline—"

She shook him off. "No, brother. I say let him have her, since you won't follow the law. That is House Monteague's price for this alliance. In fact, why wait for her to turn herself in? She's right here. Maybe this lich will simply leave if we strike the right bargain. Like giving him *her*."

"Stupid brat," Duke said. "Have you stopped to consider why a lich wants an elemental? What might happen if he collects more than one element, with a sylph as powerful as Arden at their head?"

"Don't talk to me like that! I'm not a—"

"Evangeline!" Troy rose now, his six-foot-something height and lean muscle doing nothing to intimidate the unshakeable confidence in her more petite form. That knot of paranoia in the back of my head tightened, and ice settled into my gut at the idea that someone might go along with her. Janae frowned, looking between me and Troy. I didn't blame her. I'd been trying to figure out where the line between cautious ally and merciless executioner-in-waiting lay for months.

I slid off the bench and walked toward the woods, leaving them to squabble, wondering if we might have maintained some semblance of cooperation without Sergei and Evangeline bringing their antagonisms and ulterior motives. We all had them, but those two were outsiders, young and rash, without Janae's wisdom and drive to be cooperative and constructive.

Or was this my fault for balking so long that we'd lost the spark that had kicked all of this off to begin with?

It's my fault.

At the edge of the picnic clearing and Janae's deterrence spell, I stopped, leaning a shoulder against a tree with arms crossed, looking to the waning moon. There was no easy way forward from here, even if I could get the alliance solid and focus them on the lich. And if I couldn't, my options for saving my friends were down to one: join the lich.

Duke had hinted once that Callista was near to being a goddess, if not actually one, so why wasn't she handling this? Something was off, and I wasn't seeing it. Something to do with the djinn. And the alliance. And me.

"I'm sorry, babe."

Roman's voice behind me, just loud enough to be heard over the argument the rest of the group was having, broke the thread I had almost tied to a connection and made me stiffen. "For what?"

"Everything. It's…hard. That you don't need my protection. Hell, that sometimes you need to protect me."

"None of that was about Ana?"

"What if it was?"

I shrugged and looked out into the woods. I doubted there would be hikers or fishers this late, but I didn't know shit about fishing. Was night fishing a thing?

"You still don't smell jealous," Roman said.

"Why would I? Whatever you had isn't about me."

"But don't you care?"

"About…?"

His heavy sigh suggested that he thought I was being intentionally dense. "Fine. Forget it."

"Roman—"

"Did he threaten your friends?"

I let our argument drop, disturbed that he seemed to think I would or should be jealous and wanting to prioritize my friends. "Yes."

"Shit, Arie. I'm sorry."

"It's my fault." I swallowed past the lump growing in my throat. Something had happened to them, because of me.

"How do you reckon that?"

"Nobody would have paid attention to Val if I hadn't dropped my card. If she hadn't become my friend. Then I went and dragged Doc Mike into Otherside but didn't properly warn him about how dangerous we are. The lich wants him, too, if he doesn't have him already."

"Now you're being silly."

Scoffing, I turned back to my scrutiny of the night sky. "Gee, thanks. Because that's exactly what I needed to hear."

"Come on. Even if they noticed Val because of you, you're not responsible for other folks' fucked-up actions. And you didn't drag Doc Mike into Otherside. He was already a part of it. He just...hadn't been shown the door is all."

I didn't answer, turning an ear back to the center of the clearing. Duke and Evangeline were still squabbling, with the occasional shit-stirring interjection from Sergei. "I need to get back over there before Evangeline does something stupid."

"You're not worried about Sergei?"

I was, but Roman had been clear in not wanting to hear about it. I wasn't about to fall into the trap of bringing up Sergei's betrayal now, not when we needed unity. "Sergei doesn't blame me for killing his high school crush," I said, deflecting. "Or anything, really, except not wanting to sleep with him. Right?"

He grunted. "I guess."

"So. I'll deal with Sergei once the homicidally heartbroken elf is back in her box."

Roman caught my hand as I started back for the picnic table. I looked back in question, and he pulled me to him with a little tug. "We'll get through this, babe." After planting a small kiss on my forehead, he let me go. My heart lifted a little; we weren't fixed, but at least we were talking.

"I won't argue this with you further, little princess," Duke said as we returned to the group. "We cannot give Arden to the lich."

"And *I* won't—"

I slapped my hands down on the table. "Enough."

Satisfaction flickered in me, seeing Evangeline's outrage at my interruption, but I was careful not to let it show on my face.

"Evangeline, even if you wanted to beat me up and give me to the lich, you'd have to catch me first. There are enough people here who want to keep using me that you'd have to take me alone, maybe you and your brother, and I'm much stronger with Air than I used to be." I resisted the temptation to draw on it now to make the point.

Evangeline bristled like a cat. "You—"

I ignored her and turned to Troy, allowing my temper to show. My friends were in danger. I'd had enough. "Monteague, I'm assuming she's here because your grandmother sent her for some kind of training exercise. If she can't be a grown-up and set aside her irrational personal grievance with me, I'll blow your car off the road and be done with you both. Understood?"

Silence fell over the clearing. I stood taller to shrug off the weight of everyone's eyes on me. I wouldn't do it, although I was pretty sure I had the strength now, but it looked like they were all taking me seriously as a force and not just as their gofer. Both elves stared at me as though I'd grown horns, and Troy's hand hovered over the empty knife sheath at his hip. Duke winced and shook his head in disapproval at my heavy hand. I ignored him too.

"We don't have to like each other, but there are bigger fucking issues to deal with," I said, exasperated with my own inability to strike a balance. "Like a lich lord threatening the Triangle, attacking Othersiders with zombies, and sending the mundanes into fits of violence. We have to do something. And it starts with settling this alliance. Now. What do you all want? And Sergei, if you say me one more time, you and me are gonna take a walk to the overlook and have a serious come-to-Jesus moment."

Sergei drew himself up, puffing out his chest. "But I—"

"Stop. You made your play. It's not happening. What. Else. Do. You. Want?"

Janae cleared her throat. "The witches want a full seat at the table and a voice in all decisions. We're tired of being afterthoughts to the rest of you simply because we embrace non-violence. We will not do harm, but we will open our homes to offer healing and neutral ground as sanctuary for those who need it."

I blinked. "That's quite an offer, Ms. Janae."

"We know. I told you, child, I'm not of a mind to play games, and neither are my coven leaders. The Reveal is coming and we want a say. *Before* it happens, not after. Our kind were burned at the stake, drowned, hanged, and tortured for years. We will not allow it to happen again."

"Thank you, and thank you for setting this example." I looked around the table. "Anyone else care to follow it?"

"The wolves want territory. In Durham," Sergei said, glaring at me.

"No," Maria and Troy said in unison.

"We won't abide more predators." Maria stared stone-faced at Sergei, then narrowed her eyes at Roman. "It's bad enough the leopards and jaguars are already here and have formed a pact. Adding the wolves tips the balance. No."

Troy scowled as he looked between Roman and Sergei. "We have enough to cover up without adding more big predator kills. Plus, the Reveal means the mundanes will be looking for things like that," he added. "If you expect the elves to leverage our political standing to keep covering up all of your mistakes when the humans know what to look for, think again."

I studied Troy, wondering how much of their efforts to cover up Otherside's missteps stemmed from a need to cover up some predation of their own. If nobody knew about their second row of teeth, nobody would look at them in a big predator kill. He caught me looking and lifted his eyebrows, a warning to keep my mouth shut.

"We do well enough taking care of our own messes," Maria retorted.

Troy sneered. "Like you did last winter, with the bitten elves recovered by mundane police? Sloppy work. Do you know how much we burned in money and favors killing that medical examiner's report?"

Rolling her eyes, Maria said, "Then you should have found them first, given it was one of yours drowning them."

"You should have just killed the medical examiner," Evangeline said, her eyes on me.

I fixed her with a steady look. "Back off, Evangeline. Grown folks are talking." I wanted to add that Doc Mike was my friend, but he'd already been targeted for that once. "Come on, y'all. Everyone is gonna have to give up something."

Sergei said, "What are *you* giving up?"

"Anonymity, peace of mind, time, and a fuckton of goodwill," I snapped. "Possibly my life. I'm painting an even bigger target on my back than being a sylph has already made me. Duke asked a good question. Why would a lich want to collect elementals? Don't you think there might be more of that going around if it gets out? But no, everybody wants to act like that's somehow my damn job and I should just slap a smile on and do it."

"Easy, babe," Roman murmured.

I shrugged off the hand he rested on my shoulder as the resentment that had been flickering in my heart flared into a flame. "No, I'm done with 'easy, babe.' I've bowed my head and said yes sir, no ma'am to every party in the Triangle. I've stifled my own powers, my own *needs*, to let all of you feel safe, all while taking on more work for Otherside. I'm a private investigator for the *mundanes*, but fuck me if one of you wants to come into my office or order me to your lair, and wave money and threats in my face."

The sun had set, but I could still make out their faces in the semi-dark. Taken aback, suspicious, angry, disdainful, disappointed.

I threw my hands up. "This is clearly not going to happen tonight. Go home, think about what you're each willing to trade to establish a new balance of power, and be ready to come back for a real negotiation tomorrow."

Nobody answered me, so I threw in one last admonishment, since it was on my mind and it looked like I'd be doing this myself.

"Don't forget, it's not just the lich lord we'll have to tackle. There's also Callista and the rest of her Watchers. If that's too much for you, leave me the fuck alone. You're either in as much as I am, or you're on your own. Don't look to me if the Reveal goes sideways."

Roman reached for me as I fled the picnic clearing, and I dodged his hand, mad at him all over again. Neither he nor anyone else was truly on my side, all while expecting me to fight on theirs, and the lich's words dug a little deeper into my heart.

Chapter 23

After threatening to blow Troy's SUV off the road, I figured a practice session was in order. Only a fool makes an empty threat, especially one of that magnitude to an audience that powerful.

My backyard had become too limiting for my sessions as my powers had grown. My control had improved, but control only did so much when I drew on enough Air to blow down a section of my fence and one of the small trees growing alongside it. Lately, I'd saved my heavy practices for when there were storms in the area, in case I surprised myself or overdid it and lost control of a chord again.

In a good stroke of timing, thunder rumbled as I made my way out back. I left a towel by the door just in case it actually poured instead of just blowing through. I had a flashlight hooked onto a belt loop on my shorts with a mini carabiner but picked my way through the night without it. I knew where I was going and could see well enough in the dark. Plus, the gloom and uncertainty matched my mood.

As I climbed over the downed section of my fence, I made yet another mental note to fix it. It was a simple point and blank stockade privacy fence, but between the tree that had crashed over it needing cutting and disposal first and my caseload picking up earlier in the spring, I hadn't been able to get to it.

With the lich making threats, the gap in my security bothered me. Not that it would be hard for any of my enemies to get around a wooden fence even when it was whole, but its presence made me feel better. Maybe Zanna would help me with it if I threw in some extra beer or a few good cigars.

A few feet from the edge of my backyard, the land sloped down toward the Eno River. Most of the park and river was accessible to paddlers, hikers, campers, and picnickers, but they tended to use the marked trail heads and river access points. My little corner of paradise was in a narrow section connecting the two main areas, off a gravel access road so small that Google didn't bother sending a car down for Street View. There might be the occasional adventurous hiker or unleashed dog owner going off-trail during the day, but nobody came out here at night.

Just to be sure, I stopped and listened. Woodsy sounds reached me. Frogs croaking, the faint scratching rustle of raccoons or possums prowling, leaves rattling in the gusts of wind, the hoot of a barred owl, the soothing ripple of the river tumbling over rocks. The only scents were the damp air, the river, the dirt and vegetation, and the trace of a deer that had used my trail to navigate the forest. I had the woods all to myself.

Calm stole over me as I took the broadest path through the beech and hickory trees, careful not to trip over the scattered fragments of granite boulders littering the ground. Being in nature and exercising my power were both things I needed to feel good and whole. I'd neglected practicing since the disappearing bodies case had first hit my desk. Reaching for Air and welcoming it fully felt like peeling off a sodden wetsuit, shedding a reluctant tightness to let my skin breathe for the first time in days.

When I reached the small clearing I'd made at the river's edge, I inhaled, filling my lungs with night air and my power, filling myself to my limits and past them. The brewing storm winds licked and teased me, their energy adding to what I could naturally call until I thought I'd burst if I didn't direct the power. So I did, solidifying the molecules and wedging them hard under a boulder at the river's edge.

It wobbled. I grunted, straining, wondering how close it was in weight to an SUV. It was half my height, a solid chunk of granite that must have started life higher up in the hillside if the hollow upslope was any indication. Dirt cradled and embraced it. I had no power over Earth, but I'd learned to find the gaps and seams—or at worst, to drive a shim of Air under my target and force it up with brute strength.

The ground separated with a sound like an old man sucking his teeth. The boulder wobbled. I pushed harder, straining with clenched fists, pushing my Airy wedge deeper, leveraging the boulder up as sweat poured down my face. Its weight pressed against the compacted molecules of Air, seeming to weigh against my soul as well, a symbol for everything I'd shouldered since my secret had been revealed to the rest of Otherside.

Forget Callista's Big Reveal. Mine had already happened. Even if the humans discovered me, they couldn't want any worse for me than the elves did.

Lightning cracked as I managed to roll the boulder. One side of it splashed partway into the river as thunder rumbled and I dropped to the ground, bouncing up and shifting to the side as my ass found a pointy stone. I dropped my head and heaved breath like I'd run a long race as fast as I could, trembling with exertion and praying that I really was alone. If an elf, vampire, or Sergei came on me now, self-defense would be a struggle.

"Not good enough," I muttered. My enemies wouldn't just stand back and wait for me to recover. I had to learn how to push through. It would hurt like hell, but it wasn't like I could burn myself out. Give myself a stroke, maybe, but I wouldn't lose my power.

Gathering myself, I reached for Air again, grasping at stormwinds for help. It was cheating—if I was trapped and fighting in a building, the air conditioning unit wouldn't do much for me by comparison. But this was practice. Baby steps.

Winds swirled around me, and I wove them into a cocoon of Air, a millimeter thick but enough to block physical attacks. Aether would have been able to slip through, and I'd learned the hard way to leave small gaps for air to breathe, but I would have had protection from an enemy relying on weapons or fists.

While holding the cocoon, I tried something I'd been attempting for months: slipping one chord of Air through another. Unlike Aether, elemental magic was tied to the physical world. Even undirected Air would hit something solid and push it forward or knock it over. Managing conflicting chords was like managing a sail in crosswinds—difficult. The necessary focus and control had evaded me since I'd thought to try it. I didn't even know if it was possible, but it wasn't like anyone was around to teach me.

I failed. A trickle of blood trailed from my nose to my lips as I pushed too hard.

"Fuck." Letting it all go in a whirlwind burst, I fell back and tilted my chin to the sky, tasting copper and defeat. I'd progressed further than I'd ever dreamed possible, but it still wasn't enough. I had to do more. I had to be better. Stronger.

Hot tears leaked from the corners of my eyes. I swiped at them and the blood on my lip. Would I ever be strong enough to stand alone? To not be easy pickings for whoever wanted to command me?

Maybe...if I joined the lich. But that wasn't an option. The lich was evil. I wasn't.

Thunder rumbled again, but no rain fell. I stayed where I was. It was nice here, even if there were rocks digging into my back and mosquitoes out for my blood. Nobody was trying to kill or pursue me. The trees, the river, and the rocks wanted nothing from me. Neither earth nor water held any pull for me beyond the comfort of nature.

Fire might. I remembered the arrow of lightning Mixcoatl had shot at me. A fire pit would be nice. Illegal, given I was on state land, but pleasant. I could make this clearing an escape from even my own home, a refuge for when I couldn't bear the slightest hint of civilization. It was about time I carved out space for myself, rather than forcing myself to fit the space everyone else had defined for me.

The rain started as I made my way home and mounted the stairs to my deck. Fat drops pattered to the ground and splatted against my face. Lightning cracked and thunder rolled so close together that the storm had to be less than a mile away. I darted into the house, exhausted but feeling complete for the first time in far too long.

"No more," I muttered, grabbing the towel by the door.

"What no more?"

I jumped, having missed Zanna's presence at my dining table in my exhaustion. She had the case of beer I'd left by the door at her elbow, one of the bottles open and half gone.

"Limits." I crossed to the counter where the bottle of Rioja I'd opened yesterday? The day before? sat waiting for me to finish it. After chugging a glass of water, I poured a large serving and joined Zanna at the table. "I'm done being less so that everyone else in this fucking town can feel good enough."

Zanna studied me, dark eyes half-hidden behind wild curls that would be the envy of any eighties model. "It's for you or them?"

"What is?"

She rolled her eyes like I was dense and swigged her beer. "You want to be more for you? Or more against them?"

"Is there a difference?"

"If it means calling storms and blowing rocks in the woods? Yes."

Had I drawn the storm closer? I frowned. Zanna was usually too busy with whatever kobolds did to lecture me on my doings. She wouldn't be making this point unless it was important. "I don't get it."

"You're the wind."

This was too philosophical for my level of fed-upedness and power exhaustion. "What are you trying to say?"

She shrugged, gathered the cardboard box containing the rest of her compensation and slid off her chair. "Wind just is. Others use it for power but never own it. And it can always turn its own way."

Zanna might be half my height and look like a child, but she was wiser than I gave her credit for. "Thanks. I needed that."

"More of this beer." She hefted the box. "This one is good."

"Noted. And hey—if I got the materials, would you be able to help with the back fence?"

"Materials and maple candy."

I blinked. "Sure. Maybe some honey, too? Or mead? I can get it at the farmer's market."

Her broad grin lit up the room. "Yes. I'll start as soon as materials arrive."

She let the door slam behind her, like always, and I winced but didn't scold her. She'd fix it if she broke it, like she had the porch rail when she'd tripped over the block of Air I kept in front of the door and crashed through it.

Sighing, I tried to just enjoy my wine. I should have had more water after that practice, but I needed the self-indulgence and hoped that a glass would inspire some kind of creative solution to the jam I was in. I let my mind wander over it, eyes half-lidded and as my vision unfocused, allowing it to seek whatever connections it wanted, jumping from worry to task to relationship.

Some of the remaining tension lingering in my shoulders eased with the wine and the mental exercise. One of the things I'd learned in my years as a private investigator was that sometimes, forcing yourself to think directly toward a solution would only ensure you kept hitting the same damn walls. There was always a solution if you were flexible enough to stop charging toward it.

I didn't like the one my mind kept circling toward though. It made a nasty, knotty feeling in my guts. I tried to gently empty my mind, focusing on the wine's bouquet, the mild sting of alcohol on my tongue, the mental image of peaceful woods, but whenever I let it wander back toward what I could do, it kept landing on one thing.

Join the lich.

It wouldn't be for real. He was evil, true evil, and had kidnapped people I cared about. But I'd been chasing my tail for days. The connections between my problems all looped back to him. I'd found the places he'd been but was no closer to finding where he was. I wouldn't be able to carry out my plan to search the archives for cemeteries, call around to all the possible sheriffs, and investigate a shortlist by the day after tomorrow. The way things were going with the alliance had me doubting that I'd be able to get them to set aside their differences in a day, even if I was able to sneak in and gather intel.

But I could fix this all by myself.

I veered away from the thought again. The same idea had come to me when I went alone to the abandoned boat warehouse where Leith Sequoyah and his co-conspirators were holed up, planning their revolution against the elven matriarchy. I'd volunteered to go in alone, gotten captured, and ended up drowned. That might have been Troy's plan all along—I'd never asked him—but regardless, things were different now.

Weren't they?

Otherside knew who and what I was. All I had to do to make sure I didn't go in alone was get a handful of them to agree to an alliance. This was in everyone's best interest, and they knew it. I just had to get them to agree to it. I *would* get them to agree to it, tomorrow.

I finished my wine, washed the glass, and went to bed. The storm passed outside, raging and wild. I lay there, weighing how far I would go to save Val and Doc Mike if—despite everything I'd done—I couldn't bring the alliance together.

Would it really be evil to join evil, if my intentions were good?

Chapter 24

I hadn't decided on an answer to my moral quandary when I woke the next morning, but I had more immediate concerns. A power hangover thundered behind my eyes and twisted my stomach with nausea so intense that breathing seemed likely to trigger vomiting. Had I gotten drunk after my practice, the wine would have mitigated the effects of power, but I'd stopped after one glass. I was still trying to find the balance between being wine drunk and power drunk, and a single glass of red was not it after how much I'd done, even though my limits with Air had increased with my strength.

When the headache and nausea had receded enough for me to think of something other than not dying, I forced myself out of bed and into the shower. Because I felt like shit, I slathered on some of the fancy lotion I usually saved for date night. I regretted it as the scent of amber and lotus smacked me hard, bringing the nausea back. I breathed through my mouth long enough to wipe some off, annoyed at the waste, before dressing in cut-off black denim shorts and a drapey green camisole. In a few more minutes, I had a pot of chamomile and spearmint tea and was hunched over my computer at the table.

Focusing on the Otherside angle of this case meant that I'd neglected Raleigh PD, who'd pitched it my way in the first place. The only silver lining in the whole mess was that they were so overwhelmed with the spike in violence, arson, theft, and road rage-driven car accidents that non-violent crimes like finding out who'd robbed a morgue was not even on their radar. I shot off a quick email to my contact anyway, letting him know I was expanding my search to other grave robberies. I couldn't tell them that it was a lich, but I had to tell them something if I wanted to get paid and called back for another job. Maria's twenty grand would keep me going for a good while, but taking jobs for Othersiders was not going to become a thing.

Why not?

Rubbing my forehead, I leaned back in my chair to consider that. It sure as hell paid better, and I'd more than earned my new place in Otherside society. Did I have all the respect I deserved? Not yet. But I would…as soon as I had enough power.

There it was again. The lich's offer echoed. If my intentions were good but I also went along with the ruse because I genuinely wanted the power to make people listen to me or leave me alone, did that negate the good intentions?

My phone rang, another unknown number to my personal line.

"You said I had two days," I snapped.

"Look, ma'am, I don't know who you think I am, but…"

The caller was male, with a heavy Southern accent and a rich, deep voice, not one I recognized. I tried to tone it down a notch. "Who is this, and how did you get my private number?"

"Roman Volkov gave it to me. I'm Terrence Little." He didn't sound pleased, but I wasn't either.

"Why did Roman do that?"

"Because I'm the duly elected obong of the wereleopards of the Carolinas, and he wanted to offer us a deal. May I presume I'm speaking with Arden Finch?"

Shit. I scrambled for a balance between diplomacy and boundaries, not wanting to punish Terrence for Roman's overstep but not intending to become the doormat for yet another group in Otherside. "I see. Very few people have this number, Mr. Little, and the last person who called without my knowing the number made threats. I'm sure you can understand my concern."

"Noted. Now, if you're definitely the sylph PI who's handling negotiations for the new alliance…"

I sighed, trying to keep it quiet but unable to keep it in, and a breeze whispered through the house with it. How much had Roman told him? "That's me. What exactly did Roman promise you?"

"A seat at the table, to start. An equal voice, if we agree to cede a portion of the lands between Eno and Falls Lake to the wolves."

"Anything else?"

"There might be. But we'll bide." A deep satisfaction rumbled through his words, and I could only imagine he had a leopard's cool patience and confidence. Take the target of opportunity, striking with an ambush from the superior position when an opening presented itself.

His arrogance irritated me, and I reached for patience. I didn't need to step on more toes. "Fine. None of this gets back to Callista though."

"We respect Callista's mandates, but I don't see why we'd volunteer anything. For now."

Another lazy swat of a threat, hinting but with no real impetus behind it, testing the limits of my posturing. "Callista will keep." My voice stayed low and even. "It's me you need to worry about."

"I see that. Well then. You have my attention, ma'am."

Ignoring the whiff of mockery in the words as cat confidence, I gave him the time and place for today's follow-up negotiations. We'd be back at Raven Rock, and I could only hope that everyone arrived in a better mindset than they had last night.

As soon as I was done with Terrence, I dialed Roman. "What the actual fuck, Roman?"

"Umm…hi, babe."

"You're giving out my private number to the wereleopards? I thought we were on the same page with this."

"Oh. That."

"Yes. That." I paced my kitchen, fuming, daring him to defend it.

"Look, I needed something to set Sergei chasing his own tail instead of mine. Now he can worry about Terrence."

His smug tone sent my temper from boiling to superheated. "Seriously?"

"What?"

I took a moment to breathe, trying not to blow up. "First, you drop my name to your pack without even telling me you'd opened negotiations. Then you're making deals with your brother, which I'll be expected to enforce, again without telling me. Now you're handing out my personal information to a wereleopard I didn't even know existed? He knew everything about me, Roman!"

"What was I supposed to do? We're trying to negotiate the first new balance of power in hundreds of years! I had to give him something, or he wouldn't have trusted me enough to agree to come to the table."

"You were supposed to *ask me*!" My voice broke as I both fought back the return of the power hangover and struggled not to cry. Why was this so hard for him to understand? "We're supposed to be partners, Roman. I need one person on my side. That's it. Just one. And I needed it to be you."

"I am on your side, Arie. How could you say I'm not?"

"Because every time I turn around, you've done something that solidifies your position in Otherside while making mine harder, without *talking* to me about it."

He didn't reply for long seconds.

"Right, because you're the only one who gets to try to find a better place for themselves." Bitter anger coated every sentence.

My heart clenched. "You know that's not what I'm saying."

"Do I?"

"At least if I need your help, I ask first. I don't just throw your name out there and tell people everything about you."

"What an asshole I am for thinking you'd be there for me."

I gasped at the feeling like a knife twisting in my gut, trying to figure out how we'd gotten to this tangent. Why had things gotten so nasty between us lately, so quickly?

And then it hit me. The lich.

Violence had spiked among the humans, but what about Otherside? If anyone snapped, we'd all assume it was due to spillover tension from all the extra blood, high passions, and fear being pumped out by the humans. We were so used to covering up our own messes, dealing with sharp tempers and sharper fangs, that every faction was probably hiding at least one "accident" from the last week. I doubted that the vampires or weres would have thought to say anything. I was almost certain the elves would keep a mishap to themselves. Maybe that was why Evangeline had slipped with her teeth? Was it just the human spillover, or was the lich magic starting to affect all of us now? Would an Othersider with less powerful magic, like Roman, be more affected or affected sooner, than a more powerful being?

Roman was still silent, though I could feel the tension though the phone. He was a wolf waiting for the rabbit to startle and flee.

"I think we need to take a step back," I said, consciously gentling my tone. "Something isn't right here."

"You're damn right it isn't. I am sick and tired of being everyone's bitch, and I'm fixin' to do somethin' about it."

216

"I hear you."

"Don't patronize me. I won't—"

"Roman!" I waited until I was sure I had his attention. "Something is *wrong*. All of us are extra salty lately. You and me picking at each other and being nasty—"

"I'm not being nasty. I'm being straight up."

I sighed, pressing the heel of my palm into my eyes to try to hold off the resurgent headache. I wasn't getting through, and the more I thought on the lich's power, the less I thought it likely that I would. "Okay. Let's just…I'll see you later, all right? We can talk in person."

"Fine." He hung up, and even though I knew it was probably lich-driven irritation, it still needled me.

"Fine," I said to the empty air as I slumped to rest my forehead on my crossed arms on the table. I let myself wallow in misery for another minute before sitting up. The whole day stretched before me, and even though I knew it was futile, I had to keep working to find my friends.

In the hours that followed, I went over to the archives in Raleigh and worked on narrowing down options for my graveyard theory. Even limiting my search to the band between Clayton, southeast of Raleigh, and Calvander, northwest of Chapel Hill, there were far more sites than I would have expected—the unmarked or forgotten burial grounds for enslaved Africans, Civil War casualties, and the American Indian victims of smallpox and colonialism.

We weren't allowed notes or anything that could mark records in the archives, so I paid for a stack of copies and went to a cafe to mark locations on a fold-up paper map I'd brought along. The place was strangely empty, the baristas practically snarling. The energy in the archives had been tense as well but muted somehow, as though there'd been a spell of protection over the place. Out in the street, people bustled past with faces twisted in fear, loathing, outrage, or shame.

If this lich wasn't ended soon, we might see a police murder, the kind that turned another innocent person of color into a hashtag. It had happened elsewhere for far less. I might be a sylph, but I presented and passed as a Black or mixed-race human. The elves weren't the only people I had to worry about coming after me for features I had no control over.

Holed up in my house or driving around the Triangle trying to fix everything, I hadn't taken the time to just sit and observe. It was almost worse than seeing the aftermath on the news. I had to do something before the area exploded, dragging the local Othersiders with it and forcing us out in the worst way possible. We'd kept everything hidden during the horrors of the Inquisition, the colonial period, and two World Wars, but new technology and a lich lord might be the perfect hellstorm we should have anticipated and hadn't.

Those thoughts stayed with me on the drive over to Raven Rock, tugging and tumbling. The park seemed to be at the southern edge of the lich lord's sphere of influence, with the drivers getting less ragey the closer I got. Of course, it helped that there were fewer cars going my way.

The more I thought about it, the more determined I was to get this alliance to work. It had to. We couldn't afford to act like the humans I'd seen today, not if we wanted to be accepted into mundane society rather than wiped from it.

Chapter 25

When I stalked into the clearing, Janae was already there sitting cross-legged and meditative on the ground, heedless of the sandy soil. "Hello, child," she said without opening her eyes. "My, but there's a weight and a shadow on your soul this evening."

I crunched to a stop and slouched onto the bench of the picnic table nearest her, straightening reflexively when she opened her eyes. "I think the lich is starting to impact Othersiders," I said, confessing my biggest worry. "And—"

A figure at the edge of the picnic area caught my attention, half-formed and misty. At first, I thought it was a djinni, but I would have sensed if a djinni was using Aether, just like I could sense when elves were preparing a spell. It also lacked the smokiness of a djinni in their true form, appearing instead to be manifesting halfway between planes. As I focused on it, it grew more distinct. Power radiated from it, enough that Janae turned around.

"Shit," I said, with feeling.

Janae scanned the clearing, missing the specter the first time despite feeling its power. I could tell when she switched to her unseen senses because she went rigid. "Is that…"

"A goddess, I think." Swallowing past the lump of fear in my throat, I took a step toward it. If an Old One was here, they were probably here for me. The apparition flared, showing me a red sash and a *was* scepter before disappearing in a burst of savage amusement. "That was Neith."

The witch whipped her head to face me so fast I thought she'd twist her neck. "Just how many times have you been to the Crossroads that one of the oldest faces of the Goddess can manifest to you on our plane?"

"Enough, apparently. She's taken a special interest in me."

"How special? Did she get blood?"

"No—umm. Actually. Maybe." I rubbed my scarred shoulder and remembered the bite of her ankh as it cut into my cheek. "Damn it."

"Indeed. Time grows shorter than I thought if we have that kind of company."

"My thoughts precisely," Duke said as he materialized with his back to the same tree he'd leaned against last night. I swear he chose it because of how handsome his umber-dark skin looked in the fading light. He'd always been vain, and I wasn't in the mood for any of his shit today.

"Don't do your vision thing, Duke," I hissed. "We've got enough to worry about."

"What are we worried about?"

I looked toward the source of the voice, knowing it was Terrence Little from the phone but not having a face for the name. Terrence was the even brown of acorns with a gaze like tiger's eye gems: hard, smooth, and deep. He was about my height—five-six—and lean almost to being scrawny but carried himself with the self-assurance normally seen on much bigger men. A Marine tattoo peeked out from under the sleeve of his T-shirt.

"You must be Terrence," I said.

"And you must be Arden."

"And what the fuck is a leopard doing here?" Sergei surged into the clearing a few steps ahead of Roman, who said, "I invited him."

The brothers stared each other down, with Sergei looking away first. That exchange gave Maria time to arrive, moving in the clockwork steps that told me she was a little too close to the dangerous side of her nature and probably needed to feed. Troy arrived without Evangeline, frowning at the quiet. Terrence watched it all, clever and calculating, giving away no reaction other than his interest.

"Ladies and gentlemen, boys and girls," I bellowed in my best announcer's voice. Smirking at the pleasure of having both wolves jump, I said at a more appropriate volume, "If that's everyone?"

Suspicious glances, folded arms, stiff faces, and hard eyes were all I got from everyone except Janae and Terrence. The witch stood with her usual unflappable patience. The wereleopard looked bored and unimpressed.

"All righty then. Welcome to Terrence Little, obong of the wereleopards of the Carolinas."

Terrence saluted, turning it into a little wave.

"Let's make sure everyone is on the same page. When we left last night, Ms. Janae had generously offered the sanctuary and healing of the witches in exchange for a seat at the table and a voice, particularly as pertains to any alliance-facilitated Reveal." I glanced at her, receiving a nod in return. "There were no objections. The wolves demanded territory in the Triangle. This was rejected by the third of the Master of the City of Raleigh and the princess of House Monteague. Where is Evangeline, anyway?"

Troy scowled and shook his head.

"Fine. Monteague's price was turning me into the lich, and you can damn well—"

"That is withdrawn," Troy said.

I leveled a don't-fuck-with-me look at him. "Do tell."

He shrugged. "My sister was rash. But we stand by our objection to more wolves in the Triangle."

"Reckon that's not your call, Prince." Terrence hooked his thumbs through the belt loops of his jeans. "For the same price as the witches—a seat and a voice—the Acacia Thorn leopards and our allies, the Jade Tooth jaguars, will cede land to the Blood Moon wolves."

"It's not land we're worried about," Troy said, frowning.

"I figured." Terrence crossed his arms.

"Then by all means, let the other shoe drop," Maria said. "And tonight. Some of us are hungry." She looked Terrence up and down, long and slow.

He returned the look. "Oh, darlin', is that your price? A drink?"

"Whore," Sergei muttered, a snarl curling his upper lip.

If he'd intended it to set Terrence off, he failed. The wereleopard grinned. "I call it being a good leader. But I guess a spoilt pup like you wouldn't know anything about that."

His slash landed solidly. Roman snagged the sleeve of his brother's polo shirt as Sergei took a menacing step toward Terrence and snarled.

"I told you I'd do what I had to," the older Volkov said. Anger still thrummed through his energy, but he'd spent so long containing it and controlling himself that Janae was probably the only one other than me who would sense it. "If your pride won't let you hear reason, you'll eat crow."

I looked at all of them, knowing it wasn't just Sergei's pride in the balance and weighing what had just happened. Sergei had made the same demand—territory for support—last night and been rebuffed. Roman had gone around the pack's official representative and brought in a third party, a local one that the vampires and the elves would have a harder time pushing back on. As far as I knew, the leopards and the jags had limited influence as individual prides, but together, they had enough to command the respect of the groups represented here. Besides, weres had zero chill when it came to territory. You didn't push unless you were ready to get pushed way back.

Maria broke the tense silence. "Will Ximena agree to any terms you negotiate?"

"I didn't know we were making agreements tonight." Terrence's cat smile was getting on my nerves. He turned it on me, as though he'd read my mind, before returning his attention to Maria. "I'm here to see if this is worth our time."

The vampire narrowed her eyes. "I want to know what else you want, first, pussycat. Your kind plays the long game."

Roman grimaced, and I looked to the sky in exasperation. He was clever enough to outmaneuver his brother but hadn't considered the other layers.

Terrence tilted his head. "That's rather mistrustful for a potential ally."

"Cut the shit, Little," Roman said. The flush on his neck betrayed his embarrassment at the one he'd intended to use as a tool turning around to use him in turn. "Do you want something else?"

Terrence studied the group. He noted everyone's position, pausing on Janae standing closer to me and Duke almost completely out of the group. The Volkov brothers were side by side but with palpable strain between them, while Troy and Maria had edged closer, though not close enough that they could be called allies. As representatives of the Triangle's two biggest players, they were probably more accustomed to dealing with each other than anyone else here.

"We don't want to be Revealed." Terrence looked more serious than he had all night. "Black and brown folks got enough problems these days with being shot for no cause, or thought of as dangerous animals, without it coming out that African and Mesoamerican legends of leopard and jaguar gods had a root in real life. We don't need to add big game trophy to our long list of troubles."

"That will put more pressure on us," Roman said, scowling.

Terrence shrugged. "Werewolves are the legend most people are familiar with. I'm not gonna pretend there'll be less danger in it, but you didn't see any wereleopards in the last big monster movie, now did you? Let folks get used to weres with what they think they already know. Besides, wolves aren't the only others. There's a good number of coyotes and foxes out West, and a bear clan or two along the Canadian border. Work something out with them."

"They don't have nearly the numbers of wolf, leopard, and jaguar."

Another nonchalant shrug. "You asked what else we're gonna want in exchange for handing the wolves a sizable chunk of prime territory in what is poised to be the new capital of Otherside. That's it. We don't come out, and y'all help keep it that way."

"Big ask," Troy said.

"It's nothing more than what the elves are already doing with your political placements, your lawyers, and your hackers. This just changes the dynamic to one where you don't get to act like you're the martyrs of Otherside anymore, since you could formally call on us for help in return."

Troy pressed his lips together in a thin line but didn't clap back. Duke smirked from his position at the edge of the clearing, and Janae shifted her feet. My stomach soured, though I couldn't say why. This seemed like progress.

"Your deal with the Blood Moon clan isn't binding on the rest of us," Maria pointed out. She'd dropped the flirtatious flapper girl mien she usually bore. "Why should we agree to your terms?"

"Because either way, we'll find someone to work with or work through. Then they'll be here, and you'll have to work with all of us anyway. Times are changing, and those who change with them will come out on top."

"This is fucking outrageous," Sergei said. "Are all of you seriously considering this?"

"I see nothing in his request that troubles the witches," Janae added. "And our offer stands."

"Yes, we'll consider it," Maria said flatly. "Though the commitment to help keep the leopards and jaguars hidden will need to be taken back to my master."

Terrence grinned. "Give Torsten my fond regards."

Maria frowned but didn't ask the obvious question, probably wary of airing dirty laundry in front of present company.

Sergei wasn't willing to drop it. "If they don't come out, why should we?"

Rolling her eyes, Maria scoffed. "Do you honestly think the mundanes are going to believe that vampires, elves, and witches exist but not werewolves?"

"She has a point," Troy murmured. "Although none of this considers the fae. Or the djinn." He glanced across the clearing at Duke, who smiled.

"We can be whoever we want or need to be, whenever we need to be it." He demonstrated, shifting from the laughing-eyed Black man to an overweight grandmother, an all-around average ginger man, and to give everyone an Aetheric middle finger, a goat, before resuming his usual shape with a wide smile.

I barked a laugh. "And I'd love to see someone go and convince my kobold landlord that she needs to do anything other than whatever she damn well pleases."

Troy frowned, looking as though he was filing the information away. "Also a fair point."

"Fuck your points. It's not fair. What about elementals, for that matter? What about *her*?" Sergei pointed at me, red-faced in his fury.

Shaking his head, Troy said, "Elementals are too dangerous—"

"Sergei," Roman interrupted. "Shut up. This doesn't change from what we were already planning for."

"It changes everything! One group gets special demands—"

"In exchange for *us* getting something *we* want. Think, brother!"

For not having seen it coming, Roman was handling the turnabout well. A flash of resentment streaked through me. Why couldn't he be as equanimous with me? All I'd asked was to be consulted before being used in plans of wolf power and territory expansion. Was that really so much?

No. It's that getting back to his family means that much. It's not about you.

I shook myself and forced my mind back to the present, setting aside Troy's comment for the moment. It didn't sound like a defense of me. I didn't know what it was. A threat? An excuse, for when he finally did get around to cutting my throat?

Clearing the throat in question, I said, "Sounds like we're going to need to take all this back to our respective decision-makers before we can finalize the points of agreement. Duke? You've been quiet. Anything you want to add? Any special requests from the Council?"

"No more bottles and no wishes, not from Othersiders. We punish our own and favor who we choose."

"I'm sure we can all agree that's fair enough," I said when Sergei opened his mouth to go off again. The stars had come out while we talked, easier to see out here in the country with no light pollution. The night was darker as well. Even in my little patch of Eno it didn't get this dark.

My heart sank as I realized this wasn't going to happen before the lich called for my answer. "We're running out of time for the Triangle. I don't know how many of you have been out and about lately, but the mundanes are close to breaking. If there's a shooting, a riot—if anything pushes this kettle to boiling over—it will escalate fast, and the human government will send more firepower than we can handle. Talk to your people but be quick."

Eyes darted. We all had excellent night vision, though all of them except Janae would have far better than mine. Making out expressions was difficult under the waning moon, but the energy was biting.

With a nod, Roman gripped his brother's arm and steered Sergei out of the clearing. *I guess we won't be having that chat tonight.*

Duke shifted planes with a shimmer. Terrence and Maria left together at a murmured word from her. Janae looped her arm in mine and steered us toward the path to the parking lot, strengthening my suspicion about her night vision. I didn't like it, given that it meant she could taste my aura if she wanted, but she'd asked permission before and I didn't feel the telltale prickles of life magic.

"So, what will you do about the lich, now that you don't have an alliance to fall back on?" she asked.

I stiffened. "Are all witches so prescient?"

Her teeth flashed in a smile in the dark. "Only the ones who care to be. We're as fallible as anyone else."

We walked in silence, the parking lot's overhead lights penetrating the thinner trees and giving us something more to see by.

"He has my friends," I said when we'd nearly reached our cars. "I'll do what I have to."

"That, my dear, is what scares me. But it's also what gives me hope for this alliance."

"What, that I might be suicidal?"

"No. That you hit a wall and don't allow it to give you an excuse."

When I didn't answer, she released my arm, patting it before she drifted toward her car. I don't know what I'd expected a witch to drive, but an aging silver Mercedes wasn't it.

"You'll figure it out," she said over her shoulder. "One way or another. And the gods aren't done with you, child, though whether that will help or hurt remains to be seen."

I thought about what Janae had said and Neith at the edge of the clearing the whole long drive home, sick to my stomach at both her faith and the reminder of the gods' interest.

Chapter 26

The djinn had taught me the trick of lucid dreaming as a child when I kept casting in my sleep and neither throwing water on me nor beatings stopped it. It's how I knew I wasn't in a dream when I smelled meringue and fresh cut herbs. The confusing thing was that if I wasn't having a nightmare, there was no reason for me to be smelling elves in my sleep.

Unless there was.

I snapped awake with a gasp, and a hand clapped over my mouth. An arm with muscles like iron bands wrapped around my body and pulled. I tumbled out of the bed, tangled in the sheets. My fingers brushed the enchanted knife I kept under my pillow and missed. It tumbled to the floor with a clatter as my knees hit with bruising force.

My scream cut off in the compression of my diaphragm, but it didn't stop me from fighting back. A masculine "ooph" was my reward for a well-placed elbow, followed by a hissed, "Calm down!" as I was hauled to my feet.

Telling someone to calm down has never worked in the history of anyone or anything ever, and it didn't work here. For an elf to have made it past Zanna, he had to be one of the Darkwatch. I knew what they were capable of, and I wanted none of it. I tried again with my elbow.

"Dammit, Finch, don't make me spell you!"

Only one elf called me by my name rather than something intended to dehumanize me: Troy. He could slip my shields and spell me into submission almost as easily as he breathed. I knew because he'd done it at least three times despite my best efforts.

Like I said, it had to be one of the Darkwatch.

With an effort, I overrode the budding panic attack and forced myself to stop struggling. As soon as I stilled, he released me and went back to the bed, scooping up a pillow from the floor, shoving it under the covers, and fluffing everything.

I stood, fists clenched in outrage that he'd break into my house and pull me out of bed in the middle of the night, and then be all up in it. "What the—"

He dashed back to me and pushed me back into the corner. My heart thundered as his body pressed full-length against mine, close enough to kiss or to kill. He covered my mouth again and hissed, "Stop. Talking. And don't move."

I started to clap back when the chill hit me, colder than ice and darker than death, like the vision Duke had of me earlier this year. Troy eased back around to face the room, too slow to be real, his back to me and arms wide to stop me from going around him. We both watched as a black shadow crawled in, hanging upside-down from the ceiling and slithering over the lintel. It paused just over the entry to the room. Evil radiated from it, a pure malice and intent to harm that I hadn't ever experienced, even from Leith Sequoyah as he'd used Aether to command our bodies to shut down and die.

For three long seconds, I stood riveted by a fear so powerful all I could do was pray to every facet of the Goddess that it didn't see me. All of me seemed to run in reverse. My stomach backed up into my esophagus. My blood chilled. My breath was too much out and not enough in; I was choking on carbon dioxide.

My mind forgot what it was to be sentient and remembered only the basest instincts: fight or flee. Or die.

Not moving suddenly seemed like a fucking ridiculous idea. I didn't want to be anywhere near whatever it was. I definitely didn't want it in my room, and if it had hurt Zanna on its way in, we were going to have a serious problem. If I survived, anyway.

Troy's body blocking me was the only reason I stayed there long enough to watch the shadow ooze down from the ceiling, extend a single, long claw to test the not-me form made of pillow and sheets...and shred my bedding to scattered fluffs of down and shreds of cotton, squealing with unearthly outrage as feathers filled the air instead of blood.

That should have been me.

Troy had prevented it. A damn elf had just saved my life.

"What the fuck!" exploded out of me as I reached for Air.

"Finch, no!"

The shadow turned and, with a subvocal screech like a car crash, metal on metal blended with smoke and gasoline, it flowed toward us.

With an elven hunter's speed, Troy had his longblade out before I could recover the breath I'd used to scream. A smooth motion blocked the nightmare's swipe toward us—toward me?—and steel shrieked against the thing's claws like nothing I'd ever heard before. I covered my ears and searched the room for something I could use.

My Ruger was in the nightstand, too close to the darkness personified for me to reach it. I'd have to use Air.

I reached for my power, my heart hammering in both fear and exertion as I pulled on more of my magic than I ever had before.

Troy blocked another slash. "No! Don't—"

Whatever I wasn't supposed to do, I was doing it. With a snarl, I pushed everything I had at the thing. A solid yet swirling block of Air smashed into the monster—and whooshed straight through it, blowing out my bedroom window and creating a gale of shredded sheets, downy tufts, and sparkling shards of glass.

I froze, blinking and gasping in terror, as it refocused on me with the full weight of its gaze. Maggots crawled under my skin, and the taste of rotting meat in the back of my throat made me gag, hard. I dropped to one knee, muscles spasming and fingernails gouging the wood floor, fighting to find a piece of *me* left under the raging death and rot and horror.

Impact to my left side. I tumbled, sprawling, choking, still trying to breathe past overwhelming dread and the certain knowledge that I was about to meet the Goddess herself.

An image came to me. True helplessness. Bound and enchanted and drowning. It was me in Jordan Lake, terrified and dying. "No. No!"

I dragged a breath in. Another flashback, this time of Grimm pressing me hard in the shape of an Akkadian rabisu, like this demon, as everything in me tried to get away, down to the single hairs standing straight out from my body.

Salt and courage had forced her back then. Would it work now?

Trembling so hard my muscles spasmed again, I forced myself to crawl under a slash of Troy's blade as it met steely claws. Out the bedroom door. To the kitchen. I pushed myself to my feet, telling myself that it was only a nightmare.

Only a nightmare in the flesh, hunting me.

For real this time, not Grimm or Duke or Callista. Not training. No chances to stand up, wipe the blood from my mouth, and have a do-over if this went poorly.

An eleven-ounce canister of salt beckoned from the kitchen counter. Baby blue and yellow had never been such powerful colors—the girl in her yellow dress, carrying her umbrella, was a warrior on my side. I prayed that the fact the salt was "lite" and iodized wouldn't lessen its effect and poured a heaping handful into my palm.

"Get the fuck outta my house!" I shouted as I stormed back into my bedroom, drunk on adrenaline and hurling the whole amount at the darkest shadow.

Again came the sub-vocal screech. Troy bellowed and pushed forward, knicking the nightmare with his black blade.

"Get. Out!" I pried the lid off and hurled more salt at the thing, pushing with Air as I slipped back around to stand closer to Troy and farther from the route it had taken into the bedroom. The salt hitting it made it solid enough for the Air strike to knock it half off the ceiling. My doorframe cracked from the impact, and everything on my bedside table clattered to the floor.

With a last frustrated shriek, it flowed backward over the lintel, taking a swipe at me as it passed.

I ducked so hard and so fast that I fell back on my ass. Undignified, but either way, it missed me.

The salt rolled from my hand, leaving a spiraled trail of white granules, and the absence of fear was so powerful that I dry heaved before collapsing, every nerve and muscle in my body wrung out to exhaustion. Grimm's training was *nothing* like the real thing. Not even close. She might be a djinni, and djinn might have ambiguous morals, but pure, unadulterated evil couldn't be faked.

Is this what Janae meant when she said other beings would find a way through?

Troy glared as he checked a gash in his shoulder. "I told you to be quiet and not move!"

It took me a few gasps to find my voice. "There was a fucking elf and a motherfucking rabisu in my bedroom in the middle of the night, and you want me to be quiet and not move? Are you on drugs?"

"No, I'm disciplined," he snapped. "And it's a lesser demon."

"That's what I said, asshole. Rabisu. Doesn't explain what you're doing here."

"Other than saving your life?"

"The question stands, Monteague. Not many people would be too put out if I died, including your grandmother, which means you're on another mission." I crossed my arms, willing the bitterness in my own statement to turn itself into anger. I was about to be used by Troy Monteague. Again. "Keithia said I had until the new moon."

"So I should have just left the one elemental we know of for sure run around unmonitored?"

My blood went cold. "For sure" implied they knew there were others. I prayed that I hadn't led him to Val, or that he hadn't recognized her as a dea. "What the hell does my being an elemental have to do with a rabisu and you, of all people, being in my bedroom?"

"It smells like a lightning strike for a full quarter mile. You've been practicing."

"Get to the fucking point!"

"How much do you know about liches?"

I pointed in the direction of the front door. "Get out. I'm done playing twenty questions."

"You owe me."

"I don't owe you shit because you didn't do this for me. You did this for whatever mission you're on and your hard-on for duty. Explain or get out."

Troy glared, holding my gaze as he wiped his blade on the remains of my mattress and sheathed it.

I bristled, but it wasn't like I could sleep there. "Wait. Where's Zanna?"

"She's fine."

"You're terrible at answering questions."

"She's tied up outside. I didn't need her getting in the way."

That set me back. "What is so fucking important that you'd risk a kobold's curse and a rabisu?"

"Avoiding a second Atlantis." The only thing harder than Troy's voice was his expression as he stared at me.

Shock stole my words. Atlantis, an elven city, had drowned when elementals bound themselves together at the behest of the djinn, combining the four natural elements to destroy it. Nobody could remember why they'd turned on half their parentage in favor of the other half, but it was what had prompted the ban on elves mixing with djinn and started elves hunting down and killing every elemental they could find. Until me.

"A lich with enough strength can force a binding of elemental power, which can then be used however he damn well pleases. The Darkwatch has suspected there were elementals in the Triangle for years, but you're the only one we've managed to confirm. For a lich to be drawn here suggests there are more."

"You've got to be shitting me. Maria's scroll didn't say anything about that." Was that why the gods wanted the lich stopped?

"Torsten's library is good, but his only reason to focus on liches is the undead angle. We have broader criteria."

"Because Atlantis."

Troy nodded. "You're obviously strong enough to draw his attention, although I don't know what possessed you to think practicing like this was a good idea."

"Well, let's see. Your grandmother has you haul me into her presence and threatens me with murder, your sister blames me for the death of her boytoy and threatens to kill me for

235

something *you* did, you follow me around the Triangle with still more fucking threats, and you think I'm just being reckless?"

I shook my head, utterly disbelieving. Every time I thought I'd seen the full extent of Troy's jackassery, he revealed a new level. "I would love to live in whatever privileged alternate reality allows you to ignore every single fact of my fucking existence to arrive at *that* conclusion, so let me drop another F-bomb. Fuck. You."

"Finch—"

"Don't you fucking 'Finch' me. I don't care what you just did, you *will not* 'Finch' me in my own fucking house. Get out. And let Zanna go before you get off my property."

"Listen to—"

"*Get out!*" A breeze stirred with the force of my outrage.

Raising his hands, Troy backed up. "Tell me what you've learned, and I'll help you with the lich, alliance or not."

I leaned forward, fists on my hips. "You want to bargain with me to do the right thing?"

"Right and wrong are subjective."

"Goddess. As if I needed another reason not to like you."

Troy stayed where he was, quiet and wary, waiting for me to come to the conclusion that was hurtling to the fore. I had to go in, and I think he knew it. I also suspected that he'd try to infiltrate the lich's lair if he could, as he had with Leith, but I was the one with the in. I was his ticket. And it would be more than a little rash to go completely alone, not telling anyone. Val and Sofia were counting on me. I couldn't fuck this up going cowboy again, even if it meant trusting Troy—which was also not smart but all I had right now.

"Fine," I said.

"Come to the safehouse. It's warded."

"No. I remember your wards. I couldn't leave." Anxiety tightened my skin as I remembered the full-body cramps that had dropped me when I'd tried passing the door's threshold.

He crossed his arms and sighed like I was being dramatic. "I took that down. You're not a prisoner this time."

"What am I then?"

"An ally. If you want to be," he said with a small tilt of his head.

I couldn't read the gesture or the flat tone he delivered the words in, but it had to be better to make a deal with this devil than the one that was the lich.

Chapter 27

Zanna was spitting mad when I cut her free of the ropes Troy had bound her with, subsiding only when the elf explained himself, promised not to do it again, and offered ten cases of beer.

"Should still curse you. You, your House, your ancestral home, and all who dwell there," she grumbled, rubbing ostentatiously at where the ropes had been. "Would do for anything less than a demon."

She and I covered the broken window with a tarp I kept in the back of my Civic hatchback, nailing it into place. Glass crunched underfoot from the broken window and the mug of tea I'd had on the nightstand, both now shattered on the floor with the weak smell of chamomile and lavender. I made Troy wait outside while I secured my home as best as I was able, unable to bear another invasion. My bedroom reeked of a blend of fear sweat, ozone, musty herbs, and marshmallow burnt to ash, and crawled with the remnants of evil. I'd have to have Janae come out to cleanse it on top of paying for repairs.

Good thing I've got Maria's cash payment. Maybe I shouldn't be so quick to rule out working for Otherside. It put me in more danger, but I'd been working a human case when I first encountered lich complications. If I kept racking up this kind of damage, I'd have to set up a retainer with Torsten's coterie or the Monteagues or both.

My head spun at the idea. What the hell was my life coming to that I'd consider working for either party?

I grabbed Duke's callstone and my weapons before we left. The elf-killing knife I'd commissioned from a tomtar smith went into a sheath I strapped to my thigh. Eight inches of fae-enchanted lead and steel would give anyone pause, even if the combination wasn't fatal to their particular species. My Ruger pistol went into an inner-pants holster at my left hip. The shotgun I kept for home protection went into a heavy canvas duffel, along with a first aid kit and a few of the ratty old towels I kept for washing the car.

When I was ready, Troy led the way to his safehouse. I thought about calling Roman and asking to crash there, but the way things were going lately made my guts clench at the idea. I wasn't ashamed to admit to myself that I was also trying to avoid Sergei—and any reports he might make to Callista.

"You better deliver on that beer," I told Troy when we got to the Chapel Hill apartment. I wouldn't mind if Zanna carried out her threat, but I needed to distract myself from the fact that I was back at a place where I'd awakened half-dead and feverish and then been held prisoner for another two days before managing to convince Troy I needed out.

He looked at me funny, though that might have been as much for my obvious nerves as my comment. "I keep my word. Always."

"Says you." Weak clapback, but I was fighting off an anxiety attack, complete with short breath, a palpitating heart, and sweaty palms. What the hell had I been thinking to agree to coming here?

Troy rolled his eyes and didn't bother answering as he opened the door and went in.

I swallowed my fear and followed, shutting the door behind me as I hefted my weekender duffel, not sure where to put it, where I'd be sleeping, or whether this might be the new low point in shit that had happened lately.

"What's your plan for getting in?" Troy called from the kitchen. He reappeared in the archway with a mini-bottle of San Pellegrino. Plain, not the good lemon-flavor one.

I grimaced and dragged my brain back to business. I'd had enough practice working through fear this past winter. Just needed to get back in the knack of it. "Umm...honestly, I was just going to tell him I accept."

"What was the exact offer? All you said at the negotiations was that he'd made an offer and you had two days to decide, which I assume runs out tonight."

"Tomorrow," I said, still standing awkwardly in the living room. This was weird. I didn't like it. "How the hell can you just stand there, sipping your fancy water, like the last time we were both here wasn't because you'd thrown me in a half-frozen lake?"

He blinked. "Because it wasn't personal."

Resentment curled through me. "You're not the one who was sentenced to death for being what you were born as."

Troy froze, then took a breath and scrubbed his free hand over his eyes as though to hide the odd reaction. "I'm going to take a shower. Put your bag down somewhere and decide where you want to sleep."

"Are you staying here too?"

"Kind of hard to make sure there isn't another attempt on you if I'm not around," he said drily.

"So, what, you're the only one who gets to try to kill me?"

"Something like that."

I danced away from him as he passed me, flipping him off when he smirked. He grabbed some clothes from the bedroom and slipped into the bathroom, shutting the door behind him. If I'd been confused about what my life was turning into before, I was utterly lost now. Troy changing roles between executioner, parole officer, and bodyguard all in the name of whatever elven law or mission was most important on a given day was screwing with my head.

"Stay practical," I muttered to myself as I stomped into the bedroom and dropped my bag with more force than was necessary. If the elves needed me to live today and he was determined to play bodyguard to make sure his people got what they wanted—or avoided what they didn't want—then he could sleep on the couch near the door. I still expected him to betray me at the end of all of this, but better to face an elven prince than a rabisu. I'd already killed one of the former. I didn't have to like any of this, but I was a survivor. I did what I had to do. My options had just gotten stranger in the last few months.

Didn't mean I had to be naive about sleeping in the lion's den.

I pulled on Air just long enough to build a thin but solid wall of it in the bedroom doorway, cracking a window so that I'd have enough airflow to feel comfortable. I also wanted to test what Troy had said about me being able to leave if I wanted this time.

It was true. My fingers touched the breeze outside without a hint of the cramping that had had me writhing on the floor when I tried to leave during my last visit.

As soon as they crossed the threshold of the window sash, the bathroom door slammed open hard enough to jar the walls. A naked Troy, his black longknife in hand, burst out of the bathroom and plowed full-on into my wall.

I busted out laughing so hard I had to bend over, then squat, then finally fall on my ass with tears streaming down my face as

I completely lost my shit. It was like watching someone run into a sliding glass door, but better because it was this pompous naked ass.

"What the hell is going on?" His shout came through my wall muffled, as though he were on the other side of a closed door. By the time I had enough control over myself to wipe the tears from my face and answer, he'd found a towel for his waist but was still dripping wet.

"You forgot that I could do this, huh?" I grinned, fear gone for the moment.

"Take it down, Finch."

"Nope. You said pick a room. This one is mine now." Usually I forced myself to be the grown-up around him, but this was too precious to waste.

He slammed his fist against my wall. "Take it. Down."

I resisted the childish urge to say, "Make me." Leith had shown me that Aether could get through Air, if there was enough focus behind it. Troy was even more single-minded than Leith, so between that and the tag he'd put on me, he could probably get me to do it with enough time.

Instead, I lifted my eyebrows and said, "Your wards won't let anything evil in, right? Nothing from another plane?"

He must've scowled for a full minute before nodding, sending drops of water shaking from his hair. It gave me time to wonder what had made the long, jagged scar on his chest, dark against the tawny brown of his skin. Looked like someone had tried cutting his heart out the hard way at some point.

"Okay then," I said. "Now you know nobody from *this* plane is going to get at me if they make it past you."

Something ugly flitted across his face. "Leith broke you."

"He broke you too. Which of us killed him, in the end?" I snapped, my amusement morphing to anger at the reminder.

Yeah, I probably needed therapy to deal with all that, but there was no one to go to. "Good night."

Ignoring him, I went about getting ready for bed again. I needed another shower after the fight, but that could wait until morning, when I was less tired and hadn't just made a big deal over not taking my wall down.

I didn't sleep the rest of the night. A call to Doc Mike went to voicemail, and I had to assume that if the lich had sent a demon to make a point to me, he must have sent something after Doc Mike as well. If he had, that meant all of my friends were being held prisoner. My house was so trashed I couldn't sleep in it. I'd failed to get an alliance together and was left with Troy as my one ally because Callista had twisted the Volkovs away from me.

Troy. Of all people.

Curling into a ball, I swallowed hard to keep myself from crying. Elves had good hearing. I didn't need the bastard knowing I was at rock bottom.

From the look he gave me the next morning, my face gave it away anyway.

"How do you want to do this?" he asked, more gently than I'd expected.

"I don't know." I traced a swirl on the table, still trying to reconcile the last time I was here with now. "We can't trust the wolves. Vampires are no good against a lich lord."

"What do you mean, we can't trust the wolves?"

I looked up at the sharpness in Troy's voice, wincing as I realized he didn't know about Sergei. "Roman's brother is working with Callista."

Troy paled. "And you let him come to the negotiations?"

"What the hell was I supposed to do? All I have for proof is a scrap of paper with an Asheville area code, a phone call from a vampire saying they had a wolf of their own, and Sergei's guilty reactions. Roman wouldn't hear it."

"So you said nothing to anyone else?" He scrubbed his hands over his face. "You let us all just sit there and talk about how we were going to make our own alliance, in front of him?"

That stung because he was right.

"I was hoping to talk him back around!" I hated how defensive I sounded. Hot shame prickled down my neck. I hadn't thought Roman would bring Sergei. But I also hadn't thought to insist against it. I was screwing up left and right, and I didn't know how much longer my friends had. I needed to do better than this.

"Finch, I need you to tell me everything you know."

I crossed my arms and looked away.

"We don't have time for that. I have to find…a plan." I'd need to tell him about the other elementals eventually, but the longer I kept it to myself, the less time he had to plot something.

"I have to figure out damage control, or there won't be anyone left to fight the lich with you. I don't know how Callista found out that the Sequoyahs had been covering for Leith, but she did everything except burn the Sequoyah family house to the ground and salt the earth. The Lunas and the lesser Houses are sitting this one out, and the queens are inclined to let them."

My stomach soured even as I fought a smirk. I'd given Callista information after Keithia thought she'd mazed me into forgetting it, and I wasn't sorry about it. I didn't want that happening to any of my people though.

"It's all speculation," I said.

"Tell me anyway."

When I'd finished laying everything out, Troy just stared with sick admiration. "It's a good plan," he said when he'd wrestled himself closer to neutrality. "And it all fits."

"*Thank* you." I slapped the table, feeling vindicated. "Now, please tell me you're not going to war with the Volkovs over it."

"Nothing to gain and too much to lose," Troy said, rising to refill his coffee cup. "But we have to shore up the vampires."

"No. I need to do something *now*."

"What's the rush? What does he have on you?"

I just looked at him, my jaw bunching as I gritted my teeth.

"Fine," he said. "The coterie needs to do something now as well, if Torsten's enemies are being funded by the Volkovs and have been infiltrated by a witch-born vampire." He leaned against the counter and gave me a hard look over the coffee mug. "This is what happens when you try to go it alone, Finch. Whatever the threat is, it obviously matters to you. But how many people will die if Torsten is overthrown and these Modernists rush a Reveal?"

My throat closed, and my chest tightened. "Don't—"

"This is what it means to lead. You're in charge of the alliance. You have to make the tough call. That means shutting down the Modernists, right now, before they get more zombies."

I lowered my head to my hands, breathing shallowly to keep myself from throwing up. Maria was betrayed. Roman wasn't speaking to me. The enemy I was relying on to be my ally had just served up the harshest truth I'd ever had to face.

Unfortunately, he had a point. My friends were important. But with all of Otherside and the Triangle in the balance, I wasn't sure I could say that two or three people were more important than many.

Something in me died as I said, "I need to stop at home first. I'll meet you at Claret."

Chapter 28

The feeling that I was being pushed and manipulated again burned like acid in my veins and belly as I drove back home. Hot tears blurred my vision. I couldn't help but think that this was why I'd risked taking the Sequoyah case in January—so that I wouldn't have to bend over a barrel and compromise myself to solve everyone else's problems.

Sure, there was a necessary element of give and take in any relationship, including this alliance. But why was it on me, a sylph, to sort out a problem that Torsten should have dealt with months ago? This wasn't an interspecies issue. At best, I was nothing to the vampires except a convenient bit of leverage to be used against the elves. A growing soft spot for Maria didn't mean I was obliged to set my problems and my friends aside to fix shit they'd let slide so far that they found themselves splitting into Old versus Modern vampires.

"What fucking business is it of mine?" I muttered to myself as I pulled into my driveway. I got out of my car and stormed into the house, blowing through like a tornado as I geared up with everything I hadn't taken with me already. "None. It's none of my business. But here I am."

A gust of wind snapped from me, knocking a framed picture from the wall and making me even more cross as I stomped through the house.

My stock-up brought me to my bedroom for another knife. Zanna must have cleaned up, because the broken glass and tea mug were gone, as were the remains of my bedding. My anger cooled as I called out my appreciation, just in case she was in the crawlspace under the house. The longer I looked at the bare bedframe and boarded-up window though, the more anger flickered to life again, burning hot somewhere deep inside.

This lich had kidnapped my friends and then attacked my house. My *home*, my refuge from all of the bullshit I'd been putting up with. I couldn't even stay here because of him. Aside from my shattered bedroom, the sense of evil layering the house was still thick enough to make my skin crawl—and I was about to spend more time solving the vampires' problems instead of my own?

"I'm a fucking doormat," I said to the violated room. My words echoed strangely, the air not following the patterns it used to with the furniture in disarray. Even my power wasn't working as I was accustomed in here.

Unable to tolerate it any longer, I snatched my phone out of my butt pocket and redialed the number the lich had used.

"You said I had two days," I said in a tone so harsh it hurt my throat. This was the last thing I wanted to do. Sometimes, that was the thing you had to do first.

He has my friends. No more wasted time.

"I lied. Besides, my pet liked the taste of your magic," he replied in a voice like termites chewing through rotting wood. "And I like the taste of this doctor of yours."

My guts went cold. He had Doc Mike. And he kept the rabisu as a pet? "You admit to lying? How can I trust that you'll let my friends go if I come to you?"

"You cannot." He sounded far too cheerful. "But you can be certain I will cut them into tiny pieces to use in my spells if you do not come."

Fear prickled over me, tight barbs of dread and certainty. "That, I believe."

"Good. You can be taught. Now, did you have something you wished to say?"

A cold sweat broke out on my skin despite the warm air. My stomach churned so hard I thought I'd be sick. "I…"

The lich waited. If he breathed, I couldn't hear it.

"I'm on my way," I forced the words out in a strangled whisper.

"Excellent." He gave me the location, and the phone clicked off before I could say anything else. The area was one I'd shortlisted in my research so I would have found him sooner or later. This was just faster. At least, that's what I told myself.

I muttered the directions to myself as I dashed into the kitchen and grabbed a pen and paper to scribble it down then jotted a note of appreciation to Zanna for the clean-up. I didn't know if she'd be back, but failing to acknowledge the fae was inviting trouble and that, I didn't need more of.

As I headed for the door, I double-checked everything. Reluctantly, I pulled my father's pendant from around my neck and went back to the bedroom, tucking it away behind the tied-off wall of air with Leith's pendant and the lightning arrow Mixcoatl had shot me with. That arrow was still live, and it sparked as though it recognized my magic. I grimaced and restored the wall.

That done, I repeated all my checks. I was stalling and knew it, but how the hell does anyone prepare to go serve a lich lord in the hopes of freeing their friends? I was talking to myself as I locked up, trying to convince myself I was doing the right thing. I couldn't help feeling like I should have gotten the alliance together before a crisis hit. Then none of this would have been necessary. Maybe it wouldn't even have happened.

Turning, I stopped short on my porch. My heart leapt into my throat. Troy was waiting in the driveway, leaning against his Acura MDX hybrid.

"You just did something foolish, didn't you?" His sandstone-and-moss eyes were harder than I'd ever seen them, and my yard reeked of Aether. How had I missed him pulling into the drive and drawing on enough Aether to shatter my shields? Where was Zanna? She must have gone to the woods. The house reeked of the rabisu's evil and she wouldn't want to be anywhere near that. Hell, I didn't want to be near it.

"That's none of your fucking business," I said, going for aggressive and hoping it covered my fear. "Shouldn't you be on your way to Raleigh?"

"You won't mind me following you down there then."

"I don't need a babysitter."

He scowled. "You're avoiding the question."

"Imagine that." I jumped down, skipping the steps, and went for my car. He was blocking me in, but I might be able to squeeze around him.

Something twinged at the base of my skull. I ducked and whirled, feeling silly until I came up and found Troy much closer than he had been and looking hella frustrated. I must have looked pissed off because he raised his hands.

"You're committed to getting this done. I get it," he said. "You were always going to go for it over anything anyone else came up with unless we—the alliance—came with you."

I crossed my arms and cocked a hip, not answering but willing to listen because hell, he was right.

"Call your boyfriend. Send him to Maria. Tell him it's a chance for the wolves to claim a favor from Torsten. He can strongarm the alliance without Sergei, and you'll have thrown him a bone to get over whatever you two are disagreeing over. You and I can handle the lich."

"Not that Roman and I are your business, but that's actually pretty smart."

"I know. It's almost like I was bred for it."

His blank face didn't match the bitterness in his voice. The combination stopped me from getting saucy. Something else was going on.

"Why are you insisting on going?" I asked instead. "What do you get out of this?"

"I have a duty."

"Fuck duty, this isn't a video game. What's your upside?"

He stiffened, almost imperceptibly. "You have your business. I have mine."

"Last time we did *business*, it didn't end well for me."

"For the love of the Goddess, will you let that go?"

Scoffing, I said, "Why? Because you were just completing a mission?"

"Yes."

I gave him a one-fingered salute and smiled sardonically.

Troy looked like he might explode. A flush darkened his neck, and his shoulders tensed. "I need leverage."

"Now we're getting somewhere. Against other elves?"

He gave me a tight nod and nothing else.

I studied him. Troy had too many allegiances for a man who was consumed by duty and loyalty. Species, family, the Darkwatch, who knew what else. From what I'd seen, he kept nothing for himself, which would bite him in the ass one day. Not my problem.

Trust was my problem. "I need assurances."

"You're still alive."

"I said *assurances*, Monteague, not threats." When he tensed again, I grinned cheekily and added, "And if you're fixing to draw some kind of blade on me, we'll find out if I've practiced enough to wrap your car around that tree. I bet that would be fun to explain to your insurance carrier."

"You never do what—Never mind. Fine. Go along with my plan and I won't let my grandmother or Evangeline have their way."

"So, I bend over backwards, and you'll be a decent son of a bitch? Nah. I like carrots better than sticks, and lemme tell ya, I am fucking tired of sticks from the rest of Otherside. You want this? Make it worth my while."

Aether crackled, and the scent of ashy marshmallows and burnt herbs flared as his fists clenched. "Do you have to be difficult? I know you haven't exactly been part of Otherside politics before, but this is not—"

"Bo-ring," I said in a sing-song as I spun on my heel and went for my car again. "And not an offer. Move your car, or I'll move it for you."

"Damn it, Finch," Troy said bitterly. "What do you want?"

That was interesting enough to pause. I looked back over my shoulder. The normally cool and composed elf was desperate, eyes pinched and nostrils flared. Very interesting, indeed. "You get Keithia to sign on to the alliance. No more bullshit and no games. The witches, weres, and djinn get their demands, no quibbling. If the fae want in, you accommodate those demands as well."

Troy's lip curled. "And what do the elves get? What do *I* get?"

With a sweet smile, I stepped back within his reach, trying to act like I wasn't afraid of him despite my pounding heart. "You get whatever the fuck you drove out here for. A shot at the lich and whatever leverage that gets you." I tilted my head. "You know, for the good of the mission. Which I'm sure will be for the good of the elves somehow. It's all you care about."

I don't know why I added that last statement, but it landed. Blood drained from his face then flushed back up. He opened his mouth, no doubt to say something nasty and intended to cut me down to the little elemental-sized box he thought I should shrink myself to fit into, then swallowed it. Progress, at last.

"Do we have a deal?" I asked.

Looking like he'd rather eat glass, Troy said. "We do."

We shook on it. A spark leapt between our palms, and I pulled back, shaking it. "What did you do?"

"Nothing. This time."

He was looking at me with enough suspicion that I believed him. "Fine. Give me a few minutes to call Roman, and then we'll go. You can follow me most of the way there, but you can't go in with me. I won't risk my mission for your honor and duty or the stick up your ass."

When he nodded, I turned away and pulled my phone out. Roman answered as the phone was clicking over to voicemail. He always had his phone on him, which meant he'd been close to just ignoring the call. Ignoring me. I pushed aside the hurt and repeated what Troy had said in a neutral tone.

"Help the vampires to preemptively demonstrate the value of the alliance," Roman said when I was done. "I can't decide if that's clever or stupid, Arie."

"Yeah, well, take it or leave it. I'm just trying to help."

"Why aren't you going, again?"

I sighed and hoped he took it for tiredness rather than frustration. "Because I have to take care of something for the mundane cops and I'm trying to do what I can to make up for…whatever you're mad about." When all he did was breathe at me, I added, "I don't understand why it bugs you so much that I can handle my shit and yours, but I'm trying to offer you a chance to *help me*. Like I thought you wanted. And in so doing, help yourself. Is that wrong?"

"No. I just wasn't expecting you to stop being so damn stubborn." Roman's voice was lighter than it had been in days, and some of the knots in my shoulders eased. "All right. I'll round up Terrence and Ximena."

"But not Sergei."

"Dammit, Arie—"

"Please, Roman, just please trust me on this. I know he's your brother. But something isn't right. What's the harm in going without him? Especially if it re-establishes you as the top wolf?"

After a few tense seconds, Roman said, "Fine. But you and I are gonna have a talk about it later."

"Okay," I said, purely out of the hope that saying it would manifest a later. "Be safe. I...I love you."

"Love you too." He almost sounded like he meant it.

I hung up. Troy was pretending to watch the chickadees squabbling in one of the pines in my yard when I turned back to him.

"Let's go," I called.

His bright eyes and tight smile in response scared me, reminding me that elves were hunters with sharp teeth and sharper minds, and this one was particularly dangerous.

Chapter 29

When we were a mile out from the abandoned historic cemetery Google Maps said was at the address the lich had given me, I flashed my hazards and pulled off the empty road. Troy pulled off behind me. I got out and rapped on his window. Cool, herb-scented air swirled out, mixing playfully with the heat of the day. I resisted the temptation to play with the zephyrs. No need to set off the elf.

"Wait here," I said. "Give me at least an hour."

"Is this the part where you tell me what he has on you?"

I crossed my arms, hugging myself as I looked down the road.

"Friends," I said in a quiet voice. Saying it aloud made it feel more real, and I hated it. "He has friends of mine. I don't need the lich doing something to them because you decided to charge in."

Troy pursed his lips and flicked his gaze over me emotionlessly then nodded as though that made sense. "Where would I be charging in to?"

He didn't give a damn about my friends or me. I decided to consider that a good thing. I dug in my pocket for the scrap of paper I'd written the address on, pinching it between my fingers when he tried to take it. "Wait here. I mean it, Monteague."

"You always do. You're as stubborn as you are reliable."

For him to consider me reliable meant something, even if I didn't want it to. Somewhat mollified, I released the paper and started back for my car.

"Finch."

When I looked over my shoulder, he was extending something small and black my way. Intrigued, I returned and stuck my hand out to receive a dot the size of a dime that weighed nothing and felt like plastic. "What is it?"

"Earpiece."

"No way." I peered at it, flicking it over with a fingernail. "Darkwatch tech?"

Lips pressed together and eyes tight, Troy nodded. "If you're caught with it, I'll say you stole it."

"Super-secret Darkwatch tech then. Cool." Butterflies fluttered in my belly. I loved new tech, but this was dangerous shit. Troy must really need this leverage to hand out something this valuable. It put me in a tight spot though, and I narrowed my eyes at him. "You just want to know who my friends are."

"We already suspected there were other elementals in the Triangle," he said, gaze suddenly hard as stone. "If the Darkwatch or the queens cared, they'd be dead. You're the only one powerful enough to be worth keeping under surveillance."

My guts squeezed in on themselves at the acknowledgement that not only did he know who the lich had, but that he had indeed been keeping an eye on me, as I'd suspected. I couldn't hide the anger in my voice as I said, "I'm flattered, I think."

He looked skyward and sighed. "Rub behind your ear and stick it there. The adhesive is waterproof, so don't try telling me you got sweaty and it fell off. I expect to get it back when we're done."

I did as he said, then pulled the tiny plastic tab covering the adhesive side and balanced the earpiece on my index finger like a contact lens to press it behind my left ear. "Like that?"

Troy's fingers were cool as they pressed against my jaw to turn my head, and I shivered at his touch.

"Perfect." He fiddled with a black box the size of a cigarette carton in his lap. "Say something."

"Troy Monteague has a stick up his ass and some awesome toys."

He scowled as he adjusted something. "I think I preferred it when you were scared of me."

"Of course you did." No need to tell him I still kind of was, even if we kept finding ourselves working together. "We good?"

"Good."

I checked my rearview mirror every quarter mile until I got to the cemetery. If he'd broken his word and followed me, he was good enough not to be spotted. I stopped at the rusting chain strung across the dirt turn-off, though it was practically useless with the rot in the wood fence it was wrapped around. The little track could have led to any abandoned farm or ramshackle house, but the creeping, stomach-churning sense of evil said it had to be the path to the lich's lair.

Ignoring the subconscious urging to turn around and leave, I took a few deep breaths of air scented with pine and tasting of decay as I unwrapped the chain, conscious of the fact that Troy could hear me and was probably judging me. Fuck it, he'd get his share of the crawling evil soon enough.

Loblolly pines had never seemed threatening before. As I drove slowly under interlaced branches, the late afternoon sun seemed to dim. The ground had an uneven roll to it on either side of the dirt track. Some of the lumps looked fresh, with uprooted plants and disturbed pine needles sticking out stiff and brown. My gorge rose as I realized they were graves. The entire area was a grave site, and whoever had been at rest here was no longer. Where were the bodies?

"Goddess," I breathed, counting. "Monteague, he's got at least two dozen zombies to work with, if the graves are any indication. Assume a hell of a lot more. Hard to tell exactly with the way all the trees have grown over everything. Hope you have a flamethrower in your bag of tricks."

I was suddenly glad to have the elf as backup—someone capable but I didn't give a damn about. This was not going to be pretty, and I wouldn't worry about Troy Monteague dying by lich. Either he wouldn't die, or I wouldn't particularly care.

After another quarter mile, a clearing spread wide. Dead, brown grass surrounded the tumbled remains of a large stone cross on a small rise. An opening yawned in the mound, lined with yellowed bones. I pulled up next to it, got out, and was immediately assailed by an even stronger sense of the same sickening feeling that had assaulted me at the last crime scene.

The clearing was cooler than the road had been, and utterly silent and still. That set my hair on end as much as the antlers pricking from the grass and feathers fluttering across the clearing with tufts of fur. It was as if everything that crossed the clearing died, including the sun and the wind. I reached for Air, and it was like pulling a hair out of chilled molasses.

"This is messed up," I muttered, trying to alert Troy but conscious of the fact that the lich might be listening, too. "How the hell is he dampening Air?"

I debated leaving my weapons behind and settled on a compromise. The Ruger and the elf-killer would come with me. The shotgun would stay in the car as backup. Someone would probably go through my shit at some point, so I wanted to spread it out.

The opening loomed. I hated going down into dark spaces. Visiting the lower level of Claret was enough to make me feel like I was suffocating. The air underground always felt smothered by earth and sometimes water, trapped when it wanted to move freely. I'd be at a disadvantage both psychologically and metaphysically even without whatever the dampening effect was.

Nothing for it. Doc Mike, Val, and Sofia needed me. With a last, soul-steadying breath, I ducked my head and went into the earth.

A single path with a downward slope took me deeper and it wasn't long before I needed to use the flashlight on my phone to see. Skulls peered from the dirt walls at even intervals, though whether they were magical or simply to mark distance, I didn't know. My skin crawled too much to have any chance at sensing magic like I did at Janae's house. Light beckoned, and I pocketed my phone, using a trailing hand on the wall to guide me. After a minute or two, the path abruptly opened into a cavernous space lined with rune-carved bones and lit candles. I stopped and stared, momentarily forgetting my fear.

"You arrived early. I am pleased that you are so eager to serve, little sylph."

I jumped, and the fear I'd controlled flooded back as a cadaverously thin creature, its pale skin stretched to translucence over bones that were a little too long, emerged from another passage. Long, lank strands of white hair clung in patches to an age-spotted skull. Pristine robes that were probably blood red in full daylight hung from his frame, as though they mocked the shape they graced. A grey sphere wrapped in silver hung on a chain around his neck, flashing incredible purples and golds as it caught light from the candles. His soul stone, maybe. Power radiated from him, like it did from Torsten, only instead of the thudding, warm heartbeat of glamour, it was the nauseating sense of a ragged fingernail across your soul.

I swallowed twice before I could speak. "I was worried about my friends."

Not what I'd intended to say, but the cleverness had bled out of my tongue.

The lich lord clapped and smiled broadly, showing rotted teeth. "You take me seriously. How delightful! Come, my dear. As a reward, you may see my other guests. After you hand over any weapons you brought with you, that is."

Once I grudgingly handed over my enchanted blade, he led me deeper into his lair, not thinking or bothering to search me further. The Ruger weighed heavy against my hip, hidden under my clothes. It would be useless against an undead lich lord, but it was better than nothing.

The witch-born vampire didn't make an appearance. I hoped that meant he was young enough that he still needed time to recover from the gunshot wound I'd given him at the morgue.

As we walked, I peered at the strange, thin pattern etched into the walls at random angles.

"Oh my god. Those are finger marks," I blurted. Someone— or more likely, many someones—had dug this tunnel. With their hands.

"Indeed. The old dead are delightful workmen. Well. As long as their sinews hold their bones together." He kicked a bone out of his path, as though it had upset him. "Discovering the necromancer was pleasing. It would have been better if he had control of his powers, but he serves ably enough as a conduit." The lich looked at me over his shoulder, the glint in his dead eyes telling me that something about using Doc Mike as a conduit had been intended to hurt me.

I bit my tongue so hard that I tasted blood.

"I am pleased that my lord is pleased," I finally said, forcing every syllable in a rough voice. It was infuriating and humiliating, but my friends mattered more. I had to play this fucker's game until I found them.

"You learn more quickly than I dared hope," the lich said. "How fortunate for you. The others needed to be coerced."

"My cooperation is dependent on their being alive," I reminded him, anger flaring to chase away some of the fear. Anger with him and with myself for being in another messed up situation.

"Oh, they are. Just maybe not all in one piece."

Bile rose as we entered another chamber smelling of unwashed bodies and old blood. A flame danced in the air, seemingly without fuel or support and casting a strange silver light. Chest-high cages lined the walls, making me wonder how long the lich had been here that he'd been able to literally dig a lair out of the ground and furnish a chamber like this. How long...and how many zombies we were dealing with.

"Arden?" a broken, male voice called. "Oh, please God, no. Not you too."

"Doc!" I darted to the cage his voice had come from and reached through the bars.

The hand that reached back for me was crusted with dried blood, showing dark marks where some of his fingernails had been pulled out.

"What did you do?" I said, too angry to be afraid as I turned back to the lich.

He stepped closer, and Doc Mike whimpered, dropping my hand and scrabbling back. "I told you, he needed convincing. Or rather, proof that his Christian god is not interested in saving him."

Dizziness swayed me. "And my other friends?"

The lich shrugged. Annoyance pinched his eyes as he gestured to the other cages.

I knelt before each one. A woman I didn't recognize was in the one next to Doc Mike. Brown hair fell over a pale face streaked with dirt. Hard blue eyes stared back at me, wary and mistrustful. Something about her said elemental, though not Air or Fire. An oread, maybe, given the solid feel of her aura.

Val was in the next pen. Her tan skin was yellowed in the strange light, and she was unconscious. I reached through the bars to see if she was still alive.

Another woman's voice snarled from behind me. "Don't you touch her!"

I turned, spotting a young woman locked up across from Val. She was haggard, and a dirty bandage wrapped her left hand, which looked to be missing its little finger.

"Don't you dare touch her!" she said again, flinching back with a cry as the lich shifted his attention toward her.

"Do I need to provide another lesson?" the lich said.

"No." The woman's voice was barely a whisper, and she clutched her maimed hand protectively. Fear blended with fury and pain in a face that was a rounder, more feminine version of Val's.

"Sofia?" I said. "Is your name Sofia?"

"How did you know that?" she asked in a small voice.

I crossed to her and knelt, gripping the bars. "I came to find you. Find all of you. I—"

Fingers twisted in my hair and wrenched me up.

"That is quite enough," the lich said as I hissed in pain and barely stopped myself from drawing on Air to attack him. "You have seen your friends. They yet live. And shall, so long as you do my bidding like a good girl."

So long as you have use for all of us. I choked the thought down, alongside my rage and despair. How the fuck was I going to get all five of us out alive, even with Troy's help?

Chapter 30

The question echoed in my mind as I was dragged back to the main room. The finger marks in the walls took on a new meaning as I thought about putting my hands out to stop our movement away from the people I cared about.

"Where's your friend?" I asked, trying to refocus my mind. I had to hold it together. Whether Troy came or not, I needed information. "The witch-born vamp? He's your buddy, right?"

"Finding a meal for my pet. Fear not, you shall meet him soon enough."

I shuddered, both at the confirmation that the accomplice was strong enough to heal a bullet wound and to imagine what a rabisu ate. "Is your…pet…around?"

The lich waved a hand in a vague motion. "I can summon it back from the other plane, if you are so eager to reacquaint yourself. It will need to eat one of your friends though."

Remembered fear unsettled me as much as the boredom in his tone. "I wouldn't want to trouble you." I fought to keep my words steady. "So why am I here and the others are in cages?"

"Play with toys too much and they tend to break."

We arrived back at the main chamber and he halted, freeing me so abruptly that I fell to my knees.

"Good, you know the correct postures already. From here forward, you are chief among my tools in reshaping the world. I have allowed you leeway up to now because magical tools tend to twist in the hand if not treated properly, but know this: seek to turn, and you will watch your friends suffer."

My heart twisted and cold, invisible fingers slid over me. "I understand."

"Do you? You are remarkably pliant. I had expected more fight from one rumored to be as powerful as you."

"I just want my friends to be okay."

"So you say. *I* say that you are playing a long game." He smiled. "Play away, my dear. I have all the time in this world and the next to watch you fail. In the meantime, you will serve."

"Why remake the world?" I blurted out.

The lich tilted his head, studying me. "I will answer that. You should know my purpose if you are to serve it." He started pacing. The candles didn't flicker with his passage, which weirded me out as much as anything else about all this. "This world is broken. The humans have corrupted it. Poisoned it. The elves have failed in their charge, and the witches hide behind pacifism. But not me."

He clenched his fists. The knuckle bones cracked like whips.

"I will wipe the stain of humanity from this earth. I will turn their dead to my purpose, level their cities and restore the balance of our Mother Gaia. When I am finished, Otherside will be in balance with those humans who see the light of my reason. We will have harmony." His lips stretched in a grotesquely benefic smile.

I wanted to vomit. He truly thought he was the hero of this story. In a sick, twisted way, I couldn't deny that he might be. How many of us wished we could start over somehow, for some reason? His scale was just grander than most—and more horrific in cost, both to himself and the world. This wasn't the way. Raising the dead. Twisting the elements to rain destruction.

According to Neith and the scroll I'd found in Torsten's library, the gods wanted something similar. "We won't be denied our hunt," the goddess had said. I was a chew toy caught between a mastiff and a pack of wolves.

"Fuck," I muttered.

For an undead guy, the lich moved fast. I barely saw his hand before the slap rocked me back on my ass.

"Lesson one," he said. "I will not have such language. You will keep a civil tongue. That includes addressing me as 'my lord' or Master Gideon."

Lacking anything clever or wise to say, I nodded, working my jaw. He raised his eyebrows and I forced myself to say, "Yes, Master Gideon."

"Excellent. Lesson two. Your power serves mine. If it serves well, I shall reward you. I have already told you what will happen if it does not."

"Yes…Master Gideon." I hated everything about this. It burned in my blood, and the humiliation of it redoubled when I remembered that Troy was listening to everything.

"Good." The dampening effect lifted, and I breathed deep—until he said, "Now blow out the candles."

I looked at them, sensing a trick. His hand came up again, and I embraced Air. I'd learned with Leith Sequoyah that being slapped silly wouldn't help anyone, least of all me. Keeping my eyes on Gideon, I sent a gust of Air strong enough to bend a sapling to the ground toward the candles. It should have extinguished them all. They barely flickered.

Gideon grinned his rotten smile and made his way to a throne made of femurs and ribs against the far wall. "Again."

I threw almost everything I had at the candles. One went out, sending purple smoke twisting downward. The bizarre behavior gave me my first hint. This wasn't any kind of magic I'd encountered before, which meant it had to be soul magic. But whose souls?

I changed tactics and tried depriving them of air, sending the molecules fleeing. That earned me applause, but no more candles went out. I tried smothering them with more pressure. Cracking a whip of air at them, breaking the bony shelves they rested on...nothing worked. I was being defeated by some goddamn candles, to the point of trembling with fatigue.

How long had I been at this?

I stopped and moved closer to the freaky fucking things, trying to sense them the way I did Aether. I could tell when a djinni was coming, if I wasn't distracted or tired, by the way Aether and matter shifted. I could also read the shape of elven use of Aether, the way it tugged on something I could sense but not see. Janae's life magic gave me goosebumps. If a djinni could teach soul magic, surely I—being half djinn—could learn its shape?

The flame of the nearest candle shifted colors as I focused on it, from a normal, cheerful orange-yellow to blue and purple. I gasped, not knowing what it meant but allowing myself to fall into it. I needed to find the key to destroying the soul amulet. If the lich was inclined to teach me to achieve his own dream, so be it. I'd take the lesson.

Something in the flame called to me. Fire and Air blended, wrapping around something else. A negative space? I pushed that to the side. If it was Aether, I could only manipulate it as Chaos—the two halves, elven and djinn, blended. But the essence of any candle was Fire. I thought of the fire Mixcoatl had kindled in his hands, trying to remember the shape of it. I'd used Fire once, sort of, when I'd pulled Mixcoatl's lightning arrow from my shoulder. I rolled that shoulder now, looking for the spark of Fire in the remembered pain.

I found it.

Burning agony washed over me as I grabbed for it and tried to pull it from the flame. Howling, I dropped to the floor, slapping at the heat of invisible fires licking over my aura, sending all the air from me as I tried to stop burning with metaphysical fire.

Heat disappeared in a wash. I laid on my back, shaking with pain and exertion as Gideon toed my shoulder. "What an unexpected result. Splendid, my dear." He stared down at me, the parchment-thin skin of his face drawn in thought. "That is enough practice for today. It is time to rejoin your friends."

I tried to find the energy to fight, but I was a quivering mess on the verge of being unable to hold my shields. All I could summon was a glare, delivered through the straggled curls that had come loose from my bun and stuck to my face with sweat.

"You hate me. Good. It will keep you focused on improvement." Gideon smiled, his thin lips stretching in a rictus that didn't match his honey-sweet voice. "After all, if you get good enough, you might defeat me one day."

He echoed the thought I'd come into this with, spitting it back at me with cutting mockery and cheerful scorn as he reached for me.

"Don't touch me," I said, snarling. My stomach knotted and plummeted as I pushed myself unsteadily to my feet.

Amusement kept him from punishing me for the outburst. With a chuckle, he bowed and swept his hand toward the tunnel leading to where my friends were caged. "After you, my lady."

When we got back to the prison room, I balked as he opened an unoccupied cage on the end and pulled an incongruously new-looking padlock and key from somewhere in his robes.

"What, no room with a view? I thought I was special," I said. Troy might be coming in behind me, or he might not. I couldn't rely on him. That meant being free.

"Earn it," Gideon taunted. "With loyal service. Or resist and be an animal like these others. It will be your choice, sweet sylph." When I didn't move, his face contorted, and evil lashed me. "Move."

I retched as it curled around me, and obeyed. The lich lord hummed a jaunty tune as he tucked the key into his robes and left.

"Bastard," I said when he was out of sight...but not too loud. At least if I was here, I could check on the others. Silver linings in a shitheap. "Val?"

A groan answered me.

"She's been in and out," Sofia said. "She kept fighting that...thing...so he's using her to power whatever that light is."

"I didn't realize she had that much juice," I said, eyeing the silver flame.

"That's why she's unconscious. She doesn't. None of us do." The bitterness tingeing Sofia's voice sharpened. "Except maybe you. You're Arden, aren't you?"

"Yeah."

"Thanks for this."

I looked at her, peering through the bars of an empty cage to hers. "Excuse me?"

"If you hadn't shown off with the elves and reminded folk what we were capable of, do you think we'd be here?"

"That's enough, Sofia." Doc Mike shuffled closer to the front of his cage, kneeling to lean against the bars. "No one should have to live in hiding. Not you, not me, and not Arden. Bickering amongst ourselves resolves nothing."

I swallowed the lump in my throat, touched by his words. "Thanks, Doc."

He nodded, his face drawn with pain and exhaustion. "Now please tell me you have a plan. I—I don't want to be used anymore. I won't."

"Okay then. Time for full disclosure." I paused long enough to read the air currents, looking for any sense that something was moving. Gideon didn't breathe, but he did fidget with his pendant. It was hard to tell with the dampening effect back in place, but I was reasonably confident we were alone. Still, I lowered my voice as I said, "There might be an elf coming behind me."

Terror washed over the face of the woman I didn't know, and Sofia looked around as though Troy might appear from another plane like a djinni.

"As if this could get any worse!" Sofia said.

"He already knows there are other elementals in the Triangle," I snapped, tired of her attitude. "It's my head he wants. I just happen to be more valuable alive for the time being."

"An elf, Arden?" Doc Mike sounded doubtful. "Like Santa's little helper?"

"More like Legolas as a commando," I muttered, equal parts tired and amused at the mental image of Troy in Christmas get-up.

"He's *Darkwatch*?" Sofia cried.

I ignored her outburst and focused on Doc Mike. "Look, Doc, I will answer every question you have. *After* we get the fuck outta here."

"I'm in," Val said groggily. "And so is Sofia. What's the plan?"

"Glad you're still with us," I said. Relief loosened some of my muscles. I fought my exhausted mind and tried to remember what Troy had said about liches. "Apparently, if a lich lord has enough strength, he can use his magic to bind elemental power for his own use. From what I just saw, he's already working on it. Gideon said he wants to remake the world, so I assume that means our quiet friend is an oread?"

"I'm Laurel. Laurel Kerr," the woman said in a faintly accented voice. Scottish, maybe. "And yes."

"We're in your element," I said, waving at the hard-packed earth walls. "Is there anything you can do? Or read?" I didn't know much about how the other elements worked, but if I could read Air, I had to assume the others could read their own elements.

"He's dampening it. That damn bauble around his neck seems to control everything."

"It's soul magic," I said. "We need to get that stone. It's not just the key to the dampening magic. It's the key to killing him."

"That's it? Just get it from him and we can leave?" Doc Mike asked.

I winced. "Um. No. We have to destroy it. To become a lich, a corrupted sorcerer severs his soul from body and mind. It goes in the stone. The first catch is that it takes a djinni to do all this and the same djinni to *un*do it, unless one of you knows how to wield the powers of primordial creation. The second catch is that the gods won't be forgiving if I tell them I have the stone but not the djinni."

"Gods. Plural?" Doc Mike asked.

"Djinni? You're involved with elves *and* djinn? And which gods?" Sofia said on top of him. "Val, you never said—"

"Shut it. Both of you." The flame overhead flickered as Val fought to stay conscious. "Options, Arden?"

"I think I'm your option."

Troy's voice came from a spot of shadow along the darkest wall, one I hadn't noticed before he spoke.

I jumped, and hope flickered in me—not something I'd ever expected to feel around the Monteague prince. I smothered it. Collaborating with him would cost me something. It always did.

Sofia made a small *eep* and Laurel swore as the shadows fled, revealing Troy.

"That! That's what I saw at the—"

"Not now, Doc," I interrupted. Too many people's business was getting aired, and I didn't need my friends added to Troy's hit list for knowing too much.

Chapter 31

Troy crouched in front of my cage and examined the padlock before pulling out a lockpicking kit. "Nice job on the intel," he murmured as he worked the lock. "I guess that means I keep you around another day."

I frowned, not sure if it was a joke or a threat blended in with the compliment. "Thanks. I think."

The lock clicked open, and he pulled the door wide. I wrestled with exhaustion and won, dragging myself out and leaning against the cage.

"You don't look so good," Troy said, pressing the kit into my hands as he studied my face. His focus on me suggested that he was being very careful not to see anyone else in the room. Decent of him. "Are you up for this?"

I nodded once. "Gonna have to be."

"Good. You free them. I'll get that amulet before the demon comes into play."

"No! What are you—" I cut off with a disgusted noise as he wrapped himself in shadows again and disappeared. "Fuck! This is why I work alone," I muttered as I worked the locks on each of my friends' cages in turn.

We were a ragged little bunch. Sofia and Laurel supported a woozy Val between them. The flame overhead flickered, threatening to go out and plunge us into darkness as Val moved away from it. Doc Mike danced from foot to foot, looking from them to the tunnel. "Unless y'all can work shadows, you're going to need to be real damn sneaky," I said in low tones. "As far as I can tell, the lich's only weaknesses are that he's certain he's superior to us and he doesn't get, or think about, modern tech."

I handed Doc Mike the cell phone and car keys the lich hadn't thought to search me for. "Get out of magical range before his apprentice comes back and call Roman or Maria. Tell them everything you've just heard."

"How far is magical range? And what about you?"

"Just get as far as you can, okay? You can hide out at my house. The address is programmed into the car." Janae's would be better, but I didn't want to risk sending the lich her way if we messed this up. Zanna could go to ground if there was trouble.

A roar of outrage accompanied a wave of Aether. We all froze. Val, with her first responder's training, recovered first, then me.

"Let's go!" I said as Val shook her sister. I darted ahead of them, praying to all the faces of the Goddess that the accomplice was with the vampires and that Gideon would be too busy with Troy to notice us—or summon the rabisu.

When I ran into the chamber, my jaw dropped as I skidded to a halt. All of the damn candles were an eerie green. Sparks flashed as Troy battered with Aether and his black longknife at a dark, auratic shield surrounding the lich. That the blade was holding up suggested it was both meteoric steel and enchanted. Troy bellowed spells, sending Aether to sting at the shield, only to be repulsed.

Shit. He was good, real fucking good, at making it through shields. It looked like the lich's magic played by different rules. Troy was even stronger than I'd thought if he was still fighting against what I sensed being thrown back, but this wasn't something he could handle alone. He was in over his head.

I pulled on as much Air as I could hold and pushed it at the lich in a massive punch when Troy stumbled back from a counterspell. The creature staggered, turning on me with fury in his eyes. "How dare!"

"Shit!" I dove to the side as a slash of magic I could only half sense streaked toward me.

The distraction gave Troy an opening. He pressed his advantage, forcing Gideon back, trying to get the lich down. I picked myself up, groaning, and tried to figure out how I could help without knocking out Troy in the process.

The amulet.

Troy's Aether stings couldn't get through, but what if Gideon's stagger meant his shields were attuned to Aether and not the elements?

The lich was shouting in some language—ancient Greek, maybe. Not one I spoke. If I were him, I'd be calling zombies or the rabisu. We didn't have much time. I fought off exhaustion to focus, staying in the shadows along the edges of the room and using the wall as a guide. I don't know if Troy saw me moving, but their fight shifted so that I was facing Gideon's back.

Time slowed as I steadied myself. With the fastest, steadiest whip crack of Air I'd ever loosed, I snapped the fastener holding the chain around Gideon's neck. The stone dropped to the earthen floor, unnoticed as the lich lord snarled in pain and refocused on Troy. Blood trickled from my nose as I eased forward, a sign that I'd used far too much Air today and was pushing myself beyond limits I was still figuring out. If I could get the amulet away from his auratic field, that had to help. Maybe Doc Mike's necromancy could work on it in the absence of a djinni.

"Oh, honeysweet. Of course you got yourself mixed up in this. And this time, you've damned your friends as well."

I whirled, heart jumping into my throat, to face Grimm. "No. Not you."

Duke had said a djinni had to have been involved in creating the lich. I'd thought her lack of interest at Torsten's library was just typical self-interest—as in, there was nothing in it for her. I was wrong. If she was here now, that meant there was *everything* in it for her. She'd been misdirecting me, and I'd fallen for it.

She grinned, her eyes flashing ruby and staying there as she strode forward like an avenging empress. "Why not? I'm sure Duke told you how much a soul goes for on the *sūqu*."

I danced back as she swiped at me with clawed fingers, her blood red hair swinging. "What could be worth breaking the Détente?"

"Being mistress of a new world, of course. One where the Détente won't stop me from taking back everything I've lost."

I stabbed at her with an arrow of Air, but she went misty, shifting to the smoke and fog of her true form to evade it. Smoke and fog…both were made of air interspersed with solids or water. I had to be able to use that, even if using more Air would hurt.

Troy and the lich fought with Aether and soul magic in the background, spell and shouted counterspell clashing like swords. When Troy had fought Leith, the elven princes had been silent except for mutters and whispers, the way Othersiders had been taught to fight amongst themselves to avoid notice. I could practically taste the desperation from both of them though. Gideon must not have expected to face a challenger so soon, but Troy had probably never encountered soul magic. Troy's life energy flared against Gideon's undeath, only to be washed under in turn.

"Grimm, stop this." I tried a whirlwind, hoping to scatter the air in her if I couldn't topple her solid form, but she was too fast, shifting from this plane to another and back to evade me. "We were like sisters!"

"And you chose the elves." She came at me harder than she ever had in training, shifting to a furious sandstorm, then a bird-headed woman with wings and curved talons in place of her fingers. "You ungrateful little bitch! We kept you safe!"

I drew the Ruger, still hidden in its inner pants holster, and fired. It was loaded for elf or human, not djinni, and the lead bullet would barely slow her down, but at least she'd know I was serious. The only person here who had a chance was Troy, and that assumed his blade was actually meteoric iron and not just fancy black steel.

Ichor dripped for all of a heartbeat before the bullet wound healed. With an ugly, hateful look twisting her expression, Grimm lunged for me.

I scrambled backward. "Monteague!"

Grimm's fury flashed to horror as the black blade erupted from her chest. Her ruby eyes flared bright as she screamed and fell. Behind her, Gideon's cry echoed hers.

My heart stopped, and I looked up from where she lay clawing at the sword to see Troy borne down with Gideon's hands around his throat as he reset his body from throwing the blade. The elf bellowed as soul magic crested. Before I could think about what I was doing, I bent and wrenched Troy's sword from Grimm's back, dashed over, kicked the amulet as far from all of us as I could, and skewered the lich.

The longknife crunched through Gideon's ribs. He twisted his head around at an impossible angle to look at me. "You wretch!"

I withdrew the longknife and stabbed him again, then dared a grab past him when my elf-killer fell out of his robes as he fell and started writhing. With his djinni sponsor wounded and lacking the amulet's power, the lich was a reanimated corpse with terrifying magical strength—but still a corpse. Corpses could be incinerated.

My hand burned as I tugged the bone shelf holding some of the strange candles. A shoulder blade came loose from the wall, spilling a rainbow of fire over Gideon. He screeched worse than before.

However badly he was hurt, he wouldn't die until and unless the amulet was broken. Leaving Troy to recover his breath or his wits or both on his own, I scrambled for the amulet. Icy cold seared me as I grabbed the chain and carried it back to where Grimm lay gasping on the floor. Bubbles popped on her lips with every breath.

"Break it!" I shoved it in her face.

Dark blood stained her teeth and spilled over her lips as she sneered a smile. "No."

"Dammit, Grimm, why—"

She lunged at me again. I danced back, but she caught my ankle and tugged me down, pinning me by the throat as she drew a dagger from the air. Grimm's being weakened by the unhealing wound in her chest was the only way I blocked her first stab, losing my hold on Air as bronze skidded past my guard and bit into my forearm. Troy's blade spun out of my grasp. She twisted and started another strike, aiming for my thigh and the big artery there.

"Grimm, don't!" I caught her arm and wrestled with her.

"I've been waiting for years to put you down. Ninlil was a fool to lay with that fucking elf. To bear his filthy child!"

My fumbling reach for Air connected, and I swept her arm to the side. The bronze knife sank into the dirt as I scratched at Grimm, wondering why she took it and didn't go misty.

Aether crackled. Grimm snarled and turned to face it—and Troy opened her throat with a sweeping blow from his longknife.

"No!" I screamed, pushing to my feet.

A subsonic boom rumbled, and I rolled to shield my face with my arms as shards of smoky quartz burst from what had been Grimm. On the other side of the room, Gideon screeched again.

We'd need to deal with him somehow, but I was rooted to the spot in shock, staring at the crystalline glimmers in the light of candles that were now crimson and black. "Why, Troy? We needed her to break the amulet!"

He frowned, breathing heavily. "I had a choice. You or the djinni. Would you rather it'd been you?"

"But—"

"Look at it this way. You killed Leith. I killed her. Now we're even. There has to be another way to destroy the amulet."

I stared up at him, feeling utterly lost. Grimm had been a manipulative, psychopathic bitch. She'd hidden more from me than I'd ever know and had directly harmed me on more than one occasion before this one. But she'd also had a hand in raising me. Her death meant that Duke and Callista were the only ones left who knew my full story and that they'd be less inclined than ever to sell me a piece of it.

A new, breathy screech from dozens of throats interrupted my attempt to process that Grimm, and any hopes I might have harbored toward figuring out why the hell the gods were so interested in me, were well and truly dead.

Footsteps pounded toward us.

"Arden!" Sofia burst into the room, panting and wild-eyed. The others stumbled in behind her.

"We couldn't get out," Val said. "Zombies are swarming."

Laurel was supporting a rattled-looking Doc Mike. "I tried, Arden," he said. "God help me, but there are too many of them and I don't..."

"Great," Troy said, raising his longknife and peering into the dark. "Until that amulet is broken, the lich can reanimate and his zombies won't die, even if the necromancer could lay them to rest. Can you do it, Finch?"

A hollow ache grew in my chest and tears of frustration burned. The djinni who'd created the amulet was dead, scattered to crystalline shimmers in the dark. Troy was right—there was another way. But I couldn't wield the primordial forces of creation. I didn't even know what they were. All I knew now was that if I didn't try something, we'd be overrun by zombies.

I picked up the smooth stone. The icy burn was lessened now, so that it felt like it had just been in the refrigerator and not in some sub-zero nitrogen container. "I don't know."

The screeching echoed again.

"Try. Make it fast," Troy said as he moved to stand in front of the rest of us.

Val hesitated before joining him, bringing a small flame to life in each of her palms.

I ignored him, trying to fall into the stone like I had the candles earlier. Blood dribbled over my lips again as I traced the magic within. Soul magic made a void that I couldn't see and didn't understand. Life was blended through it as well, a brightness I could see but not touch. But as with the candles, the elements were present. Earth made up the stone. "Laurel, come here!"

She dropped to her knees beside me. "What do you need?"

"Can you, I dunno, lend me some Earth? Or find an anchor for it in the stone? Guide me into it somehow?"

"I can try." She rested a cool hand over mine.

Hisses and roars filled the chamber as zombies poured in. Val grunted and threw flames that the zombies didn't seem to notice until they consumed a limb. Troy fought like a whirlwind, hacking off pieces that kept crawling toward us or their fallen master.

I fell deeper into the stone, guided by the framework Laurel built. She couldn't touch the soul magic either, but her power created a structure that I could follow, making it easier to find the gaps. A dismembered hand clutched my thigh and I recoiled, losing concentration. Doc Mike darted in, praying to Jesus and all the saints as he pulled it off and *pushed* with a force I could feel but not comprehend. A clear space opened around us.

As I tumbled deeper still, I found the heat in the stone. It had been born of magma. Fire. Like the arrow of obsidian and lightning. Val had said Fire was sympathetic to Air. "Val! I need you, too!"

The bursts of flame stopped as the dea settled on my other side. I extended my free hand, and she clasped it.

"Show me the Fire," I gasped, drawing hard on Air then harder still. I thought of feeding oxygen to a roaring flame, of sparks in the night, of volcanic lightning. I remembered tracing the chords of Air and Fire as I drew the arrow from my shoulder. Finding lightning in it.

"Hurry, Finch!" Troy slashed and snarled a word of Aetheric power. The zombies roared, and Troy roared back as he was swarmed and carried to the floor. Aether crested, stung—and went out, extinguished.

I couldn't worry about him. I almost had it.

Fire and Earth curled through me, flowing like lava through tubes of Air, carving new channels in my soul. A bolt of lightning zapped from my palms, burning as it sank into the amulet and erupted, blowing the sphere into pieces in my hands. Chips of hot stone narrowly missed my eye, biting into my right eyebrow and tearing my hands to shreds. Laurel and Val fell back with shouts of surprise and pain. Zombies screamed. The candles blew out, and the room fell utterly silent except for the sound of my breathing.

"Are y'all okay?" I whispered.

The voice that answered was not any of theirs.

"That was a clever trick," Mixcoatl said from somewhere in the darkness. "An elemental with *two* elements?"

"Perhaps she is a worthy Mistress of the Hunt after all."

I didn't recognize the new, androgynous voice, but it had the same resonant weight as the other gods.

"Perhaps." A ball of flame bounced into existence, leaping to dance on Mixcoatl's fingertips. The other god shifted to stay in the shadow, and the galaxies spinning in Mixcoatl's eyes created a light of their own as he knelt to examine first me, then the other elementals, then Doc Mike and Troy, all now unconscious. I wasn't dead, so unless I was delusional, he was here, on this plane. That couldn't be good. What had changed to make that possible?

"And perhaps not," he said, swiping some of the blood from my face before I could stop him. First Neith, now Mixcoatl. Two gods with my blood.

"Offer me this as sacrifice, and I'll burn this chamber for you," Mixcoatl said with a sly smile. "You've done the hard part. Give me my due, and I will do the rest."

I took a breath to answer and swayed.

"What's the catch?" I asked when the dizziness had passed.

"For me to know and you to find out." The deer hoof spools in his ears trembled as he laughed silently.

"Then no. I'll do it myself." I'd made enough shitty deals in the last two days.

Mixcoatl shrugged and licked his fingers clean like a cat. "Your loss."

"Hey!"

"Mmm. Tastes of power. You have potential after all, sylph. We'll see how far it takes you." Then he was gone. No shimmer or fade, like a djinni, just...gone. The fire went with him, leaving me in rot-scented darkness.

Chapter 32

Earth weighed overhead, seeming heavier now that the lich was gone and his magic was snuffed out. Kneeling there in the endless dark, unable to sense anything, made me feel as though the roof might fall at any moment. With the addition of exhaustion, the gods, the pain in my hands and face, the silence, and the darkness, I was hovering on the edge of what I could take without breaking. I'd be trapped here, under the ground, never to feel the brush of Air again. I had to get out.

First though, I had to find my friends and destroy whatever remained of the lich. My sense of direction was fucked, and the first step I took landed on a fallen zombie, turning my ankle and tripping me. Whether Troy or Val had taken it out, or it had dropped like an undead puppet when the lich had died, I didn't know. When I caught myself, the burns and shards of stone in my hands sent more pain lancing up my arms. I allowed myself to cry out and the threatening tears to fall. I could be strong again once I'd gotten out.

I pulled shards from my palms by feel, sniffling as I tugged them free and threw them aside. Fortunately, the amulet hadn't slivered. That would have been worse. My hands still hurt, but I patted the floor until I found the Ruger. I holstered it, then found my knife and gripped it, doing my best to ignore the spikes of pain.

One by one, I found the others and shook them awake. Doc Mike quaked like an aspen under my hands as he found his feet. Laurel didn't seem much better. Sofia, who seemed the least shaky of the four, lent Val an arm.

"Do you still have my keys?" I asked Doc Mike.

"Yes," he whispered.

"Good. Take my car and go. With the amulet broken, I should be able to destroy what's left of the lich." *And figure out what to do about the elf who now has confirmation of elementals in the Triangle.*

They didn't argue. As their feet shuffled away down the main passageway, a groan and the sound of shifting bones made me freeze. I held my breath, trying to figure out what it was and where it was coming from.

A rough voice said, "Finch?"

My breath shuddered out. Troy was still alive.

"Finch, are you—" He broke off with a grunt and a hiss of pain.

My knife seemed to spark. It was eight inches of lead-infused steel, crafted by a tomtar smith and imbued with fae magic to protect me from elven hunters. I'd baptized it in Leith Sequoyah's heart. I could use it again and be free of Troy.

I wavered, unable to convince myself that he still deserved it. He'd drowned me and he used me at every turn. He'd only helped me here because it served him and his fucking mission. His grandmother wanted the lich dead, so he'd condescended to fight with me.

But that was the key thing: he'd fought with me.

Protected me and my friends instead of taking the first opportunity to escape when Grimm and the lich went down. We were elementals. He shouldn't have given a damn about us.

Heat curled through my chest, too hot as the conflict raged within me. I opened my burnt hand and released it, screaming as my palm blistered anew and a splash of Fire ignited the far wall. It hit the still-twitching Gideon and started consuming the lich's body.

Troy's sharp intake of breath pulled my attention back to him. Blood and filth smeared his handsome features in the firelight. A mark too dark to be a bruise circled his throat in the pattern of strangling hands. His breathing was too short, and he was clutching his left flank. He was wounded, badly, and half-pinned under fallen zombies.

I could finish him. Protect my friends. He knew who they were now. Saving us today didn't mean he wouldn't follow his duty and kill us all tomorrow, if he was given the order.

His eyelashes fluttered as he realized the same thing. For the first time, I saw fear in him. Fear of me. And it felt fucking good. It would be so simple to end him, right here, right now, then walk away. I had two elements now, apparently. Who else could say that?

"Finch." Troy's eyes darted from my face to the knife and back. He didn't plead or beg, he just looked at me.

Something niggled in the back of my mind, and I shook my head to clear it, squeezing my eyes closed, pressing the heel of my unburned palm to my forehead and wanting to be out of this hole and back in the free air above. Free. Air.

My mind shoved those two words together over and over. If I killed Troy, my friends might be safe—for now—but I'd have to deal with Evangeline and Keithia. They didn't want me breathing any air, let alone using it. They certainly wouldn't want me at the head of an alliance that would provide me with my own power base in the Triangle, and they wouldn't just ignore my fellow elementals.

Like it or not, the prince had kept up his end of the bargain. He'd spoken for me when Evangeline had demanded my head as the price of the alliance. I had to trust that that was enough.

Troy slumped when I opened my eyes.

"Remember this," I said as I knelt and put the point of my knife under his chin. He tipped his head away, snarling soundlessly, and I shifted to keep the knife tight enough to draw a bead of blood. The points of his second set of teeth flashed as outrage burned in his gaze. I locked eyes with him. "Leave my friends alone. They were never here. They don't exist."

"What friends?" he said in a growl.

I took that to mean we had an understanding. Rising, I sheathed the knife, shoved a zombie off of him with my heel, and extended my hand. With a wary look, he gripped my forearm. I gritted my teeth at the abrasion of his clothes against my palm and pulled him up, settling his arm over my shoulder.

"I want what you promised. House Monteague, in the alliance. No fuckery. No more threats. Or I finish this." I elbowed him and was rewarded with a pained grunt.

"My word is my bond," he replied grimly when he'd gotten some of his breath back.

We staggered out together, our path lit by the evidence of my growing power blazing behind us as fire consumed the lich and his zombies. Troy nudged me in the direction of his car, hidden amongst the pines as mine had been at Jordan Lake.

Ruptured graves lay everywhere, spilling open like burst abscesses. The clearing was already starting to warm as summer's heat broke through the dispersing magic. It would probably stink to high heaven in a day or two. Any humans who dared come near to investigate would be turned back, subconsciously, by the lingering sense of evil. But eventually, someone would discover this site.

We had to accelerate the Reveal, before this or another incident forced our hand. And if I let Callista lead it, she'd do something to screw my little group in the process. Not only that, but the lich's accomplice was still out there somewhere. I could only pray that the rabisu stayed on its natural plane without someone to summon it and the source of evil gone.

"We can't let Callista finish her negotiations with House Sequoyah," Troy said as we reached his black SUV, his thoughts apparently paralleling mine. He leaned on the door and unlocked it with a touch.

When he tried to get in on the driver's side, I used the arm I was supporting him with to tug him away. "You're not driving."

"It's my car."

"You can't even walk, and you think I'm gonna let you drive me anywhere?"

He glared down at me. Our faces were too close for anything more than an impression of ire, but I stared right back at him until he acquiesced. "Fine."

When we were settled in the car, he dug in a bag at his feet, coming up with a drug store first aid kit. I snorted a laugh as I turned us around and got us on the road out. "Seriously? The Darkwatch can give you next-gen tech but not like, some kind of mini field hospital?"

"Shut up and drive. And don't mess with my seat settings."

I snickered and tapped through the car's heads-up display, wincing at every touch with my burned fingertips, until I found an address for Chapel Hill, one that seemed like it should be his safehouse. He grunted and didn't protest, looking silly with his torn shirt hiked up around his chest, a square of gauze between his teeth as he tried to clean a nasty-looking bite mark just above his belly button with an antiseptic wipe.

"I didn't expect you to actually help us," I said as I pulled back onto the main road, curious about his motivations in spite of myself. "You could have been rid of me and some—of my friends."

"The greater good, Finch," he muttered around his gauze. "Hunting weak elementals wasn't the mission, and believe it or not, it's not all about you. Or them. But while we're on the topic of you, how long have the gods thought you had potential?"

"Uh…" I grimaced. "I thought you were out for that part."

"Hard to miss an interplanar visitation." He transferred the gauze from his mouth to his belly and taped it over before rolling his shirt down. Hazel eyes flicked to me before he continued his self-evaluation and tended to a set of gashes that looked like nail tracks down his left forearm. "If we're going to work together, I need to know things like that."

My gut clenched like I'd been kicked. "Since when are we working together?"

He snorted. "You're setting up an alliance. You take my advice and send Volkov to the vampires. I jailbreak you. We're working together." When discomfort didn't let me answer, he added in a grave voice, "Don't worry. I don't like it either. But we've still got a rogue sorcerer and maybe a demon to hunt, so I'll take you and an alliance over doing it myself. Or trusting the Conclave to find it worthwhile enough to do something about it before the Triangle burns."

"How generous," I said, letting myself sound as utterly unimpressed as I felt.

He didn't answer. The miles fell away as we made our way back to Chapel Hill. Troy made me avoid 540, pointing out that the toll road had cameras and his people had access to all the footage. It made the journey longer but I was just as eager to avoid being seen in his car as he was.

I did call Roman from Troy's phone on the way back. "Hey, it's me," I said when he picked up. "You're on speaker."

"Babe? You all right? Whose phone is this? I got a fucked-up call from your medical examiner on your number. I can be there in—"

"I'm fine, Roman. Thanks." I smiled and something icky and tight in my chest eased. He hadn't been this warm in days. We'd be okay. Especially now that the lich was burning. The evil should start to fade across the Triangle. "We got the lich, but the witch-vamp and possibly a rabisu—a demon—are still out there. Are you okay?"

I could hear the savage smile in his voice when he said, "Hell yeah. Good fight. This alliance might work after all."

That eased another knot. "Good. Great. Is Maria okay?"

"She's looking at me like a stoner eyeing a hot pizza, but we'll manage. Say hi, Maria."

In the background, Maria snapped, "Tell that fucking elemental to get her ass back to Raleigh. I want this deal finalized. Now. And then I want to go kill something."

"Something else, she means," Roman said with a little chuckle. "How soon can you get here?"

I glanced at Troy and winced when I found him watching me, studying my face like he was learning something. He shook his head and pointed at the heads-up display when I lifted my eyebrows. "I'm, ah, I'm actually heading to Chapel Hill first. Can you have Janae send a cleanup crew to the lich's lair? It's a pyre. Open graves, burning lich. I can't read the magic, but they should be able to." I swallowed as the pain of Grimm's death rose up. "There's also a dead djinni."

"Aw, shit, Arie. Anyone you knew? Wait—Chapel Hill? You're with that fucking elf bastard. Did he hurt you again? Did he make you call me?"

"That's *Prince* Elf Bastard, thanks," Troy interrupted in a surly tone. "And I haven't touched her. If we're talking alliance, I need to get Evangeline. Finch gave her car away and has insisted on chauffeuring mine."

I pressed my lips together to stop myself from laughing. I hadn't known Troy had a sense of humor. Maybe the alliance was encouraging him to be less of a dickhead. Or maybe it only came out when he was hurting and snappish. He frowned at me, and I forced my face smooth.

"Hurt yourself?" Roman taunted.

"Goodbye, Volkov," Troy said more calmly despite the pinch to his brow.

"Thought so. Arie, where we meeting ya?"

"Umstead is about as neutral as we're going to get, if we're trying to keep it close and fast," I said. The state park was right next to the airport, technically in Raleigh but close enough to neutral ground in RTP that everyone should be satisfied. "The Reedy Creek shelter? Midnight?"

"Gates'll be shut," Roman pointed out.

"Are you trying to tell me you can't pick a padlock?"

"Ha. Fair. All right, I'll tell Maria and the other weres."

"And the witches," I said, cheered by his laugh for all of a second before sobering again. "I'll...figure out something with the djinn."

"And the witches." He paused, as though weighing his words. "Be careful, Arie. Love you."

"Love you, too," I said, face burning. I didn't say the words often and had never said them where someone else could hear. But I'd nearly died today, and Roman had gone to fight on my advice, so Troy could suck it.

"I could consider that a conflict of interest," the elf said when I hung up.

I clenched my hands on the steering wheel. My healing abilities had kicked in, and my palms itched as they started to heal. "Wanting me dead and putting a magical tag on me is also a conflict of interest. Love and hate are two sides of the same coin, Monteague." I took my eyes off the road just long enough to bat my lashes at him.

"I don't hate you," he said, sounding even more tired than he looked.

"Funny, that didn't stop you trying to kill me."

He shrugged and looked out the window. "I don't make the laws."

"You seem to break them when it suits you."

That struck a nerve. He shifted slowly to face me again. "Luckily for you."

This was going to be such a fun drive.

Chapter 33

I was ready to kill both Monteagues by the time we arrived at Umstead. Troy had admitted broken ribs and a few wounds he couldn't tend in the car with a drugstore first aid kit. Between those and his sister's pointed comments, he'd worked himself into a shitfit. With his insistence that Evangeline make the alliance work she wasn't far behind, and that was before I used the callstone Duke had given me to contact him from the car.

Roman's battered Ford F-150 waited in the trees, just out of sight of the gate and hard to pick out in the waning moonlight. I slowed the car and rolled down the window as he ambled up and peered in.

"Arie. Princess. Prince Elf Bastard," he said with a nod and a sly grin.

Evangeline and Troy just stared back stonily, which made Roman smile wider until he sniffed and caught a whiff of me. "Lupa's teats, y'all smell like death."

"Roman, please," I said, letting him see how frazzled I was. "It's been a long day, and I would really, really like to get this wrapped up and get to bed."

"Sure, babe. Y'all are the last ones. I'll go shut the gates. You head on up."

"Duke came?" Given his stiffness on our call, I hadn't been sure he would.

Roman shrugged. "Yeah, but Arie, he's really not in a good mood."

I winced, and my stomach churned. "It'll get worse. I'll see you up there."

As Roman jogged for the gates, I pulled forward. We parked up at the Reedy Creek lot and made our way to the picnic shelter the direct way, going cross country over the hilly landscape for the short distance rather than sticking to the meandering trail.

A light beckoned through the trees. Evangeline jogged ahead, flowing over the rocky ground as easily as if she was on a sidewalk. Troy's jaw was tight when I glanced at him, though whether it was more from his sister or his injuries, I couldn't tell.

Evangeline was already sizing up Terrence and a woman I assumed was Ximena in the light of an LED camp lantern when Troy and I trudged into the clearing.

"Miss Arden," Terrence drawled, nodding. From the way Evangeline stiffened, she hadn't gotten the same respectful greeting.

"Obong Little," I said, grinning despite my exhaustion. The leopard's attitude was less grating when it bugged Evangeline.

I nodded to Ximena as well. She was even smaller than Maria, with broad features and long black hair, dressed in jeans and a magenta T-shirt with sensible hiking boots. Her accent was as Southern as Terrence's when she spoke. "My prowl call me Jefa, but you can call me Ximena," she said with an easy smile. "Seeing as we ultimately have you to thank for being included here."

I shook her extended hand and inclined my head. "An honor to meet you."

Glancing around the small clearing, I nodded to everyone else as well. Janae sat tranquilly at a picnic table, appearing as though she was communing with the spirits. Duke leaned against the big bulletin board with the park map—at the edge of the group, as usual—his carnelian eyes and the fog around his feet signaling that all was not well. Everyone gave him a wide berth.

Troy stayed by my side with his arms crossed rather than joining his sister, which struck me as an odd choice. Paranoia sparked at the back of my mind. Would she try something? Would he stop her if she did? I was too tired and there was too much at stake for me to have to wonder, and it made me both nauseous and grouchy. Keeping my face smooth with my thoughts roiling faster than my stomach was an effort. If I was lucky, he was just reminding people that he'd gone to fight along with me and had earned the right for an elven presence, just like the weres had.

While we waited for Roman to return, I crossed my arms and kicked a toe at the dirt, avoiding everyone's gaze. That I'd been willing to join the lich when this didn't look like it would come together was something I'd have to examine later. For now, I just felt gross.

"Where's Sergei?" I asked Roman quietly when he jogged up.

He scowled and leaned close. "You were right. As soon as we scattered the rogue bloodsuckers, he confessed. He's at his hotel now, shit-scared about what I'm gonna do when I get back. Arie…I'm sorry. I should have listened to you."

I nodded, vindication and sadness filling me in equal measure, then clapped and launched into the highlights of the fight against the lich when I had everyone's attention. Troy let me tell it, and I made sure to give credit where it was due, although I left out the other elementals and Doc Mike. I stumbled a bit as I got to the part about a djinn casualty. Everyone carefully avoided looking at Duke, especially when his form slipped from man to smoke for an eyeblink.

Next, we heard from Maria about the attack on the New Vampires. The three weres stood proudly as she acknowledged their aid and formally accepted the ceding of land to the Blood Moon wolves, subject to agreement from the Acacia Thorn leopards, the Jade Tooth jaguars, and House Monteague.

Terrence and Ximena lifted their chins and exchanged cat-like smiles as Terrence said, "So agreed. We'll have a private ceremony later to formalize it."

Everyone turned to Evangeline. The younger elf pressed her lips together, looking at each of us in turn—except me.

"Evangeline," Troy prompted.

She glared daggers at her brother. "I have some points of clarification."

I sighed. It would be wheeling and dealing, which could take all friggin' night. As a solo party who was supposed to be playing arbiter, I had nothing to say until they'd attempted to work shit out for themselves, so I wandered away to give them all space and remove myself as a possible point of contention. Evangeline would be trying to push some demands, and Terrence seemed to enjoy baiting her. She didn't need the reminder that an elemental would be the nominal guiding party in all this.

Exhaustion tugged at me and turned my eyelids to sandpaper. I prayed they'd wrap shit up quickly now that we'd all publicly demonstrated that we were willing to go to bat for each other, but I doubted it.

"You two should just hate fuck already."

I jumped and turned to find Maria behind me. "Excuse me?"

"You and the elf and whatever weird energy is going on between you two. You both tense every time you're in the same space, looking like you're ready to poke each other with your little knives, then go into battle together and turn up here looking like lifelong allies. Just fuck. It'll kill the tension."

"I'm not going to fuck Troy Monteague."

"What about me?" Maria smiled, charming and wide enough to show fang.

"Ummm. No."

"Why not?"

"Because I'm with Roman?"

She grinned even wider. "He can join. I know you find me attractive."

"Doesn't mean I'm going to do anything with you."

"Your loss, poppet." She pouted then made her way back to the others.

I glanced at Troy, praying he hadn't heard any of that. Then a piece clicked into place, and a cold knot settled in my belly.

Troy turned the instant it did, frowning at my expression before looking around, seeking the threat he thought I was reacting to. It confirmed my suspicion.

"Whatever he put on you, it's sympathetic magic. And it's evolving, I can't say how."

Janae's words rang in my mind, swirling with Maria's talk about connections. The tag Troy had put on me had become more than a simple tracker. Now it also told him my emotional state. As I focused on it, I realized it told me where he was in space. Which meant that it was probably also feeding me something of *his* emotional state. All those times I'd felt off, the weird paranoia and distraction…

Bastard! I stalked over to him and pulled him a step away from where he was keeping an eye and an ear on Evangeline.

"You were there." I hissed, outraged.

He blanched and gave me his full attention. "What are you talking about?"

"You were at fucking Claret!"

Maria's head snapped around. "Excuse me?"

295

The weres looked up, and I waved them off, annoyed at having underestimated vampire hearing. When they went back to their negotiations with Evangeline, I glared up at Troy and said quietly, "This, this whatever the fuck you tagged me with. There was no reason for you to turn around just now. Unless you *sensed* something."

I danced back as he advanced on me and Maria darted to my side, hissing with bared fangs.

Troy took the warning and backed off. "Whatever you think is going on, this is not the place or the time, Finch."

"Oh, I very much think it is," Maria said. "What is she talking about? I won't have elves trespassing at Claret. Not after the Sequoyah mess."

Troy's glance at Evangeline arguing with Ximena told me he knew exactly what I was talking about, and that whatever it was, he didn't want Keithia or the Monteagues or the elves at large knowing about it.

"The tag," I said. "It's sympathetic magic, isn't it?"

"What's sympathetic magic?" Maria asked.

Janae had looked up at the sharpness of my words and wandered over at Maria's question. "He's the net's weaver?"

"Yes." I glared at Troy, remembering the moment it had happened. I'd confronted him in the parking lot of a Harris Teeter, and he'd slipped through my shields with a zap. Then he'd done it a second time when I tailed him through Chapel Hill. Maybe a third time. I didn't know what he'd done until later, when he'd told Leith that he'd tagged me. All I'd known at the time was that Aether had stung me without the usual pain of shield breakage, and I reflexively didn't like it.

Troy grabbed my arm and steered me away from the vampire and the witch. "Stop talking about this."

"About what?" I asked, snatching my arm free. "The fact that your tag backfired? And I can track you if I try?"

"You can—what?"

I smirked as I stared up at him, beyond satisfied to finally have a card to play in our odd relationship. "I thought it was overactive paranoia or intuition, but then poof, you'd turn up right as it peaked. *Months* of this shit, Monteague. Then, just now, you turn around when I start freaking out."

"It shouldn't work like that," he said, disbelief and frustration coloring his tone.

"So I'm right."

"I didn't say that. I'm just saying—"

"No. You don't get to backtrack. Something went wrong with your tag, and now I can sense you." Even in the dim light I could see the blood drain from his face. It made me laugh. "You're screwed, huh? Take it off."

Troy stared at me, face blank.

"Take. It. Off."

"I can't."

"You—excuse me?"

"Frankly, Finch, I assumed you'd die before I had to worry about this."

It was my turn to stare. "Are you saying I'm stuck with you riding around in the back of my head?"

He folded his arms and looked at the ground.

"Seriously? What is it? What did you do?"

The skin around his eyes tightened and a muscle in his cheek twitched. "Nothing I have to explain to you."

"I'm sure Evangeline would love to hear about this."

Fury pinched Troy's face as he glanced between me and his sister the royal bitch. He might be a prince, but elves were matriarchal. She was already crown princess and would outrank him when she reached her majority—which meant she could sentence him.

297

"Too many secrets, hey, Monteague?" I said in a low voice, careful to keep a teasing note out of it. "You can't tell me about the tag, but you can't have Evangeline find out, especially if she also discovers who really stabbed her boyfriend through the heart. I can only imagine what would happen if I mentioned magical trespass."

Though it sounded mild, magical trespass was a grave crime. If I understood the nature of tag, Troy had essentially bonded me without my consent, even if he hadn't meant to do it. The elven Conclave of Queens might overlook it, since there was no intent, he'd done it to complete a mission, and they all considered me less than nothing. But the balance in the Triangle was precarious, and secrets were worth a life.

He started to answer, then shut his mouth as he searched my face. "You'd accuse me. For an accident."

"Bet your ass I would. To the highest bidder. If I make a new deal, I don't need you."

Troy steered me farther away from the group with a firm grip on my upper arm.

"Arden?" Roman called.

"We're fine!" I turned to flash him a smile and wave. "Right?" I asked Troy.

"Right," he said grudgingly. "Look. I—" He looked down at the ground and toed it.

This had to be the most anxiety I'd ever seen him display. It freaked me out. "What? What the hell did you do?"

"It's just a tracking tag. It should have faded and broken. On an elf, it would have."

"But?"

"But it's mutated somehow."

I stared, mind completely blown, before I could shake off my shock enough to say, "It's *what?*"

Troy spun away from me and walked to the closest tree then back. I glanced at the group to find Roman watching with a frown as he tried to work out what the hell was going on and keep his attention on the negotiations with Evangeline. Janae's lips were pressed tightly together as she pretended not to look, and Maria had her eyes narrowed in speculation. Everyone else was busy bickering over the points of the deal.

"I regret how I handled you," Troy said, "but—"

"How you *handled* me?" I barely kept myself from shouting as I stepped closer, my chest nearly touching his. "Take it. Off."

"I told you, I can't. It's designed to break by itself. My guess is that you have enough Chaos influence that it's warped somehow."

I was pretty sure he was right, given my heritage, but I'd be damned if I told him. Rage throttled me with hot fingers, choking every coherent thought that came to mind. "I hate you," I finally got out. "Highest bidder it is."

"Finch, stop. Think!" He reached for me but stopped when I looked at the offending hand like it was as foul as the lich. "If you tell them now, someone will move against House Monteague, and the alliance is shattered before it can be anything. Everything we've worked for."

"Don't you fucking dare act like there's a 'we' here."

"Fine. But do you really want to throw it away? Give me six months. I'll figure something out."

"Are you kidding me? Six months?"

"Do you think I like it? I wish we'd never crossed paths."

"Difference is, it's not my crime. Whether you meant for it to happen or not, I'm owed, Monteague."

He ground his teeth so hard I could hear them. "I acknowledge the debt. It will be paid."

A chill ran over me. I hadn't expected his sense of honor to kick in. I already had amnesty from his House. Could I get more? "This is a killing offense. It's paid by the rule of three. Pulling me out of a lake you threw me into and breaking into my bedroom don't count."

"Be reasonable. The rabisu counts."

I was winning. "It doesn't count because I didn't know what you'd done. Debts are paid *after* they're acknowledged. Swear it." When he hesitated, I leaned into his ear and whispered, "Swear it, and be glad I don't demand the debt in Monteague blood. I could ask for Keithia's head instead. Or Evangeline's. That would be the smarter option."

We both knew I wouldn't be that bold, if only because we couldn't afford to upset the balance in the Triangle further after the fall of House Sequoyah, but it was a truth Troy couldn't risk testing.

The bond flared hot as he said, "I swear that I will pay my debt in life, three times over."

"On your honor as a prince of House Monteague and an agent of the Darkwatch."

He repeated the words, glaring bloody murder at me. The knot of magic in the back of my mind was seething with a sickening roil of outrage and bone-deep shame. I was willing to accept that he hadn't meant for his mission to take him this far—and me along with him—but I was done being everyone's bitch after the Sequoyah case. I was owed, and I'd claim every hateful scrap of the debt.

"Nice doing business with you, Monteague." I walked back toward the gathering and let my triumphant satisfaction slap him through the bond. No, I wasn't above a last nasty dig.

I'd earned it.

Chapter 34

Duke jerked his head to the side when Troy and I returned to the group. "Since we're doing sidebars, I want a word," he said. "Now."

Triumph fled, and my heart thudded as I followed him a short ways off. "Duke—"

"Where is Grimm?" he asked in a dangerously calm voice.

A thousand answers formed and shattered. I kept myself in a ready stance. It wouldn't do much good against a being that could dematerialize and reappear wherever I managed to dodge but...instincts.

"I know she's dead," he said. "The gong rang in the ethereal realm, and she's the only one who can't be accounted for. Did you kill her?"

"No," I whispered.

"Then it was that thrice-damned elf." Duke was gone before I could blink.

"Monteague!" I hollered.

Both Troy and Evangeline looked up. Evangeline's eyes widened, and she drew a dagger as Duke rematerialized behind Troy. The elf prince ducked and whirled, coming up with his black blade drawn. Duke, as a furious cloud, smacked Troy and sent him hurtling back into a tree. The longknife flew from his hands as he cried out in pain.

The scent of burnt marshmallow choked the clearing as Evangeline snarled something in elvish. Duke disappeared and flashed back into existence behind her, choking off her spell with crystalline fingers wrapped around her throat. She stabbed at him ineffectively. Unlike Troy's, her blade was simple steel and silver. The few parts of Duke that were solid healed as quickly as the knife was withdrawn.

Maria, Janae, and the weres stayed back, though Maria looked ready to join the fray. Torsten's coterie had worked with House Monteague for at least as long as I'd been alive. They might only tolerate each other at the best of times, but that was better than starting over with another House if both heirs died.

"Arie? What now?" Roman said. His gaze darted from Duke throttling Evangeline to Troy gasping as he tried to get his wind back with his busted ribs.

Our alliance was going to break before it was even formalized. Callista would continue setting the terms in the Triangle for the next thousand years, driving a Reveal that would exclude the wants and needs of half of Otherside. She'd do whatever she pleased with me after that—but only if I let this happen.

"Arie?" Roman was one dead elf away from a shift, and if he went, Terrence and Ximena would likely follow. Then Maria. But Duke was family, or at least as close as it came for me. He was all I had left with Grimm dead and Callista estranged.

My heart broke as I made my choice. I dove for Troy's knife, scooped it up, and scratched a simple eight-pointed star in the dirt and dead leaves. With a toe on the converging lines at its center, I said, "Nebuchadnezzar, I order you to *stop!*"

Giving him an order without a talisman shouldn't have worked, even with invoking his true name, but the star and our blood tie was enough to get his attention. He froze, dropping Evangeline to cough in the dirt. I slid between him and the elves.

"Stop, Duke," I said again, quieter, keeping Troy's longknife between us as I raised the arm Grimm had grazed and pulled away the hasty bandage I'd slapped on while waiting for Evangeline earlier. It hadn't started healing. He'd know what that meant, but I spelled it out for our witnesses. "She had bronze. Monteague didn't have a choice, not if we were going to end the lich. Grimm...she made the lich. She was trying to kill me, and be sure of it."

"Lies. What are you covering up?" He swirled, trying to edge around me, a dark cloud with sharp teeth and fiery eyes.

I moved with him, feeling his words like a punch in the gut. Tears burned. How could he gaslight me like that?

"I should ask you the same thing." I forced the words out of a throat tightened by loss. "She said she wished she'd killed me sooner."

"She was being dramatic. As always." He glared at me as though I had overreacted, then narrowed his eyes. "If Grimm made the lich, as you say, how did you stop it if you killed the holder of its debt?"

Troy shifted in the dirt behind me and spoke in a voice heavy with pain and short on air. "Finch destroyed the amulet and killed it. With Fire."

Someone gasped. I didn't turn to see who or give Troy the kick in his broken ribs that I really wanted to. I'd hoped to keep that quiet until I'd had a chance to talk to Val. It seemed like it shouldn't be possible for an elemental to handle an element not their own. That I could, even if I burnt the shit outta my hands in the process, scared me.

"With Fire," Duke repeated, clearly having heard the difference between a lighter and an elemental power. "Oh, Arden. The gods won't be able to overlook this, or what you might become. What have you done?"

"Maybe if y'all had fucking explained things when I'd asked, I would know!" I clenched the longknife almost as hard as I gritted my teeth to stop the tears of frustration from breaking free. What did he mean about what I might become? Had I somehow tapped into powers I wasn't meant to have—the primordial forces mentioned in that old book?

From the look on Duke's face, he wasn't about to tell me now.

"Fate's edge, a blade in your hands," he said, his eyes flicking to it and back to mine. "Just as I saw. I knew it wouldn't end well, but I didn't think you'd turn on your own people. Now you'll never know."

I lowered the longknife and let my broken heart sing its sorrow in my voice. "Would I ever have known either way?"

Duke looked at me as he shifted back into the form of the lithe young man with dravite eyes. Tears streaked his cheeks in the light of the camp lantern. "That is not something I was gifted to see. I tried, Arden."

"I know," I whispered.

He was under at least one geas, probably set in place by Callista. Damn the woman. I'd thought it would be enough to get out from under her thumb. Now I understood that I needed her gone—for good.

I shook my head, resolving to deal with that later, and squared my shoulders. "Duke, I'm sorry, but you can't have the Monteagues."

His eyes shifted back to carnelian again. "The djinn are owed, Arden."

"No. You're not. In creating a lich, Grimm was in violation of the Détente. In trying to kill me without a particular grievance, she was being even more of a bitch than usual."

Duke's form started smoking. "She was blood. To both of us."

I wanted to ask then who Ninlil was. My mother, given the context, but who was she to Duke and Grimm? But this wasn't the time or the place, and neither time nor place would ever come again if I sided with Troy. What did I want more? My past? Or my future? I bowed my head.

"Don't do this, Arden," Duke said.

I forced all of my emotions into a box, crumpling them and shutting the lid tight, before I lifted my chin and spoke to everyone.

"If this alliance is to survive, no one is above the law, and no law is greater than another." I turned to give Evangeline and Troy a hard look. "Djinn Council law says that I give Troy to them, regardless of what Grimm was doing. Her quarrel was with me, not Troy, so blood is owed. Elven law says one of you two takes my head, or that of any other elemental, for something that happened millennia ago."

Before I could tell myself I was doing something ill-advised, I tossed Troy's longknife to Evangeline's feet and knelt, lifting my chin. "You can have me. But you give Troy to the djinn in exchange. Both laws are obeyed, or neither of them are."

"Arie, no!" Roman barreled forward. I embraced Air, threw up my hand and a wall, and tied it off, ringing the two elves, Duke, and me. Roman hit it so hard he bounced, stumbling away with a savage curse that was lost in a wolfish snarl.

I ignored the sound of his bones cracking as he shifted, forcing my tone even as I spoke to the princess. "Choose, Evangeline, knowing that you decide the fate not only of your House but of the Triangle."

Troy used a tree to help himself to his feet, the other arm tight against his ribs. He held his tongue and kept his expression blank, sensing the knife's edge we all walked. The bond between us was quieter than it had been in months. Even his emotions were locked down.

Evangeline picked up her brother's knife. She hardly seemed to breathe as she looked down at me, cold, calculating, and with eyes far older than her years. Then at her brother. Then at Duke. A chill gripped me as I realized she'd be a terrifying queen one day, when her tempestuousness was cooled by wisdom and control.

This might have been a mistake. I'd assumed she wouldn't give up Troy, but now I wasn't so sure. My heart thundered, and a cold sweat chilled the spring night as I prayed she wouldn't make an ass—or a corpse—outta me.

"To give a prince of House Monteague to djinn justice is intolerable," she said so quietly we barely heard her over the crickets and cicadas. She twisted her wrist and flipped the knife over it, catching it by its edge to hand back to Troy hilt-first. "You and your ilk keep your lives, sylph. But I will be watching closer than the gods for your betrayal."

I shuddered at the close call as I rose. We all turned to Duke.

"No," he said, shaking his head and morphing back to his true form. "No, I do not accept this elven bitch taking choice and justice both. I say, blood is owed!"

He dematerialized.

Troy's back was to a tree, so I scooted in front of him as fast as I could.

"I say, it is not," I roared in Duke's face as he popped out of the ether in front of us. "And you *will* listen!"

Force was the only thing he'd listen to, and Air didn't impress him anymore. I channeled all of my frustration, my disappointment and my heartbreak, into Air and Fire. Fire recognized me this time. It didn't want to come alone, but it would blend with Air.

When I pushed my hands forward, lightning crackled. I yelped in pain as it jumped from my hands and danced through the cloud that was Duke like heat lightning on a dry day.

Duke roared and fell away, smoke roiling furiously as he tried to expel or dampen the lightning. When it dissipated, he made himself ten feet tall.

"You dare!" he thundered.

"You're damn right I do! I have had *enough* of everyone acting like their laws and their agenda are the most important and that I should give my time and my fucking life for shit that actively harms me. I'm *done*, Duke!" I fisted my hands, throwing more energy into another crackle of lightning as blood dribbled from my nose and over my lips. "It was your idea for me to be arbiter. You don't get to decide you don't like the result now, not and have the djinn be a part of this!"

For long heartbeats, we stood at an impasse. Then, with agonizing slowness, Duke shifted to his man-form. When he just stood there, I sent the lighting to the ground. Dead leaves and pine needles smoked, but the earth was damp from recent rains and nothing ignited.

"Do you accept the judgement?" I said, voice shaking.

Hatred shifted to disappointment as Duke turned his gaze from Evangeline to me. "On behalf of the Djinn Council, I accept this judgement and the terms of the alliance, so long as the djinn terms are also respected. No more wishes. No more bottling." Bitterness twisted his full lips. "On behalf of myself…you're dead to me, Arden. Call me again, and I'll hang you from a tree by your intestines when I appear."

With a shimmer, he was gone, leaving me heartsick, nauseous, and full of doubt. Had I done the right thing? Wouldn't it feel better if I had? I bowed my head, just trying to breathe. All I'd wanted was to belong. To have a place of my own in Otherside. It shouldn't have cost this much.

The sound of banging fists reminded me that the wall of Air was still up. I pulled myself together and released the tied-off chord of Air after scrubbing away the trickle of blood. That was getting tiresome. I needed to rest before I temporarily lost the ability to handle Air. Everything hinged on my being able to bluff my way out of a corner with the threat of elemental power. No power meant no bluff—and I'd be fair game for anyone who wanted me.

Roman raced to my side as soon as his fists stopped meeting Air, squeezing my arms and shaking me. "What the hell were you thinking?" he said, love and fear and anger blending in a wolf's snout to make the words harsh.

"Easy, wolfling," Maria said as I pulled free. The weighing look she gave me held equal parts respect and consideration, as though I'd done a trick she hadn't seen coming. I suppose nobody would have anticipated the lightning, but I had a feeling it was more than that. Her expression became cunning when she looked at Evangeline, but all she said was, "Wise choice, princess."

Evangeline pulled herself up to her full height and nodded back coolly.

"Can we wrap this up now?" I desperately wanted to sit at one of the picnic tables, but Troy's battered ass was still standing, which forced me to stay upright to maintain appearances.

"I just need to know one thing," Evangeline said. Everyone turned to her. "If we're circumventing Callista, we need to beat her to the Reveal. Not only that but do it better. Monteague and Sequoyah aren't on good terms just now." She glared at me, as though it was my fault. "So who's going first?"

"So tetchy for one so young," Maria said. "Not to worry, summer child. Torsten has agreed the vampires must go first."

"That was too easy," I muttered.

Maria pinned me with her gaze, and I shut my mouth. "You only think that because you didn't lose half your coterie cleaning house," she said sharply. "We stopped the Modernists this time. We need to get ahead of them. My people may not be the healers that House Sequoyah could offer to dazzle the mundane masses, but vampires hold a kind of…fascination for humans."

Evangeline tilted her head, considering. "Your price?"

Maria inclined her head in a salute. "The alliance's help in rooting out every last one of the fools who sought to undermine Torsten and recusal without prejudice from the hunt for the rogue sorcerer."

"The first part sounds like it's Torsten's problem, not ours," Terrence said, echoing my earlier thoughts. "Especially given how much we've already done. I'll concede the second part. It'd be suicide to bring the undead to fight a witch who may have trained as a necromancer."

Ximena and Roman nodded their agreement. Janae kept her eyes on me and Evangeline.

Maria tilted her head. "Normally, I'd agree. It is our problem. But if the coterie's energy is going toward preparing for a Reveal—which, may I remind you, will be for *all* of Otherside— we need our allies to drain the traitors while they think we're occupied elsewhere."

Nobody answered her as they turned inward or to their most likely ally in the group to consider the implications. Getting involved in the internal management of another faction was unheard of, both in the asking and the doing. Shifting the power balance to our side meant intertwining the factions in a way that would have been anathema a few months ago.

Now? With the lich's near-takeover of the Triangle fresh in everyone's minds, along with Sergei's meddling and the threat of the genetic test developed by Verve Health Solutions? Asking for help and getting involved might be the only way we'd ensure our survival.

If there was anything Othersiders were good at, it was survival. We'd lived with humans this long by either pretending to be them, staying beneath their notice, or turning their minds and bodies. Announcing that their stories were real would open a Pandora's box for which none of us could anticipate the consequences. We'd need each other. And that meant transcending boundaries.

Everyone else seemed to come to the same conclusion. Faces firmed and shoulders squared. But rather than looking to Maria, they looked at me.

My heart pounded, and I clenched my fists to stop my hands from shaking. After months of limbo, they were all ready. And they wanted me to make the final statement. Me, the newbie, the least experienced in this kind of power brokering.

Peace comes at a price, I reminded myself. If I wanted everyone here to protect my right to exercise my considerable and growing power—if I wanted them to sympathize with me and see me as an ally, not a threat—I had to be part of the community. Not a disgruntled outsider carrying grudges. Not a quiet loner trying to forge my own path. Troy had steered me through the muddle that had sent the weres to aid the vampires, but if they were all looking to me, I couldn't rely on him for this or anything else in future. I had to lead, and lead by example. I had to be part of this, visibly, in action and not just in words.

My mouth went dry, and I looked at the ground, hoping it looked like I was deep in thought when really I was just trying to find enough spit to speak.

Maria tensed when I looked at her.

"I agree with the request. And I will help," I said. "On one condition. Any elementals who are currently or in future, resident in or visiting the Triangle, are not subject to the agreements here unless they agree individually. They are, however, protected. No more bounties on elementals."

"Already a different rule for the wereleopards and the werejaguars, and now for elementals," Evangeline said with a scoff, rolling her eyes. "And that's if we forget that we already have to ignore elven law in their favor."

"Evangeline," Troy said in a warning tone.

"What? What, brother? I speak the truth."

"You speak *your* truth," Troy pointed out, shocking me to hell and back. "We've hunted the elementals to near extinction. Finch is the only one left who's powerful enough to be worried about. I'll keep an eye on her, and our Queen has an agreement with her. Consider the future and let it go."

"It's not an equal arrangement," Evangeline said.

Terrence crossed his arms and frowned at her. "Equal and equitable are two different things, princess. We're not all starting from the same position. Some of us need a little time and a little help is all. Once we've caught up, we'll all be stronger for it. We'll all prosper, or at least be in a better position to integrate with humanity."

Evangeline's lilac eyes seemed to flash in the harsh light of the LED lamp. The muscles of her jaw bunched as she pressed her lips together, and I wondered if she was having trouble controlling her secret set of teeth again.

"Fine," she said at last. Haughty arrogance dripped from her posture and tone as she said, "House Monteague is in agreement. We expect the same commitments should *we* call for aid."

"The Blood Moon wolves are in agreement," Roman said, as soon as she'd finished.

"Acacia Thorn leopards as well."

Ximena grinned, her eyes lighting up. "And the Jade Tooth jaguars."

"The witches stand ready to offer aid, as we've promised. Starting with the lich cleanup and healing the Prince of Monteague, here," Janae said, pointing her chin at Troy. "You look like you're hurting, son."

I swallowed my fear of putting myself forward in the spotlight and said, "The djinn have agreed. I speak on behalf of the elementals and myself. The fae are not present, but they will be welcome should they seek to join their realm with this plane and the alliance."

Nobody objected. Energy quivered between all of us. I drew my knife and made a quick slice across the heel of my palm, then squeezed it over the center of the circle we'd made and let a few beads of blood drip to the ground.

"And so it is," I said.

The others followed me. The weres used claws and Janae had to borrow my knife, but we sealed the alliance with a blood pact. On impulse, I scooped up an acorn and pressed it into the ground at the center, squatting to cover it with a little dirt. Janae nodded, as though I'd done something right.

It was done. After months of negotiations, shitfits, battles, and pain, the alliance was agreed. By some miracle or curse, they all looked to me to lead us into the next evolution for Otherside.

Chapter 35

Roman drove me back to his place and made a 3 a.m. snack of steak. I tossed salad greens with some tomatoes and cucumbers, then joined him. We ate a few mouthfuls in silence. I was just tired as hell, but something seemed to be on his mind. It made the food sit badly in my stomach.

"What are you considering how to say?" I finally said, trying to keep my voice light.

He grimaced. "We can talk tomorrow when you've had some rest."

"I won't get any rest if I'm laying awake wondering what has your face all pinched up like that."

My nerves sharpened as he picked at a piece of steak, slicing the fat off with unusual precision.

"I'm leaving. At the end of the week," he said to his plate.

I frowned. "Like...for a job?"

"I'm *leaving.*" He didn't look me in the eye, focusing instead on wrangling the bit of rare meat onto his fork. "I'm going back to Asheville. That was the deal Sergei offered in exchange for my not telling the family about his misstep with the vampires and staying out of the last meeting with the alliance. He never wanted to be involved. Pops forced him to go instead of sending Vikki, and it got out of hand when Sergei got involved with Callista. So, I go back. He sponsors me. I pass a few tests. I settle down. With Ana, seeing as that accord still hasn't been settled and Sergei won't say why."

I set my silverware down, not sure I'd heard that right. "You've given Sergei a pass. And you're going to marry Ana."

He flinched. "We were betrothed. Before my...defect...was discovered."

That Roman had been separated from this Ana for years and hadn't mentioned her before his brother had appeared meant nothing to me. There was no reason for him to talk about a past relationship with someone he'd never expected to see again. But everything I'd had with him—and Sergei's betrayal—didn't mean as much as finding a place within his clan, whether I'd known it or not. Whether *he'd* known it or not.

I understood. Sympathized, even. I ached to find a place for myself and had sided with the Monteagues over the djinn to create one that included all of the Othersiders in the Triangle, not just the djinn and Callista. Knowing how Roman felt about his treatment growing up, he'd do something to make a place for others who didn't have enough magic to complete their shift, create an option other than murder or exile. He'd have a chance to do some real good at a point when the were community really needed to evolve to keep up with the changing times.

That Roman was only doing what I'd done to Duke didn't stop it from hurting. When he reached across the table, I jerked my hand away, grabbed my glass of lemonade, and took a long drink. Logic warred with angst inside me.

"Come on, Arie, don't be like that."

"Don't—don't be like that?" I hissed as angst won.

My heart was breaking for the second time that night. I'd told myself, over and over again, not to fall in love with Roman. I was an elemental in hiding and always someone else's tool. He was an exiled werewolf alpha with abandonment issues and a burning desire to return in triumph to the family that had cast him out. Our relationship was supposed to have been business and pleasure, not love, and yet here I was, childishly resenting him for not choosing me after he'd convinced me to choose him.

I closed my eyes and breathed. I was better than that. We all had hard choices to make, and they'd get harder with the Reveal. Roman going back to the mountains meant the werewolves would be stronger, and I'd have an ally there where I wouldn't have had one in Sergei.

This is what it means to be part of something. You don't always get to have shit your way. I scrubbed my face and resolved to be happy for him.

"I'm sorry, babe." Roman reached across and tipped my chin up, though he could only hold my gaze for a moment. "I'll always love you."

"It's fine," I said. "It's better this way."

His brows drew down, and he pulled away. "How can you say that?"

A frown pinched my brow so hard I thought it'd give me a headache. I was trying to be grown up about this, to be happy for him, and he was mad again? I'd thought it was the lich's corruption driving the tension in our relationship, but maybe it was just us.

"You're the one who's leaving," I said, careful and confused.

"What, by Lupa's teats, am I supposed to do? You're not even going to ask me to stay?"

I didn't answer. I didn't know what he was supposed to do. It wasn't my place to say, and if he stayed because I'd asked, it'd hang between us forever. This was his choice. I'd known when we started getting involved that it might come down to this but gone along with it anyway. I'd taken what I wanted—a shot at stability and safety—and now I would pay for it.

"Would you wait for me to see how things work out?" he asked, voice rough and eyes sad.

I recoiled as my heart clenched. "Roman, don't ask me that. It's not fair. Not when you're going home to be with someone else."

"You know what's not fair? Banishment at fifteen for something that's not your fault, like being born less than everyone thinks is 'normal.' Or, you know, I coulda stayed and fought to my death." His voice became even more bitter, even more savage, and his expression filled with wrath. "Should I have done that? Should I have stayed and fought and killed until I died?"

"Stop it."

"Would you prefer that? That I was dead and we'd never met?"

"*Stop it!*" The words echoed in his trailer.

I got up from the table and went to the kitchen, clenching my fists and turning away so he wouldn't see how much I was shaking. How much his words broke my heart. How could he ever think I'd wish him dead, or that we'd never met? Even as I choked back tears, the private investigator in me saw what he was doing, consciously or not. He was making this my fault, picking a fight so he wouldn't have to feel as bad for not choosing me when maybe, deep down, he really wanted to. I sniffled as a tear fell.

"Shit," Roman muttered behind me. His chair scraped.

I flinched as his heavy sigh tickled the back of my neck and his hands rested on my arms.

He didn't let go, even when I tried to tug free.

"Arden…"

"Let go of me."

"I need you to listen."

I jerked again, and he let me go.

"I'm sorry. I shouldn't have said those things."

"But you did," I said, unwilling to let it drop. I'd been manipulated for years by the djinn and Callista. Roman had been my haven. Only now, he wasn't. He was just another person who wanted me to fit myself in a box for him. Somehow, that hurt the worst of all.

The muscles of his jaw bulged as he gritted his teeth. "I did. I'm sorry."

"How long?"

"Huh?"

"How long were you going to ask me to wait?" Heat coiled in my chest as I retreated into anger, done with trying to be understanding. "Until you got back into your family's good graces? Until you were welcomed back onto Volkov pack territory? Until you got *married*? How long did you plan to ask me to put my life on pause for you to work things out? When did you foresee me getting my life back and moving forward again?"

He just stood there, looking like I'd slapped him, and I crossed my arms, glaring off to the side. Our food sat on the table, the fat on the steaks congealing as it cooled. The salad was wilting a little in the warmth from the window he'd cracked open to let in fresh air.

"I'll always need you," he said. Something in his whisper made me look at him. "Arie…" Roman reached for me again, and this time, I let him gather me into his arms, too heartsick and tired to stop him.

"Would you stay, if you passed whatever test, and they offered?"

"Yes."

"At least you're honest." Bitterness choked me, even as his woodsy-musky scent soothed me.

He didn't answer except to lean away and tip my head up for a kiss. That was always his solution, to smooth the sharp edges of our relationship with passion.

Fine. There was nothing left to say. I'd play his game one last time.

I bit his lip when it met mine, and he jerked away. Startlement gave way to determination at whatever he saw in my face.

When he leaned in again, I bit him again but didn't push away.

"It's like that?" Roman asked, something dangerous in his stormy grey eyes.

In answer, I raked my fingernails down his back. He snarled, a wolf's growl from a human throat, and pushed me back against the counter.

Whatever was between us, I still trusted him not to hurt me. He wasn't one of my elven captors. There was no burnt-marshmallow scent, only the musky cedar scent of werewolf. This was how we'd started things, with a mutual attraction, no strings attached, and more than a little bite in the sweetness of our lovemaking. I fell back on it now, allowing him to pin me and claim me.

We stripped with rough movements and jerks of fabric. When he carried me to the couch, I wrestled him for the top position, settling on him with a groan of frustration. It shouldn't feel this good to fuck someone I was mad at, but it did, and I rode him hard.

He gave as good as he got, moving with my rhythm, until we were both panting with exertion as sweat rolled down our bodies, mine dripping to his chest, his soaking the cushions beneath him. I arched back, and he pinched a nipple. He closed his eyes, and I dragged my nails across his chest. Neither of us drew blood, neither of us pushed beyond what we knew the other enjoyed, but it was the roughest we'd been with each other since we started dating. A release of all the frustrations great and small, giving pain even as we took pleasure.

"Arie, I'm sorry," Roman said again after we'd finished and dozed a while, my head on his sweat-sticky chest.

"I know. Me too. But you're going to do what you have to do, and so am I."

"I hate this."

I shrugged, my skin sliding against his. There was nothing to do and nothing to say. We might love each other, but love only stretched so far when blood and justice entered the mix. After both of us had been denied the comforts of both for so long, how could I begrudge him the chance to find them? "So do I, but I understand what this means to you. Just go with Sergei. Be happy."

"You mean that?" When I didn't answer, he lifted me with gentle hands on my shoulders. "Babe?"

"Do I think he's going to screw you over? Yes. Is it my place to stop you from claiming what should have been yours? Hell no."

"Even if that means I have to take their bargain? All of it?"

I shrugged again and repeated what I'd already said. "We're both going to do what we have to do."

Roman scowled, looking angry and disappointed. "How can you just…let go like that?"

"You think this is easy for me?" I tugged the thigh trapped between him and the couch free and stood, peeling our skin apart. I crossed my arms as I stared down at him. "I'm not 'just' letting go. I'm doing what I have to do as arbiter of this alliance and, fuck, just for me. I will *not* sit around and wait while you work out whether you're going to marry your childhood sweetheart so you can become alpha."

Something died in his eyes, even as it died in my heart.

When did I fall in love with him? Stupid, Arden. So. Fucking. Stupid.

"Stay the night?" he asked.

I nodded, unable to speak around the lump in my throat. When he rose and wrapped strong arms around me, I let him, needing a last little bit of the comfort I'd come to take for granted.

Chapter 36

I left at dawn, sneaking out before Roman woke, trembling and nauseous with an Air hangover that beat at my brain like yesterday's zombies.

Maybe I was a coward. Maybe he knew I was leaving and was being equally cowardly by pretending to be asleep. I didn't know, and I couldn't let myself care. I'd been strong enough through the whole ordeal with the lich. Everyone else had gotten the best of what I had to offer, and I had nothing left to give. I sat in the back of the Uber choking on tears that wouldn't fall, grateful that the driver had caught my mood and wasn't talking.

My car was in the driveway when I got home, but I assumed Doc Mike and the elementals were long gone. For the moment, I was too numbed by Grimm's death, Duke's disowning me, and Roman's decision to care.

Whenever I felt lost, I went to the woods. I didn't even go inside when I got home, just got out of the car and headed straight for the path down to the Eno River. If Zanna was home, she didn't come out to ask where I was going, which suited me just fine. I didn't want to talk. I just wanted to walk and be soothed by the taste of the wind moving between the beech trees.

The sun was rising as I reached the river path. I followed it to the boulder I'd heaved over with Air. A small pool had formed where the bulk of it had lain before, fed by a rivulet that made its way back to the larger river. I tested the rock's stability and climbed up, finding a flat spot crusted with dried mud. After kicking the worst of it off, I sat, arms folded across my upraised knees, and watched the sun come up over the river.

A belted kingfisher called, and a great blue heron flapped slowly through the mist rising off the water. I closed my eyes, seeking peace and reminding myself that, although there had been heartbreak and there was still more to do, I'd won. I'd gotten what I wanted: an alliance that could counterbalance Callista and give us all a voice in coming out—or not—to the humans. We'd determine our own futures. I smiled, finding satisfaction in that victory and settling into calm.

"He left you, didn't he?" Troy said from somewhere to my right.

My sense of peace shattered. I scrambled to a crouch, heart pounding, and wrestled past my hangover to pull on Air. He was leaning against a sycamore, in fresh clothes that suggested he'd gone home sometime between the alliance having been decided and now. I snarled at him. "Goddess, are you fucking stalking me now?"

He smiled, his usual smugness tinged with sick shame at the edges, and didn't draw on Aether despite my aggressive posture. "Just testing something."

"You couldn't test outside my woods? Without sneaking up on me?" I released Air, since he seemed more inclined to jab at my peace of mind than my body. "What do you want?"

"Did you sense me?"

Blinking, I frowned at him, then swallowed my extreme irritation and took a mental look at the space in my mind that I'd come to associate with the paranoia that signified his tag. It wasn't gone, but it felt like he was sleeping somewhere far away. "No," I admitted. "What did you do?"

He shrugged. "Good. That's good. For what it's worth, I didn't sense you coming either."

Which meant he'd been waiting somewhere in the woods and I'd been so preoccupied with myself that I'd missed him. I had to get over this Roman business, fast, before it got me killed.

"Does it buy me time?" he asked.

"Depends on how seriously you meant what you said to Evangeline about keeping an eye on me."

Troy sighed and gestured to my rock. "Can I join you?"

"Wow, you're actually asking instead of just doing whatever the hell you want. I might be impressed." When he lifted his eyebrows, I turned back to the river and said, "I'm not in the mood for company. But fine." Might as well reward him for asking. Maybe he'd do more asking and less pushing in future.

He grunted as he pulled himself up. Probably his ribs, still. The Monteagues weren't the gifted healers that the Sequoyahs were, and he was proud enough that he'd probably refused Janae's offer. "You shifted this?" he asked once he was settled, carefully not touching me.

I considered not answering, but if anyone had an idea of my strength—and could stand a reminder—it was him. "Yep."

"So you weren't bluffing about blowing my car off the road."

"Nope." The kingfisher that had called earlier zipped up the river. I watched it, wishing I could follow.

"Good."

That wasn't the response I'd been expecting. I side-eyed him. "You hate elementals. Why is that good?"

He shifted and scowled. "I never hated elementals. Feared, yes, and still do. Especially you. Elves have long lives and longer memories. But hate you? No. I didn't believe there were any elementals left. Besides, you're just so…lost, most of the time."

That made me grouchy. "You could have fooled me."

The memory of being tossed into the icy water of Jordan Lake rose and I slapped it back down, but not before my muscles clenched and my chest tightened in remembered fear.

Troy sighed. "That was a mission, Finch. We've been over this. More than once. And either way, I was following elven law. Not that it matters anymore, with the alliance."

I leaned away and sneered at him. "The law doesn't say what's good or right or moral. It just says who has power and who's controlled."

That finally sparked something in him. "I know that now!"

The burnt marshmallow scent of Aether tickled my nose, and I slid off the rock, choking down a retch as I drew on Air again.

Troy jumped down to face me, wincing and holding his ribs as he landed. "You have no idea—"

"I have every idea! I was raised by Callista and the djinn to fear elves. To fear *you*! Do you see me drowning people or putting magical trackers on them and treating them like criminals? No! I mean, Goddess, we're standing here arguing like civilized people because I choose not to let other people dictate how I behave!"

Troy glared at me, hands fisting. "I guess that makes you better than me. Congratulations."

That wasn't what I was trying to say, but as he said it, that was how I felt. "You know what? You're damn right it does."

The press of Aether crested. A breeze fluttered around us as I drew in more Air, stirring the leaves overhead. "Do you really want to come at me, Monteague?"

He held my gaze for a moment that felt like a year. "No."

The pressure fell so suddenly I gasped. An errant gust of Air split a rotting log and whipped the leaves overhead.

Troy jumped, but didn't reach for Aether again. "The Reveal is here, and we both know something even bigger is coming. We need to be allies."

I rolled my eyes and crossed my arms. "That was the point of last night."

"I mean you and me. The alliance is only as strong as its weakest links. If we're busy fighting each other, someone else will exploit it."

"You need to admit I'm a person."

He looked at the ground. "You're a person. You always were. That's what made all of this so hard."

I recoiled, feeling as though he'd punched me. "What? Then what the hell was..."

I waved my hands, at a loss for the words to describe our interactions to date. His icy disdain and emotionless threats, the tag, the dragging me before Queen Keithia, who most certainly *did* hate elementals in general and me in particular.

"I needed distance. I needed you not to be a person so I could do my damn job and uphold my oath." Troy glanced up and away again then slumped, looking ten years older. "I can't anymore, Finch. You have every quality I was raised to admire, stuffed into the form of my people's worst nightmare, but I can't pretend..."

Swallowing, I asked, "Pretend what?"

"Nothing."

"Then that's the most backwards-ass apology I've ever heard."

Eyes hardening, he advanced so quickly I didn't have time to move away. "Is that what this is about? You want an apology for me trying to do my job? Completing my missions?"

"Yes," I whispered past the lump of fear in my throat at the invasion of my space. "You don't get to say you were just following orders. I deserve better. Much better."

He held my gaze.

I stared up into moss and sandstone and stood my ground.

"I'm sorry."

I blinked, not having expected him to actually say it.

"I'm sorry I wasn't wise or brave enough to find another way. I'm sorry I used you. I'm sorry the tag warped. I'm sorry that you're so afraid of me right now that your eyes are glowing like the sun and I'm waiting to get blown away by a freak tornado."

I took a shuddering breath and let go of Air, not realizing I'd taken hold of it again, and Troy backed up.

"Okay," I said.

"Okay?"

"Yeah."

We studied each other. I had no idea what this meant, other than that maybe I would have one less reason to be looking over my shoulder. Adrenaline drained from me, and I rubbed the goosebumps from my arms. "Doesn't mean I forgive you. You pulled some fucked up shit, and that's on you to atone for. It definitely doesn't mean we're friends."

"Can we be allies? For real, and not just because of circumstance?"

I took my time considering him and my answer. "Yeah. I guess we can." I didn't fully trust him, but we both had bigger enemies. "Until you try to kill me again."

He scowled. "I won't try to kill you again. I wasn't even trying to kill you the first time, or I would have succeeded."

"Coulda fooled me," I said again.

"You're infuriating."

"You're a dick." I smiled sweetly. "Does this mean you'll help me get the Lunas and the Sequoyahs off my ass when we're done with the rogue sorcerer?"

"Will you stop bringing up the Goddess-blasted lake if I do?"

"Maybe. No promises. You don't just get to forget that you hurt people."

"Somehow I'm sure you'll make sure I don't," Troy said drily. When I flashed my eyebrows up and down in agreement, he extended a hand. "I deserve that, so I guess I'll live with it."

"And do better?"

"And do better."

I shook his hand and managed not to jump at the tingle of magic that always seemed to jump between us. I suspected he'd come here more because it benefitted his people and his House than because apologizing was the right thing to do and I didn't like it, but that would have to do for now. Otherside had to put aside differences if we wanted to survive the Reveal. As bad as we were toward each other, humans were worse. Allowing ourselves to be divided was a recipe for disaster and, eventually, the end of Otherside.

That's if the gods didn't finish us all off first.

Triumph and pride nestled alongside trepidation and the broken pieces in my heart as I watched Troy disappear into the forest. I might have lost Duke, Grimm, and Roman, but sometimes growth meant letting go of what or who you couldn't take with you, to make space for something bigger. The alliance was bigger than all of us, and having it meant that I and other elementals might have room to breathe for the first time since Atlantis. The world was changing. I was doing my best to change with it and claim something for myself in the process.

For the first time in my life, I'd have a voice in what happened to Otherside—and to me. I chose to find the silver lining and chalk this up as a win.

Acknowledgments

I was admittedly overwhelmed (in the best way) by the support I received for *Elemental*. So many people shared it, bought it, read it, and reviewed it. Some were people I hadn't expected, or hadn't heard from in years. Each and every one of you helped heal a piece of my heart that past experience and mental health struggles had broken. You showed me that people *will* be there for me and do want to help. From the bottom of that healing heart, thank you for taking a chance on me and my story. Thank you for restoring my faith.

The biggest thanks go again to my family. The books I write aren't the kind they usually read, but they not only cheered me on and bought T-shirts (literally), they also took the time to read the book. To have that kind of support as I worked on *Eldritch Sparks* meant the world.

All my friends and extended family using their platforms and connections to talk up my book, thank you.

A big thank you goes to Jeni Chappelle, who edited *Eldritch Sparks* and helped me work out a few thoughts for future books whose seeds needed to be planted here, as well as offering so much support.

A thank you also goes to Stephanie, who beta read both *Elemental* and *Eldritch Sparks*, providing the pointed, insightful feedback authors need to improve early drafts.

I would be remiss not to acknowledge the effects of George Floyd's death and the rising adoption of the Black Lives Matter movement in the attention my writing and I have received. *Elemental* launched a few days after Juneteenth 2020, in a period when people were suddenly looking for more Black authors and stories. I know that some of my success rides on the pain and guilt of others. It's an inextricable part of what it means to be a Black writer in the US. *Eldritch Sparks* will launch shortly after the US general election in 2020. All I can do is vote, and keep writing, and pray that in my writing, non-BIPOC will connect with characters like Arden. Pray that you see us. Pray that you support our lives—not just our human right to live, but our livelihoods, our work, our ideas, our voices. Thank you.

Also by Whitney Hill

The *Shadows of Otherside* series
Elemental
Eldritch Sparks

The *Flesh and Blood* series (as Remy Harmon)
Bluebloods

Praise for Elemental

"Arden is a winning protagonist, pushing against PI stereotypes in small but telling ways, and the denizens of Otherside—particularly the vampires and djinn—have well-developed personalities. Hill also has a fine ear for dialogue and a good sense of timing, and the story builds steadily and believably, resulting in a genuine page-turner." —*Kirkus Reviews*

About the Author

 Whitney Hill writes adult sci-fi and fantasy from her adopted home of Durham, North Carolina. Her worlds feature the diversity she has lived as a biracial woman of color and former migrant to Europe's political and financial capitals. She draws on these life experiences to write characters trying their best to find a place for themselves.

Outside of writing, she enjoys hiking in North Carolina's many beautiful state parks and learning about world mythology.

Learn more or get in touch: whitneyhillwrites.com
More books by Whitney: whitneyhillwrites.com/original-fiction/
Sign up to receive email updates: whwrites.com/newsletter

Join her on social media:
- Twitter: twitter.com/write_wherever
- Instagram: instagram.com/write_wherever
- Facebook: facebook.com/WhitneyHillWrites

Learn more about the publisher, Benu Media, at benumedia.com, or sign up to receive newsletters with the latest releases at go.benumedia.com/newsletter.

One Last Thing...

If you enjoyed this book, please consider posting a short review, recommending it on Goodreads, or telling a friend who might also enjoy this story. Thank you for reading, and for your support!

CPSIA information can be obtained
at www.ICGtesting.com
Printed in the USA
LVHW091650210122
708857LV00016B/421